BLOOD REIGN

THE SAGA OF
PANDORA ZWIEBACK
BOOK 2

STEVEN
A. ROMAN

StarWarp Concepts
www.starwarpconcepts.com
NEW YORK, NY

StarWarp Concepts
P.O. Box 4667
Sunnyside, NY 11104

Visit our Web site: **www.StarwarpConcepts.com**

Visit Pan on the Web at:
www.PandoraZwieback.com
www.facebook.com/pages/Pandora-Zwieback/122630931125833

Library of Congress Control Number: 2010921106

ISBN: 978-0-9841741-2-6 (trade paperback)
ISBN: 978-0-9841741-6-4 (e-book)

First Edition: February 2015
10 9 8 7 6 5 4 3 2 1

Cover painting by Bob Larkin
Based on a sketch by Eliseu Gouveia
(after a painting by Larkin)

Frontispiece by Eliseu Gouveia

Edited by K. C. Winters
Cover and interior design by Mat Postawa

Printed in the USA

PRAISE FOR STEVEN A. ROMAN AND BLOOD FEUD, THE FIRST PANDORA ZWIEBACK NOVEL

"Roman has written an incredibly enjoyable teen supernatural urban fantasy, with a dark and edgy tone that doesn't try to play light with the sensibilities of younger readers just because they are younger."
—Melissa Voelker, **HorrorNews.net**

"Roman knows how to structure a story to bring out the most in a scene, and I found that I couldn't put down this book once I started reading."
—**Dwight Jon Zimmerman**, *New York Times* bestselling coauthor of *Lincoln's Last Days: The Shocking Assassination That Changed America Forever*

"*Blood Feud* is one of those fabulous books that manages to straddle the young adult/adult fiction divide . . . catering equally for teens and more, ahem, 'mature' readers alike with a light touch that makes it a joy to read."
—Kell Smuthwaite, **BCF Book Reviews**

"Roman has an incredible gift for running lateral plotlines that intersect with a glorious crash. . . . Highly recommended."
—Sheila Shedd, **Monster Librarian**

"Roman's writing is wonderfully crisp, drawing us into a hidden world that is great fun. Definitely recommended."
—Andrew Boylan, **Taliesin Meets the Vampires**

"The characters are beautifully developed and relatable. Pandora is so three-dimensional that you feel you've known her your entire life."
—Ashleigh Mayes, **Krypto Dies!**

"Charmingly fun, addictively energetic, explosively violent, and almost terminally endearing. Oh, and highly recommended."
—"The Dome," **Sci-Fi Saturday Night**

This one's for
the Panatics

Thanks for your patience,
your understanding,
and your words of encouragement

Hell's vengeance boils in my heart;
Death and despair blaze around me!

—Wolfgang Amadeus Mozart
and Emanuel Schikaneder,
The Magic Flute

1

Her chest ached.

Eyes closed, Pandora Zwieback grimaced and gently massaged the spot above her heart, but it did little to ease the throbbing pain. It felt as though the world's biggest gas bubble had settled dead center inside her rib cage, and it wasn't in any hurry to pop. Pan grunted. If the damn thing persisted, she'd never be able to get back to sleep.

She forced a tiny belch, but it did nothing to alleviate the pressure on her heart. Pan sighed. The last time she'd suffered indigestion this bad, she'd been gorging on the Hungarian dishes her paternal grandmother, Erzsébet, had made for her fifteenth birthday. Total P-I-G behavior, but the chicken schnitzel and stuffed cabbage rolls and spicy liptauer had been *so* good it was almost worth spending half the night trapped in Bloat City.

Almost worth it. When the gas bubble formed, waking her up at three A.M., the pain was so intense she'd thought she was having a heart attack. Her mother, Karen—somehow aware that her only child was suffering—stumbled out of bed to stay up with Pan, rubbing her back, calming her nerves, helping her get through the crisis. And in the morning, after the bubble had dissipated and she could breathe normally again, Pan purposefully strode into the kitchen and finished off the stuffed cabbage for breakfast.

"You never learn, do you?" Mom had asked playfully.

"Sure, I do," Pan said around a mouthful of rice and ground beef. *"But no stupid gassy vegetable's ruling my digestive tract."* She pointed her fork at Karen. *"You gotta show these things who's boss, Mom—y'know?"*

Then she'd belched, and grinned broadly.

Mom sighed, walked over, and kissed the top of her head. *"That'll do, pig,"* she said warmly. *"That'll do . . ."*

Pan chuckled at the pleasant memory. "Thanks, Mom . . ." She smiled and opened her eyes—to find herself gazing up at a bloodred sky.

". . . the hell . . . ?" she muttered.

Pan sat up and gasped. This wasn't her bedroom, she realized—she was lying in the middle of a street.

Surrounded by bodies.

Most of them were adults: men and women of varying ages, half of them attired in expensive suits, the other half adorned in frills and lace, as though for a fancy costume party. A few were engulfed in flames, their burns so horrible it was impossible to distinguish gender. Clamping a hand over her nose and mouth, Pan turned away before the stench of roasting meat that filled her nostrils and singed the back of her throat caused her to throw up.

There were others, she now saw, who were not so nattily dressed. Adults and teens, senior citizens and children, police officers and paramedics—all just as dead as the partygoers, sprawled around the sidewalks and curbs with their features frozen in expressions of shock and outright terror.

"What is . . . what is going on?" she asked, all too aware of the way her voice nervously jumped a couple of octaves.

Pan scrambled to her feet and looked around. She recognized the area—Astoria, Queens, about a half block from Renfield's House of Horrors and Mystical Antiquities, the museum owned by her father, David—but not like this: not as a war zone. Cars were on fire; windows in every building had shattered, littering the streets with glass shards; the air was thick with the tang of smoldering metal and burning flesh. And except for the bodies, she was completely alone.

Alone with the dead.

Her heart suddenly began racing; her head throbbed; it became difficult to breathe. She knew what that meant, what all the signs were pointing to.

A panic attack.

"No," she said hoarsely—and then, more forcefully, *"No."* She couldn't lose control now. She needed to calm down, to make sense of this bizarre scene; maybe later she could waste time freaking out. Closing her eyes, she took a deep breath and slowly released it through her nostrils, willing her wildly beating heart to slow down, her pounding head to end its drumbeat. Then she began whispering the coping statement that her psychiatrist, Dr. Farrar, had taught her to get through a crisis: "It's just a bump in the road, it's not the end of the world. It's just a bump in the—"

A sharp twinge in her heart doubled her over, and Pan clenched her teeth to keep from screaming. It didn't stop a low groan from pushing past her lips, however, but she was able to fight the excruciating pain before it drove her to her knees.

She exhaled sharply and pressed the palms of both hands against her chest, moving them in slow, circular motions over her heart. Gradually, the ache eased a tiny bit and she was able to straighten up.

Pan took her hands away from her chest—and froze. Her palms were stained a bright red. Confused, she looked down at the black T-shirt she was wearing. Mom had presented her with the T a couple of days ago, and Pan had been proud to show it off. Printed on the front was a full-color, silk-screened image: a cartoon drawing of a devil girl's face with a Band-Aid across her nose and a bruise on her cheek.

Its eyes were bleeding.

"You're a reg'lar friggin' mess, ain't ya?" said a rough voice beside her. "But I guess I ain't much to look at, neither."

Pan looked up and yelped. One of the charbroiled corpses—a man not much taller than she and wearing the remains of a dark suit—was standing a few steps away. His features had been burned away, his throat had split open like the skin of a baked potato, but he was somehow still able to communicate. Pan found herself mesmerized by his exposed vocal cords, and how they vibrated when he spoke. The nasally pitch of his voice reminded her of the movie actor Joe Pesci.

"Had yerself a little run-in with the dark lady, did ya? Ha! I know what *that's* like." He flashed a shark-toothed smile and gazed around at the destruction. "Don't know why that broad had to go stickin' her nose in where it don't belong, anyway. I mean"—he gestured at the bloody and smoldering corpses—"considerin' how eager we all was to go rippin' into each other for a chance at the Prize, who needs La Bella Tenebrosa around to do the killin'? Am I right?"

"I . . . I guess," Pan muttered, not having a clue as to what he was yammering about.

He turned back and frowned at her; the skin around where his laugh lines should have been cracked, flaked off, and settled on his tie. "Thing is, little girl, you ain't one'a my clan's members—that friggin' piece'a crap punk outfit you got on is a dead giveaway—"

"It's not punk," she said. "It's Goth."

"Whatever. Anyways, you ain't part'a House Orlock, an' you ain't frilly enough to be one'a those House Otoyo mopes from Japan . . . so just what vampire clan *do* you belong to?"

Pan started. "*Vampire?* I'm not a vampire." Besides, outside of movies and TV shows and books, there was no such thing as a real vampire—everybody knew that. Although . . . now that she considered the matter, something told her that wasn't exactly true . . .

My Undead Cousin Vinnie snorted derisively. "Oh, yeah? Well, if you ain't a vampire, you mind tellin' me what yer doin' with that thing in ya?"

"W-what thing?" Pan stammered.

"The *stake*, sweetheart," he replied, pointing at her. "If you ain't a vampire, then whattaya doin' with that hunk'a lumber rammed through ya?"

"S-stake . . . ?" she managed to croak. For a moment she fought the urge to glance at the focus of his attention, but slowly her eyes tilted downward.

There was a broken wooden handle poking out of her chest.

Pan bit down hard on her bottom lip to block the scream that tried to vault over her tongue. This, she realized, had been the source of her pain all along—but how could she have missed seeing it? And how could she still be alive with something like that piercing her heart?

The most important question, though—one she was hesitant to ask herself— was, *was* she alive?

Pan rolled her eyes. Of *course* she was alive! How stupid a question was that? This was probably some kind of weird dream she was having after watching another all-night horror movie marathon. *You keep watching all those vampire movies,* her maternal grandmother, Ellie, used to say, *and one day you're gonna turn into one!* At the time, Pan thought that would be the coolest thing ever.

Now, though, with a wooden stake rammed deep into her chest? Not so much . . .

She gazed at the burned man standing before her, then at the other corpses, which were beginning to stagger to their feet. Most of the . . . vampires—if that's what they really were—appeared angry at finding themselves here, although a few seemed downright frightened by the situation. As for their human victims, even from a distance she could tell how scared and confused they were, especially the children.

Pan glanced down at the stake, and shuddered. *Not as much as I am . . .*

She took a deep breath to calm down, then exhaled shakily and raised a trembling, bloodstained hand to touch the splintered wood with her index finger. A tiny blue spark of electricity crackled at the contact point and she gasped as—

It all came back to her in a flood of memories: The Albany Megamall, where she'd punched that mean girl, Nikki Van Schrik, in the face for badmouthing Pan's parents. Mom sending her downstate to stay with David until Nikki's family stopped freaking out over their little darling getting—in Pan's opinion—a long-deserved beat-down. Meeting the shape-shifting monster hunter Sebastienne "Annie" Mazarin—the "dark lady" the crisped vampire had alluded to—and her friend, a hot teenage boy named Javier Maldonado, in the train tunnels beneath Pennsylvania Station as they chased a trash-stealing monkey. How Annie had made her realize that the "monstervision" Pan had been experiencing for the past ten years was really a special talent for seeing past supernatural creatures' human disguises. Then later that night, Dad had unveiled a weird skeleton—and the same wooden stake stuck in its chest that Pan now had ownership of—that he'd bought from some collector in England. The next day Annie explained that the skeleton was not only the remains of an old boyfriend, a fallen angel named Zaqiel, but that the stake was actually the tip of the Spear of Longinus, the weapon used by a Roman soldier to stab Jesus Christ while he hung on the cross. Following that revelation was the gun battle between rival vampire clans that erupted right on this very street, and Zaqiel's resurrection. Then Mom's capture by the vampires. Pan grabbing the spear and rushing to her aid, only to arrive too late and finding her dead. The mocking tone of the fallen angel, her mother's blood still moist on his lips, ringing in her ears as she wept over Karen's body. Pan, consumed with hatred, charging forward, spear held high. Zaqiel disarming her—before impaling her with the ancient weapon.

Before killing her.

Her legs suddenly weakened and Pan leaned against a car for support. "Oh . . . Oh, God . . . ," she gasped. "I'm . . . really dead?"

"Hey, we're *all* dead around here, sweetheart," Count Pesci the Vampire said. "Some of us more'n once. I guess in your case, it's like they say: there's a first time for everything, right?" He chuckled at his little joke, then frowned when the girl didn't join in.

"But . . . but what about Mom?" Pan asked herself, ignoring the cinder-caked monster. She looked around in a slow circle, calling out, "Mom? *Mom!* It's Pan! Where are you?" A twinge of panic plucked at her severed heart. Why wasn't Karen answering?

She scrambled onto the car's hood, then stepped onto the roof. From here she could see the entire area—and more. She hadn't noticed it from ground level, but at a slightly higher elevation it was apparent that the war zone had a distinct border—a sort of shimmering heat haze at the end of each street, similar to what she'd observed the first time that Annie had encouraged her to open her eyes to the magic-laced realm that had always existed around her, side by side with the human world. This time, as she gazed at the wavering, transparent barrier at the end of the block, her special sight revealed glimpses of other people, in other places: a fog-blanketed road on which blazed a multicar pileup, the accident victims screaming as they burned; next to that, soldiers, riddled with bullets, sprawled across the dirt floor of a mountain stronghold; to the right of that, a woman lying on a moldy carpet in an abandoned building, a makeshift crack pipe beside her. And on and on and on, in all four directions—kaleidoscopic tableaux of death upon death upon death.

Pan felt pity for them all—people she had never known and never would, yet lives ended all too soon. Like her own. Like her mother's.

"*MOM!*" she wailed.

"Whattaya whinin' about now?" the vampire asked. "Yer *mother*? Little late to be cryin' fer Mommy, don'cha think?"

Pan angrily wiped away her tears and snarled at him. "I don't see her. Why don't

I see her?"

"Hey, how should I know? I don't even know who you're talkin' about." He waved a dismissive hand at her. "Whiny little punk . . ."

"Sure you do. The one the angel . . ." She swallowed nervously, barely able to get the words out, then gestured toward a spot on the asphalt a couple of yards away. "He killed her, right there, in the middle of the street."

The dead man appeared confused—a neat trick, considering he didn't have much of a face left to pull off such an expression. Then his black eyes widened just a hair. "What—the broad in the Harley-Davidson T-shirt? That blonde the angel was nibblin' on? That who you mean?"

"Yes!" She hurriedly climbed down from the roof of the car. "Did you see her?"

"What the hell'd *she* be doin' here? She ain't dead." He paused. "Leastways she wasn't last time I seen her—right before that friggin' Knight, Alexander, put a couple'a incendiary rounds in me." The vampire snarled. "Ruined a friggin' five-hundred-dollar suit . . ."

Pan started. No, he couldn't be right. She'd knelt beside her mother, stared in horror at the blood dripping from her punctured throat, felt Karen's skin, icy to the touch . . . "You're wrong. I—"

She suddenly halted and thought back to her final moments of life, after Zaqiel had impaled her with the spear. Knowing that death was only seconds away, she'd wondered if she'd be reunited with her mother in the afterlife, only to hear:

"Pan! Oh, God, no!"

Mom's voice.

Clear as day. Unmistakable.

Karen Bonifant—very much alive, and screaming for her only child.

"PAN!" But then had come the sounds of her struggling with someone. *"Let me go! Let me—"* A loud thump, like a heavy punch, cut her off, followed by car doors slamming and tires squealing.

The vampires had taken her away.

Pan gasped. Mom *was* alive—still in terrible danger, but alive and in need of rescuing. Yet . . . who was going to *do* the rescuing?

The smile faded. *Not* you, *dead girl. You're* waaay *past saving anybody.*

Her lips twisted into a snarl. *"No,"* she said aloud. "Mom *needs* me. I *promised* I'd come get her."

How, though? Mom was back in the real world, and Pan was . . . wherever. She looked around. It didn't appear to be heaven—although, really, how would she know for certain—but it didn't appear to be hell, either. Pan ignored the growing curiosity of her inner horror fangirl—who, if given half a chance, would want to see just how accurate Dante Alighieri had been in describing the Devil's furnace room when he wrote his *Inferno* back in the fourteenth century.

Okay, not heaven or hell, but maybe purgatory? That seemed more likely. The spiritual no-man's-land where souls were supposed to hang out indefinitely until a decision was made as to who was getting invited into God's penthouse suite, and who was getting tossed into Satan's overheated basement. For her and the victims and vampires here, the celestial hangout resembled the very street in Queens on which they had died, but the other locations she'd spotted through the barriers meant the landscape changed to reflect whatever settings those other people had died in.

All those men and women and kids, they died today—*like me,* she thought morosely, then quickly shook her head to dispel the wave of depression she felt lapping up against her mental shoreline. Yes, it was totally sad, what happened to all those people, but she needed to stay focused—for Mom's sake, if not for her own. No matter what part of the afterlife she'd wound up in, the bottom line remained that she was here and Mom was on Earth, and Pan needed to get back and help her. If there *was* a way to get back.

I wonder if Annie knows any magical resurrection spells? Pan thought, then grunted softly. *Nah. With my luck, I'd come back as a zombie wanting to eat everybody's brains, and then somebody'd have to shoot me in the head and I'd wind up right back here. That would* totally *suck.*

She climbed onto the hood of another car and sat down to consider the situation. In the short time she'd known Annie, the huntress had opened Pan's eyes to a world of supernatural wonders and living, breathing monsters. A world the teen Goth had spent the better part of the last decade believing was a figment of her monstervision. On top of that, when Javier had been injured during his pursuit of the trash monkey in the Penn Station tunnels, she'd been able to treat a bump on his head, *with just the touch of a finger.* Annie had said that meant Pan had healing powers, on top of possessing monstervision. Then, the next morning, Dad had jokingly threatened to kill her for staining one of his bath towels with the black cream she used to color her natural-blond hair, and Pan had said:

"Then I'll use my new magical superpowers to come back from the dead . . ."

Her eyebrows shot up. Could she really do something like that? Before yesterday she would have thought the notion absurd—but after everything she'd experienced in the past twenty-four hours? It didn't seem quite so crazy.

. . .

Well, no crazier than sitting in an afterlife waiting room with a makeshift stake poking through her heart.

"Only one way to find out . . ." She closed her eyes, crossed her legs Indian-style, and placed her hands palms-up on her thighs. It was one of those yoga positions Pan had seen her mother perform countless times when she wanted to relax. She used to think it look ridiculous, like when Doctor Strange did the same thing in his Marvel comics so he could project his astral form out of his body, but right now maybe Mom and the Master of the Mystic Arts were on to something. Problem was, it was really hard to concentrate with the Spear of Longinus wiggling in her chest every time she drew a breath. Pan grunted, opened her eyes, and glared at the ancient wooden handle. "Stupid spear."

She grabbed the broken wood with both hands. Blue-white lightning flared around her hands.

"Now what the hell're you doin'?" the vampire asked.

Pan gritted her teeth and began pulling. "What's it *look* like I'm doing? I'm getting this thing outta me." Trying to, at least. It was really stuck all the way through her—she could hear the rasp of the iron tip as it scraped against the lining of her leather jacket.

She pulled harder, and was rewarded by the spear moving a couple of inches, followed by the most intense pain she'd ever felt in her life . . . next to the pain she'd experienced from the spear going in, of course. Pan bit down on her bottom lip to keep from screaming.

"Stop being such a baby," she growled at herself. "Just yank the damn thing out."

Eyes tightly shut, screeching through clenched teeth, she doubled her efforts, dragging the weapon back through her body. Tears flowed down her cheeks; her mouth filled with blood; her skin and muscles crackled as the mystical energies generated by the spear fought her every inch of the way. The pain threatened to overwhelm her, yet she refused to give in. She was already dead—anything else, she figured, including the unbearable agony, was just an inconvenience; an obstacle blocking her path back to Mom. The spear shifted a little more and Pan opened her eyes to watch its progress—

—and saw her father right in front of her.

David Zwieback's face was inches away, eyes wide in surprise. She couldn't see the rest of him—it was like he was peering at her through a small window. His face was smudged with dirt and the tracks of dried tears; fresh ones glittered along the edges of his bloodshot eyes.

"Dad!" Pan cried, and reached out to him.

He yelped and jumped back in fright. Now she had a better view of him: he was sitting on the real-world version of this same Queens street—next to her corpse, she assumed, which would explain why her viewpoint was tilted on one side: her body was still lying where it had fallen.

My body . . . Pan thought sadly, then gasped. *Oh, my God! I'm back in my body!*

Behind Dad crouched her best friend, purple-haired Sheena McCarthy, and Annie's godson, Javier. From the horrified expressions Pan saw on their faces, she had no doubt they'd heard her, too—and it was seriously freaking them out.

You and me both, guys, Pan thought. She turned her attention back to her father, who was inching away from her. "Dad, please! It's me!"

Dave paused, tilted his head to one side in confusion, and then slowly leaned forward. "Pan . . . ?" he whispered.

Sheen gently placed a hand on his shoulder. "I . . . I wouldn't go doin' that, Mr. Z."

Despite her situation, Pan had to smile. Leave it to a fellow horror fan like Sheen to realize how stupid it was for *anybody* to lean in close to a suddenly vocal corpse.

Dad should have known that as well, considering he ran a horror-themed museum, but given it was his *daughter's* corpse that was doing the talking, Pan was willing to overlook his mistake.

Dave ignored Sheen's mild attempt at restraining him and moved closer. "Pan, is it—"

Anything else he was about to say was drowned out by a blast of sound —a single musical note that seemed to explode all around her. Pan released the spear to clasp her hands over her ears, and in doing so lost the connection to the other side.

Then the bloodred sky ripped open, and through the rift swept a phalanx of winged men and women in what appeared to be riot gear. Her first impression was that they looked like a bunch of comic book fans cosplaying in Hawkman and Hawkgirl costumes; then she realized they could only be—

"Angels," Pan whispered in astonishment. "Those are angels."

One of them was carrying what she thought was an oversized trumpet, but then she remembered seeing a similar instrument in her friend Tommy Guerrero's apartment; his dad played one in a weekend jazz band. A flügelhorn, it was called. The angel raised it to his lips and blew another eardrum-rattling note, probably to get everyone's attention. Or to sound the charge. Or to scare the crap out of the humans and vampires. That last choice was definitely what *she* was feeling.

"Great. Like my friggin' day wasn't bad enough . . ." Crusty the Vampire shook his head in a forlorn gesture, wisps of charred scalp spiraling away like black snowflakes. "Gonna start cryin' fer yer mommy again, little girl? 'Cause if ya thought yer day sucked up to *this* point . . ." He threw up his hands in exasperation. "*Pffh.*"

"Why? What's going on?"

He jerked a thumb toward the sky. "Looks like His Majesty up there wants t'clear the field," he replied with a sneer. "Prob'ly expectin' more souls to come poppin' up, if the fightin's still goin' on, so he sent the goon squad in to do the groundskeepin'. Now they're gonna start dishin' out the pain—and believe you me, little sis, ain't nothin' these holy mothers like better'n kickin' a little vampire ass."

"So? Like I already told you, I'm *not* a vampire."

"Yeah, like that's gonna make a difference to *them*." He pointed to the Spear of Longinus—which, to the casual observer, would no doubt appear to be exactly the sort of wooden stake one would expect to see jutting out of a vampire's chest.

"Oh," Pan said in a small voice, and glanced at the broken handle. If what the thug said was true, then this thing *really* needed to come out . . .

A scream from someone across the street brought her attention back to the celestial security force, and she watched as the angels' methods for "clearing the field" quickly became evident. They hovered above the war zone, studying the souls that cried out to them for salvation, and those—both human and vampire—that shrank back in fear. Then they swooped down to pass judgment. Humans who had obviously passed the "good" test during their lives were taken by the hand and carried into the sky, through the rift toward what Grandma Ellie would probably call their "just reward." The ones who'd probably spent every waking moment acting like total d-bags were herded toward a sinkhole that had suddenly formed in the middle of the intersection. From her perch on the car hood Pan could see down into the pit—it seemed bottomless, but the shrieks and wails that drifted up from the shadows, and the stench of sulfur that wafted up to irritate her sinuses, made it quite clear that a bottom did exist. She had a pretty good idea what was down there. Her inner horror fangirl demanded a closer look, just to be certain, but Pan thought they were both fine right where they were—for the moment.

As for the vampires . . .

Whether they stood their ground or ran away, the undead clan members were struck down by fiery swords that the angels pulled from golden scabbards attached to their weapons belts. One slice and the vampires were instantly reduced to ashes, which swirled in the air before being sucked down into the hellmouth.

That was the point at which Pan decided it was time to move a safe distance away from the sinkhole. Her inner fangirl didn't argue.

Not that Pan was out of danger. As she slid off the car hood, a male angel swooped down and landed close to the vampiric goodfella. He was taller than her dad, so that probably put him around six foot six or seven. He had strong, chiseled features and full lips, like the kind you'd see on a top-level male model, and the steroid-pumped physique of a body builder. And based on the manner in which he stared daggers at the shark-toothed gangster, he appeared to be in a particularly foul mood. Maybe he hated vampires a lot. Or maybe he really hated working the cleanup shift.

The angel slowly drew his sword. Bright red-and-gold flames ignited along the blade as soon as it cleared its sheath.

The vampire snorted disdainfully. "Think yer pretty tough with that sword an' everything, don't ya? Well, you can take that pigsticker and shove it up—"

The sword strike came at warp speed, the blade cleanly separating the vampire's head from his neck; a moment later, both head and body erupted into flame before disintegrating into ash. Pan watched, openmouthed, as the goon's remains swept past her on a sudden breeze and made their journey down to hell.

Then the angel turned and snarled at her—the girl with the wooden stake stuck in her chest.

Pan swallowed nervously. "Hey, now, look, before you get all, uh, judgmental and stuff—"

"*Demon*," he growled, and strode forward.

"No, wait!" Pan cried. "I'm not a vampire! I'm just a Goth chick!" She backed away, tugging with all her might on the damn spear that would just. not. come. *out!* Bluish electricity flared around her hands, then surged up her arms. She tried to ignore the pain, but when her eyeballs started tingling it took a supreme effort to avoid freaking out and maintain her grip on the wooden handle.

Then, miraculously, she felt it shift forward; not a great distance, maybe six inches, but at least she'd gotten it moving. Now if she just had another minute or so to completely work it loose . . .

The angel wasn't about to give her that time, though. He followed her retreat, stalking her step for step. "Undead parasite or painted harlot, it matters not. You are a sinner—of that I am certain. And there is always room in hell for one of your kind."

"Aren't you listening?" Pan asked. "I said— Wait." She snarled. "Did you just call me a *harlot*?"

The celestial warrior raised his sword as he closed in for the kill.

"Oh, crap!" Pan yelped, and jumped away as the fiery blade swung toward her head—only to lose her balance by tripping over a piece of rubble. Arms pinwheeling, she stumbled wildly for a few steps, until finally slamming backward against the side of another vehicle—

—at which point, amid a flash of blue lightning and a loud crack of thunder, the spear finally popped out.

The ancient weapon clattered on the ground as Pan bounced off the car and fell to her hands and knees. She rubbed her sore chest and breathed a heavy sigh of relief. "Oh, God, that is *so* much better," she said, and looked up—

—into the disbelieving eyes of her dad, Sheena, Javi, and a female paramedic. They were sitting on the ground about five feet away, mouths hanging open, their expressions a mixture of confusion and fright.

Startled, Pan looked around. The street was still a war zone, still littered with corpses and stinking of burnt metal and flesh, but here there were no angels trying to cut off her head, no sinkhole leading to hell. Instead, an army of very human-looking police officers, firefighters, and emergency medical technicians had descended on the area. Crowds of bystanders and reporters pressed against NYPD wooden barricades, attempting to get a closer look at the chaotic scene. The air was filled with wailing sirens and grating car alarms and the angry buzz of swarming police and news media helicopters.

She was back among the living.

A shrill giggle eased its way past her lips, one eerie enough to make all four onlookers gasp and draw back a little farther. The sound scared Pan, too, when she realized it was coming from her. She clamped both hands over her mouth before the giggle could grow into a hysterical laugh, and forced herself to calm down. It took some effort, but when she at last felt a bit more in control she lowered her hands.

"W—" she began to say, then had to turn her head and spit. A wad of blood-thickened phlegm smacked onto the asphalt, and she wiped her mouth with the back of her hand.

"Wh . . . where's Mom?" she croaked.

No reply. They were obviously too weirded out to answer, but Pan wasn't in the mood to wait until they got tired of making googly eyes at her.

"*Where's. Mom?*" she asked loudly, then grimaced and clutched her chest. Raising her voice like that had sent a wave of pain through her heart; it felt as though the spear was still lodged in it. She drew a sharp breath through clenched teeth. "It's just . . . ," she gasped, "just a bump in the . . . in the road . . . not the end . . . end of the world . . ."

"Zee . . . ?" Sheen croaked.

Pan waved her off; slowly, the pain subsided. Damn, she thought, this coming-back-from-the-dead stuff hurt—a *lot*. "Just . . . just tell me."

"She . . . That angel, Zaqiel, and the vampires took her," Sheen slowly replied.

"Yeah," Javi said. "But . . ." He nervously cleared his throat. "But Annie went after them."

Pan nodded weakly. "Okay. Good . . . that's good . . ."

Dave Zwieback scrambled forward and knelt beside her. Gently, he brushed aside the tangled, blood-matted hair that had fallen over her face so he could look into her eyes. "Pan? Is it . . . is it really you?"

She wasn't surprised by the question. A major horror fan had just witnessed his daughter rise from the dead—of *course* he was going to wonder if her body had become the home for something far more diabolical than his monster-seeing child.

"Y-yeah. It's me, Dad." A sickly smile quirked the corners of Pan's mouth as the ache in her chest flared up again. "P-pretty wild, right? I guess I—" Another twinge, even more painful than the last, made her gasp. "I guess I really *do* have magical superpowers, huh?" she whispered hoarsely.

Then her eyes rolled up in her head and the world spun away into darkness.

2

The angel was going to die—of that Sebastienne Mazarin was absolutely certain. She'd killed him once before, almost two centuries ago, during his attempt to unleash hell on Earth; she would have no trouble doing it again. Only this time she'd make sure his death was permanent.

The problem, though, was in getting close enough to accomplish her goal. The traffic situation in front of her car had a lot to do with that. Not to mention all the bullets being fired.

It wasn't the fallen angel Zaqiel who was doing the shooting, but his vampiric descendants: the gun-toting members of the Otoyo and Orlock clans, respectively of Japan and Central Europe. And they weren't shooting at her specifically, but at the NYPD squad cars pursuing their vans and limousines through the streets of Astoria; Annie just happened to be bringing up the rear. The undead thugs didn't bother with the swarm of police and news helicopters that tagged along, though their presence was impossible to ignore.

Keeping pace behind the wheel of her souped-up 1969 Ford Murena GT, the dark-haired monster hunter had to marvel at how well the two clans were working together, running interference and laying down cover fire for the limousine carrying Zaqiel. Minutes ago, they had been warring against one another for possession of the much-sought-after "Prize": a legendary ultimate weapon that would give its controller the power to rule the world. Now they were united in their efforts to protect that prize from harm, even though it turned out to be not an actual weapon but one of God's former messengers who had a burning desire to wipe out humanity—his idea of taking revenge against the Almighty for being cast out of heaven and sealed up in a volcano with his traitorous brethren for thousands of years.

He was also one of Annie's old boyfriends.

Still, their past relationship had little to do with the current situation—at least that's what Annie kept telling herself. She was supposed to be a professional slayer who didn't allow emotional baggage to get in the way of her work, but she couldn't help but admit that she'd take some degree of pleasure in watching her ex suffer before she annihilated him.

It was only fair, she thought, considering all the suffering he had inflicted on others—and her, as well.

She'd witnessed a bloody, partially drained Karen Bonifant-Zwieback being shoved into the same black stretch limousine into which Zaqiel had been bundled by Lady Kiyoshi Sasaki, the leader of House Otoyo's forces, but Annie had been too slow to intervene. As incredible as her magick-enhanced healing ability was, not even the immortal huntress known as La Bella Tenebrosa, "the beautiful, dark one," could shrug off the wounds inflicted by an exploding rocket-propelled grenade fired by one of House Orlock's members. Even now it was taking a great deal of concentration to ignore the searing pain and focus on her driving.

Her aches and cuts, though, meant little when compared to what that monster Zaqiel had done to Karen's sixteen-year-old daughter, Pandora: cold-bloodedly killing her with the Spear of Longinus, the very weapon Annie had used to end his life. The anger that now consumed her, the guilt that tore at her for failing her young friend, made any physical pain Annie felt seem petty—but she was more than willing to share it with her angelic ex-lover.

A loud crash brought her attention back to the road. One of the vans was lying on its side, T-boned by a FedEx truck at the intersection of Steinway Street and Twenty-Eighth Avenue. Two cop cars peeled off from the motorcade to secure the van's occupants—the human ones, at least. Now that they were out of the fight, the vampires would probably hightail it back to their respective clan-chapter houses. And with any luck, Annie thought hopefully, the Otoyos and Orlocks would forget their momentary alliance on the way home and kill each other before they reached Manhattan. It would certainly make her life easier.

Two blocks later, at Astoria Boulevard, one of the NYPD cruisers slammed into the left corner of the remaining van's rear bumper, spinning the vampire's conveyance around in one of law enforcement's traditional remedies for high-speed chases: the PIT—Precision Immobilization Technique—maneuver. Tires screeching, the van pivoted a full 180 degrees before coming to rest half wrapped around a lamppost. It cleared the path for Annie and the others to power through the intersection and turn Astoria Boulevard South into a drag strip along which she and New York's Finest vied for the leader position behind the limousine. She growled at the SWAT van that weaved from side to side directly in front of her, blocking her every attempt to get around it.

Then, as the convoy roared up the entrance ramp for the Grand Central Parkway, Annie stomped on the Murena's accelerator and squeezed past the SWAT team, smiling pleasantly at the cop behind the wheel who flipped her The Bird. Let him curse her all he wanted, she thought. Zaqiel was hers to deal with, and nothing was going to keep her from that goal.

Besides, she wanted a closer look at the limo's occupants before she unleashed hell on them. Killing Zaqiel would go *much* easier if she knew the seating arrangements.

"Well, now, isn't *this* cozy," Elden remarked cheerfully as Lady Kiyoshi Sasaki pressed into him again, this time as the limousine swung hard to the right as the driver tried to avoid scraping the guardrail that separated the parkway's westbound and eastbound lanes. The scarecrow-thin British vampire leaned in close to Kiyoshi's ear to murmur: "I'd watch out if I were you, your ladyship. If word ever got back to Japan that you and I had become so . . . intimate in the back of your limousine, it would be an absolute scandal." His playful grin grew even wider as the leader of House Otoyo snarled at him.

Kiyoshi forcefully pushed off from House Orlock's strike-team leader to resume her seat, then snapped at the chauffeur in Japanese, "Fool! Watch how you drive or I'll tear out your throat!"

A delicate hand settled on her knee, gave it a gentle squeeze. Kiyoshi turned to face her sister, Miyuki, who sat on her other side. Miyu smiled shyly, a tiny uptick of her lips as her gaze shifted from her clan leader to the other occupants of the limousine, then back—enough of a warning gesture for Yoshi to understand that she needed to calm down. Losing her cool—especially in the presence of their exalted ancestor, Zaqiel of the First Reborn—would only make her appear weak in front of their clansmen . . . and more important, their enemies.

Kiyoshi looked around the cramped interior. Zaqiel—still wearing the tattered velvet pants and leather boots in which he'd been buried more than a century ago—sat alone on the left-hand couch, his wide, black-feather wings making it impossible for anyone to sit beside him. Next to him was the vehicle's minibar, its bottles of liquor and chilled blood clattering against tumblers and champagne flutes with every swerve the limousine made. Across from Zaqiel sat two of Elden's subordinates: Noureddine, a bald, black vampire wearing diamond studs in each earlobe, and an unkempt Russian named Alexi whose lantern jaw was almost outsized by the thick handlebar mustache that trailed down to it. Toward the front of the vehicle, on the seat against the partition separating the passengers from the chauffeur, sprawled Hiromi Takami, Kiyoshi's second-in-command, and Emiko Matsuda. Though their Elegant & Gothic Lolita outfits—Emiko's tailored suit and Hiromi's ruffled dress—were dirty and frayed from the street war in front of the museum, their muscles were taught, their expressions determined as they glared at their vampiric rivals. One tiny gesture from their leader and they would move like lightning to eradicate House Orlock's three hunters. Kiyoshi was sorely tempted to give the signal.

Zaqiel suddenly stiffened. "She is coming."

It took Kiyoshi a moment to figure out who "she" was, before realizing there could be only one woman to whom the fallen angel was so attuned that he could sense her presence.

La Bella Tenebrosa.

She shifted around to gaze out the back window, and through the smoked, bulletproof glass spotted what appeared to be a hearse-turned-racecar bearing down on them. Behind its steering wheel, Sebastienne Mazarin flashed a predator's smile.

"Headstrong and beautiful—and as overconfident as ever," Zaqiel murmured. "I see some things never change. Excellent."

No, Kiyoshi thought darkly. This was far from excellent.

At first Karen Bonifant thought it was her head that was jingling so loudly as she regained consciousness. Eventually she realized it was the sound of bottles and glasses clanging against one another that was making her skull ring. And, based on the screech of tires, the close-by roar of an engine, and the honking of horns, she concluded she was in a fast-moving vehicle.

Then something even more important came to mind.

PAIN!

Ignoring the throb of her head and the ache in her jaw where one of the vampires had punched her, Karen cautiously opened her eyes halfway. She found herself sitting in the front passenger seat of a limousine that rocked from side to side like a boat caught in a violent storm as it sped down some highway; a sign that flashed past clued her in it was the Grand Central Parkway. Yet it wasn't the reckless driving that riveted her attention, as much as a familiar face she saw reflected in the rearview mirror.

The Japanese vampire queen, Lady Sasaki, was perched on the backseat, barking orders at the driver through an open partition. Karen's lips drew back in a fierce snarl. That evil, Alice-in-Wonderland-garbed girl and her sister had brought their similarly attired clan to the museum owned by Karen's ex-husband, David Zwieback, in search of some "prize" that turned out to be the skeletal remains of a supposed fallen angel. An angel the vampires had wasted no time in resurrecting, and who'd drunk Karen's blood to revive his flagging strength—before murdering her daughter by plunging a wooden stake into her heart.

The same angel Karen now spotted sitting near the vampire girl.

Her first instinct was to crawl over the partition and tear out *his* heart with her bare hands, but she quickly tabled that option. The distance from the front to rear seats was too great, with heavily armed vampires between her and her target. Besides, she was alone and frailly human, while her captors were the sort of superstrong monsters that Pan had insisted for the past decade she could see. Monsters that Karen had never believed in—until they killed her baby girl. Her Panda-bear.

Monsters . . . with the exception of the driver.

From the corner of her eye Karen observed the panicked expression that contorted the young Japanese man's features; the sweat that poured down his face and soaked through the front of his shirt, even though the air-conditioning was on full blast; the accelerated breathing that bordered on hyperventilation. Here was a man terrified beyond measure—either because he was driving like a maniac and fearful of plowing this four-wheeled aircraft carrier into another vehicle, or because his passengers were a group of living corpses with short tempers and big guns. Either way, it meant he was paying no attention to the woman slumped beside him.

Karen gazed out through the windshield, to see a large green sign:

Exit 5

La Guardia Airport

Marine Air Terminal

Her lips twisted into a confused frown. The airport? What were the vampires expecting to do there—pull up to one of the terminals, then board a plane without being noticed by the veritable army of Transit Authority cops and National Guard soldiers that were stationed there?

Apparently not. The driver floored the accelerator; the limo shot past the exit ramp and swung into the lanes that, farther along, merged with the Whitestone Expressway. Now Karen was really confused. If not LaGuardia, then where could they possibly be going? JFK? No, the route the driver was taking had them entering the College Point section of Queens, so perhaps he was angling for the entrance to the Whitestone Bridge that led into the Bronx—except that by now such an obvious escape route would be blocked by police cars.

So just where the hell are we going? she wondered.

Flushing Airport—that's where the limousine was going, Annie realized as it screeched across three lanes toward the Exit 15 ramp. Or at least that's what the single-strip airfield was called during the five decades it had been in use, before it degenerated into a marshy wetland. Officially, the airport had been closed and abandoned in the 1980s; unofficially, it was still in use by the majority of the vampire clans' tristate-area chapters. One of the few places in the world, in fact, designated a no-combat zone by the Otoyos, the Tepeses, the Ch'ing Shihs, and the Baitals. The other houses, from what Annie understood, never agreed to the arrangement but grudgingly accepted it, since a private runway was advantageous to all, in an era of heightened airport security. This way, there was no need to tolerate pat-downs and full-body scans and prying questions from nosy TSA agents. Annie cursed sharply. For years she'd repeatedly petitioned City Hall to have the hangars bulldozed and the grounds blessed to prevent any future use of the facility by the undead. Unfortunately, the clans were far more politically connected than she. Bureaucracy, as always, remained the one monster not even a professional huntress could kill.

She eased the front bumper of the Murena against the right corner of the limousine's rear bumper and gave it a push, hoping to imitate the PIT maneuver she'd witnessed earlier. No such luck—the vintage speedster didn't have the weight required to spin the vehicular battleship. As the chase continued onto the service road, Annie remembered the .45-caliber Megastar she kept in a holster under her seat; she could use that to blast the tires. It meant she'd have to shoot left-handed while driving, but better that than playing tagalong until the vampires reached their destination.

Annie swung the Murena onto Twentieth Avenue just behind the limousine and took her eyes off the road, just long enough to reach for the handgun.

That's why she didn't see the city bus until it hit her.

From her slumped position, Karen stared wide-eyed at the limo's passenger-side mirror and watched as the westbound Q20 slammed into the car that had been chasing them and flipped it. The supercharged hearse rolled four times as it crossed into eastbound traffic, where a UPS truck smashed into it, bringing the car to rest on its roof. Karen lost sight of the accident scene as the limousine swung on to the southbound service road, back toward LaGuardia, though the driver bypassed the expressway's entrance ramp. He sped on, zipping past a postal service depot.

Behind Karen, the vampires laughed.

"So much for the notorious La Bella Tenebrosa," one of them lightly remarked in a British accent. "She may have been many things—but a good driver? Apparently not one of her stronger talents."

"Dear, sweet Sebastienne," Zaqiel said. "I shall mourn what might been . . . for the opportunity to kill her myself has been stolen from me." He snarled. "I owed her a great deal of suffering."

Karen gasped. Annie was in that car?

She felt eyes on her, and slowly turned her head.

The chauffeur was staring at her.

Looks like the cat's out of the bag, as her mother used to say. It was just as well— if Annie really was dead, then it meant only Karen could prevent her daughter's murderer from escaping. And there was only one way she could think of to accomplish that.

As the driver opened his mouth to alert his masters, Karen surprised him by jumping across the wide seat for the steering wheel.

Sirens—that was the first sound Annie heard as she regained consciousness, followed by the squeal of brakes. It was all a bit muffled, though, by the ringing in her ears.

She opened her eyes and wondered why the faces peering at her through the cracked windshield were upside down; then realized that *she* was the one upside down, the seat belt shoulder strap cutting into her chest. The bones in her left hand felt loose, her neck ached from a serious case of whiplash, and she could feel blood flowing into her hair from a deep laceration across her forehead, but broken and bloody was always better than stone-cold dead. After a few fumbling attempts to undo the belt the latch popped open; she was rewarded for her efforts by dropping out of the seat and banging her head on the overturned roof. Now she could add a concussion to her list of injuries, if she didn't already have one.

Annie crawled from the wreckage and found a throng of onlookers—the driver of the UPS truck she'd collided with, the bus driver who'd plowed into her, other motorists, shoppers clutching plastic bags from the nearby Target store, police officers involved in the high-speed chase—gathered around the Murena. More sirens in the distance heralded the approach of fire trucks and probably an ambulance or two.

Helping hands reached for her, but Annie waved them off as she staggered to her feet. "Where'd they go?" she asked weakly as she rested against the Murena's chassis. She dragged her broken hand across her eyes to wipe away the blood flowing down from the forehead cut.

"Who? That *other* crazy driver?" replied an elderly black woman in what Annie assumed was her finest Sunday-go-to-meeting white dress, the matching wide-brimmed church hat tilted at a chic but not rakish angle. And why not? It *was* Sunday, after all. "They took off down the service road like a bat out of— Well, you know what I mean."

Annie glanced in the direction that the woman indicated. The police vehicles that hadn't stopped at the crash site were continuing the pursuit of the limousine, which suddenly veered to the left across the asphalt, then back to the right. Had the chauffeur lost control of the car, or was he having second thoughts about helping his monstrous passengers escape, and had decided to allow the NYPD an opportunity to catch up? It mattered little—Lady Sasaki's group was close enough to the airport that they could run for their plane.

Not if Annie got there first, though.

"Thank you," she said to the church lady and pushed off from the Murena to set her trembling legs in motion, stumbling toward a chain-link fence that formed the boundary of the airport-turned-wetland.

One of the cops jogged after her. "Hey, where d'ya think *you're* going?"

"To kill an angel," Annie growled.

She ignored the church lady's loud gasp.

Karen smacked her elbow into the chauffeur's face, breaking his nose, then yanked the steering wheel toward her again. The limousine swerved so abruptly that both right-side tires momentarily rose off the ground, only to slam back down before the vehicle could flip over. The driver responded by biting her arm; she paid him back by punching him in the stomach. The car slalomed back and forth across the service road before roaring into a parking lot that was adjacent to a *New York Times* printing plant. A high chain-link fence at the far side of the lot loomed ever closer, yet neither combatant would give up control of the wheel.

Hands reached through the partition and grabbed fistfuls of Karen's hair; she cried out as the vampires dug their nails into her scalp. Still, her fingers remained locked around the wheel even as her head was pulled toward the rear compartment. She felt the tendons in her neck tighten to the verge of snapping—

And then the limousine cannoned through the fence. The vampires lost their grip and fell backward as the vehicle bounced over dirt mounds, flattened endless rows of tall weeds, and skipped across large pools of standing water. Karen had only a few moments to wonder who'd come up with the bright idea of sticking a swamp in the middle of Queens, before the limo powered through a final thicket of scruffy foliage and came to an abrupt halt—on the remains of an airfield she'd never known existed.

The tarmac was cracked and partially submerged under a foot of oily, mosquito-infested water, and the two hangars and a small luncheonette on the opposite side of the landing strip were empty, rusted shells on the verge of collapse, but the site wasn't entirely abandoned. A heavily armed ground crew was taking up defensive positions behind an SUV and a fuel truck near the cyclone fence that separated the airport from the street.

There was also a private jet parked on the runway. With its engines running.

This was the vampires' escape route, Karen realized—but there was no way in hell she was letting her daughter's killer get away. Especially not when the police were so close behind; she could hear sirens approaching from beyond the fence on the far side of the landing strip.

She glanced at the chauffeur, who was slumped in his seat with blood from his broken nose covering the area around his mouth like a crimson goatee. He'd banged the back of his head pretty hard against the partition when the limo crashed the fence, so odds were good he was too dazed to be of any further trouble.

The sound of the rear doors opening caught Karen's attention and she reacted immediately, snaking her left leg past the driver to stomp the accelerator. *Let's see them fly out of here after I've taken out the plane's landing gear,* she thought.

The limo's back tires squealed as they spun wildly, but the car refused to move forward. Karen pounded the steering wheel in frustration. The damn thing was stuck in the mud. She mashed down even harder on the gas pedal. "Come on, come on!" she urged.

A shriek of tearing metal made her jump, and she turned to see the passenger-side door being ripped from its hinges.

Zaqiel snarled at her through the opening, then reached in and grabbed her right arm. He dragged her from the vehicle and held her by the neck in one hand, inches off the ground. "You're as insolent as your bothersome offspring," he commented, then flashed a sadistic smile. "Your *late* offspring, I should say."

Karen spat in his face.

Zaqiel growled and tightened his grip. Karen gasped for air, lashing out with punches and kicks, but her struggles only made him laugh. It was a blood-chilling sound.

"This is the New York Police Department!" an amplified male voice suddenly boomed. *"Drop your weapons and lay flat on the ground!"*

Surprised, Zaqiel stopped crushing Karen's throat and looked up. So did everyone else.

Through the spots dancing in front of her eyes, Karen observed a swarm of police helicopters forming a rough semicircle above the airfield. "Finally," she wheezed.

"I repeat," the voice roared from a loudspeaker mounted on one of the helicopters, *"drop your weapons and lay flat on the ground!"*

Zaqiel released Karen and turned to the Japanese clan leader in the black, Victorian Era ruffled dress. "Since when can humans fly?"

Sitting on the tarmac while she rubbed her bruised throat, Karen thought that was probably the oddest question anyone could ask, given the circumstances. Yet it prompted one of her own: before his resurrection a short time ago, Annie had related the story of how she had fought and killed Zaqiel, but had deliberately avoided saying just when that had occurred. If the angel was unaware of manned flight, which would indicate his death predated the Wright Brothers . . . Just how old *was* Annie?

Karen shook her head. Annie didn't look a day over thirty, maybe thirty-five at the most. No way could she be over a hundred years old. That was just too hard to believe.

Like vampires and fallen angels and shape-shifters, K?

Like Pan's monsters?

"My lord," Lady Sasaki replied, "I will be more than happy to discuss the subject with you—once we are airborne." She gestured at the plane. "Please . . . ?"

"Very well." Zaqiel began striding toward the jet—until Karen jumped on his back.

She attempted a choke hold—the sort of takedown move her mother, Eleanor, had tried to teach Karen when she was a young girl. Ellie Noor had been a six-time female wrestling champion in her 1950s prime, so who better to teach her daughter how to defend herself against bigger opponents? Karen wrapped one arm around Zaqiel's windpipe while locking it in place with her other hand behind his head; then she squeezed. It seemed to have no effect on him.

Karen bit her lip. Was she doing it right? She'd never enjoyed Mom's fighting lessons; when she was Pan's age she'd been more interested in being romanced by boys than in learning how to beat them up. Oh, God, she thought with growing panic, did a fallen angel even *need* to breathe? She snarled and squeezed even harder. Whether he did or not didn't matter—this son of a bitch had killed her baby girl and she had to stop him from getting away.

That steely resolve quickly shattered when the vampires began tearing into her.

Head still pounding from the concussion, leg muscles now trembling from exertion after slogging double-time through the wetland, covered in mud and dirt and blood, Annie crashed through the weeds that towered over her. After leaving the scene of the accident she'd morphed into a falcon in order to fly to the runway—forgetting that a broken hand denied time to heal properly would transform into a broken wing. She'd barely cleared the chain-link fence surrounding the wetland before the pain overwhelmed her concentration, forcing her to shift back to human form in midair. It made for a sloppy landing.

Yet in spite of her injuries, she'd made fairly good time crossing the marsh. With a final burst of energy she shoved her way past the final tangle of wild growth and stepped onto the airfield—in time to see Karen trying to choke the undead life out of Zaqiel.

Regardless of the severity of the situation, Annie couldn't help but smile. It was easy to see from where Pan had gotten her strong will. Then the smile fractured and became a teeth-baring snarl, as she thought of the poor girl lying dead in the street.

Karen screamed as Lady Sasaki raked her black-lacquered nails across the woman's back, slicing through T-shirt and skin with ease. Stripes of blood soaked into the white cotton as Karen lost her grip on Zaqiel and crumpled at the vampiress's feet.

Annie ran forward, reaching for the leather sheath hanging from her belt as her sneakers splashed through the fetid water soaking through the tarmac. Before the shoot-out in Astoria, she'd armed herself with a pair of specially made KA-BAR serrated tactical knives, edged with silver, that she kept in the mini-arsenal stored in the Murena. One of the knives had fallen off her belt during the crash, but she still had the other available.

A reed-thin male vampire in an elegant black suit was the first to hear her approach, but by the time he turned to face Annie she'd already hurled the weapon at him. The nine-inch blade punctured his throat before he could utter a warning— but in dying his finger spasmodically squeezed the trigger of the Glock he was holding. The single shot was all the warning Kiyoshi and her party needed to learn of Annie's arrival.

She dove for cover behind the limousine as three male vampires—the representatives from House Orlock—opened fire. Kiyoshi and Miyuki took Zaqiel by the arms and bustled him toward the plane. It took some effort to get him moving— from the expression of rage that he flashed at Annie, it was clear he wanted to stay. Probably wanted to reminisce with his ex-girlfriend about their apocalyptic breakup back in 1820—when she'd impaled him with the Spear of Longinus and cut off his head. Good times.

The third female vampire scooped up Karen and ran after her clan leaders. Annie stepped out from cover to try and intercept her, but the cover fire was too intense. Annie had no choice but to retreat as the male trio hurried to board the plane, which started taxiing before the scarecrow in the dark blue suit had made it through the hatch.

Annie charged out from behind the limo and scooped up the Glock owned by the vampire she'd knifed. As the plane picked up speed she ran after it, firing round after round at the tires and windows.

That's when the NYPD apparently decided they'd sat on the sidelines long enough and moved in. Forcefully.

A Bearcat-model armored car slammed through the chain-link gates, flattening them as it roared toward the airstrip. Behind it came a SWAT van—perhaps even the one Annie had sped around on the parkway—and a pair of police cruisers. Other cop cars screeched to a halt inside the entrance, creating a barrier to prevent the plane's ground crew from escaping.

Escape, however, seemed to be the last thing on the minds of the vampires' helpers. They opened fire with semiautomatic weapons as soon as the Bearcat had swept the gates aside. Bullets pinged off the armored vehicle and then it was past the shooters, churning up a wake of loose gravel as it swerved onto the crumbling tarmac to join Annie in her pursuit of the jet. The ground crew turned their attention to the SWAT team and the shoot-out began in earnest.

The end of the runway was fast approaching, and Annie exhausted the Glock's ammunition clip by firing the last two rounds at the plane's tail rudder, though that did nothing to slow the jet's progress. She tossed the gun away. Bulletproof glass had prevented her from smashing the windows, but she'd hit the landing gear at least a dozen times—without effect. Apparently the wheels were run-flat tires that remained inflated even when punctured. She would have needed a higher-caliber weapon to damage them.

The nose lifted as the plane began to take off, but Annie didn't slow down. She'd made a vow to kill Zaqiel, and she was determined to honor it. Instead of giving in to despair over his apparent escape, she concentrated on reconfiguring the bones and muscles of her body into powerful wings that sprouted from her shoulder blades. What she expected to do, unarmed, against a private jet was a question she chose to ignore for the moment. First, she had to catch up to it; then she could worry about how to force it to land.

From the corner of her eye she saw the Bearcat pull alongside as her feet left the tarmac. A hatch on the roof flew open, and an Emergency Service Unit police officer in full tactical gear popped up, holding a Colt M4A1 assault rifle.

Seeing the military-grade weapon made Annie smile. *What was that about being unarmed . . . ?*

The cop gawped with saucer-size eyes at her wings for a couple of seconds before he found his voice.

"Uh . . . get down on the ground!" he barked.

Annie swooped over and plucked the M4 from his hands before he could target her. "Thanks!" she called back as she soared upward. "I just need to borrow this for a second! I'll bring it right back—promise!"

She banked northward on an intercept course. The jet, flying west, would have to turn north as well, giving a wide berth to the area around LaGuardia Airport to avoid crossing flight paths with commercial airliners. She smiled as the jet did exactly that, and increased her speed.

Annie landed on the south tower of the Whitestone Bridge and braced the M4's stock against her shoulder, then used the sniper scope mounted on the upper receiver to draw a bead on the pilot. She had no intention of shooting the man—the last thing she wanted was the plane crashing with Karen aboard—but she figured the threat of being shot would be enough to make him turn back.

What she *didn't* figure on was the plane's door opening in midflight—and a body being tossed out. Blond hair flashed golden in the light of the afternoon sunlight.

"Karen!" Annie screamed. She dropped the rifle and dove off the bridge, angling her powered descent to place her between Karen and the river that seemed to be rising to meet them.

They collided twenty feet above the water with an impact so jarring it shattered Annie's concentration, causing her wings to revert to their natural skin and bone. Flightless, the two women plunged into the East River.

Annie was the first to surface, and she quickly reached down to pull Karen's head above the water. Karen gasped, then went limp. Annie breathed a sigh of relief. Alive and wet was always better than dead and waterlogged.

An NYPD powerboat came roaring over from nearby Flushing Bay, but the huntress was more interested in the dark metallic speck that soared higher into the bright June sky.

Enjoy your resurrection while you can, Zaqiel, she thought. *It's going to be a short-lived one.*

Annie brushed the hair away from her friend's face. "Karen?" she asked softly, and gave her a gentle shake. "Karen? Can you hear me?"

Karen's head lolled back and she opened her mouth to release a low moan.

Sunlight gleamed along the jagged edges of her new sharklike teeth.

3

Soft music was the first thing Pan became aware of as her eyes slowly opened: one of those "golden oldies" Grandma Ellie liked to listen to. This one involved a woman singing about how Mama said there'd be days like this, but Pan doubted either the singer or her mother had ever experienced *anything* as weird as Pan had, even on their worst day.

Her vision was a tad out of focus, but as it cleared she spotted birds hovering above her in a pale-blue sky. *So pretty,* she thought drowsily, but when they didn't flap their wings yet continued to remain airborne, her brow furrowed in confusion. It took her a few seconds to realize she was staring at a painted ceiling; the birds were part of a mural in a large oval frame set directly above her.

Okay, so she wasn't outside as she'd first imagined but she wasn't home, either— the ceiling in her room at Dad's apartment was off-white and one corner was a little water-damaged from an old leak in the apartment on the floor above. Which raised the questions of whose bedroom this was, and how she'd come to be in it. Interesting questions, to be sure, but neither concerned her as much as knowing where her parents were.

The woman singing about her mama was replaced by a babble of male voices, followed by the mellow wail of a saxophone and the soothing voice of Marvin Gaye as he launched into "What's Going On?"; Pan recognized it from her dad's collection of Motown albums, and smiled. *What's going on?* She couldn't think of a better question to ask, given her situation.

She turned her head toward the source of the music. On a nightstand beside the bed she was lying on was an antique wooden radio, big with sides that curved to a point at the top, large dials, and a giant speaker behind a cloth grill. Next to the radio were a box of tissues, a plastic bulb-shaped, lavender-scented air freshener, an empty drinking glass, and a silver pitcher. Beyond the nightstand was a large window, through which she could see that it was raining outside, storm clouds roiling above a park across the street. "Good staying-in weather," as Grandma Ellie liked to say on overcast days.

Her maternal grandmother would like this place, Pan thought as she looked around. Along with the ceiling mural there were antique furnishings: a dresser with mirror, a pair of upholstered straight-back chairs, even a tall potted plant with big droopy leaves in one corner. The decorative style reminded her of Mom's home, back in Schricksdorp—*Our* home, Pan reminded herself. She'd already done enough to make Karen feel miserable about transplanting her daughter to the Bonifants' Upstate New York hometown after she and Dad divorced; from now on, she promised to be more grateful for the time she and Mom spent together. Once they'd been reunited, that is.

Pan inhaled deeply, appreciative of the fact that she still *could* breathe after what she'd been through, and caught a whiff of a familiar tang in the room, one the air freshener couldn't completely disguise. Something clean . . . antiseptic.

A hospital smell.

For a few moments her heart raced wildly—given her history as a psychiatric patient, waking up alone in a strange hospital was never a good thing—but she quickly snapped out of her panic when she realized that Dad wouldn't have just dumped her into some unknown psych ward and headed off who-knew-where. If anything, he probably would have bullied the paramedics who'd arrived at the war zone into taking her to the best medical facility available. That had always been his way—when it came to his daughter's health, civility tended to be the least of his concerns. And since she didn't see him passed out in a chair beside the bed, she could only assume he'd taken a bathroom break, or something. Even overprotective dads had to pee sometime.

Still, she'd like to know where she was. Pan raised her head and discovered she was attached to a half-dozen medical devices: pulse monitor clipped to her right index finger; IV drip poking into her left arm; electrodes for the heart monitor and brain scanner stuck to her chest and temples; some other machines she didn't recognize. *Doesn't all this bring back some memories,* she thought glumly. *All that's missing are the restraints . . .*

Reminiscing about calamitous psych ward visits could wait for another day, though. She'd made a promise to find Mom, to rescue her, and she had every intention of keeping it. Lying around like a boneless chicken wasn't going to help her accomplish that goal.

Pan sat up—or tried to, anyway. The quick ascent made her light-headed. She closed her eyes and waited for the dizzy spell to pass, refusing to give in to the fatigue that was trying to lull her back to sleep.

"Hold on, now, where do you think you're going?" a female voice asked. Pan opened her eyes and through spotty vision saw a white-garbed, twentysomething African-American nurse enter the room. She reached out to gently push her patient back. "You need to lie—" Pan emphatically waved her off and she held up his hands in surrender. "Okay. Fine. But if you're going to insist on sitting up at least let me raise the bed." Pan nodded and the nurse pressed a button on the side of the bed frame; the top half of the mattress rose to support her.

Pan opened her mouth to offer thanks, but her tongue felt heavy and glued to the bottom of her mouth. She grunted in frustration. The nurse, however, seemed to understand what she was trying to do and picked up the pitcher, filled the glass with water, added a bendable straw, and sat on the edge of the bed to direct the straw into her patient's mouth. As she took big sips, Pan's gaze drifted from the woman's kindly face to a small metal nametag pinned to the left side of her tunic: CHRISTA. Below that was embroidered a small, ornate design: a braided golden rope that formed a circle around a sky-blue field; in the center floated a seven-pointed star, below which hung a sword with a golden hilt and a silver blade. The symbol looked familiar, but Pan couldn't remember why; she'd seen it recently, though, and it hadn't been embroidered. Something metallic . . .

She felt her tongue finally loosen and pushed the straw away. "Thanks," she gasped. "Where . . . where's my dad? I've gotta talk to him about—"

"Your mother? She's safe," Christa assured her. "Ms. Mazarin got to her in time." Pan started. "R-really?"

Christa nodded and Pan breathed a quavering sigh of relief. "Thank you, Annie," she whispered as she wiped away the tears that flowed down her cheeks. When she got out of this hospital, the first thing she was going to do was offer some token of her appreciation to Annie—wax her hot-rod hearse every week, pick up her dry cleaning forever, paint her a portrait . . . whatever. She owed Annie more than she could ever express through any good deed, but she was willing to give it a try.

And yet . . . she couldn't help but worry about what sort of condition Mom had been in when Annie "got to her in time." What did "in time" really mean? "How . . . how is she? Did the . . ." *Don't say vampires, you'll sound like an idiot.* "Did they do anything to her?"

There was a momentary flicker in Christa's eyes—she knew something—but then she smiled awkwardly and turned her attention to smoothing out the bedsheets. "She's recovering in another part of the hospital. And your father's in the next room, sleeping. Poor man didn't sleep a wink until the doctors told him you were stable, then Ms. Mazarin finally convinced him to go lie down. He got to bed about an hour ago."

Poor man was right, Pan thought, remembering the horrified expression on Dad's face when she'd started talking to him from beyond the grave. And when she knocked the spear out of her body it'd been a wonder she hadn't given him a heart attack.

Speaking of hearts, she suddenly realized that hers wasn't aching anymore. She lifted up the neck of her gown and found her chest sporting a white, vertical scar about three inches long—roughly the size of an ancient spearhead, turned on its side.

Pan frowned. Before the all-out vampire war, Annie had explained that, in addition to possessing the ability to see the monsters that really and truly existed in the world—what Pan had called "monstervision" for the past decade, but her mental-health therapists regarded as schizophrenia—the girl was also a healer: a supernaturally gifted, walking, talking first-aid kit. Or something like that; Annie had said it was sort of like being an extreme biofeedback expert. So, Pan wanted to know, if she was a healer how come she had this stupid scar?

Could it be the healing power didn't work on its owner? No, that didn't make sense—something had to be keeping her alive, and it wasn't any of these beeping, booping scanners she was glued to. Maybe surviving her escape from purgatory had drained most of the power and she needed to reenergize, like a cell-phone battery, and the scar wouldn't fade until she was back to a hundred percent.

Or maybe never being able to wear a V-neck top again was the price she had to pay for coming back from the dead. That would suck.

Pan dropped the gown and took another sip of water that Christa offered. "So, what hospital is this?"

"Agostino Gabrino Memorial. It's on the Upper West Side."

In Manhattan? It seemed a long way to go from Queens just to get medical care, but if this nurse knew about Annie it probably meant Pan's new friend had pulled some strings with the administrators. Pan had never heard of the place, but that didn't mean anything. Unless she was a "guest" in their psychiatric wards she paid hospitals as little attention as possible.

"And how long've I been here?"

"Three days."

Pan started. *"Three days?"* She threw back the sheets. "I want to see Mom."

Christa eased the covers back into place. "You can't right now. She's in isolation."

A chill spider-crawled up Pan's spine. "What's wrong with her?"

Christa flashed another awkward smile. "Let's concentrate on you first, all right? You just went through a terrible ordeal and—"

"I was *dead,* okay?" Pan snapped. "My mother got kidnapped by a bunch of vampires and a fallen angel, and he *killed* me. Sorta. For a little while. Now I find out I was in a coma for three days and my mom's in an isolation ward. 'Terrible ordeal' doesn't even come *close.*"

"All right, so a poor choice of words," Christa replied, apparently unfazed by conversing with a formerly dead girl about vampires and angels. "But really, Pandora, there's nothing you can do for her."

"Not right now, anyway," Pan muttered. She felt winded and dizzy from that little outburst. Frustrated, she pounded the bed with her fist. She hated being sick. She hated being unable to help. Why couldn't this stupid power hurry up and reenergize, or whatever?

Christa patted her hand consolingly. "You know what the best thing you could do for your mother is?"

"Yeah," Pan said glumly. "Get better."

"Right. So you're going to stay right here in bed and do just that, and let the doctors take care of your mother."

Pan folded her arms across her chest. "And what if I don't want to stay in bed?"

Christa tilted back her head, to look down her nose at her patient. "Oh, but you *will*," she said archly.

"And why is that?"

She glanced over her shoulder, to make certain they were alone, then leaned in close to whisper, in a deep, overly dramatic voice, "Because the Power of Christa *compels* you."

An *Exorcist* joke, of all things. Pan laughed and settled back on her pillow.

"You better not be laughin' about *me*, Vampira," warned a familiar voice, "or I'll clobber you."

Christa stepped back so Pan could see into the hallway. Standing just outside the door was Sheena McCarthy. Her purple hair and makeup were perfectly styled, as always, but couldn't draw attention away from the bags under her eyes; it seemed that, like Dave Zwieback, she hadn't slept much in the past three days. Sheen clutched a dripping umbrella, and wore black boots under distressed jeans, with a black zip-up hoodie over a Poizen KP T-shirt. The cartoony, silk-screened image on the shirt was that of a zombified Panda bear with half its brain exposed.

Pan smiled. "Hey, Jungle Queen. Nice T."

Sheen flashed a big grin. "Yeah, seemed like the appropriate thing to wear. When I saw it in the shop the other day I instantly thought of you, so I *had* to buy it. Nice of you to finally wake up so you could admire its awesomeness."

"I'll leave you two alone," Christa said. "But I'll be back after I let Dr. Carlyle know you're awake. Would you like some soup?"

"How about a burger?" Pan asked. "I am *starving*."

"Let's start with something lighter," Christa replied. "Just to make sure you can keep it down."

Pan sighed dramatically. "Okay, fine. Soup, then."

"How 'bout split pea?" Sheen suggested. "It'll look really colorful when you barf it up."

"It's chicken noodle soup," Christa replied. "I'll be back with it in a few minutes." On her way out, she paused and lightly placed a hand on Sheena's shoulder. "Just don't get her too worked up, all right?"

"Yes, ma'am," Sheen answered in a respectful tone . . . before grinning devilishly at Pan when the nurse departed. She walked over and sat on the bed beside Pan, then reached out to brush a few stray blond strands away from Pan's eyes. "How you feelin', Zee?" she asked gently.

"Pretty good . . . for a zombie chick just back from the dead. But I sure am hungry." She grinned wickedly as she eyed her friend—"Bet you taste like chicken."—and smacked her lips. "Nom nom nom."

Sheen frowned, apparently not in the mood for jokes, and gave her a hard nudge. "No, seriously, Zee. How do you feel?"

Pan flashed a tiny smile. "Alive."

"Yeah," Sheen said quietly—then threw her arms around Pan's neck in a tight hug and began sobbing. Pan returned the embrace. And the tears.

"You scared the *crap* outta me," Sheen scolded. "Don't you *ever* do that to me again, you hear?"

Pan smiled, and rubbed her best friend's back to comfort her. "Sure," she replied wryly. "I'll definitely keep *your* needs in mind next time I feel like getting staked by a vampire-angel thing." She paused, listening as Sheen's crying settled down to a contented sigh. "You better not be getting snot in my hair, or I swear to God I'll kick your ass."

Sheen gave a phlegmy laugh. "Too late."

Pan grunted. "*So* dead." And yet she gave no indication of making good on her threat, or even of letting go, so they sat there quietly until Pan eventually forced herself to pull away before they both melted into puddles of tears.

Sheen grabbed some tissues from the box on the nightstand so they could clean up. As she wiped her runny nose she asked, "So you gonna tell me what happened? I mean, I *saw* you, Zee. You were . . . y'know."

"Dead," Pan said softly. A tiny shiver ran up her spine. It felt so weird—and frightening—to say it out loud, but it was also kind of exciting, in an unsettling, creeptastic way. She thought back to the mad fit of giggling she'd experienced after her comeback. Pandora Zwieback: The Girl Who Laughed at Death.

That worried her, too, because she should be the last person laughing about dying. And yet it *was* kind of funny—wasn't it? Stabbed through the heart, her soul cast into purgatory, yet refusing to stay down because she'd made a promise to Mom to rescue her from the vampires. Maybe not The Girl Who Laughed at Death, but The Girl Too Busy to Die?

Pan nervously bit down on her bottom lip. *God, what am I becoming . . . ?*

She swiped at the fresh tears running down her cheeks with the tissues she'd unconsciously crumpled into a ball. Then she realized that Sheen had been talking the entire time Pan had been lost in introspection.

"—and I got so freaked out when I saw you just . . . just layin' there with that thing . . . that spear in you . . ." Sheen paused on the verge of crying again, and drew a shuddery breath. Pan reached out to give her hand a gentle squeeze.

"I heard you yelling for help," she said with a warm smile. "Thanks."

"Just wish I could've done more," Sheen muttered.

"Hey, you looked after my dad when I ran after Mom, didn't you?"

Her best friend shrugged. "Yeah, but it wasn't like those vampires were gonna come back to the museum after—"

"Sheen, *quit it*," Pan interjected. "Look, I know you've always looked out for me, and you know I love you for it, but right then you and Javi protecting Dad was way more important to me than—"

"Gettin' yourself killed?"

"*No.* But more important than you backing me up while I was doing something crazy-stupid 'cause I was worried about Mom."

"Like gettin' yourself killed."

Pan sighed. She could spend all day arguing about her motivations but, really, Sheen had a point. "Yeah, like getting myself killed," she finally agreed. "But I mean, I already thought I'd . . . lost Mom. I couldn't have taken it if something happened to Dad, too. So . . . thanks."

Sheen nodded. "You heard Annie got your mom back?"

"Yeah. Christa, that nurse that just left, told me and said she's in another part of the hospital. She mentioned an isolation ward. She also said Dad's sleeping next door. I wanna check on him first, then I've *gotta* see Mom."

"Uh-huh." Sheen eyed the medical devices hooked up to her friend. "And how you plan on doin' that with all'a this stuck to you?"

Pan lowered her head, grinned wickedly, and stared at her friend from the tops of her eyes. "Moo-ha-ha."

Javier Maldonado had just stepped off the elevator onto Pan's floor when alarms began sounding at the nurses' station at the end of the hall.

The nurse sitting behind the desk—a cute blonde named Dina—jumped up from her chair and hurried down the corridor into one of the rooms. Javi heard footfalls approaching from behind and pressed against the wall to allow a pair of nurses— one of them Christa, who placed a bowl of soup she was carrying on a small table next to the elevator—and Dr. Carlyle to go racing past him. It took Javi a couple of seconds to realize everybody was heading in the direction of Pan's room. Then he took off after them.

"Oh, man, *now* what?" he muttered.

Ever since they'd met while chasing the monkeylike orang pendek in the tunnels below Penn Station, Javi had been struck by two things about Pan. One was her strength of will. This was a girl who wasn't going to back down to anybody. Monsters, fallen angels, or high school mean girls—if they got in her way, she wasn't afraid of taking them on. Even death couldn't hold onto her, apparently, although no one—not even Annie, who was immortal—had been able to explain how that was possible. When he'd called Pan a badass chick down in the tunnels, after she'd saved his life from that runaway primate who'd tried to crush his skull with an iron bar, he'd been half joking—but now? *Badass* didn't even begin to describe how awesome she was—although, he had to admit, he wasn't sure yet if all these weird powers she possessed made her even more appealing . . . or downright scary.

What if she was turning into one of those creatures that Annie was always hunting? What if monstervision and super-healing and being unkillable were just the start of what she could do, and she became even more powerful? Would Annie eventually have to . . . destroy Pan before she posed a threat to the whole world?

Javi's stomach did a nervous flip. *Man, I sure hope it doesn't come to anything like that . . .*

The other quality about Pan that had left an impression on him was a vulnerability she possessed that made him want to protect her—even though she probably didn't need the help. Sure, he'd felt the same way about other girls he'd dated (although, come to think of it, he and Pan hadn't been on a date yet), but some of them had been faking it—putting on a helpless female act to get his undivided attention. Pan was different, though. Her pain was real. Ten years of thinking she was crazy because she could see monsters like Annie could, plus all the grief piled on her from kids and adults treating her as a freak because they were too stupid to accept her for what she was, not to mention the added stress of dealing with her parents' divorce last year—that was too much drama for, like, five people's lives, let alone one teenaged girl. And Pan, as his mother would say, was a girl who wore her emotions on her sleeve for all to see. Was it any wonder, then, that he felt willing to take on the world if it would help put her troubled mind at ease?

By the time he arrived at Pan's doorway the alarm had been shut off. Javi's jaw dropped when he realized Pan had finally woken up and was standing a little wobbly on the carpeted floor, holding onto Sheena for support, with Carlyle and the nurses clustered around them. The brain monitor had been switched off—no doubt the cause of the alarm—and the electrodes removed, but the adhesive pads were still glued to Pan's temples. They looked like the shaved down stumps of antlers. The wild bed hair she had—mad clumps of black-dyed tresses sticking out in all directions—made her appear even goofier.

Javi breathed a sigh of relief; for a minute there, he'd been afraid something terrible had happened to Pan—although considering she'd been dead three days ago, how much worse could things get? Then as he gazed at her faux antler stumps and crazy hair, a grin slowly spread across his face. How could any chick that messed-up cute ever turn out to be a superpowered monster? *That was just stupid thinking. Pan ain't no monster—but man, from that look she's giving the doc I sure wouldn't wanna make her angry . . .*

As Dr. Carlyle was apparently discovering for himself.

"I just want to see my mom and dad, all right?" Pan snapped.

"You really need to stay in bed, Ms. Zwieback—" Carlyle began.

"No!" Even though the goateed, fortysomething African-American doctor was a good foot taller than Pan, she glared at him as though they were on the same eye level. "I'm *done* with staying in bed"—she pointed to the remaining contraptions she was attached to—"and I'm done with all of this. Just get this crap off me and let me go see my parents."

Carlyle smiled. "That 'crap,' as you put it, was monitoring your vital signs for the past three days, so I'd appreciate it if you'd refrain from giving my staff heart attacks by unplugging everything because you feel you have places to be." Frowning, he turned to Sheena. "Gave up on the escape plan after the alarm sounded?"

"No." Sheena jerked a thumb toward her best friend. "Hellgirl here wanted me to take out that catheter thingy next, but no way was I gonna touch it."

Pan rolled her eyes. "A little pee wasn't gonna kill you."

Sheena grunted. "So *you* say."

"Ladies, please." Carlyle gestured to Pan. "Now, Ms. Zwieback, I realize you've been through a lot in the past few days and you're worried about your parents, but it's *your* well-being I'm most concerned with. So if you'd kindly get back to bed, I'll consider disconnecting the other monitors—after I've examined you. All right?" He folded his arms across his broad chest and raised an inquisitive eyebrow in challenge.

Pan stared at him for a few moments, then lowered her gaze. "Fine. Whatever." With Sheena's help she began climbing into bed. Then she happened to look up—to lock eyes with Javi.

He smiled, trying to play it cool even though his heart was racing with excitement.

"Hey, Cookie, welcome back," he said, forcing his voice to remain level—or had it just cracked a bit when he'd started speaking?

Pan let loose a tiny scream.

4

Finding Javi standing in the doorway had been a pleasant surprise for Pan—until she realized that the back of her hospital gown was wide open and her butt was sticking out. She yelped like a dog whose tail had been stepped on and hurriedly yanked the bedsheets up to her chin. Her cheeks burned with embarrassment. The ones on her face, that is, but she was totally certain the other ones were just as red. Her whole body felt like one giant blush.

Javi blushed, too, much to her surprise. He tried to act nonchalant but it was obvious he'd taken a peek as she'd scrambled for cover, because he couldn't meet her gaze.

"Get a good look, Jeter?" Sheen asked, frowning at the boy in jeans and tight-fitting New York Yankees T-shirt. He sure did look good in them, Pan thought.

"Quit it, Sheen," Pan stage-whispered. "Thanks for coming, Javi. I really appreciate it."

"I'm just glad to see you're okay." He paused a moment. "You *are* okay, aren't you?"

"Close enough," Pan said, and smiled at her two friends. "Better now that I'm seeing you guys again."

Her gaze drifted over to a small bag in Javi's left hand; the logo for the coffeehouse chain Latte's Inferno was printed on the black plastic. She smiled, intrigued. Hot, adventurous, *and* a gift-bearer—why couldn't she have met *him* two years ago, instead of her last boyfriend, Curtis "Amadeus" Sheridan? She would have been spared the disastrous relationship . . .

"That for me?" she asked, nodding toward the bag.

"You bet." Javi walked up to the bed and held out the parcel, which Pan accepted.

"Annie told me the emergency room doctors had to, uh, cut up your clothes to get them off'a you so they could treat you, so I got you this."

Inside the bag was a black T-shirt with a colorful silk-screened image printed on the front: a manga-style drawing of a devil girl's face—that of Lilitu, daughter of the devilish mascot of Latte's Inferno. Her tongue was sticking out in a defiant expression, a Band-Aid plastered across the bridge of her nose. It was a variation of the devil-girl T Pan's mother had given to her before all hell had literally broken loose at the museum—the T, Pan now remembered, that she'd been wearing when Zaqiel had—

"They didn't have the same kind you were wearing the other day," Javi continued, "but I thought . . ."

"No, no, it's great," Pan said, pushing aside the unpleasant memory. She draped the shirt over her chest to show it off. "I love it."

"Least it's not a Yankees jersey," Sheen commented, ever the proud Mets fan.

A die-hard Mets fan herself, Pan still gave her best friend the side-eye. "Y'know, I haven't forgotten about all those boogers you left in my hair."

Sheen shrugged. "I figured you could use a snack for later. To keep off those zombie cravings you were havin' before."

Dr. Carlyle loudly cleared his throat. "If we're all done with the fashion show, I'd like a few minutes to examine my patient." He turned to the blond-haired nurse who'd come in with him. "Nurse Whithouse, would you kindly direct her friends to the waiting area and then bring me some collodion remover for the electrode glue? I wouldn't want Ms. Zwieback to start tearing her skin off because we moved too slow in taking off the pads."

"Right away, Doctor," Dina replied, and turned to Sheen and Javi. "If you'll follow me . . . ?"

"I already know the way." Sheen looked to Pan and smiled playfully. "I'll let the gang know you decided to stop layin' around like a bum. They were so freaked out when they heard what happened they wanted to come right over, but Dr. Carlyle wouldn't let 'em in."

"Well, this *is* a private hospital," Carlyle replied. "Emphasis on the 'private.' But I did allow you and your boyfriend access, didn't I?"

Pan started. "Ooo-vay's here?" Sheen's boyfriend, Uwe Kier, was of Germanic heritage, so Pan liked to rib him by over-pronouncing his name. It was an improvement, in her opinion, of the days when she used to call him "Huey," though he didn't feel the same way. Regardless, she and Uwe didn't quite get along, despite their shared interest in Goth culture—and their close relationships with Sheen, of course.

"Yeah," Sheen replied. "The poor baby's takin' a nap on one'a the waitin' room couches. Between the hours his boss has him workin' at the caterin' hall and me keepin' him up half the night on the phone while I was worryin' about you, he hasn't gotten a whole lotta sleep the last three days. But he never complained—not one time. He said he couldn'ta been able to sleep anyway, knowin' how upset I was."

Pan didn't know what to say. It always seemed kinda weird whenever she heard Sheen talk about Uwe's compassionate side—he usually tried to play it so cool that his attitude became pretty off-putting to most people. That's how she felt about him, in any case.

"Okay, Resurrection Girl, we'll see ya in a bit," Sheen remarked cheerfully as she headed out. "Love ya, Zee!" Then she and Javi were gone.

Pan smiled. "You too, Jungle Queen!" she called out.

Carlyle chuckled. " 'Resurrection Girl.' Is that your new nickname?"

"Sounds like one of those superhero comic books my brother used to read when we were kids," Christa remarked, and smiled. "You a superhero, Pandora?"

"It's super*heroine*," Pan said authoritatively, then her own smile faded as she touched the scar that ached dully beneath the hospital gown. "Actually . . . I don't know *what* I am anymore . . ."

"How you holding up?" Javi asked Sheena as they walked down the corridor.

She flashed a weary smile. "Better . . . now. I guess."

"Yeah, I know what you mean." He did. With Pan awake it seemed as though the crisis had passed—but had it, really? There were still so many questions to be answered, first and foremost being how she'd been able to accomplish her miraculous return. He knew from the firsthand accounts told by his paternal grandmother, Isadora, that as an immortal supernatural being Annie had the power to come back from the dead—Izzy used to be one of the monster hunter's adventurous running buddies back in the sixties and seventies—so was Pan immortal, too? Or something else entirely?

"Do you think Zee's gonna be okay?" Sheena asked, interrupting his thoughts.

Javi gazed intently at her face. For all the tough-girl attitude she liked to exhibit—especially in his presence, given his loyalty to the Yankees—he could see right past it, to the scared teen who three days ago had witnessed her best friend's murder, then had drawn back in fear as Pan rose from the dead right in front of her. The bags under Sheena's eyes were clear evidence of the nights she had stayed up worrying about Pan, and her shoulders were slumped as though she carried the weight of the world (as Grandma Izzy would say).

"I think that kinda depends on what you mean by 'okay.' I mean, after what happened at the museum . . ."

"Yeah," Sheena whispered.

They walked a few feet in silence before Javi spoke up again. "Can I ask you something?"

Sheena nodded.

"You've been her best friend since, like, forever, right?"

"Uh-huh," she replied with a smile.

"So you'd notice if anything was . . . different about her." *Like, if she was turning into a monster, maybe?*

Her eyes narrowed in suspicion. "What're you gettin' at?"

"I mean, you could tell if she wasn't still . . . Pan, right?"

For a moment, Sheena glared at him with unbridled fury; her lips curled in a fierce snarl. No doubt the years of defending her best friend against the kids and adults who'd treated Pan like a freak because of her so-called mental health problems had made Sheena extremely protective of her. But the anger quickly faded, replaced by an anguished expression. "I . . . um . . ." Her voice faded away.

Javi nodded glumly. He'd expected an answer like that.

Then Sheena came to an abrupt halt. Her hands balled into fists; her teeth clamped together tightly. "No," she growled.

"Yeah, me nei—"

"No!" she said loudly. "I *would* know if she was different. She's not just my best friend—I love her like she's my sister. I know her better'n anybody. And if there was anything different about her now that she's back I. would. know." She nodded her head once, sharply. "I would."

"Okay. And?"

"And she's still the same old Pan." Sheena paused a moment. "And even if she isn't, I don't care. I'm not gonna abandon her—I never did before, and I'm not doin' it now. Especially now. Zee's always been there for me, and I'm always gonna be there for her—no matter *what* kinda drama's goin' on."

"And what if . . . what if she's turning into something else?"

"Then I'll deal with it when she gets to that point." Sheena wagged an index finger at him. "And if you got any intentions of bein' her new boyfriend, you better learn to suck it up and deal with it, too. Zee's always been a . . . complicated girl. She probably told you all about that. Some guys couldn't handle the stuff she was goin' through even *before* it got weirder a few days ago. Well, now she's got some more complications. So if you wanna run off back to the Bronx before things get any more heavy, you best get to steppin'. You won't be the first loser who ever dumped her."

Javi flashed a tiny smile. For a white chick, Sheena sure did try hard to act street—a little too hard, maybe. "I'm not a loser, and I'm going anywhere. I actually think Pan is . . . well, kinda awesome. And if she wants my help, she's got it."

Sheena studied his face, obviously looking for any sign of insincerity, but Javi had meant every word of it.

"Okay, then," she finally replied.

They resumed their stroll toward the waiting room.

"So, uh . . . you been gettin' any sleep?" she asked.

"Little bit," he replied, holding up his right thumb and forefinger about an inch apart. "But I'm used to staying up late."

"Watchin' Yankee game replays on YES?" she asked with a smirk, referring to the baseball organization's cable network.

Javi ignored the jab. "Movies." He noticed her sly grin. "Not porn. The Acshun channel." That was a basic cable station dedicated to action films and repeats of adventure TV shows. According to stories Javi had read on the 'Net the weird spelling came about because the station's lawyers had explained to management that they couldn't trademark the word "action," so they devised a spelling of it that they *could* trademark. A pretty stupid idea, in Javi's opinion, but considering they ran movies uncut—even R-rated ones—after midnight, he was willing to put up with the lame spelling.

"So you stayed up watchin' movies while Zee was layin' in a coma?" Again, Sheena's eyes flashed with anger.

"No, that's how come I'm used to late nights," Javi countered in an even tone. "You asked, remember?"

The anger flared out. "Yeah," she muttered.

"Besides," Javi continued, "every time I tried closing my eyes, all I could see was Pan lying in the street with that spear in her."

Sheena released a shuddery, nervous breath. "Me, too," she whispered. "And there was so much blood . . ."

She blinked back tears, no doubt reliving that terrible moment right this second, then exhaled sharply, trying to will it from her thoughts. Javi had been attempting to do the same thing almost every waking moment, but it never seemed to work.

"Hey," he said gently, "did I ever thank you for saving my life?"

"Huh?" She stared at him in confusion for a second, taken off-guard by the question. "Uh, yeah, I think so."

During the museum siege, one of the vampire girls dressed like Alice in Wonderland—Sheena later explained it was a Japanese fashion style called Elegant & Gothic Lolita—had tried to kill Pan as she defended her father. Javi had intervened, only to become the next intended victim. It was Sheena, wielding the Spear of Longinus, who frightened away the bloodsucker before she could put her fangs into Javi's neck.

"Well, thanks again." Javi smiled slyly. " 'Course, I didn't tell my parents everything that happened. My dad'd probably disown me if I told him a *Mets* fan saved me."

"Yeah, well, I wasn't doin' it for you, A-Rod," Sheena snapped. "I was doin' it for Zee. I just didn't wanna spend the whole summer listenin' to her whine about The One That Got Away 'cause some stupid vampire chick wasted him."

Javi mentally patted himself on the back. He'd figured taking a poke at her favorite team would snap her back to normal.

"A Mets fan, fallin' for a Yankees fan," Sheena grumbled. "It's, like, a total abomination! Like—"

"Dogs and cats, living together?" Javi interjected. "*Ghostbusters* was on Acshun last week. They run horror movies, too, y'know."

A smile slowly lit Sheena's features. "That's not really a *horror* movie . . ."

And then, much to his surprise, she hugged him.

Gently, he returned the embrace.

"Thanks, Javier," she muttered into his shoulder. "Just do right by my girl, okay?"

Javi smiled warmly. "You got it."

A friendship was born.

5

"You almost killed my girlfriend."

Standing in front of the dresser mirror, Pan finished tying her hair in a ponytail and gazed at the reflection of Uwe Kerr—self-proclaimed "Goth Wizard" (whatever that was supposed to be) and "King of the Splatterpunks"—as he stared at her from the doorway.

He hadn't changed much from the last picture Pan had seen posted in Sheen's Facebook photo album: Uwe was still tall and lanky, pale-skinned and dour, his shoulder-length brown hair parted on the right side to flow over his left eye, his lips full and almost feminine. The distressed black jeans, black hoodie, and studded metal bracelets went well with the unruly bed-head and red-rimmed eyes he'd acquired from his nap in the waiting room. The purple streak in his hair was new, though, and he'd added a lip ring to the right side of his mouth.

Inwardly, Pan grimaced at the adornment—and the memories it evoked. Ammi'd had a tongue stud while he and Pan were a couple, and running her own tongue over it when they'd made out always felt like she was sucking on a ball bearing. In retrospect it was kinda gross, but back then she hadn't cared at all about love or romance or the disgusting taste of warm, saliva-coated metal—or even about herself, for that matter . . .

"Did you hear me?" Uwe asked, snapping her back to the present. "I said you almost killed my girlfriend."

"Yeah, I heard you," Pan muttered as she turned to face him.

It was his overinflated ego that had made Uwe such a turnoff right from the start. King of the Splatterpunks, indeed. "Splatterpunk" had gone out of style years ago, when the book industry—which had pretty much invented the term to describe the incredibly gory horror novels they released in the 1980s and '90s—stopped publishing them in great numbers. But, hey, if Huey liked showing off his ignorance of all things horror by using outdated phrases to describe himself, she figured that was his problem. Some people felt the need to make up titles to try and sound more important than they really were, and Uwe Kerr was no exception. His problem, as she'd once pointed out to him, was that if he was trying to impress his Goth peers he shouldn't try doing it around the daughter of a guy who owned a museum in Astoria called Renfield's House of Horrors and Mystical Antiquities. Nobody knew the genre better than her dad, she'd insisted. No-bo-dy. There was only one king of horror in the borough of Queens, and his name was David Zwieback.

Uwe started ignoring her after that, which was just fine with Pan. Unfortunately, it didn't mean he'd also stopped paying attention to Sheen; even worse, they started dating! Now, almost a year later, Pan *still* couldn't see what made him so attractive to her best friend. It sure wasn't his sparkling personality. Maybe, she'd often wondered, it was the accent that made Sheen so nuts for him. She'd had a major crush on Arnold Schwarzenegger when she was a little kid; it could be that Uwe reminded her of the Terminator—only without muscles. The boy could rent himself out as a flagpole . . .

Pan opened her mouth to greet him with some grade-A snark, but the words jammed in her throat. Uwe was absolutely right about Sheen's brush with danger. During the vampire attack, Pan had led Sheen and Javi through an underground tunnel that connected to Renfield's House of Horrors, with the purpose of reaching Pan's parents. She hadn't even thought of discouraging her best friend from joining the rescue attempt; in fact, she'd been counting on Sheen's support. It had been a pretty stupid thing to do, not to mention a totally selfish act.

"You're right," she said. "I'm sorry."

Uwe nodded once; apology accepted. "Sheena was very worried about you."

"And you, too?" she asked playfully.

"You should be so lucky."

Jerk. Pan motioned to the guest chair. "Well, come in if you're coming in. No reason for you to hang out in the hall." She sat on the bed. It was a little more than an hour since she'd woken up, but already she was feeling better. Getting rid of the mad-scientist playset she'd been hooked to was partly responsible for that condition; the rest was probably the healing power's doing. Dr. Carlyle had examined her at length and come to the decision that she could be disconnected from all the monitors, although they'd remain right where they were in case they were needed again.

Once free of the machines Pan then began nagging Carlyle to let her see Dad. Eventually he relented and she got to poke her head in next door. Dave's hair was a total mess and his jaw was dark with three days' beard growth, but he appeared to be sleeping peacefully. Satisfied that Dad was okay, she'd then demanded to see her mother.

Carlyle refused, saying that Karen had been through a major ordeal of her own and needed time to recover; when her condition changed—although he wouldn't explain what that "condition" was—Pan would be able to visit her. If she'd felt more like her old self instead of an achy zombie Pan would have pressed the issue, but even *she* had to admit she was in no shape to put up much of an argument. She let it go for the time being and allowed Christa to lead her to her room's private bath, where she showered and washed her booger-encrusted hair. She hadn't bothered making up her face; her corpselike pallor hadn't seemed to bother Javi. Of course, that probably was because he'd been more focused on her bare butt when it stuck out of the gown.

When she got out of the shower, Christa helped her dress before leaving to check on another patient. Dad had brought clothes from home, so Pan was able to ditch the gown and get back to normal attire: black jeans, high-top sneakers, and an old Black Sabbath T-shirt—a Mom hand-me-down. All in all, she thought she looked pretty good . . . for a zombie femme.

Uwe flopped into the guest seat and draped a leg over one of the chair arms. He had all the posture of The Blob.

"Comfy?" Pan asked.

He shrugged.

"Not scared to be alone with the Living Dead Girl?"

He gave another shrug at the Rob Zombie song reference. "I never felt threatened by you before."

Pan suppressed a grin. *Liar.* "Got any questions?"

"Did you see Lucifer while you were in hell? Sheena said you escaped from the pits."

Her eyebrows rose. "Where'd she hear that?"

"Apparently from you, in the ambulance on the way here. You were delirious and spouting some nonsense about sword-wielding angels and burning vampires. I assumed that meant you'd paid hell a visit."

Pan shook her head. "It wasn't hell, it was . . . I don't know—purgatory, I guess. But if I'd stuck around long enough I probably would've gotten a real good look at Satan's Fun House."

He grunted. "A pity."

"For you, maybe; not for me." A shiver ran up her spine as she remembered the angel closing in on her, his sword held high. If she hadn't lost her footing and knocked the spear loose . . .

"*Any*way," she said, pushing aside the unpleasant memory, "where's your lady?" Pan grinned. "She decide to run away with Javi?"

"No," Uwe said coolly. "They went to pick up some food. I think they're"—his lips twisted in mild distaste—"bonding."

At the mention of food Pan's stomach rumbled. She'd never gotten that soup Christa had promised, and now she was absolutely starving.

Uwe reached into a pants pocket and pulled out a cellophane package. He tossed it to Pan. "This should tide you over until they get back."

"Twizzlers!" The red, waxy candy was warm and soft from being in Uwe's pocket for who knew how long, but Pan was too hungry to care. She tore off a licorice strip and happily munched on it. Strawberry-flavored ones were okay, but . . . "Got any chocolate ones in the other pocket?" she asked between chews.

Uwe just frowned.

"Okay. Just asking," she mumbled around a second bite.

They sat quietly, Pan *nom*-ing away while Uwe looked bored. He finally broke the silence by asking, "So, what are you supposed to be, now?"

Pan stopped eating. "What do you mean?"

"Well, you died and then rose from the dead—*three days later*. That would make you either a vampire, or Jesus 2.0. So, which is it?"

She rolled her eyes. "I'm *not* a vampire—"

"And you're much too short to be a messiah. A troll, maybe."

"Nice," Pan said dryly. She studied his droll expression for a moment. "You don't believe any of this, do you?"

The shrug again. "The shoot-out I believe—obviously, because it was on every news channel while it was happening, not to mention all the cell-phone videos of it that are posted on YouTube. Your injuries, certainly. But armies of vampires fighting over some moldy old relic in your father's basement? Fallen angels? Shape-shifters? You dying and then escaping the underworld? It sounds like one of your major psychotic episodes."

Pan sneered. "Screw you." Typical Huey—just when she thought she might be misjudging him, he had to go and reconfirm her considerably low opinion of him.

Shrug. "You asked. I answered."

"So I imagine you think Sheena's crazy, too, huh? 'Cause she was there."

This time a small shake of his head. "No. I think she just got caught up in the hysteria."

"Hysteria." Pan tilted her own head to one side in confusion. "Y'know, Huey, for somebody who calls himself the 'King of the Splatterpunks' I never would've figured you to be so—"

"Rational?"

"—cynical about what went down." She flashed a condescending smile. "Or is it that you're just jealous? Vampires, fallen angels, and shape-shifters running loose in New York, finding out Gothopolis really exists—that's like a horror fan's dream come true! Oh, but you, poor baby, had to pull a double shift at the catering hall that day and missed out on all the excitement. That must've been so *terrible* for you." She made a pouty face to show just how much she empathized with the jerk—which was not at all.

That earned her a frown. "Hardly."

Pan snorted a laugh. "Liar."

Back to the shrug. "Believe what you like."

She pointed at him with a Twizzler. "What I *believe* is that you're an absolute tool who thinks he's better than everybody, when you're *so* not, and I only put up with your crap for Sheen's sake. But then I'm not the crazy girl everybody always thought I was"—*That I always thought I was, too*—"so maybe you're not the complete and utter jackass you work so hard at being. Maybe. But I doubt it."

Uwe snarled.

Pan took a bite of the licorice and gave him a big Cheshire-cat grin. Let him steam; she owed him for that snarky comment about her psychiatric history.

"You comin' on to my man, you hussy?" Sheen asked playfully as she and Javi entered the room. He carried a pair of large plastic shopping bags.

Pan laughed. "Not ever, girl. You can have him." She cut Uwe a look to signal that they ought to shelve their mutual dislike for the time being, to avoid making Sheen uncomfortable. He gave a small nod in agreement.

"What's in the bags?" he asked.

"Lunch," Javi replied as he placed them on the dresser. "There's this little Greek place over on Broadway that makes some awesome spanakopita and dolmades. I thought you'd like something better than hospital food"—he eyed the Twizzlers in her hand—"or candy."

Spinach pie and stuffed grape leaves from a Puerto Rican teen? Pan's eyebrows rose. "How do you know about Greek food?"

Javi looked away. "Um . . . well . . ."

"There was this Greek chick he used to date who lives in the neighborhood," Sheen replied. "He told me all about it after the owner recognized him. Seems him and Elektra Krankydopoulos—"

"Sophia Konstantatos," Javi interjected.

"Yeah, her," she continued without missing a beat. "They used to make googly eyes at each other over the falafel." She flashed a wicked smile, stage-whispered, "I think that's code for something," and wiggled her eyebrows.

"That was, like, a few months ago," he explained, "and it . . . didn't work out. She dumped me for some college guy with a fast car." He shrugged. "Probably for the best. Sophie was kinda . . . weird."

"Weird, huh? So what does that make *me*?" Pan asked.

"Well, you're weird, too," Javi said with a wink, "but you're the *good* kinda weird. Sophie was just . . . scary weird. It's hard to explain." He turned back to the bags and began unloading them. "Anyway, back to the important stuff. We got a couple lunch specials with salads and soup; I figured we could share so everybody gets a little of everything."

"That's the same thing Sophia used to say about him to her friends!" Sheen exclaimed with a grin.

"Quit it, booger queen," Pan warned.

Sheen stuck out the tip of her tongue in defiance. "Fine. Then where's my damn food?"

On the far side of the room, the door that led to the next room suddenly opened and through it shuffled a dark-haired, disheveled figure in jeans and a rumpled Mets T-shirt. The creature yawned mightily and sniffed the air, no doubt drawn by the mouthwatering scents of the takeout order.

"Who's got the spinach and onions?" Dave Zwieback asked sleepily. "Smells good." His gaze immediately fixated on the steaming containers on the dresser; then, slowly, it shifted to scan the teens gathered in his daughter's room.

Including his wide-awake daughter.

"Hey, Dad," she said with a gentle smile. "Enjoy your nap?"

Dave gasped sharply, as though he'd been punched in the stomach; his eyes brimmed over with tears. He tried to say something, but was too choked up to get the words out.

Pan leaped off the bed and ran over to embrace him. He gave her a hug so tight it felt as though he were afraid of letting go.

"Hey, Panda-bear," he whispered, and kissed the top of her head. "Welcome back, sweetheart."

She looked up at him with a teary grin. This time there wasn't a trace of fear or doubt of her identity in his eyes, only a powerful love for the daughter he'd thought he'd lost. "Miss me?"

A phlegmy laugh rumbled in his chest. "Always."

Sheen dabbed her own tear-filled eyes with a napkin. "Sure got dusty in here, all of a sudden . . ."

Thankfully, a light knock at the door prevented the scene from turning into Sobapalooza. Pan turned to see a tall, rugged-looking Hispanic man enter the room. He was in his sixties, with craggy-but-handsome features and shoulder-length silver hair. He looked incredibly distinguished in his dark suit—which was accessorized by one of those sword-in-a-circle pins on his left lapel—and practically radiated power; the strong aureate glow Pan saw around him was proof of that. This was a man you didn't mess with.

Something else, too. Pan couldn't place him, but knew she'd seen him before, and recently. Mentally, she shrugged. She'd figure it out eventually.

"I hope I'm not interrupting," the man said, his voice a deep rumble of thunder. "Dr. Carlyle told me his star patient was back on her feet, so I thought I'd stop by." He glanced at the takeout order on the dresser. "Also, I could smell your lunch from down the hall."

Dave smiled and waved him forward. "Hey, Alex. Come on in." He gestured toward Pan. "I'd like you to meet my daughter, Pandora."

"For the second time." Alex extended his hand, and Pan shook it.

"Second?" she asked.

Alex shrugged. "The first time was in the back of the ambulance on the way here; I wouldn't expect you to remember. You said I looked 'kinda like that guy in *Blade Runner*.' I assumed you weren't talking about Harrison Ford," he added with a wink.

Pan blushed. Jeez, just how much yammering had she done in that ambulance? Between this and what Uwe had reported, she'd apparently been a regular nonstop chatterbox. "Sorry. I was kinda out of it when I . . . you know . . . came back." Inwardly, she groaned. It sounded so ridiculous when she said it out loud like that, even if it was the truth.

"Don't worry about it," Alex replied. "Resurrections tend to do that. They mess with your head for a little while"—he fluttered one hand around his skull to emphasize his point—"but it passes."

Pan eyed him for a couple of seconds, wondering if he was being sarcastic with that remark, waiting for a condescending grin. Yet none came. He didn't appear to doubt her, as Uwe had; on the contrary, the seriousness of his expression seemed to indicate he believed everything that had happened to her. In fact, she had the oddest sensation he'd seen his fair share of people coming back from the dead . . .

Then she started. An image suddenly popped into her mind, of a silver-haired man standing atop a car in the middle of the vampire shoot-out, commanding an attack while he balanced a large boxlike weapon on one shoulder. "Wait! You were the guy blowing up the vampires' vans with that missile launcher—weren't you?"

Alex smiled. "One and the same."

"Wow," Pan said with a grin. "You were, like, a total badass."

He nodded. "So I've been told. And just between you and me? I am."

Pan laughed. She liked this Alex guy. "So, are you in the military, or part of a SWAT team or something like that? I know Annie called her son for backup before everything got crazy, but she didn't say who was coming." Her eyebrows shot up. "Hold on. I remember Annie said her son was named Alexander. Are you, like, Alexander Sr.?"

Alex chuckled. "No, I—"

"So that would mean you're Annie's husband?" Dave asked. "Funny she never mentioned that before . . ."

"Because I'm not," he replied. "Either her husband *or* Alex Sr." He didn't bother to elaborate. "I run a . . . I guess you could call us a specialized security firm."

"Okay. So do you work for Annie?" Pan asked, then added in a whispery voice, "Or maybe for some top-secret organization?"

Alex paused for a couple of moments to gaze at his audience, no doubt deciding whether he should answer the question. Finally he said, "Usually I'm not allowed to discuss the Knights with outsiders, but considering the circumstances, and the fact that Annie has vouched for you"—he glanced at Uwe—"well, *most* of you, I think it's all right to bend the rules a little."

"Cool!" Pan said, then blushed again as her stomach loudly rumbled. "But, uh, can we do it while we're eating?"

"Sure." Alex reached into his jacket pocket and pulled out a cell phone. "Just let me check in with my staff and get a perimeter status."

Pan's left eyebrow rose in surprise. " 'Perimeter status'? You mean, like the kinda things guards check on when they're watching out for something?"

"Uh-huh." Alex pressed a large red button that was displayed on the phone's screen. "Hollingsworth, you there?" he asked without raising the cell to his mouth— apparently the device had a walkie-talkie app.

"Hollingsworth," replied a female voice. "What's up, Chief?"

"Stand by." Alex looked around the group. "I'll take this outside. Just give me a minute." He turned to go.

"Umm . . . do you mind me asking what is it you're guarding?" Pan called after him.

Alex stopped inside the doorway. "No, I don't mind." He looked back over his shoulder, the hint of a smile on his lips. "It's you."

6

"So, why would you need to guard me?" Pan asked around a mouthful of peasant salad. Aware of his daughter's desire to get out of her room, David had suggested moving the lunch party to a small atrium on the first floor, then coaxed her into a wheelchair for the excursion (she'd wanted to walk). Now, Pan sat cross-legged on a couch, a plate of food balanced on her lap. Javi sat beside her, shoveling plastic forkfuls of spanakopita into his maw like *he'd* been the one unconscious for three days. Uwe and Sheen shared another couch so he could pick at her food. The sight of the whip-thin teen, perched above his girlfriend's meal, reminded Pan so much of a vulture eyeing a carcass that she had to bite her tongue to keep from laughing.

The food was pretty good, but not as appetizing as the dishes made by the Lambirises, the Greek couple whose diner was located a block from Renfield's House of Horrors. Still, a round-trip to the afterlife had made her ravenous enough to eat just about anything. Maybe her earlier zombie jokes weren't so far off the mark . . .

"Are you expecting those vampires to come after Pan?" Dad asked from a wicker chair.

Seated in a similar chair, Alex shook his head. "No." He paused. "Maybe. Although considering the leaders of that street war outside your museum have fled the country, there's little chance of that. Either way, Annie was pretty insistent that you and your family get round-the-clock protection until this matter is resolved."

"So you mean the Goth Lolis who kidnapped my mom got away?"

Alex nodded. "Back to their home base in Yokohama, Japan. Lady Sasaki probably couldn't wait to show off her latest prize to the clan elders."

"That angel?" Javi asked.

Pan unconsciously placed a hand over her heart, remembering her useless attempt to avenge the mother she'd thought she'd lost, by attacking Zaqiel with the Spear of Longinus—an attempt that ended with him turning the spear on her. Pan shuddered. She could still feel the weight of the ancient weapon as it smashed through her chest, sliced through her heart, punctured her lung . . .

A light pressure on her other hand eased Pan from her dark thoughts. She looked down to find Javi squeezing it with his own, lending support—and strength. Pan gazed up into Javi's kind eyes and smiled.

"I'm okay," she said, and squeezed back. Then she turned back to Alex. "So, about this private security firm . . ."

"Right. Well, we're called the Knights of the Apocalypse—"

"*Seriously?*" Sheen howled.

"—and we work for the Vatican," Alex concluded, then cut Sheen a look that put a quick end to her laughter. "Unofficially."

"You work . . . for the pope," Uwe said. His face still displayed its usual bored expression, but there was no mistaking the interest in his voice. "The pope has his own private army."

"Not an army," Alex replied with a chuckle. "Much smaller than that. I wish we had an army. But we get the job done all right."

"Doesn't the pope already have an army . . . or whatever it is your organization is?" Dave asked.

"The Swiss Guard? They're not trained for the kinds of threats we deal with."

"You mean you're monster hunters, like Annie?" Pan asked.

"Part of the time. Except La Bella Tenebrosa predates the Knights," Alex replied. He spotted the confused expression on everyone's faces, except Javi's. "What, the nickname? It means 'the beautiful dark one.' It's a title she picked up in her travels. When weirdlings hear La Bella Tenebrosa is around they know they're in for a world of trouble." Pan noticed he showed a certain amount of pride when he said that. Interesting . . .

Then an odd remark she'd heard popped forth in her mind: *"Had yerself a little run-in with the dark lady, did ya? Ha! I know what that's like!"*

"So, that's what he meant . . . ," she muttered.

"Who?" Javi asked.

"Huh?" Pan realized everyone was staring at her. "Sorry. I was just thinking about something a vampire said to me when I was . . ." She flashed a sheepish smile. "Y'know. He mentioned a 'dark lady' and I didn't know what he was talking about."

Alex nodded. "The dark lady, the dark one . . . there are a lot of nicknames for Annie among the residents of Gothopolis." He grinned. "Most of them I can't repeat in polite company."

"Good thing we're not polite, then," Sheen said. "So repeat away. I'll promise not to faint if you pass along something really juicy—I mean, shockin'."

"What, burned through your whole vocabulary of four-letter words already?" Pan asked with a Cheshire-grin. "Poor baby. How will you ever be able to carry on a conversation when you get to college?"

Sheen stuck out her tongue.

"Maybe some other time," Alex said good-naturedly. "Anyway, here's the story: In 1693 an Italian merchant named Agostino Gabrino saw how terrifying the world was becoming as the century neared its end—witch trials in America, Mt. Etna erupting, earthquakes in Jamaica and Belgium, a famine in Mexico, France warring with half of Europe—and became convinced that all the signs were there for the rise of the Antichrist to power."

That certainly got Uwe's attention. "Really," he said, one eyebrow spidering its way up his forehead in interest.

"Seems like that kind of hysteria always pops up when a century is winding down," Dave commented. "There was all the worrying in 1999 about the Antichrist coming, mixed up with that Y2K/end of the world nonsense. And when the Earth didn't explode, or civilization as we know it didn't come to an end, the believers insisted they'd just gotten the dates wrong, but it's still going to happen."

Alex shrugged. "What can I say? It's a popular belief."

"More like wishful thinking for the simple-minded," Dave said gruffly.

Alex laughed. "So, with the threat of the Antichrist so firm in Agostino's thoughts, he petitioned the Catholic Church to raise an army to fight the Devil's kid when he showed up . . . whenever that might be. Agostino wasn't too clear about the date," he added with a wink to Dave.

"And how'd the Church react to this?" Dave asked, then held up a hand. "Wait, don't tell me. 'Thanks for your interest. We'll be sure to take it under advisement.'"

"Words to that effect."

Dave snorted. "Typical bureaucrats."

"So what did Agostino do?" Pan asked. She wasn't sure what the Knights' history had to do with her, but it would probably make sense in the end. Besides, Agostino's story had her intrigued.

"Well, when the Church ignored his warnings, Agostino decided to take matters into his own hands. On Palm Sunday he traveled to St. Peter's Basilica in Rome and in the middle of Mass he strode right up the aisle during the singing of Psalm Twenty-four—"

"'The Earth is the Lord's, and everything in it,'" Javi said. Pan glanced at him. "My mom sometimes sings it around the house before church on Sunday. Only in Spanish."

"And when the antiphony—the call-out and response—was sung," Alex continued, "'Who is he, this king of glory?,' Agostino drew his sword and yelled, '*I am that king of glory!*'"

"Wow," Dave said. "Modest SOB, wasn't he."

"Sounds like my kinda man," Sheen commented, and turned to Uwe. "Babe, you should totally do something like that when Mom drags me to midnight mass this Christmas." She grinned. "My folks would *so* freak."

Uwe said nothing, but the sly smile he gave his girlfriend made it apparent the gears in his brain were busily clanking away as he formulated an idea. Knowing Uwe as Pan did, he probably had the perfect outfit—and sword—already hanging in his closet.

"I take it that stunt was even less popular with the Church than the anti-Antichrist militia," Dave said.

"That's putting it mildly," Alex replied. "But by the time the Roman Curia finally got around to addressing the issue, Agostino had recruited eighty 'soldiers' to his cause. The first Knights. Although they weren't actual soldiers, just a collection of laborers and craftsmen."

"So . . . the Blue Collar Knights of the Apocalypse," Dave said with a smile. "Led by Sir Larry the Cable Guy—gittin' 'er done fer the Lord."

Pan couldn't help but laugh—it *was* a pretty good joke. Javi and Sheen agreed. Even Uwe cracked a nonmalicious smile.

Alex shrugged. "As a wise man once said, 'You work with the tools you're given.' And their hearts were certainly in the right place—even if they had no idea what to do if the Antichrist *did* show up."

"Did he?" Pan asked.

Alex paused long enough for his silence to send a chill crawling up her spine. "Anyway, for the next year Agostino organized his troops, working from the shadows in order to avoid catching unwanted papal attention."

"Which probably made the pope even more suspicious of him," Dave said.

"True. Within three months the order had grown to a hundred and fifty members—too many for the confines of Agostino's estate in Brescia. Too many to remain in the shadows. So Agostino told the Knights to return to their homes and await instructions. But before they left he presented each of them with a means to identify one another." He tapped an index finger against his star-shaped lapel pin. "Seven rays to represent the book of the seven seals mentioned in Revelations. A golden thread to signify the Earth. And in the center, the sword that Christ would carry in his battle with Satan."

Uwe snorted. "What, the spear wasn't enough?"

Sheen gasped.

Pan snapped her head around to glare at him, but her reaction only made his smile widen. From the corner of her eye Pan saw Dave start to rise from his seat, and waved him off. "It's okay, Dad. Huey's just being his usual jerk self."

Sheen sharply nudged her boyfriend in the ribs; he winced, but offered no apology. "Sorry, Zee," Sheen mumbled, then snarled at him. "God, babe, why you gotta be so insensitive?"

"It's his nature," Pan said. "Like the old fable about the scorpion." She winked at her best friend—"Don't worry about it, Sheen."—then turned back to Alex and pointed at his pin. "So, can I get one of those?"

Alex shook his head. "They're not the kind of thing you just hand out to anyone—

they have to be earned."

"Said the dude to the girl who got stabbed with Jesus' spear," she replied coolly with an arched eyebrow. "And then came back from the dead. I think that oughtta earn me a whole box of them." She held out a hand, opening and closing it in a gimme gesture. "Hmmm?"

Alex smiled. "I'll see what I can do."

"Hey, you got that thing printed on a T-shirt?" Sheen asked. "I would totally wear that to school next year."

"No," Alex said with a playful frown.

"Getting back to the story . . . ," Dave prompted.

"Right. Sorry," Alex replied. "In August 1694 a woodcutter named Giorgio Molinelli was dragged in front of the Holy Roman Inquisitor and, in a plea for leniency, spilled everything about the order."

"*Judas II: The Inquisitioning*," Uwe said in a deep, movie-narrator voice. "This time he's Armageddonit."

Sheen chuckled; Javi groaned; Pan bit her lower lip to keep from smiling. No way was she giving Uwe the satisfaction of seeing her laugh at his stupid joke—not after that crack about the spear. It *was* kinda funny, though.

"How soon after that did the papal SWAT team move in?" Dave asked.

"Almost immediately," Alex replied, "because Molinelli had spiced up his testimony with some real shockers about Agostino: that he wanted to overthrow the Church; that he demanded the brotherhood marry only virgins—and not just one." He glanced at Pan. "That Agostino claimed the pope was actually a demon in disguise."

Pan started. "He could see monsters?"

"There were rumors, but no one took them seriously," Alex explained. "Least of all Molinelli and—according to him—a number of the Knights. They thought it was all part of Agostino's increasing religious fervor, seeing demons everywhere he turned."

"Polygamist Christian knights, marrying virgin brides and fighting the Devil, led by a man looking to overthrow the Catholic Church," Dave said with a grin. "How has Nicolas Cage not starred in this movie, already?"

"I would watch the hell outta that," Javi said.

"What'd the Inquisition do?" Pan asked.

"Hauled in Agostino and seventy or so Knights, for a public trial—a very short one. The Knights went to prison, and Agostino . . ." Alex's voice trailed off as his gaze drifted away from Pan. "He was locked away in a madhouse."

Pan swallowed hard, thinking back to all those years when everyone—including herself—had thought she was crazy for seeing monsters. Like everyone associated with Agostino probably had thought of him. She could just about remember the faces of the mothers who'd suggested she be institutionalized, when she'd experienced a couple of minor psychosodes while attending first grade. It would be for her own good, they'd insisted, to get the poor child the help she so obviously needed. To get the freak away from our poor babies, was more like it. It had been a devastating moment in her young life—she'd become a pariah at the age of six. A decade later, the hurt had dulled to a tiny ache, but it was still there when she thought about those days.

"Did he . . . did he ever get out?" Pan smiled weakly. "I mean, he must've, or how else would the Knights still be around so you could be one—right? And didn't you say you work for the Vatican? So he must've cut a deal with them, or something. Hell, they even made him a saint so you could name this hospital after him!"

"The Knights were officially sanctioned by the Roman Curia in 1699," Alex replied, "but Agostino had nothing to do with it. He spent the rest of his days in that sanatorium. And the sainthood was bestowed as a . . . political compromise."

"Why would the Church do th—" Pan gasped. "Wait a minute. I asked you if the Antichrist ever showed up and you didn't answer. He did, didn't he?"

Alex flashed a sly smile as he rose from his seat.

"Oh, my God, he totally did!" Sheen cried. "I bet it was the demon-pope. Could he kill people with his penance stare, like Ghost Rider?"

"I don't even know what that means," Alex replied in confusion.

"Hold on a minute," Dad said. "You said all of this happened back in the seventeenth century, but that 'La Bella Tenebrosa' predated the Knights of the Apocalypse." His eyes narrowed as he gazed at Alex. "Are you telling us Annie is immortal?"

Pan's eyebrows nearly shot into her hairline in surprise. Annie was an immortal, shape-shifting monster hunter who'd fought the Antichrist almost four hundred years ago? Really? She turned to Javi, who was trying to act cool as he nodded at her to confirm Dad's suspicions, but the delighted expression on his face practically screamed, *Isn't that awesome?*

It certainly was.

The right corner of Alex's lips curled upward in a knowing smile. "Talk to Annie when she gets back. She doesn't like it when people talk about her past when she's not around."

" 'Gets back'?" Pan asked. "Where'd she go?" She'd known the woman for a little over a day—not counting Pan's three-day nap—but Annie hadn't struck her as the type who started friendships only to drop them at the first opportunity. Certainly not after the huntress had spent all that time convincing Pan how truly special she was, and that her dreaded monstervision was really some kind of supernatural gift.

"Annie followed the vamps to Yokohama." Alex pulled back his left jacket sleeve to check his wristwatch. "Let's see . . . It's two P.M. and Japan is thirteen hours ahead, so that makes it about three tomorrow morning their time. Right about now she and a couple of members from the order should be observing some big powwow Lady Sasaki has called. Most of the major clans have sent representatives."

Dave grunted. "So she can rub the 'prize' they were all looking for in their faces." His lips pulled back in a snarl. "Bastards. After what they did to Karen . . ."

Dave froze as he realized what he'd said, and looked over to find his daughter staring at him in horror.

"What did they do to Mom?" Pan asked hoarsely.

The look of discomfort that her father and Alex exchanged was hard to miss. A knot formed in her stomach.

Pan stood up. "I heard she's in some isolation ward. Where is it? I wanna see her—right now."

"Now is not a good time," Alex replied. "She's under observation and—"

"Then I wanna observe her, too." Pan snarled. "Stop with the lame excuses and just take me to her." Her anger faded a touch, enough for Alex to see the deep concern she had for her mother—but not enough to give any indication that she was willing to back down. "Please," she added in a softer tone.

A tiny smile quirked the right corner of the Knight's mouth. "Annie warned me you were a hard case."

"You have no idea how hard a case I can be," Pan said in all seriousness.

"I've got a pretty good idea, though." He glanced at Dave. "What do *you* say, Dad?"

Dave left his seat to stand beside Pan. "I . . . ," he said hesitantly. "I just don't know, honey. When they brought Mom in, Dr. Carlyle said she was suffering from a communicable disease—something the vampires had given her. That's why she was put in isolation. I mean, they won't even let *me* in to see her."

"Please, Dad. I'll wear a mask, or one of those hazmat suits. You can even put me in one of those sterile bubble thingies and roll me down the hall. Whatever. But I have to see Mom."

"Sweetheart . . ."

Okay, so much for pleading. Pan placed her fists on her hips and set her jaw. "Dad, if you don't let me see Mom, I'll find some way to sneak out of my room when you're not around and get to her anyway. And you know Sheen'll be glad to help me do it."

Sheen nodded. "You bet I'll— Wait. What?"

David Zwieback sighed heavily, then reached out to brush a wayward strand of hair from his daughter's cheek and tuck it behind her ear. She could see in his eyes the great concern he had for her . . . as well as the trace of fear that lurked behind it. Not fear *of* her—that initial reaction caused by her return had faded long ago—but rather fear *for* her. Whatever this disease was, however badly it affected Mom, it scared him enough that he wanted to protect Pan from the truth—yet she knew he was aware that she wouldn't be content with anything else.

A pained smile curled the ends of his lips as he placed his hands on her shoulders and gave a gentle squeeze. "Okay."

7

The trip to St. Agostino's isolation ward didn't begin quite as easily as Pan had hoped; in fact, it almost didn't begin at all. Dr. Carlyle had stopped by to check on her, and when he learned of Pan's intent to visit her mother he tried to deny her access to the wing. Pan, however, wasn't about to back down, especially when she had Alex's support. All right, so the Knight had only shrugged when Carlyle asked if he was okay with this, but that was good enough for her.

"Unless you're going to set up a close-circuit monitor in her room, just let her take a peek from the hallway," Alex said.

"You could always post a guard outside her door," the doctor countered.

Alex grunted. No doubt that had crossed his mind as well. However . . . "It's her mother, John. If you were in her place, you'd feel the same way."

"You mean if it were *your* mother—and you *have* been in her place. More times than I can count, I might add."

Pan thought that was a rather strange comment, but let it pass. Right now, getting to Mom was far more important than deciphering Carlyle's hidden meanings.

"Ms. Bonifant is under level-five quarantine, Alex," he continued. "You know what that means."

"I don't," Pan said.

"It means your mother has contracted a particularly virulent bug," the doctor explained, "so access to her room is limited to medical staff and"—he glanced at Alex—"certain security personnel."

"Yeah, that's the same line you handed me when Karen was brought in," Dave said. "I was willing to accept it then, and I understand the need for precautions, but it's been three days, now, and when I ask how she's doing the most I can get out of your staff is that 'her condition remains unchanged.' Except nobody has ever bothered to say what that condition was to begin with—not even Annie, before she went tearing out of here for Japan. I'm Karen's husband, for God's sake; enough with the stonewalling."

Pan smiled. It had been so long since she'd heard Dad refer to Mom that way after the divorce she thought she'd never hear those words again. Considering that before the museum attack screwed up their lives she'd been trying to think of a plan to reunite them, it was a step in the right direction. Now all she needed was a way to keep this good vibe going after the three of them left the hospital . . .

"Ex-husband, you mean," Carlyle replied, unpleasantly interrupting Pan's thoughts. "If the information on Ms. Bonifant that you provided to Admissions is accurate, Mr. Zwieback."

Dave waved his hand in a dismissive gesture. "That's just semantics. Yes, we're divorced, but that doesn't mean I stopped caring about Karen after the papers were signed. I should still be able to see her."

"Look, if it'll make you feel better, Johnny," Alex interjected, "I'll take full responsibility for letting them in. Bishop Ironside can yell at me when he finds out; I'm used to his bellowing by now."

"*You'll* take full responsibility?" The doctor flashed a sly grin at his friend. "When did you start going soft?" He shrugged, then turned back to Pan and Dave. "Very well—but we do this my way. Because of the risk of infection you'll observe her from outside the room, as Alex suggested—there's a large window you can look through." He gazed at Pan. "And you'll stay in that wheelchair—"

Pan groaned. "Oh, come on—"

Carlyle waved a hand to cut her off. "You just awakened from a three-day coma, and your body is still healing from the massive physical trauma it experienced. I'd like to avoid a relapse because you overexerted yourself. And Nurse Araujo and I will accompany you, as a precaution."

Pan sighed melodramatically. "Whatever. Can we just get going, already?"

And so, surrounded by her entourage and sitting like a frowny lump in her four-wheel transport, Pan began her journey, pushed along by her father. The leisurely pace set by Alex only increased her anxiety about her mother's condition, and she had to fight the urge to take control from Dad and roll the wheelchair through the hallways to get where she wanted to go.

Thankfully, the group reached an elevator at the far end of the main hallway before Pan had a chance to play Speed Racer.

"Why'd we have to come all the way here?" Pan asked. "What was wrong with the elevators by my room?"

"The ward is a restricted area, so this is the only elevator with access to it." Carlyle unclipped the ID card attached to the lapel of his white lab coat and swiped it through a scanner beside the doorframe. He then punched a six-digit code into the keypad below the scanner.

"Only one elevator, and it needs a special security code? Afraid of somebody breaking in?" Pan smiled and added in an ominous voice, "Or something breaking out?"

It was meant as a joke, but the serious expression on the doctor's face made her think that perhaps she'd touched on just why the ward was separate from the hospital. Knowing that her mother was confined in that place suddenly made her stomach cramp.

The car took them all the way down to a sub-subbasement. As the group stepped from the elevator Sheen expressed some disappointment at the polished, brightly lit hallway; she'd been expecting a typical horror-movie hospital basement of filthy green linoleum tiles, flickering lights, thick cobwebs, and moldy, bloodstained walls. A clean environment, however, was just fine with Pan, who'd been dreading she'd find *exactly* one of those spooky hospital basements; the thought of her mother being locked away in Freddy Krueger's playroom had had her perched on the edge of her seat throughout the elevator's descent. Now, she felt she could relax—

Until a pair of guards wearing sidearms walked past, eyeing the group with suspicion until Carlyle nodded pleasantly to them. The tension in Pan's muscles returned.

"What're the guns for?" she asked the doctor.

"Security," Alex replied.

" 'Cause'a it bein' a restricted area, right?" Sheen asked.

"Exactly."

"We gonna run into Will Smith down here?"

Alex chuckled. "The Men in Black is a different department."

"Ms. Bonifant is down this way," Carlyle said as he took the lead. He turned the next corner, but Dave slowed to a halt before they reached it.

Pan looked over her shoulder at him. "Dad? What's going on?"

"This is a bad idea," he said with a shake of his head. "I should have come down here on my own, first. You just came out of your . . . just woke up a little while ago, and before that . . ."

"I'm not fragile, y'know," she said.

"I know you're not, Panda-bear, but . . . I think it's too soon for you. We're going back."

He started to turn the wheelchair around, but Pan hopped out and ran after Carlyle.

"Pan!" he cried.

"C'mon, slowpoke!" she called back. "Let's go see Mom!"

Footsteps pounded after her, accompanied by Dad's pleas for her to stop, but Pan ignored them—as well as the tiny ache that had suddenly bloomed in her chest— and concentrated instead on Carlyle, who was standing halfway down the corridor. She hurried past other rooms framed by large observation windows but paid little attention to their occupants, though she had glimpses of something . . . odd about the people in the beds. Her mother was her only concern.

She slid to a halt in front of Carlyle and doubled over, hands on knees, gasping for breath. The spot on her chest where the spear had penetrated was really starting to hurt. The doctor's warning about the dangers of overexerting herself echoed in her head, as did the thudding of her pulse in her temples.

Guess this healing power has its limits—which totally sucks, she thought. *I mean, what's the point in having it if the damn thing's got a cutoff? I bet Wolverine in the X-Men comics doesn't have this problem. I'll have to ask Javi about that . . .*

Slowly, the pain in her chest faded. Her heart rate ceased its galloping, yet remained a little quick. *You're just outta shape,* she told herself. *What do you expect, after . . . y'know, and then lying around for the last three days? You'll be fine. Just stop being a baby and stand up straight, or Dad's gonna drag you back to your room.*

Carlyle stepped forward. "Pandora—"

"I'm fine," she insisted, although she felt anything but. The black spots obscuring her vision were a particular pain in the ass—they made it difficult to see the physician standing right in front of her—but they soon faded. "It's nothing—really. I just ate too much of that Greek food. That stuff is *so* heavy." She flashed what she hoped appeared to be a relaxed smile.

I am not *passing out here . . .*

Dave and Javi and Christa, then Sheen and Uwe pulled up alongside her. Alex ambled along behind them.

"Honey . . . ?" Dave asked as he placed a hand on her back.

"I'm good, Dad." She tried the same relaxed smile on him.

His eyebrows shot up. "Why are you making that face? Are you in pain?"

"Oh." The what-she'd-thought-was-a-smile-but-clearly-wasn't drooped. "No, I was . . . never mind. I guess I'm just nervous about Mom. I'll be all right after I see her." She turned to the doctor. "So . . . can I?"

Carlyle swiped his card key against the reader and a large screen, about the size of an iPad, built into the wall lit up to display a document. As he studied it, Pan realized it was a digital version of Mom's patient chart with up-to-the-moment readings. How very *Star Trek*, she thought.

The doctor sighed. "No change in her condition, I'm afraid."

"Don't you start that crap, too," Dave cautioned.

"I'm merely stating a fact. I was hoping the last round of antivirals we gave her might have some positive effect . . . but apparently not."

"Did you talk to my grandma Izzy?" Javi asked. "She's got all those herbs and stuff in her botanica—maybe she's got something you could try for . . . whatever it is you're talking about."

"Isadora?" Carlyle shook his head. "Thanks, but no. I'd rather not bring voodoo into this."

Javi frowned. "She's not into voodoo, she just runs a store that has a lot of religious stuff in it. And she knows lots of cures for things—maybe even more than you," he added defiantly.

Carlyle chuckled. "Always a distinct possibility."

"Hey, how come the room's so dark?" Sheen asked.

Pan turned toward the observation window. With the mini-drama caused by her recuperating body taking up all her attention, she'd never noticed that the lights were off in Mom's room. Now that she could focus on that detail, she thought it an unusual situation . . . and somewhat unsettling.

"Ms. Bonifant's eyes have become a tad hypersensitive to light," Carlyle replied. "A side effect of the virus. We keep them off so as not to disturb her. I'll bring the lights up to half strength." He made a swiping motion across the wall display, to replace the medical chart with a touch-screen control panel. He pressed a button and then moved his index finger upward, along a 2-D lever. Inside, the ceiling lights switched on to fill the room with a soft glow.

Dad, Javi, and Sheen pressed against the glass to look inside, but only Pan reacted to what she saw; to what no one else could see. Karen Bonifant lay motionless on a bed, her body covered by crisp white sheets, her wrists encircled by padded restraints. Pan's own wrists suddenly itched as unpleasant memories of coarse fabric binding her to psych-ward beds sprang to mind, and she forced herself to push aside those dark thoughts. It didn't prevent her from scratching the imaginary itch, however.

Yet it wasn't the sight of her mother tied down that brought tears to her eyes—although that hurt deeply—or flashbacks to sometimes-nightmarish events in her childhood, but the dull glow that Karen's body emitted. Only days before, Pan had unexpectedly gained the ability to see the warm, golden light of a person's life force, and been pleasantly shocked by the brilliance of her mother's aura.

Now it was pitch-black.

A hand gently grasped her shoulder and gave an encouraging squeeze. Grateful for the support of her friends, Pan closed her eyes and drew strength from that comforting touch, then looked up, expecting to find Sheen smiling down at her.

It was Javi.

"Honey?" Dad asked. "What's wrong?"

"They bit her," she croaked as she wiped her eyes, her throat suddenly thick with emotion. "She's . . . one of them."

Dad started. "What?" He looked at the doctor. "Is that true?"

"Um . . . Yes," Carlyle replied after a momentary silence.

Standing just behind the doctor, Christa gasped. Apparently she'd been kept in the dark as much as anyone else—except for Alex, Pan noted. His somber expression made it clear he'd known all along.

"And nobody in this damn place thought that was important enough to tell me?" Dave snarled. " 'Infectious disease,' my ass. You think I wouldn't have believed the truth, after what my family's been through?"

"My apologies," the doctor said. "Most people aren't as . . . accepting of the notion of vampirism. Also, the board of administrators and I decided to wait until we were able to stabilize her condition before informing you."

"And did you?"

"Not as much as we would like."

"So now she's a real vampire?" Uwe asked. "They actually exist?"

"Having trouble keeping up with the rest of us?" Javi asked sarcastically.

"No, just making certain that this wasn't some kind of mass delusion." Uwe flashed a condescending smile. "Unlike your girlfriend, I try to avoid confusing fantasy with reality."

Beside Pan, Sheen gasped.

"What was that?" Dad growled. Uwe started to reply, only to be cut off by: "The next words out of your mouth better be an apology."

"All right." In the glass, Pan saw Uwe's reflection look toward her. "My apologies, Pandora. I realize I've said some terrible things in the past, but it's good to know that at least *this* time the monsters weren't just in your head. Good for you."

"Uwe!" Sheen snapped.

"What? I said I apologized." He appeared confused by Sheen's reaction, but Pan knew that was just an act. Inside, he was undoubtedly laughing at her.

Pan slowly turned to face him. She'd become accustomed to the grief he often gave her and put up with it for Sheena's sake, but enough was enough. Her mother was lying in a hospital bed, a victim of creatures straight from a nightmare, and Pan was in absolutely no mood whatsoever for Uwe's crap. If he was looking to get his ass kicked, she was more than willing to take out her frustrations and anger toward the vampires on him.

Dad, however, stepped toward him first.

"You insensitive little—" He clamped his mouth shut before he could launch into some colorful words to describe the teen, and pointed back toward the way they'd come. "Walk away. Now. Or so help me God I'm gonna knock your teeth down your throat."

Uwe sniffed dismissively and peeled himself off the wall he'd been leaning against. "I'm going to get a drink. Is there a soda machine around here?"

"Go back down the corridor," Carlyle said, "to the intersection. You'll find the staff lounge two doors past it."

Uwe nodded, then glanced toward his girlfriend. "You coming, Sheena?"

"No, babe." Clearly angered by his behavior, Sheen couldn't bring herself to look at him. Instead, she focused her attention on Pan, and flashed a tiny smile. "I'm right where I need to be."

Another dismissive sniff. "Very well." Uwe lumbered away.

Pan reached out to squeeze Sheen's hand before she could apologize. "Hey. It's okay," she said gently. "I know—he's a jerk who's never gonna stop being a jerk where I'm concerned, but you love him. I can understand that . . . sorta. But he's lucky Dad got to him before me."

"Yeah," Sheen agreed softly, with a blush of embarrassment. "Maybe I oughtta start thinkin' about tradin' up . . ."

Pan smiled impishly. "Well, I can always introduce you to the boys back in Schriksdork." That was one of her nicknames for Schriksdorp, the town in Upstate New York where she lived with her mother; Suckville and Stinkville, USA were high on the list, too. "They're a different breed of jerk—big and brawny, with pea brains like dinosaurs. You'll love them."

Sheen grinned. "I like dinosaurs."

"I know you do." She gave her best friend a quick hug. "We'll talk later, okay?" Pan closed her eyes, took a deep breath to steady herself, slowly released it through her nostrils, and turned back toward Carlyle. "Okay. So my mom is a vampire. What's the next step?"

"Well . . . there isn't one. There's no medical treatment for vampirism—at least none that I'm aware of." He glanced at Javi. "I don't believe Isadora knows of one, either. So that presents us with only limited options."

Pan unconsciously rubbed a hand over her chest. "You are *not* putting a stake in my mother."

"I second that," Dave added.

"That wasn't one of them," Alex said. "What Johnny meant is that either they acclimate your mother to her current condition—where she'll have to spend every waking moment locked in that room, or one like it, combating her desire for blood—or somebody destroys the vampire who turned her, which should reverse the process."

Pan snarled. "Zaqiel."

"Exactly."

"And is that why Annie went after him?" Dave asked.

"Not completely," Alex replied. "Right now she's gathering intelligence on—"

"On something that isn't helping my wife."

Alex coolly stared at him for a few moments. "There's a lot more at risk than just your wife's condition, David."

"Would killing that bastard put an end to the risk?"

"Possibly," Alex replied slowly.

"Then I don't see why you need to waste time spying on Zaqiel when Annie could just put him down right now. Don't they have wooden stakes in Japan?"

"Plenty. But it's not only the angel we have to worry about."

"He's the only one *I* have to worry about."

Sheen leaned over to whisper in Pan's ear. "Whoa. Check out your dad the badass."

Pan grinned. "Pretty cool, huh?" she asked proudly.

Carlyle stepped between the two men before the conversation became any more heated. "Pandora, you knew about your mother's condition simply by looking at her. May I ask how you did that?"

Pan swallowed, reluctant to talk about her alleged "gift"; a decade of being treated as a freak had a lot to do with that. Still, it needed to be said if she was going to help Mom. "Her . . . aura is wrong."

"You can see your mother's aura," the doctor said. He glanced at Dave. "I didn't see that noted in the medical history you gave us."

"It's a . . . recent development," Dave replied.

"Yeah," Pan said. "See, I've had this . . . this monstervision thing ever since I was a little kid. It makes me see . . . monsters all the time. Well, not all the time, but enough that people thought I was—"

"Yes," Carlyle interjected. "Your father filled me in on your psychiatric background."

"Yeah, everybody except Mom and Dad and Sheen said I was crazy because of it—like that jerk, Huey—and I believed it, too. But Annie showed me that I'm not crazy; I never was." Pan paused. She hadn't planned on being so open, but once she'd started the words had flowed in a rush. It had felt good, though, to come right out and talk about her strange ability—and not be laughed at. "But, yeah, the aura thing is new. I bumped into . . . somebody a few days ago and when we touched it kinda overloaded the monstervision. So I guess now I can see other stuff, too. Like auras. It's kinda hard knowing how to deal with this stuff without an instruction manual." She smiled awkwardly. "I'm still trying to figure me out."

Dad wrapped an arm across her shoulders and gave a squeeze. "That makes two of us," he said with a smile.

"So, what's wrong about your mother's aura?" Alex asked.

"Well, usually it's really bright—not as bright as Annie's, that's like a billion-watt bulb—and kinda golden," she explained, then added softly, "But still . . . it's really beautiful."

"And now?"

"Now it's all black and . . . and ugly." Pan snarled. "Zaqiel did that to her. But I can change that. I can fix her."

" 'Fix her'?" Carlyle asked Dave.

Dad nodded. "Another, er, recent development."

"Yeah—like with Javi." Pan turned to the boy. "Remember? When you were chasing the trash monkey in Penn Station and he jumped you, and you got a big lump on your head after you banged it on the railroad tracks?"

"How could I forget?" Javi said, and reached up to feel the top of his skull, where the lump had been. "You touched it and it faded away. Annie said you've got some kinda healing power."

"Is that a fact," Alex said. He sounded impressed.

"Uh-huh," Javi replied with a knowing smile. "And you more'n anybody else knows Annie knows what she's talking about."

Alex nodded. "True."

"So you're also a healer?" the doctor asked Pan. "I was under the impression that your recuperative powers only applied to your own injuries. But you can extend them to . . . er, 'fix' others, as well?"

"I guess. But I didn't know I could do stuff like that until the thing with Javi happened, and then Annie explained it all."

Carlyle smiled. "I haven't seen a healer in three or four years, at least. And certainly not one as young as you."

"Is that a good thing?" Dave asked. "Her being young, I mean."

"Well, it would certainly account for how she was able to survive her injuries."

"So, will you let me in to see her?" Pan asked. "I know I can help." *Not that I have any idea if what I did for Javi will work for Mom, but I'm not about to tell anyone* that. She gazed at her mother, and the black haze that surrounded her, and bit her lip. *I have to* try, *at least.*

The doctor looked to Alex.

"I'm sorry, Pandora," the Knight said, "but right here is as far as you go."

"What? No!" Pan cried.

Alex held up a hand for silence. "I agreed to let you come down here so you could see your mother; I never promised you access to her. I'm not putting this hospital at risk by opening that door and letting a vampire loose in the halls."

Pan spun to face her father. "Dad . . . ," she implored.

Dave shook his head, though it seemed the gesture took some effort. "I'm sorry, honey, but I have to agree with Alex. I know you don't think so, but it's for the best. Besides, your mother would kill me—and not in any vampire-related way—if I let something else bad happen to you."

"You're so right about that," a familiar voice said from the wall speaker.

As one, the group turned toward the window of Karen's room—to find her staring back at them. Skin as white as the hospital gown she wore, blond hair hanging limply to her shoulders, her normally green pupils glowing with the embers of hellfire, she looked every bit the living corpse. But when Karen's gaze settled on her only child, and the initial shock had passed of finding the daughter she'd undoubtedly thought she'd lost very much alive, Pan saw nothing but love shining in her eyes.

Mom smiled and placed her hand against the glass. "Hi, baby."

Two simple words that brought tears to Pan's eyes, because she'd feared never hearing them again. She stepped up to the window, choosing to ignore the sharklike teeth Karen's warm smile had put on display.

"Hey, Mom," she croaked as she rested her hand in front of Karen's. "Gonna invite me in?"

Blood-tinged tears rolled down alabaster cheeks. "Maybe later, Panda-bear. I'm a little tired right now. It's probably better if I stay in here and you stay out there until the doctors have a look at me. Okay?"

"Okay," Pan said softly.

Carlyle stepped over to address his patient. Pan noticed the tension in his body language. "Ms. Bonifant, if you don't mind my asking . . . How did you undo your restraints?"

Karen looked over her shoulder at the bed. Pan could see that the fabric of both cuffs had been torn in half. She knew firsthand that those things didn't just spring open if you pulled at them; the strength required to snap them had to be enormous.

Inhuman.

Oh, Mom . . . Pan thought disconsolately.

"I . . . don't know," Karen said slowly. "I heard all of you talking and I wanted to be part of the conversation, so I just . . . got out of bed."

Alex fished his cell phone from a jacket pocket and pressed a button on the keypad. "Ronnie, I need two guards outside Ms. Bonifant's room."

"On the way, Alex," crackled the response from the phone's speaker.

"Now wait a minute," Dave said. "What do you need guards for? You've already got Karen locked in."

"It's just a precaution," the Knight replied.

A pair of security guards—one male, one female—jogged up to the group from the opposite end of the corridor. The man—Robertson, according to his nameplate—was, Pan guessed, in his mid-to-late twenties with a trim, athletic build and a buzz-cut Afro. His partner, Zheng, looked to be in her forties—if the light streaks of gray in her dark hair were true indications of her age—but had easily outpaced him to the scene. Pan's eyes widened at the sight of the pump-action shotgun Robertson held.

"Hey. You even *try* pointing that thing at my wife," Dad growled as he stepped in front of the guards, "and I'll shove it up your—"

"David," Karen snapped. "Knock it off. You're making a scene."

"It's a Taser rifle," Alex explained.

She nodded. "That's fine."

"Yeah, well, I don't care if it's a giant water pistol," Dave said, "he's keeping it the hell away from you."

"If I were you, hon," Karen said, "I'd be less concerned about me and more concerned about him using it on the tough guy who's getting in his face."

Dave turned from his ex to Robertson, who flashed a tight and noticeably unfriendly smile. "Okay, point taken . . . ," he muttered, and stepped back.

"So *now* is it okay to go in?" Pan asked Alex. "I've got a mother to try and unvamp."

"*No*, sweetheart," Karen said sternly. "You're not coming in here."

"But, Mom, I mean . . . look at me! That healing thingy I can do, it fixed me after I got . . ." Pan swallowed hard, the words difficult to get out. She shook her head to get past the image of the vertical scar on her chest that popped into her thoughts. "Y'know. So maybe there's a chance it can reverse what . . . what they did to you . . ."

"Honey, listen to me," Karen said. She closed her eyes and massaged her temples with the fingers of her right hand, as though suffering from an intense headache, while using the other to steady herself against the window. "It's not . . . it's not safe for you to come in here. You should . . . just stay away from me. As far . . ." She winced. "As far away as possible . . ."

"Mom—" Pan began, only to fall silent as Karen opened her eyes.

Her black, doll-like eyes.

"Oh, Jesus," Dad said quietly.

"You don't understand, Panda-bear," Karen said, her voice a rough whisper, like the lightest stroke of sandpaper on a wooden surface. "Your blood—I can smell it. I can *hear* it. I can hear everyone's. It's like . . . it's like the most beautiful composition— the bass pounding of your heart, the hum of your veins as your circulation races . . ." The shark-smile widened. "I wish you could hear it—the sound just sort of . . . sweeps . . . you away . . ."

As Karen's voice trailed off, Pan suddenly realized how captivating her mother's gaze was, how mesmerizing the darkness that filled her eyes. She leaned in closer, eager to hear more about the symphony of her blood, unable to look away . . .

"K," Dad said softly. "Let her go. Please."

Just like that, the spell was broken. Pan blinked and staggered back. Karen's eyes widened in horror as she realized she'd been hypnotizing her only child, and she spun away. The glass rattled from the inhuman howl she unleashed.

"Oh . . . oh, God, no . . . ," she sobbed. "Not my baby . . ." She looked over her shoulder at her ex, her eyes restored to their natural color. "David, please, get her away from me!"

The soft whine of a Taser rifle powering up made Pan shudder. Dr. Carlyle, however, motioned to Robertson to stand down.

He studied his patient as she despondently sank to the floor. "I think the crisis has passed . . . for the moment. I'm going to need a few minutes with Karen, though."

"Not without backup, you're not," Alex said.

"Then I'm staying," Dave said, then added with a glance toward the guards, "To make sure things don't get out of hand." He turned to Pan and tried forcing a smile, but looked instead to be on the verge of tears. "Honey, could you do me a big favor and go back to your room? I'll be right up and then . . . then we can talk about this. Please?"

Pan stood frozen, uncertain of what to do. Part of her wanted to run away from that terrifying monster on the other side of the glass; part of her wanted to rush inside to hug Mom and tell her everything would be all right. Most of her, though, just wanted to cry—not out of fear, but for her mother and the hell she was going through.

As always, Sheen was there to guide her through those moments when her brain locked up. She took Pan by the hand and gave a gentle tug. "Come on, Zee."

"N-no," Pan stammered. "I-I can't . . . I can't leave her like this. Sheen, it's my *mom*."

"I know that, Zee, but you gotta let the doc do his thing. Your mom's already stressed out enough; we don't wanna add to it, right?"

Pan didn't know what to think, but if Dr. Carlyle wasn't going to allow her an opportunity to use her healing powers on Mom, then she was just in the way. Unable to come up with an alternative answer, she just nodded. "But we'll come back, right?"

"You know it." Sheen slipped an arm around her shoulders. "Come on."

Leaning against her best friend, Pan let Sheen lead her back down the hall toward the elevator, Javi in tow. They made it as far as the intersection before Pan finally broke down, turning to bury her face in Sheen's shoulder.

Sheen said nothing for the longest time, preferring to simply stand there and hold Pan, occasionally rubbing her back until the sobbing faded into snuffly hitches. Then she wiped away her own tears and said:

"You better not be gettin' any boogers on my shirt, Zee."

Pan gave a phlegmy laugh. "Too late."

Sheen chuckled softly. "Yeah . . ."

Pan hugged her before stepping back. "Thanks, Jungle Queen."

Her friend smiled. "Anytime."

Javi stepped forward with a box of tissues and held it out.

"They keep them over at the nurses' station," he explained. "I figured you might need them."

"Thanks, Javi." Pan yanked out a handful—Sheena, too—and wiped at her watery eyes and runny nose. She laughed nervously. "I am *such* a mess."

"You look fine," he replied with a warm smile.

She snorted. "Liar."

"Hey, give him a break, Zee," Sheen said. "Y'know what they say: love is blind to puffy eyes and boogery snot."

Pan's eyebrows shot almost to her hairline. Sheena McCarthy, die-hard Mets follower, defending Javier Maldonado, fan of the thoroughly reviled Yankees? Hadn't sixteenth-century visionary Nostradamus predicted that as one of the signs of the Apocalypse?

"So, how went the family reunion?"

Pan turned to see Uwe sauntering toward them from the direction of the staff lounge. He had that condescending grin on his face again—the one that made her want to knock it right off his mouth.

"Babe, don't," Sheen said in a distinct warning tone.

The Germanic scarecrow studied his girlfriend's face, noticed the same mixture of anger and sadness that Pan had, and quietly nodded. Then he walked over and drew her into a comforting hug.

"It did not go well, then," he said to Pan over Sheen's shoulder. Pan shook her head. "Then I do apologize for my earlier behavior."

"Thanks," Pan replied, although she didn't entirely believe him. Knowing Uwe, if he was sorry about anything it was for embarrassing Sheen with his public display of douchebaggery; apologizing for hurting Pan's feelings would come in a distant second. Still, there was no reason to make a big thing out of it. Besides, Pan was too drained, emotionally and physically, to argue the point.

Javi placed a hand on her shoulder. "You okay?"

Pan shook her head. "No. And I won't be until Mom is back to . . . being Mom again. But that's up to Annie, isn't it? Unless she kills Zaqiel . . ."

She glanced back down the corridor. Dad stood outside Mom's room, staring through the window, watching Dr. Carlyle and the others do whatever it was they needed to do to help Mom. Even at this distance Pan could tell how helpless her father must feel—the slump of his shoulders as he leaned against the window was evidence of that. She felt exactly the same.

Come on, Annie, she thought. *Hurry up and do something . . .*

And then something did happen—just not what Pan was hoping for . . . or could ever have expected.

It began with a skin-prickling tingle in the air that made the light hairs on her arms stand straight up, as though a static charge was running through her entire body.

"Do you guys feel that?" she asked, although the surprised expressions on their faces made it clear that they had. Her friends weren't the only ones: the hospital staff that had been flowing around them came to an abrupt halt and began looking around for the source of the phenomena. A couple of security guards placed their hands on their firearms, no doubt expecting trouble.

"What the hell is going on?" Javi asked.

The answer came a moment later, as a portal formed in midair amid a burst of powerful winds and crackling electrical arcs that knocked everyone to the floor and blew out rows of ceiling lights. As alarms sounded and emergency lighting kicked in, from the portal tumbled an Asian girl wearing a rubbery-looking catsuit, chunky leather boots, and the biggest felt witch's hat Pan had ever seen—followed by a pair of fanged-and-clawed grotesqueries straight out of her worst monstervision experiences. The witch-girl screamed as the creatures bore down on her.

The security guards opened fire, and Javi threw himself across Pan to protect her; she noticed Uwe do the same for Sheen. From behind Javi's shoulder Pan saw the bullets strike the living nightmares, who screeched and howled in pain before making a hasty retreat through the portal, which slammed shut after they'd passed through.

"You okay?" Javi asked.

"Uh-huh." She gazed into his brown eyes, which were only inches from her own. There were teeny-tiny traces of gold in them. *Pretty,* she thought, although she'd never say that out loud to him. Guys never knew how to respond to compliments like that.

The alarms cut off, replaced by the squabble of voices and the sounds of people rushing about. And the yells of one extremely worried father calling his daughter's name as he came running.

Javi smiled awkwardly. "I, uh, guess I better get off of you, huh? I mean, before he gets the wrong idea and all . . ."

"If you must . . . ," she said with a melodramatic sigh. Pan felt the biggest, stupidest grin spreading across her face as she watched his eyes widen in surprise. But Javi was nowhere near as shocked as she was by her breathy response. Where had *that* come from? Tapping into her inner femme fatale, apparently—which was totally weird, because she was fairly certain that up until this moment she'd never *had* an inner femme fatale to draw upon. At least none that had existed during her time with Ammi.

Still . . . now that she had one it felt kinda nice putting it to use . . .

Dad arrived just as Javi pulled her to her feet. "Pan, honey, are you—"

"I'm fine, Dad. Really."

He nodded slowly, taking her word for it but clearly not believing her, and looked to Javi. "I saw what you did."

Javi started, no doubt fearing what Dad would do to the guy who'd draped himself across his only child. "Uh, look, Mr. Zwieback—"

Dad smiled and clasped his shoulder. "Thank you, Javi."

The boy relaxed. "My pleasure, sir."

Mine, too, Pan thought with a small grin, then clamped her lips together. *Shut up, inner femme fatale, you're gonna get me in trouble!*

Sheen and Uwe joined them. "The hell was all that about?" Sheen asked. "Were those, like, real monsters, or was I just imaginin' it?"

"Welcome to myyyy world," Pan intoned ominously, with a wiggle of her eyebrows. "Moo-ha-ha."

"Make room, people!" Alex barked as he charged up to the scene. He barged through the crowd of rubberneckers that had formed around the spot where the Asian girl had fallen. Pan fell in step behind him, waving on her friends and father.

"Sweetheart—," Dave began.

She turned to face him and walked backward. "I just wanna take a peek, Dad. Come on." Then she spun around to continue trailing after Alex. Pan grinned at Dad's wearied sigh and eased past the final row of onlookers.

The girl, who was sprawled unconscious on the floor, appeared to be around Pan's age and was dressed in a matte black, rubberized catsuit with a pattern that reminded Pan of the surface of basketballs. A lace choker decorated with tiny silver crosses and plastic skulls encircled her throat, and a wide leather belt with a dozen pouches and a metal skull buckle hung loosely around her waist. The purple streaks in her shoulder-length dark hair perfectly matched her nail color and eye shadow. It was a very cool look, sort of like a Goth superheroine without a cape, but the outfit also appeared to have been put through some major punishment: there were rips and tears that had less to do with fashion accents and more with evidence of a vicious attack—no doubt at the hands (and claws) of those monsters that had accompanied her through the portal.

Even odder than the basketball Onesie was the black, ridiculously wide-brimmed witch's hat on the floor beside her, accessorized with a big silver buckle that fastened the bright red band to the hat's crown—and a pair of large, black-felt cat ears sewn at the broad base of the droopy pointed top. The uneven pink stitching along the bottom of the ears was evidence of an inexperienced seamstress adding a personal touch to the Halloween headgear. It was kinda cute, although the big goofy hat didn't work at *all* with the rest of the outfit's superheroine vibe.

Alex and a couple of staffers kneeled beside the girl; the physicians attended to her while the Knight kept watch. Concern for her well-being was etched deeply on his craggy features, and he breathed a sigh of relief when she softly moaned. "Natsumi—talk to me! What's going on?"

The girl's eyes fluttered open. "A . . . Alexander?" She smiled weakly. "I found you."

He smiled back. "That's right, 'Tsumi. You found me. But why are you here?"

"They . . . they've got Annie," she whispered. And then lapsed back into unconsciousness.

8

Zaqiel of the First Reborn despised waiting. He'd had his fill of it during his lengthy imprisonment: waiting decades for forgiveness that never came from the so-called "loving God" who had turned His back on His worthiest creations; then waiting centuries for an opportunity to escape the hell to which he, as well as his angelic brethren and most of their monstrous offspring, had been banished. Waiting to escape and take his revenge on the Almighty by annihilating His beloved monkey-children.

Yet once Zaqiel had gained his much-desired freedom in the early nineteenth century it had been stolen from him in the midst of his finest hour. He had sought to rescue his brothers by leading an excursion into the heart of the volcano that served as the entrance to the Fallen's subterranean prison; had gathered together an army of the night-world's greatest horrors to aid him; had watched his enemies flee in terror and felt a swell of pride, knowing that not even God would be able to stop the chaos soon to be unleashed on the world.

But then . . .

But then the lowliest of all creatures, a shape-changer named Sebastienne Mazarin, whom Zaqiel had taken as a lover, betrayed and ultimately murdered him. Ran him through with the legendary Spear of Longinus, the one weapon capable of destroying an angel because the iron tip was encrusted with the dried blood of the Almighty's only child—a spiritual leader whom Zaqiel had never met yet loathed as much as any of the other humans this "Christ" was meant to reflect. Experiencing the spear's lethal power firsthand did nothing to dispel that hatred.

Then more waiting followed as Zaqiel's soul, cast into Lucifer's pits, endured a further century-plus of unbearable pain before a group of his vampiric descendants, led by the willful Lady Kiyoshi Sasaki of House Otoyo, was able to resurrect him . . . only to have the damnable girl abandon him in the room in which he now stood. Forced to wait—again!—while the Sasaki clan gathered one floor below with their undead brothers and sisters, as well as the latest generation of weirdlings who now led the world's supernatural community. No doubt the lot of them were squabbling like children over seating arrangements before he'd be given an opportunity to address them.

Zaqiel gazed once more at his surroundings. As Lady Kiyoshi had explained, her clan owned this entire floor of this building, Yokohama's Landmark Tower, mainly using the apartments and conference rooms to entertain clan leaders and the occasional human—the latter being friends of her sister Miyuki's, she'd been quick to point out. Zaqiel could not help but notice how she'd been unable to pronounce the words "human" and "friends" in the same sentence without her lips curling into a sneer. Apparently Kiyoshi did not share her younger sibling's predilection for socializing with her meals. Neither did Zaqiel.

He stepped up to one of the floor-to-ceiling windows and gazed upon this new world in which he'd awakened. Japan had changed so much since he had last trod its lands—in 1816 or '17, if he remembered correctly. Back then the island nation practically lived in the Dark Ages, its rulers having chosen to isolate their subjects from the rest of the world. When night fell the darkness was total, occasionally broken by the soft glow of lanterns. Now, in the twenty-first century, the country was a vital part of the global community, and the night was ablaze with color—neon lighting it was called, according to Miyuki, who had been eager to show him the wonders of her city . . . only to have her plans inelegantly quashed by her clan leader. It was just as well—Zaqiel was here to raise another army, not take in the sights.

Unbidden, his thoughts drifted back to his previous visit. Wintertime, he remembered, the cold winds a welcome balm for the volcanic, superheated air he had been forced to breathe during his imprisonment. He had been wandering the streets of Osaka, on his way to a meeting with the worshipers of Jishin-namazu—a godlike catfish responsible for Japan's earthquakes—when he felt the presence of a supernatural entity close by; a presence accented by the heady scent of fear. Intrigued, he traced the disturbance to a puppet theater from which humans of all ages were fleeing, their screams bringing a rare smile to the angel's lips. That smile, however, quickly transformed into a look of astonishment when he located the reason for the stampede: onstage was a breathtakingly beautiful Japanese woman, a katana in each hand, slicing her way through a quartet of panicked demons that were attempting to abduct some of the children in the audience. At first Zaqiel had considered helping the grotesqueries in their struggles, had even started walking down the main aisle to join them—after all were they not, in some way, descended from his brothers?

But then . . .

But then, after neatly decapitating one of the demons, the woman turned toward Zaqiel, undoubtedly sensing his presence as he had hers—and winked at him before returning to her work.

And that was how he met the shape-shifting huntress, Sebastienne Mazarin.

Zaqiel shook his head to clear it, his wistful smile melting into a teeth-grinding snarl as he cast aside the memory. *I would have made her my queen—damnable lovestruck fool that I was—yet in the end she chose to turn against me. And should the opportunity present itself, I will show her what a poor choice that was . . .*

A small movement from within the enormous fish tank that stood across from him caught his eye. As Zaqiel watched, the doors of a large toy castle opened wide, and a pair of fish more than a foot in length—one with blue-and-orange-streaked scales, the other almost bloodred with black speckles—swam out. They made a full circuit of their environment before coming to a halt directly in front of the angel. Then they just stared at him, as though waiting for him to do something.

Well, Zaqiel thought, *let them wait. Then I'll not be the only one in a foul mood around here . . .*

"Admiring my tiger oscars, my lord?" a soft feminine voice asked.

Zaqiel turned toward the newcomer to find Miyuki Sasaki standing in the doorway. The girl was dressed in a pink satin kimono festooned with a veritable garden of embroidered roses. While still as cloyingly dainty and colorful as the Victorian Era–inspired dresses she normally wore, the ceremonial robe lent her an air of maturity—a hint of the true immortal that lurked beneath the surface of a young woman's body. In her hands was a dinner plate on which sat a small pile of raw hamburger. The sight of the blood pooled around the uncooked meat made his stomach rumble softly. Still . . .

"I hope that is not meant for me," he said with a hint of a smile.

The girl giggled. "No, my lord. The meat is for Toya and Chiyuki. They always know when it is their feeding time." She walked over to the tank, pausing along the way to nod in respect to her ancestor.

"Ah. The fish," Zaqiel said. "Such unusual names."

"They are characters in one of my favorite manga, *Millennium Snow*," Miyuki said with some excitement as she dropped pieces of hamburger into the tank. The fish swooped in to gobble them up. "It is about a teenage girl who meets a vampire boy and they fall in love but he—"

"Miyu," interjected a harsh, all-too-familiar voice. "Do not waste our great lord's time with your comic-book nonsense."

The girl turned away in embarrassment as Zaqiel faced the new arrival. Kiyoshi was dressed in a similar fashion to her sister's, but the clan leader's silk kimono reflected the colors of the night: black and deep blue. And just as her sister's bright attire matched Miyuki's bubbly personality, the dark robes perfectly complemented Kiyoshi's sour mood.

"Lady Sasaki," Zaqiel said coolly.

"It is time, my lord," Kiyoshi said, the tone of her voice immediately softening as she addressed him. "The heads of most of the major houses have answered your summons and assembled in the Sky Garden. What would you have me do?"

Zaqiel did not trust this woman. The subservient attitude she adopted for his benefit was completely false and meant to keep him off-guard, but he was not easily deceived. Ambition practically radiated from her every pore. Since his resurrection he'd observed that Lady Kiyoshi Sasaki bowed to no one and ruled over the members of her house—including her softer-edged sister, Miyuki—with an iron fist. Undoubtedly she saw taking a passive approach to Zaqiel as a necessary, if distasteful, means to an end: gaining his trust so that she could become a more powerful clan leader—perhaps even lord of all vampires?

What then of Zaqiel of the First Reborn? What role would she expect him to play when the other houses had fallen in step behind the Otoyo clan? Or would he be the first obstacle removed from her path?

Yes, Lady Sasaki was one to watch closely . . .

"My lord?" Kiyoshi prompted, no doubt confused—and possibly disturbed—by his silence and unwavering stare.

"You said 'most of the major houses.' Why not all?"

She lowered her gaze and paused for a moment before responding. Choosing her words carefully, no doubt. "A few masters had prior commitments that could not be rescheduled and so—"

"You mean the ones who answered my summons before now refuse to have anything to do with me. They do not wish to repeat their . . . mistakes." Zaqiel had expected as much; in fact, their reluctance was understandable. Were he in a similar position he might have been just as hesitant to throw in a second time with the celestial general whose troops had been so soundly defeated by a ragtag army of religious zealots and a shape-shifting traitress.

It didn't mean, however, that those same clan leaders would not be among the first of his enemies destroyed once humanity had been crushed beneath his boot heel. He might understand their motives, but Zaqiel had never been *that* forgiving.

"You are correct, my lord . . . although they did not use those exact words," Kiyoshi replied. "But it was only a handful, and even they have provided surrogates who will inform their masters of your plans. Still, the other houses *are* in attendance and are most anxious to reacquaint themselves with you."

The angel nodded. The parasites and the power seekers—of course they were eager to demonstrate their loyalty. He may have failed in his previous attempt to subjugate humanity, but still was he Zaqiel of the First Reborn—the first vampires— and his status carried considerable weight. They would listen, and they would follow.

"Very well." He gestured toward the door. "Please, my lady, lead on. I have much to—"

He froze for a moment, then his gaze went sweeping over to the large windows. Yokohama stretched below him, but something felt different about it. He probed the night with his senses; there was something out there that had caught his attention—

something close by.

No, he suddenly realized, not something.

Some*one*.

His lips peeled back in a fierce snarl.

"Sebastienne . . . ," he growled.

"God, do I hate vampires. You know what I hate even more? Sitting around, waiting for vampires to do something. They might have all of eternity to get things done, but I don't."

Annie lowered her binoculars, rolled her eyes in annoyance, and gazed at the pair of young Knights sitting beside her on the roof of the Queen's Tower A office building. As usual, it was Kenji Azuma who'd made the complaint, weighing down his words with an overly dramatic sigh. The tall, muscular, twenty-two-year-old Yokohama native was a recent graduate of the Knights training academy, and certainly enthusiastic about being part of the organization—not to mention coming highly recommended by the bishop of the local diocese—but Azuma apparently had never learned that patience was a virtue.

His partner, however, was quite the opposite. A few feet away from Azuma, levitating a foot above the roof in a cross-legged sitting position, was Natsumi Koiwai, a sixteen-year-old girl from Tokyo whose attitude and Goth-inspired outfit reminded Annie of Pandora Zwieback—who, according to Alex, was not only recovering from her encounter with Zaqiel but was acting as strong-willed as ever. That good news had almost eased the guilt Annie had been feeling since abandoning her young friend and her mother to chase after Zaqiel—not that the sensation had faded completely, of course. It probably wouldn't for some time to come, if ever.

And there was still the issue, unspoken so far, of the possible psychological problems Pan might suffer once the reality of her brutal death and subsequent resurrection sunk in. For a girl who had spent the last decade doubting her sanity, that knowledge—as well as dealing with what Karen had become—might be too much to bear. Annie prayed that the Zwieback family was strong enough to get through this crisis.

Annie's concern for her friends was gently eased from her troubled mind by the pleasant strains of Natsumi quietly singing in English. She had such a beautiful voice that it took Annie a full verse before she recognized the song: AC/DC's "Highway to Hell." She chuckled, imagining the surprised reaction the late Bon Scott might have had to one of his signature tunes being delivered with such sweetness.

The ridiculously large, cat-ear-decorated witch's hat perched on the back of Natsumi's head and the pouch-laden belt with skull clasp that hung around her waist were not standard Knights issue, nor did her dark, purple-streaked hair meet their grooming standards, but from what Annie had been told the Church was willing to put up with Natsumi's eccentricities as long as she maintained her usual high-quality level of work. Besides, sorceresses willing to work for a religious organization that had spent centuries persecuting their kind were few and far between, so, as the old saying went, beggars couldn't be choosers.

Natsumi gestured at a dusty, paint-stained knapsack held together with duct tape and large safety pins; a silver basin and flask floated out from the bag and into her hands. The teen witch opened the flask and poured the water it contained into the basin, then reached into one of her pouches, pulled out a pinch of dried herbs, and tossed them in as well. Gray-lavender smoke billowed up from the concoction.

"Is that your scrying glass?" Annie asked. "I thought it had to be a mirror."

"It's witch-tech my ancestors used to use. Working with water means I can use whatever's handy, even a puddle, and I don't have to worry about getting slammed with bad luck, like I would by breaking a mirror." Natsumi added a few more herbs to the mix. "Getting the spell right just takes a little longer this way, though. Give me a few minutes and I'll get you an image so clear you'll think you're sitting in on the meeting."

As patient as Natsumi was, Annie hated waiting even more than Azuma, though she would never admit it. They weren't here to dawdle, they were here to gather intelligence on the major summit of weirdling lords that House Otoyo had called. Directly across from their location stood the Yokohama Landmark Tower, the tallest building in Japan—and the meeting place selected by House Otoyo. The urge to turn into a bat or a bird and swoop over there to confront Zaqiel was powerful. She could sense his presence on one of the upper floors; she had no doubt he could sense her as well because their psychic bond as a couple had always been strong. For now, though, intelligence gathering was the top priority. She'd promised the high council of the Knights that she wouldn't just barge in and start lopping off heads and tearing out hearts until they knew what they were dealing with, so for the time being Annie remained in position.

Yet that promise didn't mean she'd wait forever for a decision. There was Karen Zwieback to think of, for one thing. The longer Zaqiel stayed alive, the greater Karen's thirst for blood would grow until it was too powerful to deny. And should that happen, should Karen lose herself and be fully consumed by the virus that had taken over her body, then Annie would have to put her down.

God help them both if it came to that . . .

Azuma yawned. Annie smiled wryly.

"Bored already, Azuma?" she asked. "Have something more important you'd rather be doing?"

"No, sensei," the young Knight replied, a touch sullenly. "It's just that vampires are so . . . commonplace. When I joined the Knights of the Apocalypse, I thought it would involve exciting stuff like fighting demons and grim reapers and monsters out of folklore . . . not sitting on rooftops and watching a bunch of old-school bloodsuckers attend a business conference."

Annie chuckled softly. If Zaqiel hadn't been involved, she might have felt the same as Azuma. For Annie, killing vampires had lost its sparkle after the first hundred years; then it became just a job. And as another old saying went, when doing what you love turns into work, it's time to find a new career. Good thing, then, there was always such a wide variety of monsters to hunt that kept her interest.

"Surveillance is part of the job, Kenji, so just accept it. And this isn't a business conference—not with Zaqiel involved. The last time he gathered the clan leaders like this, it was to convince them to join his crusade against humanity. I just hope they turn him down now."

Natsumi sprinkled a few more herbs into the basin and slowly moved her hands over it in a conjuring gesture. A pinkish glow emanated from the water. "Since when did you start hating vampires, Azuma?" she asked without looking up. "What about that darkwave band you're always howling along with, like some dying wolf?"

Azuma blushed at the harsh review of his vocal talents. "Aural Vampire? They're not real vampires. And I only got into them because my sister Kou listens to them all the time . . . but I do like Exo-Chika's singing."

"And maybe 'cause Exo-Chika is kinda hot?" Natsumi glanced at him with a knowing smirk.

"Go watch your bowl," Azuma said.

"So should you." The girl waved them over. "Come take a look."

Annie hurried over to join the young witch and Azuma, who had already reached his partner. His eyes were wide open in surprise as he gazed into the basin. "Wow! That's, like, HD quality!"

"It's the holy water I picked up from Yamate Catholic Church," Natsumi replied, referring to Yokohama's Sacred Heart Cathedral, which was the seat of their top boss, Bishop Keiichi Yoshimura. "Holy water always gives the clearest pictures."

Annie peered over the witch's shoulder, and straight into the Landmark Tower's sixty-ninth-floor observation deck—the Sky Garden. Azuma was right: the image in the water was so sharp that Annie felt as though she could reach in and tap one of the monsters on the shoulder. "Good job, 'Tsumi!"

Natsumi grinned. "Thanks. Now check this out." She sprinkled what appeared to be glitter—but in all likelihood wasn't—across the water, then opened a pouch on her belt and took out a wireless game controller that she switched on. Her thumbs nudged the device's two joysticks, and in response the image of the conference tilted to one side, then began rotating in a slow circle. "Neat, huh? Three-hundred-and-sixty-degree pan and zoom. My cousin Yoite showed me how to do this."

"I remember your cousin," Annie said. "The computer wizard." And by "computer wizard" she meant that Yoite Tanaka was a spellcaster who used electronic devices to enhance his magick. *Leave it to Yoite to adapt video game technology for eldritch spyware*, Annie thought. *Amazing. Things sure have changed since the days of bubbling cauldrons and spiritual third eyes.* She watched as Natsumi took the scrying basin through a complete circuit of the room, occasionally pausing to zoom in on certain attendees. One in particular caught the girl's eye, and she gasped.

"Omigod. Is that . . . is that Dracula?" she asked, clearly awestruck at the sight of the distinguished-looking master of House Tepes. His black hair was streaked with gray—again—and cut shorter than the last time Annie had crossed paths with him, but the aquiline nose, the bushy eyebrows, and the cruel set of his mouth were unchanged.

"Yes, that's Vlad," Annie replied. "I see he's dyeing his mustache again. Let's see who else showed up."

Natsumi returned to scoping out the room. The turnout was fairly impressive. Along with Dracula there were the king and queen of Ghana's House Mamuwalde; China's self-proclaimed "emperor" Zongtang of House Ch'ing Shih; Lady Bannerworth of House Varney; Count and Comtesse Galmier from France's House Addhema; and Northern India's lord of the undead, House Baital's Prince Malhotra. There were a number of representatives whom Annie didn't recognize; apparently those clans had undergone administrative shifts in the past decade or so. She noted that House Ruthven's caretakers had apparently passed on the gathering, as had the leaders of the Orlock clan. No doubt they vividly remembered the last time Zaqiel had approached them as allies in his war against humanity, and had little interest in repeating that epic failure. However, Annie did spot Orlock's surrogates milling about—the same three gunsels who had started the firefight in front of David Zwieback's museum.

"That is fantastic," Annie said. "Is there any chance we can hear what they're saying?"

Natsumi shook her head. "I *wanted* to set up a couple of bowls as speakers, but Kenji drank the bottled water I'd brought." She frowned and stared daggers at her partner.

"I was thirsty," he replied, sounding a touch offended.

Annie sighed. "All right. Then I need to get in there." Once she'd gained access to the tower she planned to shape-shift and become a literal fly on the wall at the conference—real old-school eavesdropping, as these kids might say.

Natsumi grinned. "Finally." She adjusted her oversized hat and jumped to her feet. "Just say when." She cracked her knuckles and wiggled her fingers, ready to do some serious spellcasting.

"Aren't we supposed to get approval from Bishop Yoshimura, first, on stuff like that?" Azuma asked, then smiled slyly. "I mean, unless you think we need to move fast and there's no time to put in a request." His gaze drifted over to his own equipment, coming to rest on the sheathed katana he'd chosen from the armory. It was clear from the gleam in his eyes how eager he was to put that weapon to use.

"There *is* no time, not if Zaqiel is here to rally the troops—but you can ask Keiichi after I'm inside," Annie replied.

"You mean after *we're* inside, don't you?" Azuma asked.

"No, I mean after *I'm* inside. The two of you are staying here."

"*What?*" Natsumi cried. "No way, Annie! We're supposed to be a team on this."

"A surveillance team, not a strike team," Annie countered. "I'm not going in there to fight, I'm going in to spy on their meeting, and I can do that much easier if I don't have you two to worry about. Trust me, you're not going to miss any excitement. Even *I'm* not crazy enough to take on a skyscraper full of monsters—this time," she added with a wink. "Now, what do you have that will get me in there?"

Natsumi reached into one of her belt's pouches and pulled out a three-inch-long plastic tube that she bent until there was a small cracking noise. She shook it furiously and a bright green light shone from within.

Annie laughed. "You're using glow sticks, now? What happened to that gnarly old magic wand you used to carry everywhere?"

Natsumi wrinkled her nose in distaste. "Too mainstream. Wands stopped being cool after the wizard craze got big and all the Hogwarts wannabes started playing with the toy versions. With these I can throw spells *and* go clubbing without idiots making lame 'Harriet Potter' jokes."

Annie glanced at the teen's enormous witch hat. *They probably don't make them because everyone must think you're a* Lord of the Rings *fan—except they don't know what to make of those bizarre cat ears.* Still, she thought it best to not voice that comment. No reason to make the girl self-conscious about her headgear when she was so obviously proud to wear it.

"Okay, here we go," Natsumi said. She closed her eyes in order to concentrate, raised her hands as though she were about to conduct an invisible symphony, and muttered a few words in an ancient tongue. The glow stick flared brightly as she opened her eyes, and she whipped her hands through an intricate pattern. Green lightning crackled out from the plastic tube, forming a rough-edged, electrically charged gateway that sparked and hummed. Through it Annie could see a small, dimly lit room lined with rows of cleaning products.

"Knowing you, I figured you'd want to go busting in, so I downloaded the tower's floor plans onto my tablet," Natsumi explained and nodded toward the opposite side of the doorway. "That's a custodian's storeroom on the seventieth floor, right above the Sky Garden. It's as close as I can get you without dumping you right in the middle of Vampire Central."

" 'Tsumi, you're amazing," Annie said, and smiled warmly. "You've come a long way from the little girl who kept turning me into a talking kitty whenever I visited."

Natsumi blushed, hiding her embarrassment by pulling the hat's wide brim over her face.

"That's why she's the brains of the operation," Azuma said.

"No kidding," Annie said wryly. "Now, remember what I said: stay right here, but let Keiichi know what I'm doing. With any luck, by the time he's done yelling at you I should be back with the information we need."

Natsumi released the hat brim to let Annie see her deep pout. "Okay," she muttered. "But I'll leave the portal open a little, in case you have to come back in a hurry. Just tap on it and it'll pop open to full size."

"Good luck, Annie," Azuma said cheerfully. "And if you need any help . . ."

"I'd call Alex, but he's on the other side of the globe." Annie winked at the young warrior, then charged through the gateway, which shrunk to the approximate size of a DVD case behind her but didn't entirely close. It just hovered, crackling softly, in the night air.

Natsumi sighed and turned to her partner, who was staring up at the Landmark Tower. "So, you gonna make that call to the bishop, or should I?"

"You know," he replied slowly, "I hear the Royal Park Hotel in the tower has free Wi-Fi. And I bet the cell-phone reception up there would be a lot better for calling Yoshimura-san—you know, so we can hear him clearly while he's screaming his lungs out at us." Azuma smiled slyly and wiggled his eyebrows.

Natsumi grinned and grabbed her knapsack. "Go get your sword."

9

They were waiting for her when she walked out of the storeroom—at least that was Annie's first impression when she came face-to-face with a pair of House Otoyo's human guards in the hallway. Judging by their stunned expressions, however, they more than likely had just been passing by as they made a security sweep of the area.

Whatever the reason for their unexpected appearance, Annie wasted no time in taking advantage of their momentary surprise by shape-shifting into the form of an oni—a Japanese ogre with oversized teeth and a demon's face—and rushing them. The sight of a ten-foot-tall beast from hell bearing down on them only added to the guards' confusion.

They were dead before they could raise an alarm or bring their Uzis into play, their throats crushed in Annie's massive hands. She carried the bodies and weapons into the storeroom, then replicated the stocky body type, powdered features, and Elegant Gothic Lolita clothing of one of the men—a much better disguise for getting around the conference. Annie caught sight of herself in a mirror above a slop sink that was next to the mops, and grinned at her pseudo-glam-punk appearance. She hadn't worn this many ruffles since her backup-singer days with Adam Ant in the early eighties.

"Stand and deliver," the Japanese man in the mirror said in her voice. She chuckled softly, then focused on her mission and replaced her smile with a deep scowl. Yes, she thought as she admired her reflection, this was a much better facial expression for one of Lady Sasaki's underlings. All business. Humorless. Like his clan leader.

She bent down and retrieved one of the guns, then removed the clip to inspect the ammunition. As she'd suspected, the Uzi was loaded with a variant of Preacher's

Rounds, the so-called "holy bullets" used by the Knights of the Apocalypse to put down weirdlings. Named after Emmett Cale—a late-nineteenth-century holy man turned Texas Ranger who'd invented them as a solution to a werewolf infestation in America's southwest—the silver fragmentation bullets contained a few drops of holy water and had small crosses etched on the tips. There had been rumors in New York's supernatural community of Gothopolis that some of the vampire clans had started manufacturing knockoff Preachers, but until the firefight outside David Zwieback's museum, Annie had never seen evidence that the rumors were true. How such monsters handled bullets whose casings could harm them probably came down to human minions loading the gun clips. Not a very effective method, were that the case; what did the vampires do when they needed to reload? More important, what priest in his right mind would be willing to bless vampire ammunition? That was a question Annie would have to bring up at her debriefing—once she made it out of here alive, of course.

Annie jammed the clip back into place, slid the gun behind her replicated blazer and under the waistband of her slacks, and exited the storeroom. She'd wanted to bring the Spear of Longinus, since it was the one weapon guaranteed to put an end to Zaqiel, but the ruling council had denied her request; not even Alexander had been able to change their minds. They considered it a holy relic, given its connection to Jesus, and therefore too precious to risk losing again. Pointing out that it had never been lost in the first place, because she'd known all along where it was stashed and just never bothered to tell anyone, had only earned her the dirtiest look she'd ever received from a cardinal. And although another had tried to disguise the gesture by scratching the side of his nose, Annie knew he was really giving her The Finger.

She certainly could have used the spear right now. Zaqiel was close; the strength of his aura was impossible to miss, radiating such power that it almost masked the presence of the multitude of weirdlings she could detect one floor below. Added to that was the problem that, given the passionate relationship she'd shared with the angel, aura detection became a two-way street—the nearer she drew to her old lover, the better chance he would have to sense she was in the building. Thankfully, he wasn't on this floor, or else her eavesdropping mission would have come to an abrupt end. Still, she wouldn't remain unnoticed for long, so the trick now was to test the limits of their psychic bond and see just how much intel she could gather before he realized his ex-girlfriend had crashed the party.

Taking the stairs in a nearby fire exit brought her to the main action. As she joined the gathering she noticed there were far more guards on this floor . . . and they were all eyeing her with suspicion. For a moment she wondered if the mix of armed vampires and humans from various houses could see who she really was, but then, as their gazes drifted elsewhere, she realized they were all sizing up one another in that manner. She was merely the latest addition to the party.

Look at them. They're like a bunch of Old West gunfighters facing off in the street, daring the other to make the first move. All it would take to set them off is the right word in the right ear . . .

Annie hid the malicious smile that started to form by scratching her upper lip, and tucked away that inspired thought in the back of her mind. Something to consider in case she needed a diversion; then these goons and their undoubtedly itchy trigger fingers could do half the monster-disposal work for her.

The smile faded, however, when she entered the Sky Garden and saw the turnout with her own eyes. Natsumi's water basin might have provided a clear view of the conference, but it came nowhere close to displaying the sheer enormity of House Otoyo's soiree. Vampire clans were not the only invited guests: there were succubi and incubi—female and male sexual demons—from Germany, dressed in scant leather costumes; trolls from Scandinavia in smelly, stained furs; a pack of bTsan, Tibetan demons in survivalist gear—an improvement over their kind's normally ruddy hunter's outfits; Albanian Kukuths, female demons known for spreading pestilence; Chinese *guei*—spirits of men and women who had drowned, and who were currently soaking the Sky Garden's carpeting with the water that seeped from their bodies—and fox-people, whose features were as beautiful as the thick, furry tails they sported; werecreatures from the Middle East in human form, but Annie could tell a shape-changing hyena or jackal when she saw one; and Malaysian *pennanggalan*—bloodthirsty witches who could detach their heads and pull out their intestines, and send them all in search of victims. The latter were deep in conversation with a group of *aswang manananggal*—Filipino vampires who were also able to separate their heads from their bodies. With so much in common, they were probably discussing plans for the after-party.

Oh, for a flamethrower, a sprinkler system filled with holy water, and an unlimited supply of Priest Rounds, she thought as she looked at the assemblage. *I could cross off sooo many names on my to-do list . . .*

Not only was the Sky Garden packed, but she spotted a number of Otoyo members moving through the crowd, recording the gala with small video cameras. Her gaze drifted over to what she'd assumed upon entering was a dance-club-style audio setup manned by a couple of deejays; a closer look revealed it as the control center for the cameras' output. House Otoyo was live-streaming the event!

Wish I'd known they were doing that before I barged in here. I could have stayed in my hotel room, hacked into the signal—all right, asked Natsumi's cousin, Yoite, to hack into the signal—and watched the whole thing from my bed.

Computer skills—or the lack thereof—aside, the bottom line was that Zaqiel's resurrection had created far more buzz than Annie ever imagined, and that was troubling. Given the disastrous outcome of his previous attempt to destroy the planet, she had been absolutely certain that Kiyoshi Sasaki's invitation for this meet and greet would be turned down by anyone with a long-enough memory. Not only had she been thoroughly off-target with that belief, it also appeared that in defeat Zaqiel had become more popular than ever, if the snatches of conversations she overheard were any indication. True, he might have failed to accomplish his goals, been impaled on a mystical spear and had his head cut off, and spent the last century rotting away in a pine box, but the bigger picture was that he had come *thisclose* to putting humanity to heel. And, it was pointed out, who among those gathered here tonight could say they'd ever been that successful? Why, if it hadn't been for the actions of his crazy girlfriend, everyone gathered here tonight would be celebrating the fallen angel's 192nd anniversary of being in power instead of merely welcoming him back to the world.

"What I wouldn't give to present the head of Lord Zaqiel's betrayer to him on a silver platter," remarked one culsu, a female demon from Italy. She held up the golden shears her kind always carried, to snip the thread of life of anyone who angered them. "I'd lop it off with just a single swipe of these enchanted blades. Return the favor for what she did to him."

"You and a pair of fancy scissors . . . against La Bella Tenebrosa?" asked an Irish sea monk, his almost human features twisted in hate at having to utter Annie's nickname. The bald-headed merman grunted dismissively. "Good luck with that, Tulia. From everything I've heard of Sebastienne, she'd be the one serving *your* head on the platter."

"Damn straight," agreed a tuxedoed homunculus around a mouthful of black caviar. "If she doesn't eat it first—the head, I mean, not the platter."

The monk snarled, clearly annoyed by the foot-tall artificial man that was loudly chewing mini toasts piled high with fish eggs—in front of a much larger aquatic creature. If the homunculus was aware of the reason for the disapproving look he was getting, he elected to ignore it and went right on stuffing his face.

"Eat my head—that's just a lot of hyped-up public relations nonsense," Tulia replied. "Sure, she's a pain in the ass; sure, she's been decimating our races for hundreds of years. But there's just the one of her, and I'm talking about overwhelming her with sheer numbers. She's good, but not even the huntress could stand up to an army of the night launching a unified attack. Am I not right, Aengus? You know I am."

"Well, when you put it that way . . ." The monk nodded and shrugged. "You're right."

"Yeah, dude's got a point," the homunculus mumbled between chews.

Tulia glared at the talking food compactor. Apparently she didn't enjoy being called "dude."

"Anyway, with the huntress out of the way," she continued, "there'd be nothing to stop Lord Zaqiel from finishing what he started all those years ago—crushing the damned human race. With all of us by his side, sharing in the glory."

There was an excited murmur of assent from the group, and that was the moment when Annie (now more popularly known as "Lord Zaqiel's betrayer" and his "crazy girlfriend") realized she was standing—alone—in a room full of monsters who would gladly tear her apart, if her identity should be revealed.

Annie smiled slyly. *I wouldn't have missed this for the world . . .*

A hush fell over the room as a side door opened and the members of House Otoyo swept into the Sky Garden. A coterie of armed male and female guards, dressed in their finest Elegant & Gothic Lolita fashions, entered first and took positions along the base of a stage that had been constructed in front of the windows facing Tokyo Bay. They were followed by the ceremonially garbed council of elders—undead men and women who'd helped build the clan, one or two of them dating all the way back to the days of Lady Otoyo herself. From what Annie knew of house politics, in general the elders were highly respected among vampirekind, but not so much in-house. Ever since the rise to power of Kiyoshi Sasaki their role in clan decisions had been greatly diminished. Vampires of Kiyoshi's generation had little tolerance for the old ways—or the old masters—but apparently both still had their uses when it came to public relations events.

The elders formed a semicircle behind a podium mounted at the front of the stage, but no one stepped forward to address the crowd. They were here simply as an impressive-looking backdrop, like the city lights that blazed behind them. The whole spectacle had the look and feel of an elaborate press conference— understandable, given the live Internet feed being broadcast around the globe. If nothing else, House Otoyo knew how to put on a show for its viewers.

The pageantry continued with the blaring sounds of some rock tune that featured a harpsichord and the chorus "beast of blood," and the entrance of a pair of human women in short-skirted maid costumes. They grinned for the audience and reached into the small wicker baskets they carried, to sprinkle rose petals on the floor and create a trail that led from the door to the stage.

Annie rolled her eyes.

Finally, the Sisters Sasaki arrived, flanked by their personal guards: Kiyoshi, arrogantly confident, in the lead; Miyuki, all smiles, trailing behind at a reverent distance. Both wore Gothic Lolita–styled *jûnihitoe*: formal multilayered kimonos of color schemes that matched their personalities. Not quite exact replicas of the traditional Japanese court dress that Annie remembered from her previous trips to Japan—for one thing, *jûnihitoe* colors never included black or, in Miyuki's case, shocking pink—but the outfits were certainly stylish in their own right. Kiyoshi's waist-length hair was piled high on her head, to form a pair of huge puffs that were undoubtedly meant to emulate the updo of a Japanese empress, but to Annie they looked more like pom-poms glued to the vampiress's skull.

"Where is Lord Zaqiel?" muttered Tulia the culsu as the sisters took to the stage.

That's what Annie wanted to know, as well. She scanned the room, but there was no sign of the angel. Waiting for his cue, perhaps, after Kiyoshi had given her speech?

Annie frowned. *I don't remember him being this accommodating to women when we were a couple—certainly not to* me . . .

Kiyoshi held up a hand to ask for silence, then leaned toward the microphone mounted on the podium. "Friends . . . revered elders . . . honored rivals . . . welcome to the dawn of a new age—the Age of The Reborn."

Not the most inspiring start to a speech, Annie thought—she'd heard better—and extremely inclusive when you considered the fact that "The Reborn" referred only to the fallen angels' vampiric descendants and not monsterdom in general, but the audience greeted it with enthusiastic roars and applause.

Kiyoshi waited for the cheering to subside before continuing.

"I know that we have had our differences, and that the quest for The Prize created an even greater rift among our clans . . . but that is all in the past." She glanced at the various house leaders in attendance, her gaze taking in the trio of House Orlock thugs who'd been involved in the New York firefight. Elden, the rail-thin leader in the dark-blue suit, raised his glass in a salute to their hostess.

"Tonight, we start anew," Kiyoshi said. "Tonight, we are united as one clan. Tonight, we welcome back a member of our family thought lost forever—a member of our family who will lead us to the greatness we have always sought. Our ancestor . . . our creator . . . Zaqiel of the First Reborn!"

With a dramatic sweep of her arm she gestured toward the large observation windows behind her. There, held aloft on ebon wings, hovered the man of the hour, looking as handsome and downright sexy as Annie remembered him. The dark William Fioravanti Bespoke Suit he wore—custom-tailored and very expensive—fit him like a second skin.

"Dayuuumm," muttered a *guei* a few steps from Annie. "That is one fine-looking angel."

Why is it always the ones who look that damned hot turn out to be the most evil of bastards? Annie thought. *And why did I have to fall so hard for this one? Because*

I thought I could change him? She shook her head. *Stupid. Mother was right, all those years ago: no matter how much you try, you can never save a bad boy from himself.*

Or, in Zaqiel's case, from the ax of a heartbroken girlfriend determined to save the world from his madness.

At Kiyoshi's direction a Yuki-onna, a Japanese snow witch—recognizable by her frost-white complexion, waist-length black hair, blue-tinged lips, and bright yellow eyes—floated over to one of the windows. She lightly breathed on the glass, then with the tip of a finger quickly scrawled a set of letters before the mist faded. Instantly, the glass turned to fog, providing Zaqiel with access to the garden. He floated through the vaporous entrance—which reverted to its original state after his passage—and landed on the stage to thunderous applause.

He always did know how to make an entrance, Annie thought with a melancholy smile—and reached under her jacket for the Uzi she'd appropriated. *Perhaps I should make his exit just as impressive . . .*

Thoughts of intelligence gathering now put aside, she eased through the crowd, moving toward one side of the stage to avoid drawing attention to herself, as a straight-on approach would be noticed immediately. The monsters paid little heed to her actions, no doubt believing the Otoyo guard in their midst was simply doing his job, watching for potential troublemakers.

Zaqiel drank in the adulation far longer than was necessary—his ego on full display—but eventually he signaled for the applause to end and stepped up to the microphone.

"My children, thank you all for coming," he rumbled pleasantly. "Some of you are known to me; it is good to see you again. Most of you, however, are new friends. I hope I have lived up to your expectations," he added wryly.

"You know it!" yelled a succubus from the back of the room.

Zaqiel laughed heartily; the crowd joined in.

Still a charmer, Annie thought—and then realized she was smiling. She immediately clamped her lips together and tightened her grip on the Uzi's stock.

"As Lady Sasaki so eloquently noted," Zaqiel continued, "we stand at the dawn of a new age—one in which no creature of the night, no weirdling, no child of darkness need ever fear extermination again. An age when it is the human race that will be forced to live in the shadows. An age in which they either serve us . . . or are served *to* us."

The cheers were deafening, but Annie blocked them out and concentrated on finding the best angle for a clear shot—and a quick getaway. That door Kiyoshi and her mob had come through seemed like a good choice. And knowing Zaqiel as well as she did, the old windbag would speak all night, if given the chance; he loved playing to crowds. If that were the case here, Annie would have plenty of time to get in position.

What puzzled her, though, was why he hadn't yet reacted to her presence. She was no more than twenty feet from the stage, but he'd given no indication that he was aware of his "crazy girlfriend."

Or could it be he was merely *pretending* not to feel her . . . ?

Get out! her intuition screamed. *It's a trap. Get out now!*

That made a great deal of sense, she had to admit. Her earlier realization about being outnumbered and outgunned in the middle of a demon convention came rushing back to the forefront of her thoughts. And with Zaqiel distracted by his hero's welcome, there would be no better time to slip out.

Still, the gun was already in her hand and he was standing *right there . . .*

No. Don't be an idiot. Just leave and call in backup. Zaqiel's not going anywhere.

That was true; if anything, he was just getting started.

"But, my friends!" the angel went on, raising his voice to be heard above the excited cries of *Served! To! Us! Served! To! Us! Served! To! Us!* "But that dawn will never come unless we take the necessary steps to make it happen. That is why I have come before you this evening—to ask you to join me on a great crusade! For only by working together can we ever hope to bring about a new age . . . to create a perfect world in which humanity at last kneels before us—and the Almighty learns to fear us!"

The response wasn't quite as raucous as before—bringing God into the equation always tended to make Satan's minions understandably nervous, especially when He might be eavesdropping. The last time the big man had gotten pissed off, so the story went, He'd done a little housecleaning by turning a hose on the world to wash away the filth and didn't turn off the water for almost a month and a half. No one in this room, Annie included, wanted to see what He might do for an encore, although anyone familiar with the lyrics of an old spiritual hymn had a pretty good idea of how things might turn out.

God gave Noah by the rainbow sign, Annie recalled. *No more water, but the fire next time.* Zaqiel was certainly playing with fire—again—if he attempted to rally the troops for another war on heaven. And if he could win over the crowd as easily as he did a century ago, if he wasn't stopped before this legion of monsters joined his crusade, then everyone on the planet was going to burn.

There was no time to call for backup. Despite the risks, she needed to end this now.

Annie began moving forward, her palm sweaty against the pistol grip. With luck, there'd be time to get off two, perhaps three shots as the creatures around her instinctively dove for the floor . . . before they rallied and tore her to shreds.

"If I remember correctly," a deep male voice suddenly called out, "God had little to fear from our kind the last time you asked for assistance in carrying out your vendetta against Him. How would this be any different?"

A stunned silence fell over the Sky Garden.

Annie halted. *What's this, now?*

All eyes turned toward the speaker as he strode forward. Vlad III, vampire king of Wallachia, Son of the Dragon, lord of House Draculesti—also known as House Tepes—approached the stage, coming to a halt mere feet from his ancestor. Annie caught a glimpse of the fierce snarl that Zaqiel flashed at the legendary count before it transformed into a tight smile.

"Lord Tepes. You are looking well," Zaqiel said through gritted teeth.

"Have you an answer, First Reborn?" Tepes asked. "Before you get too involved with mesmerizing the children among us with candied visions of a world set right, perhaps you could enlighten those of us who stood beside you on that accursed island by describing how this campaign will succeed where the last failed so spectacularly?"

"My dear Count—," Zaqiel began.

"Urr . . . I'd like to know that as well," interrupted one of the haggardly *pennanggalan.* "If it's not too much trouble, your lordship."

"I am also curious about your plans," said a were-jackel near the witch. "My pack suffered heavy losses in that war, Lord Zaqiel; it took us decades to repopulate. I mean no disrespect, but to have you lead us into another similar conflict . . . ?" He shook his head. "I would be hesitant to commit any of my followers before the campaign has been fully explained to us. And even then . . ." His shrug got the point across.

Murmurs of agreement rose from the attendees. Zaqiel looked genuinely confused by the sudden lack of enthusiasm.

Annie's eyebrows rose. This was certainly unexpected—his welcome home party had turned into a focus group, and one with growing disinterest in what Zaqiel was trying to sell them. He was losing his audience. *Maybe I won't have to do anything, right this second, if they're going to reject him.* She grunted softly. *I should be so lucky . . .*

Kiyoshi stepped forward, teeth bared. She seemed on the verge of leaping at the angel's detractors—they *were* ruining her big moment, after all—but held back when Zaqiel signaled her to stop. He turned to face the crowd.

"I see," the First Reborn slowly replied. "You have grown complacent in my absence. Directionless. *Spineless.*"

The murmuring became angry shouts to counter the accusation, and not even Annie could disagree with that reaction. Complacent these creatures might have become since Zaqiel's death, for no one in this room had ever bothered to pick up his reins after Halja's Island and continue the fight, but a longtime warrior like Dracula could never be accused of lacking a spine. If Zaqiel thought insulting Vlad and the others was the way to win back his followers, he was making a big mistake. And if Zaqiel pushed too hard, he'd either see everyone turn their backs on him and storm out—or end up inciting a weirdling civil war.

Which, in Annie's opinion, wouldn't be such a bad outcome . . . if the war could be limited to conflicts among the offspring of Satan, Zaqiel, and their fellow fallen angels. The problem with monsters was that they never just killed one another when they fought—there were always innocent humans caught in the middle.

She glanced toward the main doors to the Sky Garden, remembering the hair-trigger tempers of the clan guards clustered in the hallway. Maybe this was the perfect time to discover what might set them against one another and thereby utterly ruin Zaqiel's plans . . .

Annie changed direction and headed back the way she'd come, ignoring her intended target yet still paying attention to the chatter between the angel and his descendants. Every cutting remark generated by Zaqiel's bruised ego was just one more step toward chaos among the houses.

"Take care, ancestor," Tepes snapped. "Though I am pleased that you have returned from the grave, no one—human, weirdling, or First Reborn—has the right to call the lord of House Draculesti a coward."

"Then do not greet me with derision, vampire," Zaqiel replied. "At least I attempted to change the world. What have any of you done in my absence except fight amongst yourselves in an eternal game of one-upmanship, while the humans stood by and laughed? And then, when I offer to lead you once more along the path to greatness, you mock me." He snarled. "You all sicken me."

Annie smiled as she wound her way through the crowd, which was growing increasingly hostile toward their honored guest. *That's it, baby, keep stoking that fire.*

"Am I wrong to voice my concerns, Lord Zaqiel?" Tepes asked. "This is not the world you knew. The humans are not so easily cowed these days. They possess weapons of unimaginable power that—"

"I am aware of the monkey-children's capabilities." Zaqiel nodded toward Kiyoshi. "Lady Sasaki has provided me with a clear understanding of the opposition we may face. But what you fail to understand, Count, is that no matter how powerful their weapons, no matter how strong-willed His favorites might be, still they fear the darkness . . . and what lurks within it."

Annie halted, sensing a change in the room. The sniping and heated utterances began to fade, replaced once more with sounds of approval. He was winning back his audience; given enough time he'd undoubtedly have them chanting war cries. She quickened her efforts to reach the outer hallway. If she could instigate a shoot-out among the guards before that happened, there'd be little time for cheering while everyone ran for the exits.

"*We* are the darkness, my children," Zaqiel continued. "We are the terrors that haunt their dreams, the horrors that flitter in the corners of their vision, the monsters whose bloodied claws rake at the most primitive aspects of their brains and frighten them to the very core of their being. I ask you: How can any man-made weapon counter the power that *we* possess?" He paused for dramatic effect, then said much louder, "How can any *huntress* counter the power that we possess?"

Annie grimaced but kept walking. *Damn it, I* knew *this was going to happen if I stayed too long. Idiot.*

"Seal the room," Zaqiel ordered.

Someone in the crowd—most likely the snow witch who'd given Zaqiel access to the room by magically altering the front window—uttered an incantation, and an eldritch barrier, visible for only a few moments as a grayish-white flash of light, swept around the Sky Garden, blocking every window and door. Including the one Annie had been on the verge of using to make her exit.

She sighed. "Well . . . so much for backup," she muttered, and looked over her shoulder toward the stage. Zaqiel was staring directly at her.

"You didn't really think you could disguise yourself from me, did you, my love?" he asked coyly.

" 'My love'?" asked a horse-featured grotesquerie standing beside Annie. It gave the faux male Otoyo guard the once-over and shrugged. "Not my type, but whatever floats his boat, I guess . . ."

Annie frowned at the monster. "Jackass."

Horse-Face snorted. "Hey, no need to get per—"

The transformation to her natural form surprised Horse-Face and the ghouls around them—but not as much as the loud booms of Annie's Uzi. She fired two rounds in the ceiling above her head, and the partygoers reacted precisely as she'd expected: they dove to the floor. Now with a clear line of sight before her, she ran toward the stage, leveling the pistol at her target and emptying most of the clip into her winged ex.

At least that had been her intention. Unfortunately, Zaqiel ducked behind the podium so that the Preacher's Rounds tore into wood, not flesh. On the bright side, though, she saw a half-dozen House Otoyo elders crumple as some of the bullets intended for Zaqiel punched through vampiric heads, throats, and hearts. So, not a completely wasted effort on her part; just not the result she'd desired.

Neither was seeing the podium come flying at her, thrown mightily by the angel.

Annie jumped to one side to avoid being smashed by the projectile, but then the monsters around her rediscovered their courage, surged to their feet, and rushed her before she could get off another shot. The gun was wrestled from her hand; claws and nails tore at her clothing and skin, yanked at her hair and dug into her scalp; a tentacle encircled her throat and tightened into a slimy noose that cut off her breath.

Then the blows began raining down.

10

There was something in her right eye.

That couldn't be possible, Jenessa Branislav thought. She didn't *have* a right eye, not any longer; not after that disastrous raid on the Manhattan home of one of her clan's oldest enemies: monster hunter Sebastienne Mazarin. Jenessa had lost not only an eye but her entire strike team on that mission—battle-hardened vampires and humans who had been the elite of House Karnstein's military forces. Men and women she'd commanded and fought beside for years, creating a bond with them so tight she'd often felt more like a proud mother than their leader.

Except her "children" were all dead, now, the humans brutally murdered by the huntress, the others turned to ash in Mazarin's basement by a wall of oversized bulbs that emitted ultraviolet light. A flick of an activation switch, a burst of artificial daylight in a shadowy cellar, and—

Jenna grimaced, the pain of her loss sharper than any wooden stake that had ever pierced her heart. What made the hurt even greater was the knowledge that she had led them into that trap, had led her team to their deaths, and been the only one to come out of it alive.

Survivor's guilt, however, quickly gave way to anger—directed not just at herself and Mazarin, but at the council of elders back in Prague who'd sent their best strike team on a wild-goose chase for an ancient relic. Lives ultimately wasted in pursuit of a myth.

Known only as The Prize, it was an object sought by practically every vampire clan on the planet . . . although no one seemed to know exactly what it was, what it looked like, or what it did. According to legend whoever possessed The Prize would have access to great power . . . whatever that power might be.

Jenna had never been too concerned about The Prize; she'd often joked to her superiors that contemplating such mysteries was above her pay grade. That didn't mean she wasn't curious about it—after all, who *wouldn't* want to control an ultimate weapon? (If that's what it was.) But she was a soldier first and foremost, loyal to her clan leaders and her house. Curiosity was fine, so long as the mission remained the primary focus . . . even when the trail led to a centuries-old murderess who had once chopped Jenna into little pieces. While Jenna was fully conscious.

Based on information—mostly rumors, folk tales, and a handful of brief mentions in ancient tomes—gathered by House Karnstein's historians, Jenna had led her team to a crumbling Catholic church in the Czech Republic where it was believed The Prize had been stored for the past century. The reception they received—a hail of gunfire from rifle-wielding priests who were quickly dealt with—seemed to back up the meager evidence, yet a sweep of the church and the catacombs beneath it turned up nothing. During her interrogation of the siege's lone survivor—an elderly priest who seemed amused by her demands for the device—Jenna learned that the church had been a decoy. The Prize had never been hidden there.

Enraged by this discovery, Jenna's first instinct had been to tear the lips from that smirking holy man, but then she realized he might still be useful. After all, he knew of The Prize, had even referred to it by another name: the Devil's Heart. Thus, he possessed information she needed—and would have.

She obtained it, of course, but it wasn't entirely what she'd wanted to hear. The priest hadn't a clue to where The Prize might be found—he'd been in far too much pain from blood loss to lie—but he knew the identity of its true guardian: Mazarin. The thought of crossing paths a second time with the famed La Bella Tenebrosa— "the beautiful, dark one," as Mazarin was called in the Olde Tongue—left Jenna with conflicted emotions: excitement at the prospect of paying back the sadist who'd dismembered her all those years past; and fright at what that sadist might do to her this time if the opportunity presented itself.

Finding the huntress hadn't been a problem: the address of her Manhattan town house, along with a wealth of surveillance photos, was part of her extensive file in House Karnstein's archives. The council immediately approved the team's trip to New York; with The Prize so potentially close Jenna would have been shocked if they'd hesitated for even a moment in making that decision.

In hindsight, she wished they had.

Only Jenna had survived the battle in Mazarin's home, though just barely. As a dhampyr—the offspring of a human mother and a vampiric father—she was immune to most wards against the undead. She laughed at crosses and holy water. Garlic made her mouth water for Italian food—and Italian blood. Mirrors and running water were used for grooming. Meticulously counting scattered poppy seeds or rose thorns only happened in her dreams—a variation on counting sheep for days when she couldn't sleep. A stake through the heart would kill her, of course—silver bullets, too—but sunlight, even the artificial variety, had been only a mild irritant . . . until recently.

Her fully vampiric teammates, her undead "children," had never been as gifted, so when Mazarin activated her death trap Jenna's soldiers had burst into flame. Yet Jenna had burned, too, flesh roasted inside her latex combat uniform, right eye boiled out of her head. That was how she knew there couldn't be anything occupying the vacant socket.

Still, she could feel *something* there, so being curious, she did what any flash-fried half vampire would do and opened her eyes—both of them.

She could see perfectly. And now realized she was underwater.

No, not under water. Immersed in blood. She was lying at the bottom of a bathtub filled with blood. And sitting on the tub's edge was her closest, dearest friend, Dalibor Frantisek. He had also been part of that failed mission, but since he was no fighter Jenna had ordered him to remain in the team van, parked down the street from Mazarin's home. Yet it was Dalibor who had saved Jenna's life, shooting the huntress before she could decapitate his commander with a machete, then dragging his leader from that house of horrors.

He smiled, as did Jenessa.

She tried to sit up, but lacked the strength to do so; her hands slid uselessly along the sides of the tub.

Dalibor acted quickly. His hands slipped under her armpits and lifted her to a sitting position. His smile broadened. "Welcome back, Jenna," he said, voice tight with emotion. Blood-tinged tears formed in the corners of his eyes.

Jenessa reached out to brush them away. "Hello, Dalek," she said, addressing him by his childhood nickname. "Did you miss me?"

He laughed. "How could I miss you if you were never gone?"

"I thought I was," she said quietly.

Dalibor took her hand and squeezed it. "Not while I had any say in the matter. That is"—he flashed a wry smile—"if my taking charge is all right with you, Commander. I know how much you dislike sharing authority."

Jenessa chuckled. "Smart-ass." She wiped some of the blood off her face, licked it from the edge of her hand, and blinked a few times. "So now, Dalek," she said slowly, "about this unexpected gift of full sight . . ."

He reached over to the nearby sink and picked up a small vanity mirror—no doubt he'd been expecting this reaction—and held it before her. Her left eye was as blood-colored as ever, but a light hazel orb stared back at Jenessa from the right side. A human eye.

"It doesn't appear to match," she remarked.

Dalibor swallowed hard, momentarily at a loss for words. "I had to . . . improvise before the injuries you suffered became permanent. When I was carrying you from Mazarin's basement, I noticed Dusana's body lying in the main hall, and . . ." His voice trailed off and he turned away, unable to continue—either from embarrassment . . . or shame.

Dusana. A member of their team, and one of the only two humans under her command. Mazarin had snapped the girl's neck by throwing her down a flight of stairs. Now Jenna had a constant reminder of how she'd failed that poor girl.

She pushed aside that disturbing thought, and nodded toward the tub. "And the blood?"

Dalibor took a moment to gather himself, no doubt still haunted by his organ harvesting, then turned back to face her. "There has been a sharp decrease in New York's homeless population over the last three nights—not that anyone in the press has noticed. Considering the severity of your burns and the amount of blood required to heal the damage, I thought it made greater sense to prey on the indigent rather than the consulate staff for the supply." He flashed an impish smile. "The consul general was pleased to hear that."

Unlike most of the other clans, House Karnstein did not have a New York chapter and so made its base of operations the Czech Republic consulate on the East Side of Manhattan. Not that the consul general or his staff were comfortable with the arrangement; they just knew better than to raise objections.

"I'm sure he was," Jenna replied. "So what did I miss during my recovery?"

"The Prize was located in a museum, across the East River in Queens." Dalibor paused. "By House Otoyo."

The news struck Jenna like a physical blow. Not from learning they'd been beaten to The Prize by one of the rival clans—that had always been a possibility. It was the thought of her fallen teammates. All those lives lost and they'd still been looking in the wrong place. She felt sick to her stomach.

Dalibor leaned in close, concern etched on his features. "Jenna? Are you all right?"

His commander snarled. "Leave it to Lady Sasaki and her fashion misfits to steal all the glory. So what was it, this ultimate weapon? A tattered grimoire full of long-forgotten spells? Pandora's Box? C'thulu's old Rolodex?"

"An angel."

She started. "What?"

"A fallen angel, to be precise. Zaqiel of the First Reborn."

Jenna's eyebrows shot up so quickly they nearly rose off her forehead. "One of our ancestors?"

Dalibor nodded.

"Damn," Jenna muttered in astonishment. She gripped the sides of the tub. "All right, help me out of here. This blood's gone cold and I'm starting to prune. I need a shower and a meal—a *big* meal, I'm starving—and then you can fill me in on the rest of the story while I get dressed."

"You're saying he stopped a firefight between two houses—just like that?" Jenna asked with a snap of her fingers.

"Apparently," Dalibor replied from his seat on the corner of her bed. "Or so it appeared on the news broadcasts. Took to the air, gave a speech that was only half audible over the police sirens and the whirring helicopters and the screaming humans—something about uniting the clans, from what I could gather. Probably rallying the troops to help him take over the world—again," he added drolly. "And we know how well *that* worked out last time . . ."

Jenna *hmmf*ed noncommittally as she zipped up her new black leather jumpsuit. It felt a bit loose at the waist; no doubt her "tanning incident" at Mazarin's house had cost her a few pounds. Not an ideal method for shedding weight, and not one she would ever recommend to her clan mates, but effective. Inwardly, she shrugged. A few more meals like the late breakfast she'd enjoyed a short time ago—the soup with liver dumplings and the roast beef topped with lingonberries had both been especially appetizing—and her battle gear would be back to its usual snug fit.

"Still, he does make quite the impression," Dalibor continued. "For an ancient relic, I mean."

Jenna smiled slyly. "You mean he's good-looking for an older man. A *much* older man."

A hint of blush colored Dalibor's cheeks as he flashed a tiny, embarrassed smile. "I'll admit Zaqiel is . . . pleasing to the eye, but I was talking more about his strength of character. I've never seen anyone take charge of so chaotic a situation with such authority—present company excepted, of course," he added with a wink.

"Nice recovery," Jenna said wryly. She flopped onto the bed and sat against the headboard, then grabbed one of the embroidered throw pillows that lay beside her and began playing with its tassels, twisting the gold-colored threads around her fingers. "Impressive he might be, but I'm having a difficult time seeing how Kiyoshi Sasaki could allow Zaqiel the dominant position. I would have expected her to object right from the beginning."

"And risk angering one of the First Reborn? I don't think even Lady Sasaki is that foolish."

"Then she's trying to win him over. Kiyoshi's never been the bowing-and-scraping type, so if she's acquiescing to Zaqiel it's only because she's planning something. If he's as smart as the legends say he is, he'll watch his back."

Dalibor snorted derisively. "Not so smart he didn't fall for La Bella Tenebrosa's feminine charms. A fool in love who lost his head over her—literally."

"Even more of a reason he should be suspicious of Kiyoshi," Jenna remarked. "Because she's not the type to seduce him, or get her hands dirty swinging axes around. Her methods are far more devious." She tossed aside the pillow. "Still, that's the angel's problem. House Otoyo won the scavenger hunt, and that means we can focus on more important matters." She took a shuddery breath, slowly released it. "Like mourning our dead."

"That may have to wait," Dalibor said. "Lord Schovajsa wanted you to check in once you were fully recovered. He was quite insistent about that after I explained the . . . outcome of the mission to the council of elders. I tried to delay giving them the report until you could debrief them, but . . ."

"Don't worry yourself, Dalek, I understand. But if Schovajsa wants to tear off my head over my poor leadership, he'll have to wait until we return to Prague. Our teammates are dead but their murderer is still alive; I won't stand for that, Dalek. First Mazarin gets what's coming to her, *then* the council can have their pound of flesh."

"Except Mazarin isn't in New York. From what I've heard she followed Zaqiel and Lady Sasaki to Japan. House Otoyo is holding some lavish soiree in Yokohama that they've invited all the houses to—including ours. A victory party, I suppose."

Jenna snorted derisively. "Maybe Zaqiel is starting another recruitment drive."

Dalibor stuck out his tongue, as though he'd tasted something awful. "Ugh. I hope not. Hell on Earth is the last thing anyone—human, vampire, or whatever—needs. The world's enough of a mess already without needless wars against heaven complicating everything."

"Some vampire you are," Jenna said. "You're supposed to want humanity crushed beneath our heels."

"Crush them? And ruin my collection of Bruno Magli shoes? Never!" Dalibor said with a wink. "Look, I'm just being a realist. Humans and vampires have been battling one another almost as long as they've been battling among themselves, and the fact remains that humans continue to be the dominant species. Vampires, on the other hand, have been an endangered species since day one—and no matter how many new members we add to the population, we still constantly face extinction."

She playfully nudged him with her big toe. "Drama queen. The humans have never been able to wipe us out, even with Mazarin's help, because we're too strong for them."

"Spoken like a true warrior. No, it's because there's a balance to the universe. Humans bring new life into the world by having children; we bring only death. That whole alpha-and-omega thing, if you will."

"Or predator-and-prey, if you look at it from the other side," Jenna replied. "True, we don't have the numbers, but fewer vampires means we have an almost limitless supply of livestock on which to feed. Each new generation humans create isn't a step closer to extinction for our kind, it's another course at the banquet."

"I suppose. Either way, trying to change the status quo on a grand scale, especially by throwing in with some foul-tempered relic out to piss off"—he pointed heavenward—"you-know-who for personal reasons would just be inviting trouble— for us."

" 'Us' as in all vampires, or in all supernatural creatures?"

" 'Us' as in *us*. After what happened to you and the others in that basement . . ." Dalibor turned away with a snap of his head. "Let the clans take care of themselves," he muttered.

Jenna's eyebrows rose. She'd never heard Dalibor sound so philosophical before. Or so protective. It worried her, but it also touched her heart. "Always looking out for me, aren't you, Dalek?" she asked, trying to sound lighthearted.

He couldn't meet her gaze. "That's my job, isn't it?" he asked quietly. "To watch your back, do your bidding, clean your guns and scrub your battle gear after you've finished playing soldier?" There was an unaccustomed harshness that crept into his voice as he spoke.

She chuckled. "Well, you *are* better at doing laundry than I am . . ."

He laughed, a short phlegmy note weighed heavily by emotion. "Well, what's Dracula without his Renfield?"

Jenna smiled warmly and slid down to sit beside him. "Or Jenessa Branislav without her best friend?" She reached out to stroke his cheek.

Eyes closed, he nuzzled against her palm. Crimson tears shone brightly against her pale skin. "I just don't want to lose you, too, Jenna. You're all I have left."

Jenna felt tears of her own start to form. "Oh, Dalek . . ."

She couldn't think of anything more to say, so she drew him into a gentle embrace. They sat there for some minutes, sharing their grief, mourning their lost friends, comforting one another. Eventually she eased Dalibor back, taking his face in her hands and using her thumbs to wipe away his tears.

"Dalibor Frantisek, you are my good and true friend, and I would be lost without you. But our friends must be avenged. Mazarin must die—by my hand, if at all possible."

"But after the other night . . . and before that, when she—"

"That happened a lifetime ago, and you were there to pick up the pieces." She smiled wryly. "Literally."

Dalibor snorted a laugh, then turned his head to hide his embarrassment.

"Although," Jenna continued, "I'm still not sure you ever put all of my internal organs back in their right places." She nudged his arm. "Guess I should have held off turning you until you'd finished medical school, eh?"

He nudged back. "Oh, stop. Just be grateful I put your stomach right side up after I sewed the pieces together, so you could continue to gorge yourself on human meals—as you did a short while ago."

"Mmm, liver dumplings," Jenna said contentedly as she patted her tummy. "Still, thank the ancients I'll have someone who can reattach my head after the council gets done tearing it off."

"Now who's being a drama queen?" Dalibor asked. "Besides, I'm not so certain tearing your head off is what the council has in mind."

"And how would you know that?"

He shrugged. "Just a feeling."

"Woman's intuition?" she asked with a sly smile.

"Smart-ass," he snapped playfully.

Jenna grinned. The old Dalek was back.

"No," he continued, "it's because no one in the councilors' offices would tell me why they needed to speak with you. If they were looking to rake you over the coals they would have come right out and said it. Subtlety and the elders don't exactly go hand in hand, as you well know."

Jenna grunted. "That's an understatement." She sighed. "All right, if I can't avenge our teammates because Mazarin ran away, let's just get my ass-kicking over and done with. What time is it back home?"

Dalibor glanced at his watch. "Prague is six hours ahead, so . . . say around eight P.M. The councilors should just be rolling out of their coffins about now. You should probably wait until they've supped—they're always in better spirits on a full stomach."

Jenna waved a hand dismissively. "Screw it. Go set up the call. Why should I be the only one in a bad mood?"

Subtlety wasn't the only thing House Karnstein's council of elders had difficulty with—the conveniences of the modern era were also a problem for them. Technology, especially, was a vexation to lords and ladies born long before the advent of cell phones and computers and the Internet. Which accounted for why Jenna wasn't all that surprised when her Skype connection went through and the liver-spotted forehead of Lord Bohumil Schovajsa filled her computer screen.

"Is this thing on?" he rasped. "I thought you said this blasted thing was working."

"It is, my lord," replied a male voice that Jenna recognized as belonging to Schovajsa's human secretary, Konstantin; the exasperated tone his voice usually carried was unmistakable. "If you'll just give it a moment . . ."

Jenna stifled a laugh and adjusted her headset's microphone. "I'm here, my lord. If you could just sit back so I can see you . . . ?"

"What? Oh." The old vampire did as asked, settling into a high-backed chair. "Ah. There you are." Schovajsa was one of the true elders, a first-generation member who dated back to the formation of the clan by Lady Mircalla Karnstein. He appeared to be in his late sixties or early seventies—he'd been turned late in life—but had celebrated reaching his third century of immortality just a few years ago; Jenna remembered the party well, having been in charge of security that evening. With white, shoulder-length hair swept back from his broad forehead and sharp-angled features that always seemed to be set in a disapproving scowl, dressed impeccably in a black velvet jacket, maroon cravat, and white dress shirt, Schovajsa fancied himself the right hand of Lady Karnstein—even though she *had* a right-hand man back at the clan's ancestral home in the Duchy of Styria, in Austria.

Now that Schovajsa's head wasn't blocking her view, Jenna could see that he was in his office, not the council chamber as she had expected. This was to be a private conversation, then. High oaken bookcases framed the sides of the image being broadcast to her computer, and behind the councilor's chair, through an arched window, she could see the last streaks of sunset fading against a purple-hued sky as darkness settled over Prague. Konstantin—tall, dark, and whip thin—stood in the background, holding an electronic tablet as he waited for instructions from his master . . . or perhaps he was just making certain the old vampire didn't start pressing buttons on his computer and break the connection.

Jenna sat up straight in her chair. "I thought this would be a session of the full council, my lord."

The slow rise of his left eyebrow balanced the perpetual frown that pulled at his lips. "Oh? You were expecting the council of elders to conduct a formal hearing with you about the Mazarin incident—on a telephone call?"

Jenna averted her gaze to stare at her hands. It *did* sound ridiculous, when she thought about it. And yet . . . "I was, my lord."

Schovajsa sniffed. "I suppose it might be possible . . . but not today. Certainly not when most of the others have run off to Japan to meet the Great Zaqiel."

Jenna detected a note of derision in his voice, but thought it wise to say nothing about it. Best not to remind him that locating what had turned out to be the remains of "the Great Zaqiel" was supposed to have been her job.

"Such short memories they have," he continued. "There were six of us clan elders on Halja's Island when everything fell apart. We saw the huntress impale Zaqiel with the Spear of Longinus; we saw her take his head. And once he fell, the battle was lost. The three of us left standing were lucky to escape with our lives."

"And now that Zaqiel has returned?" she asked cautiously.

"I don't know. We will have to see what transpires . . ." Schovajsa leaned back in his chair and stared into space for a few moments, lost in thought. In the background, Konstantin took a step forward (perhaps to remind his master she was still on the line?), but then Schovajsa's gaze snapped back toward the camera. "Are you well enough to travel?"

Physically, more than likely. Psychologically was a different matter. Vampiric warriors rarely suffered from post-traumatic stress disorder, but her recent near-redeath experience, coupled with the memories of her previous terrifying encounter with Mazarin that still haunted her, had left Jenna depressed and uncertain of herself. Despite all the assurances she had given Dalibor, the former strike-team leader now dreaded the notion of returning to combat. Not that she would admit that to anyone but herself . . .

"Of course I can travel," she lied. "Am I returning home, then, for the formal hearing?"

"Ancients preserve us . . . ," Schovajsa muttered with a roll of his eyes. "A little obsessed with being reprimanded, aren't you, Commander? In a hurry to be stripped of your rank?"

"No, but I just thought—"

"Well, it isn't that; quite the opposite, in fact. You're being given an opportunity to redeem yourself—although I think trusting you with another assignment after your last debacle is unwise." He sighed. "Still, it was not my decision to make."

And not a decision made by the council, either, if the others were out of the country. Someone higher ranked among clan leaders, then. Who it might be, however, concerned her less than the realization that she was agreeing to charge back into battle when she didn't feel up to it. Well, maybe that was for the best. An old saying about getting back on the horse after it threw you galloped through her mind. In this case, put a gun in her hand and it was more than likely the old, self-assured Jenessa Branislav would return to form.

Hopefully.

"And how am I to win this redemption, if I may ask?"

"By carrying out the special mission Lady Karnstein has in mind for you."

Jenna gasped. "Lady Karnstein? She requested me?"

"Yes, though I tried to dissuade her. I don't know why she never seems to take my advice . . ." Schovajsa shrugged, then beckoned Konstantin forward. "Whatever the reason, our beloved matriarch believes that you are the ideal warrior for this situation." His permanent frown deepened. "Try not to disappoint her, Commander Branislav."

Which in Schovajsa-speak meant *I look forward to your screwing up—again—so I can say "I told you so" to Lady Karnstein, and then maybe next time she'll listen to my sage wisdom.*

Jenna held her tongue, though, and simply nodded.

His aide leaned toward the camera and held up his tablet. "I've already forwarded the mission packet to your laptop, Commander. You're to rendezvous with your new team in Pittsburgh, Pennsylvania tomorrow night."

Jenna's eyebrows shot up. "Pittsburgh? What could possibly be there to attract her ladyship's interest?"

"The Spear of Longinus, Commander." The old vampire smiled wickedly. "And you're going to steal it."

11

"Kenji and I heard the gunshots and screams as soon as we stepped through the portal," Natsumi said, "and right away we knew Annie had to be involved. So I adjusted the portal to take us to the source of the disturbance and we jumped back through."

"And that's when you saw Annie?" Pan asked.

Natsumi had already told her story to Alex after the witch had regained consciousness and been moved to a private room on Pan's floor. Now, with Alex having returned to the isolation ward to check on Karen's condition, Pan and her friends had gathered around Natsumi's bed to hear the field report for themselves. Of course, after introductions had been made there was the initial "who the hell are you and why should I tell you anything" phase to get past, but once Pan had explained about her friendship with Annie and her own experiences with Zaqiel, Natsumi had loosened up. Or as loosened up as she could get considering the injuries she'd sustained: a dislocated left shoulder (put back in place and immobilized in a sling), bruised ribs (being treated with ice packs), and a number of ugly claw marks on her arms and legs that would leave some grotesque scars. The damage could have been a lot worse, one of the nurses had told Pan, if not for the protective layers of Natsumi's rubberized catsuit, which blunted the deadlier claw strikes, bites, and punches. Still, the witch was looking at a minimum of three weeks' recovery time before she'd be fit for duty.

Which sounded supremely ridiculous to Pan, who had offered her services as a human first-aid kit to speed up the healing time—after all, why wait three weeks when Resurrection Girl could probably fix Natsumi up in, like, two seconds? But as with her plan to unvamp Mom, Dr. Carlyle and Alex put the banhammer down on all displays of superpowers . . . for the time being.

"We didn't see Annie at first," Natsumi said. "When we arrived at the Sky Garden, the whole place was filled with monsters—I'd never seen so many up close in my entire life. It was . . . frightening, and I actually froze for a few seconds. I didn't know what to do. But Kenji did. He spotted Annie being dragged from the room and drew his sword and started swinging, cutting a path towards her. And because his sword blade is enchanted iron, it did a lot of damage. I just tried to keep up with him, throwing a lot of offensive bolts that didn't do much more than knock them back and give us some space." She grunted. "If I'd had time to work up a major spell I could've turned them all to dust, but the monsters were relentless. They just kept coming at us. And then they . . . they got past my spells and swarmed over us."

She swallowed hard. Pan, sitting beside the bed, reached out to give her hand a gentle squeeze.

"I heard Kenji yell my name, but I was getting beaten and ripped up and all I could see were fists and claws and teeth and . . . and my blood everywhere. And then I screamed." Natsumi drew a shaky breath before continuing. "That's when I opened the portal—I had to get out of there."

"But why did it bring you all the way over here, to the States?" Javi asked. "Why not some place in Japan?"

"It was . . . sort of a reflex action, I guess you could say. I was worried about what might happen to Annie and Alex's face popped into my mind. I knew I had to get to him immediately, to ask for help. So I focused on his soul aura and jumped through."

Pan's inner Nancy Drew nudged her to get her attention. Why Alex? it asked. What made him so special that he'd be the first person Natsumi thought of when it came to Annie? He'd said earlier that he wasn't Annie's husband, even though the huntress had mentioned having a son named Alexander, so what was the connection?

"Alex's soul aura?" Javi asked. He looked sidelong at Pan, but she gave a subtle head shake no. This wasn't the time for her and Natsumi to start comparing monstervision similarities.

"Yes," the witch replied. "When I get to know people well enough, I can sometimes track them by locking on to the spiritual vibration of their auras, even halfway around the world." She shrugged. "It's a little more complicated than that, and it doesn't always work—I'm not at, like, sorceress level to be a hundred percent accurate—but that's the basic idea." Natsumi flashed a tight smile. "Still, it was a really stupid thing to do, considering how scared I was. I could have exited the portal in the path of a moving vehicle if Alex had been walking along a street, or a kilometer in the air if he'd been in an office building. I was very lucky."

"And what happened to Kenji?" Pan asked.

Natsumi lowered her gaze. "I . . . I don't know. I thought Kenji was right behind me, not those monsters . . ." She blinked back tears. "I left him to die."

"You don't know that," Pan said. "Maybe he's a prisoner of Zaqiel's, like Annie. I mean, that's what bad guys do all the time, isn't it? Lock up the good guys so they can gloat about their plans for world domination and stuff?"

"That's how it works in comics," Javi said. "Not to mention just about every movie with a villain who's all full of himself."

"See?" Pan said with an encouraging smile. "There's a president for it."

"Precedent," Uwe muttered.

Pan ignored his correction. "So while Zaqiel is boring Annie with a lotta B.S. about how his monster army is gonna take over the planet, all you have to do is get Alex to put, like, a team together and you could lock on to Kenji's soul aura and go rescue both of them."

Natsumi shook her head. "I can't. Not like this," she replied, gesturing to her injuries. "I'm in no condition to do anything."

"Yeah." A sly smile quirked up the corners of Pan's mouth as she glanced at Javi. "Too bad there's nobody around who could do something about that, huh?"

David Zwieback stared through the hospital room window at his ex-wife as Dr. Carlyle—flanked by the security guards—talked to her, and wished there was something he could do to ease Karen's pain. There wasn't, though, and he knew it, which made him feel even more useless and worthless than he had while sitting at Pan's bedside for the past three days. His daughter impaled on an ancient weapon he'd unknowingly purchased, his ex kidnapped and turned into a monster—when it came to protecting his family in their greatest hour of need, he'd been an utter failure. And had he done anything to help them after that? No. Annie had been the one who rescued Karen, and Pan . . .

He drew a nervous breath and ran a hand through his hair as he sharply exhaled. His little girl, his Panda-bear, had been savagely murdered and left to die on the street. He should have been there to save her, to protect her from the monsters, but he had failed her as surely as he'd failed her mother. In fact, if it hadn't been for his stupidity in buying the coffin that brought this hell into all their lives, he never would have placed either of them in danger.

Wouldn't have been responsible for their deaths.

No, that wasn't entirely true. As Dr. Carlyle had explained to him, Karen hadn't died when Zaqiel bit her; it was just that, as one of the original breed of vampires, the angel's bite was more virulent than the average bloodsucker's. Its effect on Karen had been instantaneous. But Carlyle had assured Dave that Zaqiel's death should completely reverse the transformation and return her to normal—physically, at least. The doctor couldn't begin to imagine the psychological trauma Karen might suffer afterward.

But Pan . . .

Pan *had* died. Without either of her parents at her side to comfort her when she'd needed them most. Thank God that at least Sheena and Javier had been able to reach her and talk to her so Pan would know she wasn't alone as she . . . passed. And while it was true that at the time Dave had been lying unconscious on the basement floor of the museum—the result of an attack by one of the Gothic Lolita vampires—he still couldn't push aside the guilt weighing so heavily on his mind. He should have been there.

Worthless and useless—that was David Zwieback in a nutshell. And more. Helpless. Helpless to protect his family; helpless to prevent the nightmare they'd been plunged into. And all because of some piece of crap that he'd had to own.

The damned coffin and its contents: the supposed skeleton of a real vampire—

only the remains had turned out to be those of a fallen angel named Zaqiel. When he'd seen it advertised on an antiques site Dave had initially balked; after all, there were no such things as real vampires, right? Besides, Renfield's House of Horrors had never been a gold mine, and the price listed on the seller's website should have chased him away. But in his conversation with the owner, an Englishman named Morrison Millar, they'd negotiated the price down to something closer to Dave's budget, and then Dave couldn't say no—he had to have it. And all the time he'd ignored the advice his father used to repeat over and over whenever Dave asked for something as a child: "Do you want it, or do you need it? Because if you want it, then you don't need it."

Dave placed his head against the cool glass and closed his eyes. *What I want is to wake up tomorrow morning and realize none of this ever happened, but that's just wishful thinking. What I need is for my family to be all right. That's not too much to ask for . . . is it?*

"You don't have to stand there, you know," rumbled a familiar voice. "There are seats in the waiting area."

Dave turned to find Alex standing beside him; he'd been so focused on his misery that he'd never heard the Knight walk up to join him. "Uh . . . No, I'm good," he mumbled. Alex carried a pair of Styrofoam coffee cups and offered one to Dave, who recognized the scent of French Vanilla wafting up from the dark liquid. Pan's favorite flavor.

Alex nodded toward the brew. "I didn't know how you take it, so . . ."

"No, it's fine. Thanks." Dave took a tentative sip—it was still too hot for drinking—and turned back to the window. Carlyle had turned off the wall speaker in order to consult with his patient without Dave interrupting, but even without sound Dave could see that Karen was agitated, unable to sit on the bed for more than a few seconds before standing up to nervously pace the floor, punctuating her sentences with expressive hand gestures. It reminded him of all the times she'd exhibited the same behavior when she'd argued about their finances after her husband had purchased some "ridiculous" piece of memorabilia that further strained their dwindling retirement fund. She'd had every reason to be upset with him, of course; he'd just been too blockheaded to immediately recognize how his business decisions had strained their marriage as well. And by the time he'd finally focused on the problem, it was too late.

But there was more to Karen's gesticulations and pacing than just annoyance. Even from the hallway he could see the pain etched on her features by the changes forced on her by the vampire virus. And the closer he looked, the less he saw of the loving, confident woman he'd fallen in love with all those years ago and more of the monster she'd become . . .

"Your daughter seems like a good kid," Alex said.

Dave smiled. "The best. I think she looks out more for us than we do for her, sometimes." The smile faltered. "I . . . I don't know what I would've done if I'd lost her."

"I understand," Alex replied. "I've got three kids of my own. As a parent you live in constant fear that something bad is going to happen to your child, and you're thankful for every day it doesn't. But you can't always be there to protect them, and knowing that makes it even worse."

"When I saw her lying in the street like that, and all that blood . . . I thought I'd lose my mind. And now with Karen . . ." Dave lowered his head to look away and only when his vision blurred did he realize he'd been crying. He laughed nervously and began wiping his eyes. "Sorry."

"No need to apologize." Alex placed a hand on his shoulder and gave a comforting squeeze. "But you got your daughter back, didn't you?"

"Yeah, thank God . . ." Dave smiled awkwardly. "But don't ask me how she did it, I haven't a clue." He shrugged. "At this point I don't really care—I'm just grateful to have her back."

"Amen to that." Alex nodded toward Karen's room. "And as for your ex, Johnny there knows what he's doing. He's the top cryptophysician on the East Coast, and one of the best in the world. If anyone can help her make it through this crisis, it's him."

"Cryptophysician?" Dave asked. "You mean like a cryptozoologist, only he actually treats mythological creatures instead of just studies the legends about them?" He shook his head in mild disbelief. "It's just so . . . amazing, you know? And . . . I guess you could say terrifying, too. Up until I few days ago I was just your basic horror fan, fascinated by the supernatural but not really believing that things like vampires and shape-shifters could really exist. But now . . ."

Alex chuckled. "The world's a whole lot bigger and stranger than you ever imagined, right?"

Dave nodded. "That would be a major understatement." He took another sip of coffee.

Alex studied him for a couple of moments, as though assessing him. "So you know about subjects like cryptozoology? I thought that museum of yours was just some tchotchke-filled tourist trap."

Dave grimaced. "What's left of it, you mean. After those vampire assholes blew it up." He sighed. "I loved that place."

"You could always rebuild."

That got a short, sarcastic laugh in response. "Really? You don't know my insurance carrier. I had trouble enough getting them to pay out the one time the basement flooded during the last superstorm and I lost a couple thousand dollars' worth of those 'tchothkes.' So, for 'acts of God' they'll cough up some money—under duress. But I'm pretty sure vampire gangbangers aren't covered under my policy." He glanced at Karen and gestured at the hospital around them. "And how am I ever gonna pay for all of this . . . ?"

"You're not. Annie already has it covered."

Dave started. "What?"

Alex held up a hand to stop him from objecting. "And before you say no, trust me—she can afford whatever the hospital charges."

Dave shook his head. "Listen, that's really nice of her to offer, but—"

"You don't like handouts?" Alex nodded. "I figured as much; I'm the same. But it's not a handout, it's more her way of . . . apologizing for dragging you and your family into her problems."

That made no sense whatsoever to Dave. "Her problems? *I'm* the one who bought the coffin. If anyone's the cause of the trouble it's me. Why would she think she was responsible?"

"Zaqiel's her old boyfriend, remember? Even though she killed him back in the day, she didn't finish the job by burning his remains and scattering the ashes. And because he was able to be resurrected—"

"She feels guilty and thinks she owes us."

Alex nodded. "So don't even think of arguing with her about the bills when she gets back."

" 'When she gets back'? So you've heard from her? Because when that Japanese girl showed up and said they had her—"

"I haven't heard anything. But I know Annie. She always comes back. Always."

Dave nodded in mild agreement, not really certain if Alex was trying to buoy his spirits . . . or his own. There was an unmistakable pride in Alex's voice whenever he spoke of Annie that went beyond mere admiration for a coworker, but if they weren't married then just what was their relationship? "So, is anyone going after her—a special ops team, or whatever it is you call your elite Knights of the Apocalypse?"

"Not at this point," Alex replied with a frown. "The high council had been waiting on Annie's report to decide their next move against Zaqiel. Now that they're not getting one, they're sitting on their hands waiting for the higher-ups at the Vatican to decide for them. And you know how well speed and bureaucracy go together."

"But you want to go after her."

Alex flashed a tiny smile. "It's that obvious, huh?"

"Based on how keyed up you look," Dave replied, "I'm surprised you haven't left already. You don't seem the type to stand around and wait when something important needs doing." He smiled slyly at the Knight. "So when do you head out? Because as long as that damn angel is still alive . . ."

Dave glanced toward Karen's room.

"Tonight, one way or another," Alex said. "The problem will be in finding a portal-weaver on short notice. Normally I would have asked Natsumi, but that poor girl's going to be laid up for—"

The deep-voiced cry from Karen's room cut short whatever else Alex was about to say. As did the impact of an airborne Robertson slamming against the glass.

12

"Does that hurt?" Pan asked with a nod toward Natsumi's immobilized arm.

"Not as much as before," the witch replied. "But that's probably the painkillers." With her free hand she punched the mattress in frustration. "I don't have time to be here! I have to get back to Kenji—I have to know if he's all right!"

Pan knew what she really meant was that she had to know if he was still alive.

"And find Annie," Javi added.

"Yes," Natsumi said quietly. She lay back against her pillows and closed her eyes. "I . . . I can't leave him with all those monsters."

"I could maybe help you with that," Pan said. "I'm, uh, some kinda healer. At least that what Annie says." She blushed and picked at a loose thread on the bedsheet. It sounded so ridiculous, especially when spoken out loud, but it was true. She was the very-much-living proof of that amazing power, wasn't she? Still, it was going to take some getting used to.

Natsumi opened her eyes to look at her visitor, then raised an eyebrow. "*You're* a healer."

Pan frowned. "You don't have to sound so incredulous about it, y'know. I didn't snark on you about that goofy witch hat."

Behind her, Javi whispered, " 'Incredulous'?"

"Expandin' her vocabulary," Sheen muttered. "She wants to be a writer."

"I thought she was a painter," whispered Uwe.

"Apparently she's a Renaissance woman, now." Pan could practically hear the shoulder shrug in Sheen's voice.

"Yes, I am," Pan said without turning around. "And 'incredulous' means skeptical. Like Natsumi, here." She flashed an embarrassed smile. "Not that I can really blame you. I mean, up until a few days ago *I* wouldn't have believed me."

Natsumi's eyes narrowed, and she studied Pan for a few moments. "Okay. So heal me."

Pan grinned. "Okay, then." The smile faltered. "Except . . . I'm not really sure how it works. So far it's just kinda happened when it needed to . . . but, y'know if you're willing to let me figure it out on you . . ."

Natsumi shrugged with her good shoulder. "I'm not going anywhere."

The smile returned. "Cool." She rubbed her hands together. "Let's get started." Although she hadn't a clue what form that "start" might take.

"If you make things worse I'll turn you into a frog," the witch said coolly.

Pan laughed, then halted. "Wait—can you really do that?" She waved a hand to dismiss the thought—"Never mind."—and glanced toward the ceiling as she raised her voice to include her friends. "Now everybody shut up and let me concentrate." She closed her eyes and hunched forward, not having the slightest idea how to summon up her amazing power but hoping it would just sort of happen on its own.

"You're thinkin' of chocolate pudding," Sheen murmured. Uwe snorted a laugh.

Pan opened her eyes and glared over her shoulder at her best friend.

Sheen smiled innocently. "Okay, *I'm* thinkin' of chocolate pudding."

"Quiet, you," Pan growled, and turned back to Natsumi. "Sorry." She closed her eyes again, took a deep breath, and slowly released it. *Think of the healing power,* she told herself. *Think of fixing Natsumi's injuries. Think of*—she flashed a tiny smile—not *chocolate pudding.*

And it worked. Somehow. The tingling began in her chest, then spread outward—a low-level electrical charge that built in strength as it traveled along her spine and down her arms. Her fingertips suddenly had the weirdest itch.

"*Kyaaa!*" she heard Natsumi whisper in surprise, which caused Pan to sneak a peek at what had brought about that reaction.

Pan gasped and opened her eyes fully.

Her hands were glowing. It wasn't a garish, neon-y brilliance, but rather a soft rainbowish light that appeared to be seeping from her pores, as though her aura was leaking out of her fingertips.

"Um . . . okay. That looks like . . . something." She gazed at her guinea pig. "You want me to try? 'Cause I don't know how long this is gonna last."

The witch nodded. "Go ahead. But remember what I said about the frog."

Hesitantly, Pan placed a hand on Natsumi's injured shoulder. The glow increased and the girl stiffened, although that was probably more of a reflex action than anything caused by Pan's touch. Unlike that time she'd treated the bump on Javi's head, there was no electrical discharge at the contact point. So that was a good sign, right?

Think about fixing her shoulder . . .

The glow increased to envelop Natsumi's shoulder, then her arm.

"That . . . feels really good," the teen witch said with a smile . . . which quickly faded. "Are you okay? You're sweating."

"Huh?" Pan used her free hand to wipe at her brow; sure enough, it came away moist with perspiration. She flashed an awkward smile. "No, I'm good," she lied, ignoring the tiny ache that had suddenly bloomed in her chest. She needed to finish this: Natsumi was her only lead to Annie, and Annie was the only one who could destroy Zaqiel so Mom could be Mom again. The witch was no good to anyone if she couldn't use her travel magic. *So just suck it up and finish what you started, all right?*

The sweaty hand gently landed on Natsumi's chest. The girl hissed in pain as Pan's fingers brushed across her sore ribs.

"Sorry," Pan mumbled, and wiped her forehead against her shirtsleeve. That ache in her own chest was building—as was the knot of fear twisting her stomach. She thought of the jagged scar left by the Spear of Longinus; of the agony she'd experienced after pulling the ancient weapon out of her ravaged heart, just before she'd collapsed in the street. It felt just as bad now. She knew she should stop, had to stop, before things got critical.

But then she thought of Karen, of the inhuman pain she was experiencing. Mom had always been there for Pan, had always supported her, had been the guiding light in the darkest periods of her young life—Dad, too, but he hadn't been turned into . . .

No, she thought with gritted teeth. She would not think of her mother as a monster, no matter what happened. Not ever. And not if she could do something to help change her back.

She pressed on. The glow enveloped Natsumi's entire upper body.

The ache in her chest became a frightening throb.

A hand lightly gripped her shoulder. "Pan," Javi said gently. "That's enough."

Pan ignored him. She could actually feel Natsumi's bones knitting, her muscles repairing, her wounds closing. In the back of her mind she knew she ought to be absolutely amazed that she was capable of doing this.

But all she could focus on was the pounding of her own heart.

Then Javi yanked her away from her patient.

The moment Pan and Natsumi broke contact her glowing hands returned to normal. Her heart rate slowed to a gallop. The pain subsided to a grimace-inducing buzz.

But the healing power had shut down.

"NO!" Pan yelled, and turned to shove him, though she didn't have the strength. "What the *hell* do you think you're doing?"

"Saving your life!" he snapped. "Couldn't you tell doing that was killing you? I sure could!"

"I was fine!" she snarled, though she felt anything but. "I didn't need anybody's help. And I sure didn't need you sticking your damn nose in my business. Now you've made me mess it up!"

"Pandora—," Natsumi began.

"Hey, Zee, c'mon," Sheen said, who was standing beside Javi. "Cut him some slack. A-Rod here was only looking out for you. I woulda done the same thing, only he beat me to it."

"Don't you get it, Sheen?" Pan held up her hands. "I don't know how long it's gonna take me to get this thing working again, and Mom doesn't have that kind of time! You should've just let me finish!"

"Pandora," Natsumi repeated.

"What?" Pan barked, then fell silent as she watched the girl take off the sling and rotate her arm a couple of times. "Oh," she said quietly.

Natsumi smiled. "Good as new. And look!" She filled her lungs with air, then released it through her nostrils. "I can breathe normally again. I think that means my ribs are healed, too. You did it!"

"Cool." For a moment Pan felt like crying, she was so happy. Then joy turned quickly to depression as she realized how totally wrong she'd been to blow up at her friends. After all, they'd only been looking out for her. She turned to face Javi and Sheen and took each by the hand. "Umm . . . look, you guys, I am *so* sorry about biting your heads off like that. You didn't deserve it, and you've got every right to kick my ass and walk out of here." Her gaze slid toward the floor and she sighed. "I'm such an asshole . . ."

"Damn. Is she always this big a drama queen?" Javi asked.

Surprised, Pan snapped her head up to see Javi wink at her, and Sheen grin broadly.

"Oh, Jeter, you have no idea," Sheen said with a laugh. "But at least she got the asshole part right."

Pan blushed. "You guys . . ."

That's when the alarms began wailing.

"That doesn't sound good," Uwe remarked.

Pan slid off the bed and hurried to the door. A pair of security guards went haring past, followed by Nurse Araujo.

"Christa, what's going on?" Pan asked.

"There's some disturbance in the isolation ward. I have to go help. Stay in this room until you're given the all-clear." She raced after the guards.

The knot that had formed in Pan's stomach earlier came rushing back with a vengeance. Something was wrong with her mother—she could sense it. She turned to Natsumi. "You up for doing some magic?"

"What do you have in mind?"

"Get me into the isolation ward." When the girl hesitated, Pan continued. "Look, you said you can home in on people's auras when you need to find somebody, right? So home in on Alex like you did before—he's gotta be right in the middle of whatever's going down. I gotta know if Mom and Dad are okay."

"All right." Natsumi looked to Javi. "Would you get me my belt? The one with all the pouches?" Javi nodded and walked over to the closet, then returned with the belt in hand. "Thank you." She reached into a pouch, pulled out an orange glow stick, and threw back the bed covers.

Pan handed her a bathrobe. "So people can't see your butt sticking outta that hospital gown." She cast a glance at Javi, who wisely found something outside the window to stare at.

Natsumi shrugged into the robe, cracked the glow stick, and shook it to activate the fluorescent solution. "Magic wands are passé," she said when Pan raised an eyebrow. A brief recitation of words Pan didn't understand followed—obviously a spell of some kind—and the party decoration flared brighter. The witch waved her hands in a pattern that reminded Pan of some dance move she'd probably seen on TV or somewhere, and then an electrical bolt shot out of the tube to form a doorway.

"Now *that* is cool," Sheen said. Uwe shrugged.

Pan leaned toward the magical shortcut. On the other side could be seen the hallway outside Karen's room; surrounded by medical personnel, sitting bruised and bloody on the floor, was—

"Alexander!" Natsumi cried. She charged through the portal with Pan at her heels.

Things were so chaotic in the isolation ward that no one noticed their arrival. Doctors and nurses concentrated on Alexander and the pair of security guards assigned to Karen as other guards—who looked equally battered—milled around the door to her room. Pan noticed the Taser rifle Robertson had brandished laying at the base of the wall.

Natsumi went to check on Alexander's condition as he was hoisted onto a stretcher, while Pan pushed her way through the growing crowd in search of her parents. Seeing how beaten up the Knight was made her fear for the well-being of them both.

"Mom! Dad!" she yelled, and squeezed past one of the bruised guards, who made a halfhearted attempt to stop her. Then she froze.

Her mother was gone, and the room was completely wrecked: light fixtures busted, bed overturned, walls cracked. And lying unconscious on the floor, being attended to by Dr. Carlyle and a pair of medics, was her father.

"No . . . ," Pan whispered.

A hand touched her shoulder and she jumped. Turning, she found Nurse Araujo standing behind her. "Pandora, what are you doing here? *How* did you get here?"

Pan waved off her questions. "Christa, what's wrong with my dad? And where's my mom?"

"I don't know; I just got off the elevator a minute ago." Christa nodded toward Carlyle. "You'd have to ask the doctor. But I saw a medical team pushing someone on a stretcher down the hall, surrounded by guards."

"We had to move Karen to the maximum security area," Carlyle said. Pan turned to face him. The physician's face was scratched and bruised. But there was more than pain that furrowed his brow; he appeared confused. Surprised, even. "Your father came in behind Alexander when Karen started to become more aggressive. The virus . . . I've never seen anything like it. The mutation rate alone is . . ." His voice trailed off as he was apparently at a loss for words.

Pan, however, understood what he was trying to say. The vampire bug that Zaqiel had infected her mother with was a strain the doctor had never encountered—and now its effects on her had worsened, at a speed he'd never expected.

"Your father tried to calm her down," Carlyle continued. "But when that didn't work Sgt. Robertson opted to use the Taser and . . . that's when your father stepped in front of Karen. He took the full fifty-thousand-volt charge."

Pan gasped. "Oh, my God . . . Is he gonna be okay?" She started to walk toward Dave as a pair of orderlies entered the room with a stretcher, but Christa's hands on her shoulders prevented her from getting any closer.

"He'll be fine, after he rests," Carlyle said. "He banged his head on the floor when he went down, and lost consciousness. I'm going to run a CT scan, just as a precaution."

"A CAT scan?" A chill ran up Pan's spine. Those were used to create detailed X-rays to diagnose things like severe head injuries. She swallowed hard.

"Yes, but don't worry. I'm sure he has nothing more serious than a bump on the noggin. An ice pack and a couple of ibuprofen and he'll be back on his feet in no time."

"And Mom?"

"After your father got shocked your mother lost complete control and . . ." Carlyle gestured at the damage around them as the orderlies gingerly placed Dave on the stretcher. "Well, you see the results."

Pan gazed at her father. "Let me take care of him."

"You're talking about using your healing powers." Carlyle shook his head. "His injuries appear to be minor. Letting you mess around could potentially worsen his condition. Let's just leave the doctoring to the doctors, all right?" He turned to the orderlies and his medical team. "Tell the techs I want a full head scan, and then get Mr. Zwieback an ice pack for when he wakes up."

They didn't need to be told twice. With a bark of "Clear the hallway!" from the lead orderly Dave was whisked from the room.

As she watched her father being taken away, Pan felt the knot in her stomach become a lead weight. She turned to Carlyle. "Why didn't you let me try?"

"You're still recovering from your own ordeal and—"

"And I'm not fragile. I already fixed Natsumi, so it's not like it's a big deal."

Carlyle started. "You did what?"

The witch stuck her head around the doorframe. "Did someone call me?" She pointed over her shoulder with her thumb. "They're taking Alexander to one of the examination rooms, but they think he'll be okay."

Pan gestured toward Carlyle. "Do me a favor and show him what I did for you."

"Uh . . . all right." Natsumi stepped inside the room and flapped the formerly injured arm like a chicken wing. "My ribs are healed, too."

Carlyle's eyebrows rose. "Remarkable."

"See?" Pan slipped out of Christa's light grasp. "So let me help my dad."

"Look, we'll discuss it in full later," Carlyle said as he headed for the door. "Right now I have to check on your father's scans; then I have to see about your mother's condition. The two of you return to your rooms and don't go wandering around the hospital again. I'll keep you posted on their situations."

"Can I see Mom?" Pan asked. "I mean, maybe I could help her, if you won't let me near Dad."

The doctor paused in the doorway. "I'm sorry, Pandora," he replied soberly, "but Karen is beyond that sort of treatment."

She remembered the remark he'd made about the mutation rate caused by the vampire virus, and the speed at which it had changed her mother. The lead weight in Pan's stomach felt even heavier, now.

She swallowed hard. "So . . . so you mean there's no way to turn her back?"

"I didn't say that. There's still a chance, if Sebastienne can put an end to Zaqiel. But . . . time is running out. I wish I could do more for her, but all we can do at this point is wait. I'm sorry." He turned and hurried down the corridor.

Pan felt a nervous chill start to form at the base of her spine, but forced it down by clenching her fists and gritting her teeth. That damn angel, Zaqiel—this was all his fault. And if what Natsumi had told her was right, that he'd captured Annie, then how was the monster hunter supposed to kill him? Even more troubling, what if Natsumi was wrong? What if Zaqiel had killed *Annie*? Then who was going to help Mom?

She felt a hand on her shoulder. "Come on, girls," Christa said. "I'll escort you back to your rooms." *So I can keep you from causing any more trouble* was the unsaid, but understood, part of her offer.

Pan forced a smile on her lips. "That's okay, Christa. Natsumi can just pop us back." She looked to the witch. "Right?"

"Sure." The girl dug into the pocket of her robe, pulled out the still-active glow stick, and held it up. "You ready to go?"

Pan walked toward the doorway. "Yeah . . . but let's do it out in the hallway, where there's more room." She turned to the nurse as the trio exited the room. "Could you do me a favor, Christa—check on my mom?"

The nurse smiled warmly. "Of course. I'll come talk to you later."

"Thanks." Pan crossed the corridor, slipping around some workmen who'd arrived to survey the damage, and stopped by the far wall. "Say hi to Mom for me, okay?" she asked Christa, who gave a small wave and headed in what Pan assumed was the direction of the maximum-security area.

"So, back to my room?" Natsumi asked.

Pan nodded. As the witch cast her spell to open a new portal, Pan looked around to make certain no one was watching, then reached down to pick up the object she'd spotted earlier that was still laying at the base of the wall: Robertson's discarded Taser rifle. The moment after the gateway formed she quickly stepped through, weapon in hand.

Javi was waiting on the other side. "So what happened? Are your mom and—"

His eyes widened as he caught sight of the rifle. "Where'd you get that?"

"I'm just borrowing it," she replied curtly. "I'll bring it right back when I'm done." Pan turned to Natsumi, who'd closed the portal behind them. "You wanna find out if your boyfriend's still alive?"

Natsumi started. "He's not my . . . Yes, I want to find out if he's alive."

"Then get dressed. I'm just gonna go grab some stuff from my room and then I need you to give me a lift to Japan."

"What?" Sheen yelped.

"Have you ever fired a gun before?" Javi asked Pan. "Because I remember when I wanted to borrow one of Annie's just after the vampires showed up at your dad's museum, and you gave me a speech about how we're not killers and we didn't need guns to fight them."

She *had* said that, hadn't she? And at the time that had been true. Guns in movies and video games had never bothered her—how else were you going to kill monsters from a safe distance?—but the notion of firing anything but a toy version in real life had always been a complete turnoff to her.

Still . . .

Pan shrugged. "It's different, now."

"How? How is it different?" Sheen demanded. There was an unmistakable tremor in her voice.

"Because Mom's gotten even worse and now Dad's maybe got a fractured skull and nobody will let me do anything for either one of them and we're *running outta time!*" Pan drew a deep breath, released it in a huff, and took her best friend's hand. "Look, Sheen," she continued in a calmer voice, "you heard Natsumi before: Zaqiel's got Annie. That means there's nobody else who can kill that son of a bitch so Mom can get back to normal."

"What're you talkin' about?" Sheen demanded. "What about Alex? What about all these friggin' Knights of the Apocalypse he's part of—let *them* take care of this. That's their job, isn't it?"

"Alex is laid up, too. I don't know why the Knights haven't done anything by now." Pan looked to Natsumi. "Any idea?"

"Bureaucracy," the witch replied. "From what I've experienced on other assignments, the council gets so busy arguing about what steps they should be taking on critical stuff that they wind up not taking any at all."

"That doesn't mean you're the one who's gotta do their job for them," Sheen countered. She smiled through tears that had begun to form and reached out to gently stroke her friend's face. "Zee, come on. Carryin' guns and talkin' about killin' somebody—this is so totally *not* you."

"Yeah . . ." Pan flashed a tiny smile. "But it'll be okay, Sheen. Everything's gonna all work out."

"No. No, it won't," Sheen said firmly. "Not unless I'm right there, keepin' you outta trouble."

Pan started. "What? No!"

"You think I'm gonna let you go do something that crazy-stupid without me to watch your back? After all we been through? Never in a million years, Vampira." Sheen smiled awkwardly, but it couldn't hide the fear that shone so brightly in her eyes. Pan couldn't tell if that was caused by the thought of monsters tearing her apart, or by the revenge-focused Terminatrix Sheen's dearest friend had apparently become. Maybe a combination of both.

"Sheena, what do you think you are doing?" Uwe growled. He rose from his seat and took her by the arm. "If Pandora wants to go and get herself killed—again—there's no reason for you to be involved. You came close to dying yourself, already. I . . ." The anger in his expression faded, and the grip on her arm became a caress. "I do not want to risk losing you a second time."

Pan nodded. "As much as I hate to agree with your boyfriend about pretty much anything, Sheen, I gotta say he's making total sense."

Sheen squeezed Uwe's hand. "You don't have to lose me, babe," she said, her voice sounding a little more like its usual confident tone. "You can come, too. Then you can keep an eye on me the whole time."

Uwe frowned. "That is not what I meant . . ."

"*I* was gonna go," Javi said.

Surprised, everyone turned to face him.

"Hey, Annie's my godmother," he explained to Pan. "You didn't really think I'd let you go looking for her on your own, when you don't know the first thing about rifles—did you?"

"What're you talking about? It's like they say in the movies—'just point and shoot,' right? Like a camera. And I know how to use *those*." Pan snorted and held up the Taser—with the barrel aimed right at him. "And anyway, it's not like this thing's a *real* gun."

"Real enough," Javi said. "And like a real gun"—he gently took the weapon from her—"if you don't know how to handle it the right way, you're gonna get yourself, or the people around you, hurt more than the guy you're aiming at."

"And I suppose you do?"

Javi grinned as he ejected four shells from the shotgun; he slid them into his jeans pockets. "I guess you forgot I told you back at the museum I'm a paintballer—"

"And you play those *House of the Dead* arcade games," Pan interjected. "I remember."

"Highest unbeatable score in the South Bronx," he said proudly. "But what I didn't tell you is that Annie taught me about respecting guns. My parents don't know that 'cause they'd go nuts, but I kinda nagged her into it. But anyway, one of the things she taught me is that this?" He indicated the Taser. "Ain't gonna do squat against vampires, except maybe piss them off a whole lot."

"Well, it was the only thing I could think of," Pan said huffily.

"I understand that. However . . ." He smiled slyly. "I know where we can find non-gun stuff that *will* work on them."

13

"Now that's a sweet crib," Sheen remarked as she and the rest of the Zwieback Five stood in front of a redbrick town house near the corner of West Twenty-First Street and Tenth Avenue. She looked up and down the tree-lined, cobblestoned block, which was lined with similar nineteenth-century buildings. "This place is so pretty you'd almost think it wasn't in The City."

The remnants of yellow crime-scene tape attached to the town house's metal banister and the blue NYPD wooden barricades on the sidewalk indicated otherwise—as did the police officer in the patrol car parked across the street. The rain had stopped falling, so that was a plus, but now the air felt thick with summer humidity; every breath was a small labor.

"How long do you think it will be before someone misses us?" Nastumi asked. She was back in her rubbery catsuit—the demon-claw-mark damage repaired by what she'd termed a "simple spell"—and ginormous witch's hat, both of which Pan figured must be hot as hell to wear in this June heat, but the girl exhibited no signs of discomfit. Maybe, Pan surmised, the suit had some kind of coolant system running through it.

I could use some of that myself, she thought as she gazed at her own black ensemble: jeans, leather boots, messenger bag, the new devil-girl T-shirt Javi had given her, and battered leather jacket. She'd insisted on changing outfits and doing her makeup before the gang had left the hospital, as a way of mentally preparing herself for this insane mission. Like a warrior suiting up for battle, she'd told them. It had taken a little extra preparation, though, to put on the jacket; the lining was still stiff from the blood it had absorbed while she lay dying in the street.

Uwe glanced at his wristwatch. "Given the situation in the isolation ward that you and Pandora described, I'd imagine they won't think to check in on either of you for at least another ten minutes, if not longer." He paused. "Or else they've already noticed our absence and the hospital is in lockdown until they locate us."

"Doubtful," Javi countered. "The first thing Alex would've done was call my cell to find out where we went"—he slid the phone from a pants pocket and checked the display—"and that hasn't happened. Yet. But now that Dr. Carlyle knows Pan fixed up Natsumi, it won't take them long to figure out she must've zapped us outta there."

"Then we better get a move on," Pan said.

"You *sure* this is Annie's place, A-Rod?" Sheen asked. "New York One said somethin' 'bout a gas main blowin' up. The whole block had to be evacuated."

"Yeah, it's Annie's, all right," Javi said. "The gas main was just a cover story. Annie told me a buncha vampires from one of the other clans busted in here the night before the museum shoot-out, to try and make her tell them where Zaqiel was. 'Course they didn't *know* it was Zaqiel they were looking for, just that it was some special 'prize' everybody was after, but it didn't stop them from blowing the hell outta the place while they were trying to catch her."

"I remember that," Pan said. "You and Annie called me from here before you came over to Renfield's. Didn't she say something about a bomb?"

"It was an RPG—a rocket-propelled grenade. Blew out the second-floor back wall."

"So what happened to the vampires?" Natsumi asked.

"She took care of them," Javi replied with a sly smile, and headed up the steps. "Come on."

Pan had never been inside an historic town house before, but she was pretty sure the blood spatters and bullet holes hadn't been part of the original décor.

The grand foyer was the proverbial hive of activity, with male and female workers in jeans, gray Maldonado Construction T-shirts, and colorful hard hats busily repairing the damage done by the attack. There were bullet holes in the walls to be filled, dried blood to be cleaned . . . and the tape outline of where a body had lain on the hardwood floor to be removed.

Sheen pointed to the outline. "That one'a the vampires?"

Javi shrugged. "Don't know. Annie wouldn't say, and the cops or whoever had already taken the body out before me and Dad got here. You oughtta see what it looks like upstairs. Gonna need a truckload of Spackle and paint to fix up this place." Javi grinned at Pan. "The old man practically had dollars signs all up in his eyes when he did a walk-through."

"Hey, Javi!" called out an African-American man who was descending the stairs. He appeared to be in his late fifties, with a close-cropped, salt-and-pepper Afro, and he wore jeans, a pale blue dress shirt with the sleeves rolled up, and a loosened dark blue tie. A cell phone was clipped to his belt, and in one hand he carried an electronic tablet.

"Hey, Ron," Javi called back. "Ron Harper's the foreman on the job," he explained to the group.

Frowning, Ron stepped around the tape outline, then gazed around at his work crew. "Somebody gonna pull this damn thing up? The cops gave us the all-clear— they're done poking around the house. So I want this off the floor today so we can see if the adhesive's done any damage to the finish. All right?"

There were mutters of assent in response, which seemed good enough for the foreman. He smiled at Javi and walked over to the teens. "You and your friends here gonna give us a hand?"

Javi laughed. "Nah, Annie asked me to check on a few things while she's outta town, and she said it was okay if I gave some of my friends a quick tour of the un-blown-up areas." Introductions were made before he continued. Pan rolled her eyes when she spotted the tiny New York Yankees logos printed on Ron's neckwear.

"Well, the greenhouse was untouched, so that's pretty safe," Ron said, "but stay off the upper floors—my guys are still shoring up the back walls from that . . . gas main problem." He smiled slyly and wiggled his eyebrows to indicate he knew the real story.

"The greenhouse maybe later. We were just gonna hit the basement to start—is that safe?"

"Yeah, nothing wrong in the basement. We only had to vacuum up a lot of charcoal dust that was coating the carpets and some of the walls; don't know what Ms. Mazarin was doing down there to would cause that." He shrugged. "Rich folks— who can figure them out?"

Javi chuckled. "Is Dad around?"

"Naw, he's up in Yonkers checking on the Henderson estate."

"How's that restoration coming?" Javi asked. "Looked pretty sweet the last time he took me up there . . ."

As the two continued talking shop, Sheen leaned over to whisper to Pan. "Why would A-Rod's dad be here?"

"What, the T's everybody's wearing aren't enough of a clue?" Pan asked, gesturing at the workers. "His dad's a building contractor, and all these people work for him. Major renovations mean major bucks."

"Ohh. Well, ain't you just a fountain'a information." Sheen sidled closer and lowered her voice. "Man, Zee, your thumbs must still be achin' from all that booty-call textin' you and lover boy did that night you met him." Shortly before the museum chaos, Pan had told her parents and Sheen about Javi's background, after admitting to a late-night text conversation when Papa Zwieback had gone to bed.

"Quit it," Pan growled softly.

"All right, Javi, let me get back to it," Ron said. He shook Javi's hand and nodded at the teens. "Nice meeting you kids. Grab some hard hats from the dining room if you're heading out back—I don't need anybody getting their skull knocked in 'cause they didn't see an exposed beam." As he walked away he said boisterously to his crew, "Is there some reason I'm still seeing that damn tape on the floor?"

Javi led the group to a set of stairs leading downward. "C'mon. The stuff we're looking for is in the rec room." As he descended he flicked on a wall switch to turn on the lights. Pan, right behind him, stared in wonder at the fully furnished . . . well, not a man cave (obviously), but the closest equivalent for a female monster hunter. There was a pool table, a mini kitchen, an entertainment center—complete with sixty-inch flat-screen television, video game console, CD player and turntable—and a state-of-the-art speaker system.

"Oh, wow," Pan said. "Nice rec room. The parties she throws down here must be epic."

Javi grinned. "This isn't the rec room." With the group in tow he walked the length of the basement toward the rear of the town house, and came to a halt before a heavy steel door set into a brick wall. "*This* is the rec room."

"It's inside a vault?" Pan asked.

Javi nodded. "It's a bunker that extends beyond the back of the building, built in the 1950s."

"So it's really a converted bomb shelter," Uwe said. "The kind people used to have built in case World War III ever broke out."

"And now Annie uses it to store her vampire-smashing weapons?" Pan asked.

"You got it." Javi turned to the touchpad beside the door and began keying in a string of numbers and letters. "A couple months ago she was in Germany and asked my grandma Izzy to check on something she kept in here. I got the access code when Izzy asked me to write it down 'cause she couldn't remember all of it. Then she asked me to come with her." He tapped in the final digit, the touchpad beeped, and he tugged the door handle.

Nothing.

"Maybe you punched in a wrong number?" Pan asked. "I do that sometimes at home up in Schriksdorp when I forget a couple of numbers and wind up setting off the alarm."

"That why you're on such a first-name basis with the cops up in Stinkville?" Sheen asked with a grin. "Burglary—you're doin' it wrong."

Pan sniffed dismissively at her friend.

"No, the code's right," Javi replied. He hit the clear button on the pad and stepped back to consider his next move. After a few seconds he slowly nodded. "Okay, now I remember: there was something else we had to do to get it open . . ." His gaze traveled across the pad and settled on a black metal tube beside it. He snapped his fingers. "Retinal scanner."

"So then step on up and let it scan your eyeballs, Jeter," Sheen urged.

"It's not my eye it's gotta scan," Javi replied. "It's some kinda animal one . . ." He looked over his shoulder, then set off for the mini kitchen, where he opened the freezer compartment of the refrigerator. "Yup, still here." He removed a small, ice-encrusted box and carried it back to the door. "Usually Annie doesn't need it, she uses her shape-shifting powers to imitate the look of it. But one time she got a bad case of pink eye and couldn't open the door 'cause the scanner didn't recognize her.

That's when she came up with this."

"I get it," Pan said. "It's like a spare key. Some people keep a key in a plastic rock in their garden or under their welcome mat in case they get locked outta the house, so Annie does the same thing, only with . . . animal eyeballs." She raised an eyebrow at Javi. "That's pretty messed up—you know that, right? And trust me, when a psychiatric patient with ten years of therapy under her belt tells you that it's saying a lot." She grinned at Sheen. "And my doctors all used to say *I* had issues, huh?"

"No, that was me," Sheen replied with a wink.

Javi opened the box—which was labeled JAGUATIRICA in very neat hand lettering—and gingerly pulled out the "spare key" with his thumb and forefinger. "This is really gross," he said, lips curled in disgust.

"Can I touch it?" Pan asked as she held out her hand. When his eyebrows rose at the request, she chuckled. "I'm not gonna squish it or anything, I just never, y'know, saw an eyeball outside of somebody's head before. Outside of horror movies, I mean, but those are totally fake."

"Be my guest." Javi passed it along, looking relieved to do so.

Pan brought the greenish-gold orb close to her own eyes to examine it better. "Oh, my God, it's so beautiful." She smiled gently at Javi. "But it is kinda gross." It wasn't, though—in fact, she felt an overpowering urge from the artist inside her to reproduce the stunning hues in paint. She'd called it gross only so Javi wouldn't feel like any more of an outsider among a group of horror fans. When they got back from their mission, however, she was definitely going to ask Annie if she could borrow the eye; cell-phone pictures just wouldn't be adequate enough to match the colors.

"So what's a jaguar . . . rica, or whatever?" Sheen asked, pointing to the box's label.

"It's an ocelot," Natsumi replied. "It's kind of like a small leopard that lives in the Brazilian forests. I have a cousin who works at the Osaka Zoo; they've got a pair of ocelots living there." She frowned. "But Fujiko told me ocelots are on the endangered species list. So where did Annie get this?"

"You can ask her all about it when we get her back," Javi said, then turned to Pan and gestured toward the eyeball. "You wanna hold onto that while I try the code again?"

"Not big on touching it, huh?" she replied with a knowing smile. "Go punch it in; I'll do the other thing."

Javi re-entered the lengthy access sequence. Once the final digit had been pressed Pan held the jaguatirica eye up to the scanner.

The basement echoed with the loud clang of the heavy bolts unlocking. As the door swung open on well-oiled hinges, Pan returned the eye to its box, then wiped her hand on her jeans. Captivating as the eyeball was, the goopy residue it left on her fingertips was, admittedly, kinda disgusting.

Javi grinned. "Welcome to the rec room."

A light automatically snapped on inside the vault and Pan gasped. From what she could see, the rec room had nothing to do with recreational activities like those offered by the pool table and gaming console behind her, and everything to do with stockpiling a private army.

She followed Javi inside and looked around. For someone with such an exaggerated destructive bent, Annie certainly kept a neat armory: bladed weapons—swords, knives, axes—on one side, body armor and religious artifacts on the other. Low flat cabinets similar to art files lined one wall; no doubt they contained more antimonster aids. Across from that was a wall-mounted mirror that seemed completely out of place, unless Annie was the type who liked to strike badass poses in front of it before going into battle. Pan smiled—that's what *she* would do if she had a room like this.

And everywhere there were guns. Lots and lots and *lots* of guns.

"Girl sure likes to shoot the crap outta stuff," Pan remarked.

Javi gave her the side-eye. "Yeah, but we're not here for any of those, remember?"

"I know." She reached out to squeeze his hand. "Thanks for talking me down before." He smiled and squeezed back. "So, what'd you have in mind? What does the on-the-go monster hunter rely on to get the job done if she's not using a gun?"

Javi smiled sheepishly. "Uhh . . . I'm not really sure. That one time we came in here, Grandma Izzy explained what some of these things are for, but I forget if any of them worked on vampires. I just figured, what with you guys being horror fans, maybe you could tell me."

"Terrific," Uwe muttered.

"You could start with the traditional hammer and stake," a deep male voice rumbled. "But those require getting much too close to your prey."

Everyone but Javi whipped around, looking for the source. The teen simply smiled and turned to face the mirror. "Hey, Jerome. What's up?"

Pan followed his gaze, but all she saw was Javi's reflection and her own. Then a soft violet light shimmered across the mirror's surface, and Pan found herself staring into the black eyes of a Middle Eastern man she knew couldn't possibly be standing behind her. He was *inside the mirror.*

Natsumi gasped. "It's a demon!" She reached into one of the pouches on her belt and came out with something that looked like an oversize marble, then drew back her arm with the intention of throwing the object at the mirror.

Javi raised his hands to block her shot. "Whoa! Whoa! Dial it back a couple notches, Zatanna. Yeah, he's a demon but he also lives here."

Natsumi started. "Annie consorts with demons?"

"You make it sound so filthy," Jerome said with a sly smile. "But no, there's no 'consorting,' if that will put your mind at ease—she never listens to my advice anyway. Now please put away whatever that is you're holding before you hurt someone with it"—the smile widened—"otherwise I'll be forced to devour your soul."

The witch snarled. "You're welcome to try."

"Aw, don't mind him," Javi said. "He's just trying to scare you. He does that with everybody. Just put that away—please?"

"Umm . . . okay." Natsumi lowered her arm but didn't repack the tiny orb. She didn't appear too interested in taking orders from a demon.

"So, Jerome, how come you're not in your usual place upstairs?" Javi asked.

Jerome rolled his eyes. "All that damn noise the workers are making is driving me insane. I come down here because the soundproofing provides me with some peace of mind until they're finished for the day." His eyes narrowed. "Why are *you* here, Javier? You know that Sebastienne doesn't want you handling any of her weapons, and I'm certain she never gave you permission to enter the armory on your own."

"Annie's in trouble, Jerome," Javi explained. "She went to Japan to spy on a major vampire clan meeting and got caught. And since the Knights aren't moving fast enough to do anything—"

"You decided you would be the ones to rescue her?" Another eye roll. "Ahriman preserve us from the actions of foolhardy children."

"There's nothing 'foolhardy' about wanting to help somebody in trouble," Pan snapped. "Especially when Annie was trying to stop a vampire apocalypse, or whatever it is Zaqiel's got in mind for the world."

Jerome's left eyebrow rose. "Zaqiel—the fallen one? I've heard about him from Sebastienne; she has a tendency to prattle on about some of her bad relationships in her darker moods. But I also heard Zaqiel was dead. She mentioned beheading him with that very ax on the wall behind you."

The group turned to check out the weapon Jerome indicated. At first glance it looked like one of those oversized props seen in fantasy films: a thick-handled, two-bladed battle-ax that could cut trees down with one swing. Then Pan stepped closer and saw the wooden grip wrapped in aged leather strips; the intricate designs engraved in the curved metal; the traces of dried blood along the razor-sharp edges, and knew it wasn't a prop. Annie had really used this to put an end to Zaqiel—for a time.

"Yeah, well, he got better," Pan replied.

"As did you," the demon said. When Pan gasped, he continued, "You have that just-resurrected glow about you. It makes your soul look exceptionally . . . appetizing."

"Okay, lay off her, Jerome," Javi said. "Pan's been through enough already; she doesn't need your perv talk, too. Now, look, you gonna help us out with what we need, or should we just start grabbing stuff and hope for the best?"

The demon smiled. "Perhaps I should put in a call to Alexander."

"Aw, now don't go dragging him into this—he's got a ton of other problems to handle without you adding to them."

"But Sebastienne *is* his mother."

A hush fell over the vault.

"Whaaaaat?" Sheen said quietly.

"Huh. Y'know, now that I think about it, that makes all kinda sense," Pan said.

Javi started. "Seriously? You mean you don't think it'd be pretty impossible for that to be true?"

"What, like monsters and vampires and orange-pendant monkeys with backward feet that shouldn't really exist but do?" Pan gestured at Sheen and Uwe. "Maybe we don't know from monster-fighting weapons, but some shape-shifting woman in her thirties having a kid old enough to be my grandpa? That's, like, straight outta the kinda stuff we read all the time."

"Yeah," Sheen agreed. "Even though Annie'd have to be, like, a million years old to be Alex's mom."

"She's not that old," Javi replied. "Well . . . not a million, anyway . . ."

"But yeah, it does make sense," Pan continued. "I just never put the pieces together. Like back at the hospital, when Alex was talking about Annie—he got this look on his face like he was really proud of her. And him being named Alexander, like Annie's son—who we never saw—but him not being married to her." She lightly stamped her foot. "Damn, I should've figured it out sooner." Pan sighed. "So much for the great detective skills I thought I got from reading all those Nancy Drew books."

"Well, you've had a lot of problems on your mind lately," Javi said.

"And there's more to come," a familiar voice said in a sarcastic tone.

As one, the group turned toward the doorway, to find Alexander standing just inside the armory. "Pissed" didn't even begin to describe the expression on his face.

"Somebody want to tell me what the hell you kids think you're doing?" he demanded.

Javi smiled sheepishly. "Oh, uh, hey, Alex. I, uh, I figured you were gonna call my cell first. Before you started looking for us, I mean."

"Why bother, when I've got one of the Knights stationed right outside the building, to tell me he saw you leading a bunch of teenagers into my mother's home?"

It took Pan a couple of seconds to figure out what he was alluding to; then she immediately understood. "The cop in the patrol car across the street?" Alex nodded. "You guys are *every*where!" everywhere!" She paused. "So, uh, how's your head? I heard you got knocked around when my mom . . ."

"My head's fine. Or it was until I found the five of you standing in my mother's armory." He glared at Javi. "Now it just can't seem to stop aching."

Javi stared at the floor. "Sorry, Alex," he mumbled.

"You certainly made good time from the hospital," Natsumi commented. "Did you ask another teleporter to bring you here?"

"I've got a siren on my car that clears a lot of traffic, and a lead foot. Now answer my question: What do you kids think you're doing?"

"Rescuing your mother so she can help *my* mother," Pan replied. "Somebody has to do it, right?" She held up her hand to curtail Alex's protest before he could voice it. "And before you say anything about how we're too young to get involved in this, or whatever, just remember Natsumi's our age, too, and you don't have any problems with her working with Annie on dangerous missions." She glanced at the witch. "Sorry about talking about you like you're not here. I hate when people do that to me."

"That's all right," Natsumi said pleasantly. "No offense taken."

"What you're overlooking," Alex said, "is that Natsumi's been trained by experts. But even so she's been a field operative for only the last eight months, just after she turned sixteen. What combat training do any of you have?"

An image popped into Pan's mind: her right fist crashing into the jaw of Nikki Van Schrik, one of the meanest mean girls Pan had the displeasure of knowing. Nikki—whose ancestors founded the village of Schriksdorp, New York, where Pan lived with her mom—had, less than a week ago, made the mistake of pushing the wrong button on her favorite whipping Goth, and paid the price. Because nobody badmouthed Pan's parents—ever.

"I'm pretty good in a fight," she said.

"Pretty good isn't enough when you're dealing with monsters," Alex countered.

"I'm sure you're right," Pan said, "but pretty good's better than nothing when those monsters are probably out to destroy the world and your bosses just wanna sit around with their heads up their—"

"Watch it," Alex growled.

"If anything, you should be on our side, helping us figure out how we're gonna get your mom back . . . and how to stop Zaqiel before he unleashes hell, or whatever he's got in mind." Pan gestured toward the battle-ax. "Bet you could do some serious damage to him with that thing—like mother, like son, right?"

Alex's gaze drifted over to the wall-mounted weapon and for a few seconds Pan could see in his eyes the internal battle he was fighting: the responsible Knight of the Apocalypse versus the loving son. Ultimately he shook his head. "I don't do Children's Crusades. And neither should any of you."

"Y'know, I'm gettin' real tired of you talkin' down to us," Sheen said, and stepped forward to confront him. "Yeah, yeah, I get it: we're just a bunch'a stupid teenagers with stupid ideas, ain't got a brain in our heads, don't take anything seriously, never do what we're told—I've heard all that a hundred-million times. I'm used to it by now; I'm pretty sure all of us are. And I'm not gonna deny how crazy-stupid, not to mention suicidal, it is to go chasin' after vampires and fallen angels and all the other creatures of the night after what happened at the museum. Gettin' myself killed is absolutely the last thing I wanna do.

"But here's the thing," she continued in a softer tone. "I totally understand why Zee needs to do this. Because she loves her mom like nobody's business, and her mom loves her, too. And if the only way Zee's gonna get her changed back is to go rescue Annie—"

"And Kenji," Natsumi interjected.

Sheen nodded. "—so she can put a stake in that bastard Zaqiel's heart, then I'm backin' my girl a hundred percent and we're gonna do this, with or without you. And if you love your mom anywhere close to the way Pan loves hers, then you oughtta stop lookin' down your nose at us for wantin' to do this and help us out. You wanna keep us from gettin' killed? Fine. Then come with us and show us what to do. You could be like Professor Van Helsing—"

"Or Professor Xavier," Javi chimed in.

"Yeah," Sheen agreed. "Watchin' out for his X-Men so we don't get eaten or blood-sucked or whatever."

Alex frowned, but made no reply.

"It really would be a big help," Pan said. "I mean, how much longer are your bosses gonna sit on their butts before they make a decision? They gonna wait until

Zaqiel starts an all-out war against humans? That'll be too late for Annie and Kenji ... and my mom."

"Not to mention the rest of the world," Javi said.

"*I* plan on going," Jerome said.

Alex's eyebrows rose. "*You* want to help Annie."

Jerome sighed dramatically. "Anything to get away from that infernal racket upstairs."

"But how're you gonna get around?" Javi asked. "I mean, you're a mirror demon and we can't go lugging around the one you usually live in. That thing's kinda heavy."

"I've got a mirror in my makeup kit," Pan said while rummaging through her messenger bag. She came up with a black plastic compact decorated with a silver bat sticker, then opened it to display the mirror inside. "I know it's not that big, but maybe you can scrunch yourself up real tiny?"

"If I must." Jerome rolled his eyes. "The things I do to get some peace of mind . . ."

The purple glow that suffused the glass flashed brightly, then became an arc of light that traveled from the mirror to the compact. Pan felt a powerful, mildly disorienting tingle run up her arm, as though she'd whacked her funny bone. The sensation quickly faded.

"Voilà," Jerome said.

"That okay for you?" Pan asked.

If Jerome had shoulders he probably would have shrugged them. "It's sufficient. At least the powder you keep in here has a pleasant scent."

Alex's eyes narrowed. "Does my mother know you can do that?"

"It's never come up in our conversations," the demon replied with a sly smile. "So, what will it be, Alexander? Are you joining us for this heroic adventure to rescue La Bella Tenebrosa from the clutches of evil . . . or would you rather wait for your masters in Rome to make a decision—while you pass the time composing what I'm certain will be a stirring eulogy for your mother?"

The Knight snarled. Jerome was really pushing his button, Pan thought. Maybe too hard.

But then Alex surprised her by turning to Natsumi. "We'll have to make a stop before Japan."

Awesome. Pan grinned. "Got some special anti-vampire superweapon you need to pick up?"

"Probably the ultimate superweapon for dealing with those vermin," Alex replied. "The Spear of Longinus. If we're taking on Vampire Nation, we're going to need it."

That made total sense to Pan; without the spear, Annie would never have been able to stop Zaqiel's plans for world domination the last time. On the other hand, just the thought of being near the thing that had killed her made her stomach do a nervous flip. "Okay, so where it is? St. Patrick's Cathedral? The Vatican?"

Alex shook his head. "Pittsburgh."

14

The power of faith was giving Jenessa Branislav a migraine of biblical proportions, the pressure in her skull so intense she felt certain her eyes would pop right out of their sockets. And as she sat in the driver's seat of the rented van and gazed across the parking lot at her target, she knew the pain was only going to get worse, the closer she got. Inside, it would be excruciating.

St. Anthony's Chapel, as Konstantin's mission packet had explained, was the Catholic Church's greatest repository of religious relics in the world, second only to the Vatican's. Founded in 1888 by a Belgian priest named Father Suitbert G. Mollinger, the church—named in honor of Saint Anthony of Padua, Italy—had partially served as the storage facility-slash-museum for his personal collection of holy items, from a piece of the table from the Last Supper to the skulls of various saints. Following his death in 1892, the collection continued to grow and now housed over five thousand relics. And somewhere among them was the Spear of Longinus. Or so House Karnstein's intelligence division believed.

Hopefully the information this time is more accurate than what they gave me for the wild-goose chase over that damned "Prize," Jenna thought dourly. *All that needless running around, and in the end House Otoyo was the victor and I'd lost my entire team to that murderous bitch Mazarin. Well,* almost *the entire team . . .*

A scuffing of rubber heels on the van's metal floor and the soft rattle of a weapons belt against body armor interrupted her thoughts. Somebody on the new team was getting restless.

Casper Andritsch, an explosive ordnance specialist who stank of stale tobacco and cheap aftershave, poked his head over her shoulder. "So when do we make our move?" the human asked.

When my head stops pounding like a jackhammer, Jenna wanted to say, but her immediate impression of Andritsch had been that he lacked both empathy and a sense of humor. Her opinion hadn't changed in the two hours since they'd first met. Besides, complaining about a headache served no purpose. If her skull was vibrating from the celestial harmonics emanating from the chapel and she was only half-vampire, what must they be doing to the purebred vampires on her team?

"Soon," she replied, and left it at that. Andritsch grunted, then scuffed his boot heels again as he returned to his position.

"Will it be before my head splits open from all that holier-than-thou energy coming from that church?" groused a familiar voice. "That is what I'm feeling, isn't it?" A deep sigh. "I should have packed some acetaminophen in this ammunition belt."

Jenna bit her lip to keep from laughing, and looked over her shoulder. Dalibor was sitting on the floor, backed up by Andritsch and the four other strike team members: the vampires Michelina Tagwerker, Florian Herzog, and Keenan Phibbs, and the human witch Anastasya Stogryn. To match his teammates' attire Dalibor had squeezed himself into a new black leather jumpsuit—insisting the whole time he'd struggled to put it on that he wasn't fat, vampires didn't get fat, it was just a size too small—and magick-enhanced body armor, and outfitted himself with an FN P90 submachine gun, flashbang stun grenades, and an FN Five-seveN handgun, plus weapons belt. Each jogging step he'd taken from the weapons locker to this vehicle had sounded like someone shaking a box full of rocks.

My little warrior, she thought warmly.

Jenna smiled. "You didn't have to come along, Dalek. You could have stayed at the consulate."

Dalibor sniffed dismissively. "After what happened the last time, I'm not letting you out of my sight." He leaned closer to whisper in their native tongue. "Besides, I don't know these people Schovajsa stuck us with—and they don't know us. How can I expect them to watch your back?"

It was a question that had occurred to Jenna as well. If she'd had the proper amount of time to train with her new charges, to get to know them better before they'd set out, she wouldn't feel as hesitant about going into combat as she did right now.

How I miss my children . . . , Jenna thought mournfully. Not that Zuzana, Krystof, Dusana, Sionek, and Vincenc had actually been her offspring; it was just that after working so closely with them for so long she had come to think of herself as a surrogate mother. *And now they're all gone . . .*

All except for Dalibor. And the thought of ever losing him as well was too depressing to consider, so she pushed it from her mind to focus on the mission.

She turned to face her team. "All right, the street is clear. Casper, you and I will take the front—"

"We're going straight through the front door?" he asked, surprised.

Jenna frowned. Already they were questioning her orders. Never a good sign. "That a problem for you, soldier?" she asked sternly. When Andritsch said nothing, but did lower his gaze, she continued. "Michelina, Florian, I want you to sweep those roofs"—she pointed to a pair of three-story redbrick homes bookending the chapel—"to make sure there aren't any Knights or sharp-shooting priests lying in wait. Keenan, you work the houses on this side of the street. I'd hate to get shot in the head before I've even reached the steps."

"Tell me about it," Dalibor muttered in English. He knew what that felt like, as she was well aware.

Herzog raised an inquisitive eyebrow. "Sharp-shooting priests?"

"It's a long story," Jenna replied. "Anastasya, you'll remain here with Dalibor." She cut him a glance, daring him to complain, but he merely nodded. "If anything goes wrong in there, we may need a quick evacuation."

"Why can't I just transport all of us inside?" Strogryn asked.

Jenna turned to the witch. She'd never worked with one before, and this bottled-blond girl barely looked to be out of college; too young to realize the dangers she faced. "I don't know if you can feel it, Anastasya, but there are powerful waves of energy coming off that chapel—concentrated faith, for lack of a better term. It's generated by all those relics in there—they absorb the strength of religious beliefs from the congregants like sponges, and the energy field is what leaks out of the tchothkes. It's been giving me a splitting headache since we arrived. What about you three?" she asked her vampiric teammates. The trio nodded. "So if all that concentrated faith is causing us pain at this distance," she continued to Strogryn, "what do you think might happen if you teleport us right into the middle of the church?"

The witch paused a few seconds to consider the question, then placed the fingertips of both hands against her temples and flexed them away from her skull while making an explosion sound with her mouth—the universal gesture for someone having their mind blown.

"Exactly," Jenna said. "Only this would be literally. We do it my way, we can avoid all that mess. Now, places, chil—" She stopped to correct herself. "Places, everyone. Let's make this quick so we can be on our way."

Tagwerker opened the van's side door, then she and Herzog scrambled to carry out Jenna's order. Andritsch focused his attention on his P90, avoiding eye contact with his commander.

"And once we have the spear?" Dalibor asked. "Do we immediately move on to our next destination?"

Jenna massaged her aching temples with a gloved hand. "Once we have the spear we're stopping at a Walgreen's for a bottle of Advil before my brains start leaking out. Damn relics . . ."

Jesus was staring down at her from the cross, and it was kinda creepy. No, make that majorly creepy, even though he was just a life-size statue. Especially when Pan focused on the painted wound in his right side that represented the one he'd received, according to legend, from the iron tip of what became known as the Spear of Longinus. Unaware she was doing it, Pan raised her right hand and gently rubbed the scar deep beneath her bulletproof vest—the scar that roughly matched the size and shape of the wound on the statue.

"You okay, Cookie?" Javi asked softly.

She flashed a smile. "Yeah, I'm fine," she replied, although she felt quite the opposite. But, she thought, why burden Javi with any more of her problems?

Pan turned away from the alcoves containing the Stations of the Cross—a depiction in statuary of Jesus' last steps along the way to his crucifixion—and gazed at her surroundings. St. Anthony's Chapel, according to Alex, housed the second biggest collection of religious items in the world, and she could believe it—the place was crammed with artifacts, but in a really tasteful way. There were stained glass windows and gleaming walnut cabinets; gold reliquaries and glittering chandeliers and a majestically ornate altar; and an absolute tonnage of relics, although some of them were really tiny—fingernails and teeth, bone fragments and scraps of cloth, wooden splinters and such. And all of them, Alex had said, were authentic, including the sliver of the True Cross that Christ died on.

Now the Spear of Longinus had been added to the collection—and they were here to steal it. Okay, Alex had said "borrow," but Pan knew they were totally stealing it, because the Church was never getting it back—if she got the chance she was going to ram that thing straight into Zaqiel's chest and see how he liked being impaled on it.

Well . . . impaled on it *again*. He'd already had it done to him once before, by Annie, but that was like back in the age of dinosaurs or whatever. This time, it would be Pan handing out some payback to that bastard for all the misery he'd caused her family. *Then let's see him try to take over the world,* she thought with a tiny sadistic smile.

"So where do we start looking for this thing?" Sheen asked.

"I'm not sure it's been put on display yet," Alex replied. "But look around and give a holler if you spot it." He lumbered toward one of the mahogany display cases on the left-hand side of the chapel, his battle gear rattling noisily.

Before Natsumi had magically transported the group from Annie's town house to the chapel (coordinates provided by Google Maps via the witch's smartphone), Alex had gone full-on G.I. Joe: body armor, handguns, machine gun, a bunch of other stuff Pan hadn't a clue about . . . and his mom's ax, strapped to his back. *Just in case,* he'd said with a sly smile. He'd equipped his young charges with a variety of blunt instruments—the one currently tucked in Pan's messenger bag was a foot-long, fifteenth-century Egyptian iron mace with a weave-pattern silver head—but the teens had drawn the line at donning body armor (too heavy, too difficult to move around in). They agreed to bulletproof vests, but only because Alex made it clear that either they wore them or nobody was going anywhere. His follow-up demand for protective helmets was met with derision—especially from Natsumi, who refused to give up her cat-eared witch hat for any reason—so he was forced to drop the issue. (The fact he wasn't going to wear one himself did little to help him win the argument.) The vests were bulky and heavy as hell, not to mention really hot when worn under a leather jacket in the middle of summer, but Pan figured being uncomfortable was a small price to pay when the alternative might involve receiving a set of bullet holes to offset the spear scar. She'd had enough holes punched in her chest to last a lifetime . . . or two, considering her brief purgatorial odyssey and subsequent return.

So, what are you supposed to be? Uwe had asked her back at the hospital. As her gaze drifted back to the crucifixion scene in the alcove, and the wound in Christ's side, Pan could only wonder herself.

"So, where do you wanna look?" Javi asked.

"Um . . ." Pan made a slow circle on her heels, to get the lay of the land, then turned back to her friends, who'd gathered beside her. "Okay, Sheen, how about you and Uwe take the cabinets on the right-hand side, while me and Javi and Natsumi take the altar? We'll meet back here if nobody finds it."

"Works for me," Sheen replied. She gave an appreciative glance around the chapel and smiled. "You dad would totally love this place, Zee. It's like his horror museum, but, y'know, in a church."

"Maybe I can get him and Mom to come here when we're done with all the world saving. Like those road trips we used to go on when I was little." Pan smiled wistfully. Those had been great times . . . before the memories of them had been tainted by her parents' divorce. But if she could just convince them to get together after things got back to normal, maybe they could create some new great memories—as a family again.

"That's an awesome idea." Sheen gave her boyfriend's hand a light tug and flashed a wicked, gothy smile. "C'mon, babe, let's see how close we can get to stuff before the Big Man realizes we're in here and turns us into pillars of salt or something."

"You *would* make an excellent salt lick," he growled pleasantly.

"Down, boy," she giggled, and led him away.

Pan grinned at Javi and Natsumi. The witch's cheeks glowed with mild embarrassment from overhearing the teens' conversation.

"Kids today," Pan said. "Always with the dirty talk." She reached out to take Javi's hand. "C'mon, 'babe.' " She used her free hand to take Natsumi by the elbow, then guided them up the nave—the main area of the church that was lined with rows of pews. "You, too, Kiki."

The girl's eyebrows rose. "You know about *Kiki's Delivery Service*?"

"My friend Tory got me to watch it once." Pan shrugged. "It was okay, but I'm not really into that anime stuff. I'm more into—"

"Horror movies like *Saw* and *Hostel* and *A Serbian Film*?"

Pan grimaced. "Torture porn? Not ever. That stuff's just disgusting. And it's not real horror, it's just gore for the sake of shocking people. I like old-school stuff like *The Exorcist*, and some of the new scary movies." She paused. "Although I gotta admit the first *Saw* was really clever . . ."

The girls looked to their male companion. "How about you, Javi?" Pan asked.

He smiled sheepishly. "Uh . . . I'm more into the superhero stuff—y'know, like *Avengers* and *X-Men* and that—but I check out some horror movies every now and then. The last one I saw was probably *Ghost Rider 2*."

Which was totally not a horror movie, but Pan wasn't going to correct him; his attempt to fit in with the Goth crowd he'd been flung into by hanging around her was way too cute to stomp on. Instead, she nodded. "Yeah, *Avengers* was pretty—" She came to a halt and looked around. "Do you guys feel that?"

They had reached the base of the altar, where Pan had experienced a mild jolt of . . . something. Like a low electrical current that ran through her body and made the hairs on her arms and the back of her neck stand on end. It was kinda weird but strangely . . . familiar.

"No, wait!" Pan cried. "I'm not a vampire! I'm just a Goth chick!" She backed away from the sword-wielding angel, tugging with all her might on the damn spear that would just. not. come. out! Bluish electricity flared around her hands, then surged up her arms. She tried to ignore the pain, but when her eyeballs started

tingling it took a supreme effort to avoid freaking out and maintain her grip on the
wooden handle.

"It's the spear," she whispered in awe, then laughed a short, barking note. "I can feel the spear's power, Javi!"

"That your newest superpower?" he asked with a grin.

She grinned right back. "I guess so."

"Can you lead us to it, then?" Nastumi asked.

"I think so . . ." Pan slowly moved her head from side to side, trying to pinpoint the source of the power like a supernatural Geiger counter, only instead of detecting radiation levels she was on the hunt for celestial energy. The tingly sensation, she noticed, was strongest when she looked straight ahead, at the incredibly ornate mahogany-and-glass cabinet that towered behind the altar. "It's on one of those shelves . . . I think."

She walked around the altar, noting a heavy wooden door to the left side that presumably led either outside or to the rear of the building, and gazed at the display assembled in the apse—the vaulted, semicircular alcove right behind the altar. Its five shelves were lined with golden reliquaries of various designs, including a few that looked like representations of the chapel's exterior. Each of them emitted a slight hum of power that Pan knew only she could hear, but none gave her that electrical buzz she'd come to associate with the spear . . . until she took a step back to take another look at the display and her heel accidentally brushed against an object underneath the altar. Then the mild jolt she'd felt earlier became a surge of current that ran through her body from the bottoms of her feet to the top of her head.

"Found it," she croaked in a singsongy voice.

As Javi and Natsumi moved to join her, she turned and crouched down to see what she'd bumped. It was another reliquary, but larger, wider, and quite different from the others in the cabinet: this one had a lid fashioned with a golden representation of Jesus lying on a platform, his head supported by pillows; his eyes were closed, his arms folded across his chest. So, not resting but post-crucifixion; the phrase "lying in state" popped into Pan's thoughts. Her gaze lingered for a few seconds on the wound etched into his right side.

"Is it in there?" Natsumi asked breathlessly.

"Only one way to find out, right?" Pan had tried to sound nonchalant, but the thought of coming into contact again with the means of her death made her voice crack. She took a couple of nervous swallows before opening the lid.

"Jackpot," Javi said.

The spear tip, including its broken, makeshift handle, lay on a purple velvet cushion. It didn't glow or do anything special, like mystical artifacts in an Indiana Jones or Hellboy movie, it just lay there like any other rusting piece of metal—except, as Pan well knew, it wasn't rust coating the iron but the dried remains of her blood.

"Wow," Natsumi said. "I always thought it would look more . . . magical, like with cuneiforms carved in the metal, or a spell or something really grand."

" 'Whosoever holds this hammer, if he be worthy, shall possess the power of . . . Thor,' " Javi intoned seriously. The girls stared at him in confusion. "It's from the comic books. That's the inscription on Thor's hammer, Mjolnir." He pronounced it *Mi-yol-ner*, which, if Pan remembered correctly, was dead-on accurate.

Natsumi grinned at Pan. "I think you're dating about the cutest nerd I've ever met."

Pan laughed nervously. *We haven't even got to that stage yet,* she thought with a glance toward Javi. *But, y'know, one can only hope . . .*

"Aren't you going to pick it up?" the witch asked with a nod toward the spear.

Hell, no was the first response Pan thought of, but she pushed it aside with a gruff "I guess," and reached for the ancient weapon.

That's when the front door opened and into the chapel slipped a red-haired woman and a dark-haired man, both dressed in leather or latex bodysuits and bulletproof vests . . . and both carrying machine guns.

"Those aren't Knight uniforms," Javi said.

There was something else about them, Pan thought—a flicker of wrongness to at least one of them, like her early monstervision days when she used to see monsters lurking at the edges of her vision, but only people when she faced them directly. She narrowed her eyes to confirm her suspicions and, surprisingly, the monstervision worked when she needed it to, allowing her to see a graduated, light-to-dark-blue aura that shifted around the redhead like smoke in a breeze. There was nothing supernatural about the man—apparently he was a normal old human.

"Red's got a bluish aura," Pan said.

"Great, a dhampyr," Natsumi muttered and began quietly unsnapping the flaps of the pouches on her belt. Clearly expecting trouble, she was putting her spellcasting gear in easy reach.

"Dom-peer?" Javi whispered.

"It's a monster that's half-human and half-vampire," Pan answered.

"Exactly," Natsumi said. "That pedigree means they can walk into holy places that would be lethal to full-fledged vampires. And I think we can all figure out why they're here," she added with a glance toward the spear.

The soldiers didn't see the trio crouched on the far side of the altar, but the dhampyr spotted Alex at the same moment that he saw her. The Knight immediately raised his gun. So did she.

"Drop your weapons!" Alex barked. "Do it now!"

"A Knight of the Apocalypse?" The woman grunted. "You're even worse than sharpshooting priests. You're not going to try to convert me, are you?"

Alex was in no mood for snark. "I said, drop your weapons!"

The male soldier started to turn toward Alex, but then a sharp noise—the brief squeal of a rubber sole sliding across the polished tile floor that echoed like a scream in the chapel—caught everyone's attention. The soldier spun around and brought his machine gun to bear on the right-hand alcove—where Sheen and Uwe were huddled.

"Oh, crap," Sheen said, her voice cracking.

The redhead noticed the drama, then with a sigh faced Alex again. "Friends of yours, I assume. You know, you people really need to stop recruiting from high schools."

"They're not with me," Alex lied. "They're just a pair of visiting congregants."

"Really. And they just happen to be wearing bulletproof vests? Well, they've come to the right place to try them out, haven't they?"

The male soldier threw back the bolt on his machine gun.

"Now, just hold on," Alex said. "We don't need to involve them in this."

"All right, let's be rational about the situation," the woman said. "We're both here for the Spear of Longinus—and please don't try to deny it. My head is aching enough just being in here without you trying to lie about your mission. Just hand over the spear and you and your friends are free to leave. Or . . . Casper?"

"Casper" took aim at the two teens. Uwe immediately wrapped himself around Sheen, his back to the soldier, prepared to shield her from the fusillade of bullets Pan knew was coming.

"NO!" Pan yelled as she jumped to her feet.

As one, her friends, the soldiers, and Alex turned in her direction.

She raised her right arm above her head, the spear clutched tightly in her fist. "Is this what you're looking for? Then come and get it!"

And like a shot she took off for the side door.

Thankfully, it wasn't locked, otherwise her attempt to lead the soldiers away from her friends would have been extremely short-lived . . . not to mention she would have looked like a total moron bouncing off a locked door. She pushed it open and stumbled into a narrow alley between the church and a redbrick building she figured was the rectory.

The sudden roar of gunfire in the chapel prompted her to go back, but as she turned around she found Javi racing after her.

"Move, Cookie!" He grabbed her by the shoulder and gave her a not-so-gentle tug.

Pan yanked her arm back and halted. "Wait! What about Sheen and Uwe?"

"I saw them running out the front as soon as Alex started laying down fire," Javi replied, just before another burst of gunfire erupted—followed by a small explosion and a high-pitched male yelp. "Natsumi's backing him up. Sounds like she took out the dude."

Unless that was Alex yelling in pain . . .

Javi gave her arm another tug. "Come on, Cookie. They're doing this to buy us time. Who knows how many more of those guys are getting ready to swarm this place? And besides, we gotta keep the spear away from them—it's the only thing we've got that can stop that angel."

Pan nervously chewed her bottom lip for a few seconds. On the one hand, Javi was totally right: Natsumi and Alex were professional fighters, trained for firefights and stuff like that, and they wouldn't want vampires getting their hands on the spear. But on the other hand, she didn't like abandoning her friends when they needed help. In fact, the whole idea of taking off like she had was so she could give her friends a chance to escape; Alex, apparently, had thought differently.

Still, what could she really do if she went back but get in the way—or maybe get killed a second time. Or worse, get somebody else killed while they tried to protect her. She'd never be able to live with that burden.

"Okay." She shoved the relic into her messenger bag, where it clanged against the mace she'd forgotten was in there. "But we have to find Sheen and Uwe."

Javi smiled. "Deal."

They ran down the alley, emerging onto what a nearby sign said was Harpster Street. Directly across from the church was a parking lot, with a black van in one of the spaces. A van with its motor running. Pan spotted a blond-haired woman behind the steering wheel, then jumped back as the side door slid open and a thirtysomething man dressed like the soldiers—and just as well armed— jumped out.

"Oh, crap," Javi muttered.

But then, much to their surprise, the man didn't charge them; instead he ran into the church, undoubtedly to provide backup for Red.

"Umm . . . okay," Javi remarked.

Now it was Pan's turn to do the tugging. She yanked Javi's arm and turned— right into the hands of a sixtyish African-American man in baggy "dad jeans" and a sleeveless T-shirt. Beside him was his wife (Pan assumed) in a housedress, her arms full of a squirming tan-and-white Pekingese dog. And behind them was a growing crowd of neighbors who had spilled from the surrounding homes and the rectory to find out what all the noise was about.

"Hey, you kids! What were you doing in there?" the man demanded.

Pan could see in the crowd's eyes what they were all thinking: a pair of teenagers not from the neighborhood, one dressed in "lone gunman" black and devil imagery, the other Hispanic, running from a church after hours in the wake of gunshots and explosions. Obviously they must be out to cause trouble.

She opened her mouth to respond, but couldn't think of what to say. How do you explain that you're working with a Knight of the Apocalypse and a teleporting witch to steal an angel-killing relic in order to save the world from the rise of a monster empire? It sounded crazy even to someone who'd spent a decade in psychiatric therapy.

Another burst of gunfire echoed from the church. The man looked them up and down, his eyes widening in surprise. "Are those bulletproof vests you got on?"

Inside, Pan cringed. Yeah, having these on made things even worse.

She opened her eyes wide and quivered her bottom lip, going for the full-on wounded puppy look. She grabbed the man by the hand. "Please, mistah, call the police! I swear t'God me an' my boyfriend, we was just payin' our respects t'the Almighty an' these gunmen come bustin' in and start shootin' up the place!"

"But the chapel's closed at this hour," a gray-haired priest in his fifties remarked. "How—"

"Please, Faddah, y'gotta call the cops!" Pan insisted before the priest could start asking questions. "They're crazy, I tells ya! I think they're terrorists!"

"Oh, my God, George," said the Pekingese owner, wide-eyed. "Did you hear that? Terrorists!"

The T-word instantly made its way through the crowd, and just as Pan had hoped everyone forgot about the suspicious teenagers and started moving back from the church—even the inquiring priest.

Everyone, that is, except for one person. George grunted and held his ground. "Terrorists—in Troy Hill? Yeah, maybe, but how do we know these kids aren't in on it?"

The wail of sirens in the distance ended the conversation. Apparently someone had already contacted the authorities—which meant it was a good time to leave before they, too, started asking questions. Or making accusations.

Before George could stop them, the teens pushed through the onlookers and ran down the street away from the chapel. Pan caught a glimpse of Sheen and Uwe huddled under a tree in a small courtyard across the way and breathed a sigh of relief as she waved them off not to follow. Her best friend was safe and that had been Pan's main concern, even more than keeping the spear away from the dhampyr and her two-man-and-getaway-driver army. Now she could concentrate on not getting killed while she and Javi found someplace to hide. The only problem was . . .

"Why isn't anybody chasing us?" Pan asked, bewildered. "I mean, I've got the stupid thing they want right in my bag."

"Give it time," Javi replied sarcastically. "I'm sure somebody's gonna notice."

Prophetic words, as it turned out. As they passed a telephone pole at the end of the next block, a hail of bullets tore apart a metal sign nailed to it that had read NORTH SIDE SAFE STREETS. Pan thought that was sorta ironic, before she focused on the fact that those bullets had been intended to tear *her* apart. Not to mention what could have happened to all the bystanders, who were now screaming in panic and running for cover in all directions. Javi pulled her behind a parked car.

"On the roof!" yelled a man crouched behind a curbside garbage can. He pointed in the direction of the church.

Pan peeked over the car's trunk in time to see another pair of soldiers jump—or rather, soar—from atop the church and land on the rectory. The distance involved should have broken an ankle or a leg when they touched down, but they popped right up, apparently without injury. They were joined by a third soldier already up there.

"I guess somebody noticed," Javi said. "Looks like that damp-peer got past Alex and Natsumi and called in extra backup. Probably real vampires, seeing how easy they made that jump—y'think?"

"No bet," Pan replied as she wiped away the sweat pouring down her forehead. Now that they'd stopped running, she realized just how heavy and body-heat trapping the bulletproof vest was; it felt as though she was locked inside a pressure cooker. If she didn't take it off soon, she'd probably boil to death . . . or something equally humiliating.

They glanced over the car trunk one more time, to see the vampires leaping from the rectory to the roof of the home next to it. Closing in on their hiding place.

"Time to move," Javi said, and held out his hand. "You ready?"

Pan smiled as she took it. "Yeah."

They bolted from cover and turned the corner at the end of the block, where he pointed to an open area between two houses. "That way!"

The gap turned out to be a weed-claimed hill that bottomed out in the backyard of a three-story house, its windows dark. Nobody home, apparently.

"Think you can make that?" Javi asked as he gasped for air. He wiped his sweat-drenched face on a sleeve of his T, clearly feeling the effects of being dressed like a tank just as she was.

Pan, breathless herself, didn't bother to answer. She just sprinted down the hill, with Javi slipping along the grass in her wake, and dove over the waist-high hedges lining the property. She landed in a heap, crashing onto a row of live-forever plants; as an added misery, the big metal bat ornament hanging from her jacket's left shoulder smacked her in the nose. It wasn't the first time that had happened, but she refused to get rid of the ornament—it complemented the jacket's devil-and-burning-souls paint job too well.

Javi nimbly hopped over the bushes and hunched down beside her. "You okay?"

Pan rubbed her sore nose—the pain going away the moment she touched it (yay, healing power)—and propped herself up on her elbows. "I feel like a steamed clam." And an idiot for taking that spill, but she figured she could leave that part out.

She sat up, wiped off her perspiring brow with her palms, and slapped the bulletproof vest in annoyance. "I just can't anymore with this thing. I'm gonna melt away if I have to do any more running in it." She began unfastening its straps. The night echoed with the ripping sound of Velcro.

Javi looked as though he were about to object, then said, "Yeah, you're right," and removed his own. The vests thudded onto the grass. "Oh yeah, that feels a *lot* better." He rolled his head around to ease the kinks in his neck. "So what's the next step?"

"Catch our breath, first." Pan pointed to a winding set of concrete steps that led farther down the hill to another street. "Then put some more distance between us and the vampires—although I'm hoping they'll be scared off with the cops showing up—and then I'll call Sheen to see what's going on with Alex and Natsumi. I hope they got out okay."

"Me, too." Javi grinned. "So . . . 'Please, mistah'? 'They're crazy, I tells ya'? What kinda accent was that supposed to be?"

Pan shrugged. Her skill with funny voices was dubious, to say the least. "I don't know. Isn't that how they talk in Pittsburgh?"

"Mmm . . . I don't think so," Javi replied slowly. "Sounded more like somebody from Boston."

Pan playfully rolled her eyes. "I guess you'd know, Mr. Yankee fan. Next time I'll throw in a bunch'a curse words about your sucky team so you can be sure."

Javi chuckled, then flashed a sly smile. "I caught that boyfriend mention, y'know."

Her smile glowed even brighter through the blush of her cheeks. "Freudian slip."

She peeked over the hedge and saw no sign of their pursuers, but that didn't mean anything. They were freaking vampires, after all—for all she knew they could have turned into bats and were now hanging upside down from the rain gutters of one of the nearby houses, waiting for their prey to run.

On the other hand, they might have taken off. From the number of sirens closing on the chapel and the two police helicopters buzzing the area, it would make all kinds of sense for Red and her crew to make tracks out of Pittsburgh, even without the spear.

On the other *other* hand, if these vampires were anything like the ones who'd trashed Dad's museum, the last thing they'd do is abandon the spear, especially after getting into a shoot-out over it. So maybe they were still out there, somewhere, but . . .

"I'm not seeing anything," Javi murmured.

"Me, neither," Pan agreed.

"You wanna chance it?"

"Well . . . ," she replied slowly, still not quite certain about how safe it was to break cover, but then she nodded firmly. "Okay. Yeah. Let's go."

They jumped to their feet and turned to head for the concrete steps—only to find the blonde driver from the van standing behind them.

"Oh, my God," she said with a grin, "don't the two of you just make the most adorable couple."

Pan and Javi both yelped and made to dive back over the hedges, but the woman grabbed them each by a shoulder, said a word Pan didn't understand—

—and suddenly they were all heaped on the floor of the van. Surrounded by machine-gun-toting vampires. One of whom was Casper, the male soldier from the church, who up close stank of 99-cent-store cologne . . . and ass.

Javi immediately scrambled to place himself between Pan and their captors. A chivalrous move, to be sure, but pretty futile, considering Javi's lean but well-toned body wouldn't be much of a shield once the point-blank shooting began. Still, she appreciated the effort.

Figures, she thought glumly. *The* second *we take off those superheavy vests,* that's *when these stupid vampires decide to come after us—and then they cheat using magic.*

"*Told* you I could find them without a problem," the blonde said with a triumphant tone. She snatched the messenger bag—Pan immediately gripping Javi's shoulder as a sign he shouldn't put up a fight over it—and pulled out the spear with her thumb and forefinger. "It was just a matter of tracing the 'concentrated faith' leaking out of it to its source—like following a vapor trail to some skeevy dude who'd poured half a bottle of cheap cologne all over his body. All it took was the right spell." She wrinkled her nose in disgust at the spear. "So filthy . . ."

"Well, nice tracking work, Miss Witch—now *put it back in the bag,*" said a familiar voice. "It's making my head ache worse than all the other crap in that church, combined."

"Tell me about it," muttered the male vampire covering Javi with his machine gun.

The witch shrugged but did as told, then tossed the bag to the rear of the van.

Pan leaned around Javi's shoulder, to find Red sitting in the passenger seat up front. She was massaging the bridge of her nose with a thumb and forefinger.

"So much for my Advil stop," Red muttered. "Damn relics . . ."

"What do we do with these two?" Casper asked with a nod toward Pan and Javi.

The dhampyr regarded the teens for a few unnerving seconds. "Nothing right now. But if Mr. Chivalry there"—she added, pointing to Javi—"makes any trouble to try and impress his girlfriend, because I *know* that look in his eyes . . . put a bullet in *her.*"

"Oh, nice," Pan growled.

"Couldn't we just feed on them, Commander?" asked the female vampire next to Pan. She smiled broadly, flashing sharklike teeth. "We haven't had dinner yet."

So starve, *bitch,* Pan thought, frowning. *Unless you want me to knock out some of those fangs.* She wisely kept that sentiment to herself, however.

"Maybe later, Miche—" Red began to say, only to be interrupted as the van rocked wildly. Pan now realized the vehicle was racing along a bumpy street; the scream of approaching sirens told her the police weren't too far behind.

Vampires in a high-speed car chase, she thought. There's *something you don't hear about every day.*

"Steady, Dalek," Red said to the driver. "It won't help if you flip us over."

The driver—apparently the one who'd jumped out of the van when Pan and Javi bolted from the chapel, since he was the only one not back here—sighed. "I'm doing my best, Jenna, but these American policemen apparently all think they're speed demons, starring in one of those hot-rod movies that are so popular."

"*The Fast and the Furious?*" Red—or rather, Jenna—asked.

"Yes, those," he replied, with a tinge of disgust to his voice.

"I *like* those movies," she said, playfully argumentative.

"Well, *you* would," he said dismissively. "But now that she's returned, perhaps our resident sorceress might lend a hand so we can reach our destination . . . ?"

Jenna grunted. "Ana?"

"On it." The witch reached for her bag, from which she pulled out a gnarly wooden stick that looked like a small tree branch, or one of those Harry Potter toy magic wands. It definitely leaned toward the latter when Ana held it up, yelled out something that sounded like a cross between Latin and baby talk, and pointed the wand toward the windshield. A bolt of black lightning shot out, passed through the glass without shattering it, and flashed ahead of the van . . . to form a portal.

Pan's stomach fell. How would Alex or Natsumi or anyone ever find them once they went through that doorway? And if she and Javi did become a feast for these monsters, what would happen to her mom? And Annie?

Javi must have seen the worry etched on her face, because he took her hand and gently squeezed it. "We'll be okay," he whispered. He tried to give an encouraging smile but Pan could see right past it, to the same fear she was trying to hide. Fear of what might happen to them on the other side of the portal.

She squeezed back. "I know we will."

"Hang on, children!" Jenna called out lightheartedly. "Next stop: Halja's Island!"

"Dalek," if that was his real name, stomped down on the accelerator, and the van rocketed into the void.

15

"What d'you mean you don't know where they are?" Sheena demanded. "You're a freakin' witch—do some magic and find them!"

Natsumi averted her gaze and focused on staring at her hands. "It's not as simple as that, Sheena. As I explained at the hospital, I have to know a person really well for me to be able to lock on to their soul resonance . . . and Pandora and Javi are still pretty much strangers to me, like you and Uwe are. I can't just zero in on them . . . not like I can with Alex or Annie. Or Kenji."

Sheen snarled. "You're just sayin' that 'cause you wanna go save your boyfriend."

"He's not . . . never mind." The witch looked up and frowned. "Yes, I want to rescue Kenji, but it's not because Pandora and Javi mean nothing to me—I want to save them, too. But I can't just wave my hands and track them like a bloodhound. I mean, yes, I was able to for a minute or so after Alex and I got out of the chapel, but that's because Pan was carrying the Spear of Longinus—it gives off a lot of spiritual energy. That's how I could zero in on the last place they were." She gestured at the discarded bulletproof vests and the crushed live-forever plants the group had found when they'd arrived in this backyard a couple of blocks from the chapel. "But now it's like she and the spear just . . . disappeared off the face of the Earth."

"Javi, too," Sheen pointed out.

"Maybe they were taken through a magic portal?" Alex asked.

"Maybe," Natsumi replied slowly, "in which case they could be anywhere in the world, or even on some mystical plane. But it's so weird: I never heard of vampire clans using witches on their strike teams before."

Alex grunted. "There's a first time for everything. I guess House Karnstein's leaders had plans of their own for the spear and were desperate enough to hire outside the clan to get the job done."

"House Karnstein?" Uwe asked. "You recognized them?"

"The redhead," Alex replied. "Commander Jenessa Branislav, of the Prague chapter. And yes," he added before Uwe could voice the same question that Sheena was thinking, "it's the same Karnstein that Joseph Sheridan Le Fanu wrote about in his novella, *Carmilla.*"

"Except her real name was Mircalla," said Sheen, who considered the nineteenth-century Gothic story one of her all-time favorites. "She just mixed up the letters so she could make up a new identity."

"As in fiction, so in real life," Alex said.

"So maybe they took Zee and Javi to their headquarters?" Sheen glanced at Natsumi. "You could find *that,* couldn't you?"

"Knock it off," Alex snapped. " Since we lost the relic, our first order of business is rescuing Kenji. Then we can concentrate on recovering the spear."

"And our friends," Natsumi added. Alex nodded in agreement.

"What about your mom?" Sheen asked him. "You gonna just leave her hangin', like you're doin' to Zee and Javi?"

Alex snarled. "Don't you think I'm worried sick about my mother? You think my first impulse wasn't to ask Natsumi to take us right to her instead of the chapel? But if our positions were reversed Annie would do the same, and I'd just have to fend for myself until backup arrived." He turned to Natsumi. "You ready to go get him?"

"Just give me a couple minutes to get ready." She reached into her belt pouches for whatever it was she needed for her next spell.

"You think Annie's even still alive?" Uwe asked, tactful as ever. "For all you know, she could be dead already."

Sheen bit her tongue to keep from snapping at him. Knowing how dangerous it would be, Uwe hadn't wanted to come on this trip, yet he was here for her sake to offer support and protection, and she appreciated it. True, he could be an A+ asshole when he wanted to be, especially where Pan was concerned, but Sheen knew that despite his bluntness and off-putting attitude, despite her comment at the hospital that maybe she ought to consider trading up for a new boyfriend, the self-proclaimed King of the Splatterpunks wouldn't wish her best friend, or

Annie, dead.

That didn't stop him from asking cringe-worthy questions, though . . .

"Of course she's alive," Alex said confidently. "She's been getting into—and out of—situations like this all her life. You think Zaqiel is the first megalomaniac out to rule the world who ever captured her? He's just the latest in a very long line of nutjobs."

"Perhaps, but he has all those vampire clans backing him up," Uwe countered. "I doubt any of them would wish to keep her alive. I'm surprised they didn't kill her immediately at that party."

"Uwe!" Sheen said. So much for trying to not snap at him—but sometimes he just wouldn't back off a sore point. He had to be right about *everything*. "Babe, come on. That's his mom."

"Don't worry about it, Sheena," Alex said. "Doubting Thomases like your boyfriend come with the territory." He turned back to Uwe. "Here's what you have to understand: On average, monsters—whether highborn or lowborn, it doesn't make a difference—possess the same basic personality flaw: they're all raging egotists. Zaqiel is no different. You think he'd eliminate Annie before he put humanity under his heel? Deny himself the opportunity to rub his victory in her face so she could realize how powerless she was to stop him? It'll never happen. His ego won't allow it. And that's what Annie will ultimately use to her advantage to bring him down—again."

"But what about Zee and Javi?" Sheen asked. "They're not with Zaqiel, they're with those vampire soldiers. Does what you're sayin' apply to them, too?"

The Knight paused. "I don't know. Maybe not. I've read the file on Branislav—she has a reputation for being something of a free spirit, and there's been no indication so far that she suffers from delusions of grandeur. But she can be as ruthless as any full-blooded vampire when it comes to a mission . . . as you saw tonight."

"Yeah . . ." Sheen swallowed nervously, remembering the red-haired warrior—and her sidekick, who'd pointed a machine gun at Sheen and Uwe. They'd come *thisclose* to dying, and Sheen had been certain she'd never see her parents or sister again. But then Pan had stood up and offered herself as a decoy, and the admiration

Sheen had felt for her kinda-sister had never been so powerful.

She gazed in the direction of St. Anthony's Chapel. She couldn't see it from here, but the night was alive with gawking neighbors, police officers, and TV news crews. If it hadn't been for an invisibility spell that Natsumi had woven—and the distraction provided by the vampires when they busted out of the church, guns blazing, and roared away in their van—none of the remaining quartet would have made it off that block without having to answer questions from everyone from the local cops to that Homeland agency Sheen kept confusing with that TV show her sister Rachel was binge-watching these days. It was that same spell that now kept their presence hidden while they stood around somebody's backyard, waiting for Natsumi to do her witch-thing. Wasting time while who-knew-what happened to Pan and Javi.

Sheen ground her teeth and kicked at one of the crushed live-forever plants, the toe of her sneaker tearing it out, roots and all, and flinging it across the yard. *This is all my fault,* she told herself. *Zee and Javi never would've been kidnapped or whatever if I hadn't stupidly insisted on taggin' along so that I put me and Uwe in the line'a fire, which then made Pan do what she did. To save* me. She felt like crying but was too angry with herself to let any tears form.

Alex gently placed a hand on Sheen's shoulder. "We'll get your friends back, Sheena, I promise you. And they'll be okay. Javi's a smart, resourceful kid, and Pandora—"

"Wouldn't be in so much trouble if it wasn't for me, right?" Sheen asked.

Alex smiled warmly. "I was going to say, from what I've seen of her, Pandora is just as smart and quick on her feet—plus she's a fighter. Not too many people can say they busted out of purgatory."

Sheen gave a short, soft laugh. "Yeah, that's Zee, all right."

He gave her shoulder an encouraging squeeze. "I understand you're frustrated, Sheena, but don't start blaming yourself for what happened. Pandora and you are like sisters, right? I could see the bond between you. What she did, as reckless as it was, she did out of love, to keep you safe. And I have no doubt you would've done the same for her."

Sheen nodded, then removed her glasses to wipe away the tears she could no longer hold back. "Yeah," she croaked.

"Then accept the decision she made and have faith in the power of her strength—and her love."

What Alex had said was true: Pan *was* strong enough. And her love for her family and friends was too powerful for any demon or angel or vampire to destroy. She *would* find a way to hold on until rescue came. And Sheen would be the one to lead the charge.

She took a breath to steady herself, then slowly exhaled. "Okay, I . . . I can do that. Accept it. And I *do* have faith in Zee." She did, she realized. Absolute faith in her best friend.

And just like that, it felt as though a weight had been lifted off Sheen's heart.

She couldn't help but smile as she put her glasses back on. "You're pretty good at this pep talk stuff, y'know. You take confessions, too, 'Father'?"

"Me, in the priesthood?" Alex chuckled. "My mother told me to never become a holy man because they can't be trusted—they keep too many secrets. Besides," he added as he gazed into her eyes, "I'm not sure I'm ready to peer into the dark recesses of your soul. I might get lost in there and never find my way back."

Sheen grinned. "You really know how to sweet-talk a Goth chick, don't you?"

"It's a gift," Alex replied with a shrug.

He looked over to Natsumi, who was sitting cross-legged on the ground, her eyes closed; she appeared to be meditating. On the grass in front of the witch was a pair of items from her pouches: a necklace of glowing gems of various colors, wound around a six-inch action figure of a red-haired, white skinned female clad in purple bra, shorts, and thigh-high stockings, wearing black boots and clutching an oversize guitar decorated with dragon teeth. No doubt it was a toy based on some anime or manga property. Sheen didn't recognize it—Japanese pop culture wasn't really her thing, that was more her friend Tory Kwon's obsession—but it had a certain gothy appeal. Even odder than the necklace/action figure combination was that both were connected by a charger cable to Natsumi's smartphone, as though the toy were providing power . . . or maybe uploading information? Maybe. The witch was certainly riveted to whatever was displayed on the phone's screen, squeeing quietly as she scrolled through something. Sheen couldn't see what it was, but it sure seemed to make her happy.

"What's the word, 'Tsumi?" Alex asked. "We ready to get out of here?"

Natsumi looked up and grinned. "I've got a lock on Kenji's soul resonance—he's alive!" She closed her eyes again, this time to murmur something in Japanese that sounded like it could be a prayer.

Alex nodded. "Then let's go get our boy."

Natsumi stuffed the items back in their pouches and jumped to her feet. Sheen walked over to join her.

"Umm . . . look, Nat," Sheen said quietly. "I'm sorry about mouthin' off before. You got every right to be worried about Kenji, and I feel really stupid about what I said—it wasn't fair to you or your boyfriend. And I want you to know I appreciate everything you've been doin'. So if you feel like bitch-slappin' me or whatever, go right ahead 'cause I deserve it."

"He's not my . . ." Natsumi let her voice trail off, then smiled. "Thank you. And believe me, Sheena, I will do everything I can to find your friends and Annie once we get Kenji back. Okay?"

Sheen smiled. "Okay."

Natsumi gave her hand an encouraging squeeze, then looked over to Alex and Uwe. "Are you gentlemen ready to go?"

"I suppose," Uwe said blandly.

"Just get us as close to Kenji as you can," Alex advised, "and then you kids stand back. I'll go through first in case there's any trouble on the other side."

"Oh, wait!" Sheen went back to retrieve the bulletproof vests. "Better bring these along—Zee and Javi are gonna need 'em." She tossed one to Uwe, whose lithe frame almost collapsed under the additional weight.

"Smart move, Sheena," Alex said with a smile. "All right, 'Tsumi, do your thing."

Out came a new glow stick that the witch snapped to activate. With a few mystical words and a wave of the green plastic tube she formed another portal; this one opened on a dimly lit corridor that reminded Sheen of way too many horror movie locations. Water dripped from overhead pipes and a strong odor of mildew wafted through the doorway.

"This is as close as I can get," Natsumi said to Alex. "I didn't think you'd want to go charging into the middle of some vampire convention."

"That's fine, 'Tsumi. You did great." Alex raised his machine gun to shoulder level, then eased toward the threshold. He held up a hand for silence, paused at the threshold to see if there was any activity in the corridor, and cautiously stepped through. He then made a quick sweep of the area, apparently found it safe, and gestured for the teens to follow him in.

Please, Zee, hang on, Sheen thought. *Just hang on, okay? I'm comin' to get you.*

Lips drawn tight in determination, she plunged through the doorway with Natsumi and Uwe at her heels.

16

Wherever it was they'd jumped to through Ana's magic portal, the place had absolutely some of the worst roads for high-speed driving, all ruts and pits and big rocks. If they hit one more major bump as bone-jarringly hard as the last one the van had bounced over, Pan was pretty sure she was gonna hurl.

She wasn't the only one who felt that way, it seemed. Looking around at her captors, it was apparent that the witch and a couple of the undead soldiers felt as queasy as she did, which came as a revelation. Who knew vampires could get carsick?

"Dalek, slow down!" Jenna barked at the driver. "We left those police cruisers a continent back, so take your damn foot off the accelerator and pull over before you drop us off a cliff."

Pan's eyebrows shot up. A continent back? She gazed at Javi, whose surprised expression matched hers. *Where the hell are we?* she mouthed silently. He shrugged. Wherever they were, based on the sunlight pouring through the windshield it appeared to be the middle of the day, which meant they'd jumped a few time zones from Pittsburgh. The vampires flinched at the brilliance but, unfortunately, didn't burst into flames. They reached into their utility belts for sunglasses and slipped them on.

"Sorry, Jenna," Dalek replied. He did as she'd ordered and the van immediately began decelerating. "I suppose I became a little too caught up in the chase."

Jenna laughed. "Are you certain you've never watched *The Fast and the Furious?*"

"Quite certain," he replied drolly as the van rolled to a halt. "And so we've arrived. Wherever that may be." He turned in his seat to frown at Ana.

"Hey, we needed an escape route," the witch snapped. "I got you to the island, didn't I? If you'd wanted me to take you to the front door, you should've gotten me the right coordinates."

Dalek grunted. "I suppose we're just lucky you didn't drop us in the middle of the Pacific Ocean."

"I'll drop *you* in the middle of the Pacific Ocean," Ana growled.

The Pacific? Pan glanced at Javi again. *Hawaii?* he mouthed. This time she was the one who shrugged.

"All right, children, that's enough," Jenna said sternly, then opened her door. "Everyone but Ana, out. She'll keep an eye on our guests while the rest of us take a look around. Hopefully there's a paved road close by that we can get on before we snap an axle."

Ana snarled at Pan and Javi. "Why am I the one who has to babysit these brats?"

Jenna regarded the witch through narrowed eyes, clearly not in the mood to have her orders questioned. "Because if the reports I've read are accurate, there are some rather large and deadly creatures roaming this island that might require us making a hasty exit. And since you're our resident transportation expert, it's safer for all of us if you're not the one who gets eaten."

Ana blanched. "Seriously?"

"Very," Jenna replied. Her lips peeled back in a predator's smile. "But talk back to me like that again, Stogryn, and I might be tempted to let them chew on you a bit. Are we clear?" She stepped from the vehicle without waiting for an answer.

"Yes, Commander," Ana mumbled.

The four soldiers lumbered out through the side door as the driver exited through his own. It was the tinkle of metal pieces lightly colliding as he departed that caught Pan's attention.

He'd left the keys in the ignition.

She looked at Javi; he'd heard it, too. But they couldn't just jump up and drive off while they had a witch babysitting them—considering how pissed off Ana appeared, she might turn them into newts or pigs or something.

That's when Pan noticed Javi motioning with his eyes, trying to direct her attention downward. She watched as he reached into one of his jean pockets and pulled out a small plastic tube: one of the Taser shells from the shotgun she'd appropriated back at the hospital. Pan smiled. She'd totally forgotten that he'd stuffed the cartridges in his pocket when he unloaded the weapon.

Javi tilted his head in Ana's direction, indicating he needed Pan to provide a distraction while he got the mini Taser ready. Pan nodded her understanding and slid around him, blocking the witch from seeing Javi's hands.

Ana was immediately on her guard. "Where do you think you're going?"

Pan flashed a totally insincere smile. "Nowhere. I'm not looking for any trouble. I was just getting cramped up sitting over there." Ana's response was a grunt, so Pan continued. "So where are we, exactly? I heard you guys talking about an island."

"It's called Halja's Island." Ana shrugged. "I don't know why."

"And where's that?" Pan gestured toward the empty driver's seat. The keys dangled invitingly from the ignition. "Dalek, there, mentioned the Pacific Ocean. Is it near Hawaii, or the Philippines, or something?"

"No. It's at a spot in the South Pacific called the Pole of Inaccessibility, or Point Nemo—you know, after that pirate from that old book."

"Captain Nemo? From *Twenty-thousand Leagues Under the Sea*?" Pan had read that Jules Verne novel back in seventh grade. Her parents had been pleased to see her reading something other than his old horror comics and porny romances that Sheen loaned her from her mom's massive collection. The fact that it was required reading for school had only made Dad the ex-teacher happier.

The Pole of Inaccessibility, though, sounded kinda familiar. Something she'd read . . . She shrugged mentally. It'd come to her eventually, probably when she wasn't thinking about it; that kinda thing happened to her all the time.

"I think that's the book," Ana said. "I never read it. Anyway, it's supposed to be the one spot in the entire world that's furthest from land. The nearest place is, like, sixteen hundred miles away." She paused. "I looked it up on Wikipedia."

Pan felt a tiny pressure near the base of her spine. Javi was gently poking her with his finger, letting her know he was ready to make his move.

"And why're we—" Pan's eyes widened in horror and she pointed over Ana's shoulder, toward the open side door. *"Oh, my God, what's that?"*

Ana spun around to see what had caught Pan's attention, no doubt fearing it was one of those witch-eating creatures her boss had mentioned. That was the moment when Javi slid around Pan and touched the mini Taser's metal contacts against Ana's neck, just above the collar of her jumpsuit. There was a small crackle of electricity, a sort of *glick* sound that Ana made with her mouth as her body convulsed under the 50,000-volt charge, and then she collapsed.

Javi tossed aside the spent shell and checked her pulse. He sighed with relief. "She's okay. But man, is she really gonna be pissed when she wakes up."

"Then let's make sure we're on the other side of the island when that happens."

"Off the island would be a whole lot better." Javi slid Ana's prone body over to the doorway, taking care to not set the van rocking as he moved her around.

"Yeah, well, we find Captain Nemo's *Nautilus* somewhere around here I'll race you to the gangplank. In the meantime . . ." Pan moved to a crouching position and inched her way to the front of the van, where she peeked around the driver's seat. She could see Jenna and her friend Dalek standing in the road about fifty yards ahead. The redhead was using her left hand like a cap visor to shield her eyes from the sun as she slowly pivoted from side to side, looking for that paved road. A check of the driver's side mirror showed the other soldiers split between road searching and scanning the countryside with their machine guns at the ready. Probably expecting some of Jenna's giant monsters to come lumbering by.

She turned back to Javi, who was gently sliding Ana from the van to the dirt track. "You ready?"

"What's the plan?" he asked, but Pan was already vaulting into the driver's seat. She started the ignition, threw the van into gear, and stomped down hard on the accelerator.

Javi laughed as he scrambled into the passenger seat. "Well, I like it so far. You sure you can drive this thing?"

Pan grinned. "Absolutely. Got my learner's permit a couple weeks ago."

He gave a half nod. "Good enough for me."

The van shot forward—straight at Jenna and Dalek. Pan made no effort to go around them. She really didn't want to run anybody over, even if they were a monster (except for Zaqiel, if she got the chance), but if it was a choice between playing chicken with vampires and becoming their next meal, then somebody better get out of her way if they didn't want to become roadkill. But hopefully it wouldn't come down to that.

"You sure you wanna be doing this?" Javi asked hesitantly.

Pan flashed a wicked smile. "Oh, yeah."

As she'd expected, Dalek yelped and dove to one side. But Jenna stayed right where she was . . . and unholstered the sidearm strapped to her hip.

Three bullets fired in rapid succession punched through the windshield inches from Pan's and Javi's ducking heads. Both teens screamed.

"Okay, *she* wins!" Pan said, and jerked the wheel hard to the left. The van crashed through the bushes lining the road—and plunged down a slope.

"Oops," Pan said with a grimace.

She didn't lose her cool, though. As bullets spanged off the van, as the vehicle sped down the hill—chewing up vegetation, kicking up rocks, and scaring the crap out of all kinds of weird-looking beasties—Pan swerved around trees and boulders with a skill that would have shocked her driving instructor back in Schriksdorp. It surprised Pan, too.

One final tree to avoid, and the van plowed through another row of shrubs before emerging onto a wide dirt track where Pan brought the vehicle to a halt.

"*Yeah!*" she cheered, her Cheshire-cat grin in full effect, and thrust her hands into the air in a gesture of triumph—only to have her fists slam into the low metal roof. "*Oww!* Damn it!"

She tucked her sore hands in her armpits and squeezed, as though that would alleviate the pain. The pressure only made her fingers ache worse, so she took her hands back out and started blowing on them. That didn't do much, either, but at least the cool air felt nice on her throbbing knuckles.

Despite the pain Pan giggled like an idiot, amazed by what she'd just pulled off. "Oh my God, that was about the insanest thing I've ever done"—she looked to Javi—"and, y'know, with my background, that's . . . saying . . ." Her voice trailed off.

Javi was staring at her in openmouthed astonishment.

"What?" she asked.

"Where'd you learn to drive like that? 'Cause that was . . ." He grinned, clearly impressed. "Wow. That was like straight outta a Jason Statham *Transporter* movie!"

She felt the blush burning her cheeks. "Thanks. Just don't ask me to parallel park 'cause I totally suck at it."

"I don't think you'll have to worry about that out here," he replied with a wave of his hand at the jungle around them. "Wherever here is."

"Well, Ana the Teenage Witch said it was called Halja's Island. You ever heard of it?"

He thought about it for a few seconds, then snapped his fingers as something came to mind. "Sure, I have. You did, too. Remember back at your dad's museum, when Annie was telling all of us the story about how she stopped Zaqiel from taking over the world? Halja's Island is where that big battle was fought."

"Oh, right." Pan glanced around the area and softly grunted. "Not much to look at, is it?"

"Only if you're into jungles." Javi shrugged. "I guess Tarzan wouldn't mind hanging out here."

"Or King Kong."

"Yeah," he said with a chuckle. "Look, we better get going before those vampires catch up. That witch is gonna be really angry about me using the Taser round on her, and we know she can track us by following the spear."

"Where to?"

Javi looked through the windshield. The dirt track continued fairly straight for a couple hundred yards or so, then ran across a wide clearing before continuing back into the jungle. To the left-hand side, a few miles away, was a smoldering volcano that rose high above the trees. "I don't think we wanna go there . . ." He looked to the right and spotted what appeared to be a group of stone towers in the distance. "How about that temple or castle or whatever it is? Maybe there's somebody there we can ask about getting off the island. Or at least about getting in touch with the Knights."

"Somebody who isn't a monster," Pan replied. The pain in her fingers had lessened enough for her to grab the steering wheel again, so she got the van rolling.

"Somebody who's not a monster—on *this* island? Don't get your hopes up too high, Cookie. For all we know, me and you are the only humans in this whole place."

"Hey, my therapists have always told me to think positively, especially in the crappiest situation. Finding a non-monster inhabitant on the island from *Lost* might be a dream, but it's *my* dream."

"Fair enough," Javi said.

Pan reached over to give his arm a gentle squeeze. "It's gonna be okay, Javi. I know things are bad, but it's all gonna work out in the end. You'll see: Annie'll take care of Zaqiel, Mom'll turn back to normal, and the whole monster revolution thing'll be smacked down for good."

From the corner of her eye, she caught his skeptical expression. "You really believe that?"

Pan smiled wistfully, an image of Mom returned to full health appearing in her mind's eye. "I do. I have to. Otherwise what am I gonna do—sit in a corner and cry? I did a lifetime's worth of crying all those years I thought I was crazy, and I'm done. Now I'm all about the happily-ever-afters—even if I have to fight for them."

This time she caught him smiling. "Well, if you need any help with that . . ."

"Thanks."

They drove along in silence as the van rumbled into the clearing, until Pan decided to voice a question that had been lurking in the back of her mind since they'd arrived on Halja's Island.

"Hey, Javi, let me ask you something: If the big monster powwow is being held in Japan, why did the vampires want to come here?"

He thought about it for a few seconds, then shrugged. "Don't know."

"Me, either. I mean, it's gotta have something to do with Zaqiel, especially if this is where he had his last battle. Right?"

"Makes sense." Javi stared into space for a few seconds, considering possibilities. "Maybe he's coming here to pick up where he left off. After all, isn't this where Annie said the other fallen angels were locked up? He came here the last time to try and free them, only Annie stopped him."

Pan sucked in a breath through clenched teeth. "Crap. I forgot that part of her story."

"So yeah, maybe they're having a big conference in Japan, but now I'm figuring it's only a matter of time before everybody shows up on this island, to get the ball rolling again."

Pan grimaced. "That would totally suck. We're in enough trouble already just being stuck here with a bunch of gun-toting vampires and nobody knowing where to find us. I don't need that jackass and his armies of darkness making things worse."

Was that true, though? As she stole a glance at the rearview mirror's reflection of her messenger bag lying on the floor of the van—the bag containing the Spear of Longinus—Pan had to wonder if Zaqiel's coming here wouldn't be a blessing in disguise. It would certainly give her an opportunity to put the weapon to use . . .

Javi took notice of her behavior. "You think he needs the spear to help him take over the world?"

Pan shook her head. "I don't think so . . ."

"Then what's it for?"

A memory flashed into her thoughts: Mom lying on the street in front of the museum, apparently dead. Pan standing over her, surrounded by vampires. The Spear of Longinus clutched in the teen's hands as she snarled at the fallen angel who'd just fed on her mother.

"Put it down, child," Zaqiel commanded with a nod toward the spear. "Otherwise I promise your death shall be an agonizing one."

But it wasn't the tone of his voice that had caught her attention; it was the way he'd stared at the ancient weapon that had formerly resided in his chest cavity.

He was afraid of it.

And why not? It had been the means of his destruction a century ago. The thought of being impaled on it a second time probably—no, definitely made him come close to soiling his pants.

So why bring it to this island, then? Weren't all the vampire clans supposed to be falling in line behind their great angelic master? If so, and Zaqiel was coming here, then having it within any proximity of him was the last thing any of them should want to do. Unless . . .

"Listen," Pan said. "What if there's some kinda division in the vampire ranks about Zaqiel coming back from the dead?"

"You mean, like, some of them were happy with the way things were and now they're pissed 'cause he's messing everything up?"

"No, I'm thinking it's more like a power-play thing. All the clans probably had their own plans for ruling the world—that's what that whole 'prize' search was about, wasn't it? They thought they were looking for some kinda doomsday weapon or something they could use."

"Like the Ultimate Nullifier in the Fantastic Four comics."

"Is that a doomsday thingy?"

Javi nodded. "Oh, yeah."

Pan shrugged. "Okay, I don't know that one—but yeah, probably just like that. Only it turned out it wasn't a weapon, it was Zaqiel, which totally screwed up everybody's plans. 'Cause you know the first thing he was gonna do was re-establish his leadership and set out to finish what he started."

"Take over the world, himself."

"Right. Except he totally sucked at trying to do it the last time and wound up getting his head chopped off by Annie. So I wouldn't think him coming back and getting in everybody's faces would make him too popular with all the clan leaders . . . like House Karnstein's, for instance."

"So the reason their soldiers came after the spear is . . . ?"

" 'Cause they want to own the one known way of killing him."

"You mean, let him do all the heavy lifting of leading the monster armies and winning the war, and then take him out with the spear so they can run the world?"

"Exactly!"

Javi paused to consider it. "That actually makes sense."

Pan rolled her eyes. "Of course it makes sense. It's, like, basic bad-guy psychology. If you were Doctor Doom or, I don't know, Lex Luthor or the Joker . . . well, probably not the Joker, he's just a straight-up sociopath—but wouldn't you be thinking the same way?"

"Yeah," Javi replied slowly. He gazed at her, clearly impressed by her deductive reasoning. "Uh . . . don't take this the wrong way, okay? 'Cause I mean it as a compliment. But you're a whole lot . . . deeper than most of the girls I've dated."

"What? You mean up to this point you only admired me 'cause of my incredible beauty? That's sexist!" Pan grinned at her forwardness. Must be that power-of-positive-thinking preaching she'd been doing . . . or maybe there was something in the South Seas air. Whatever the source, she liked this more confident version of herself.

"I am an Artichoke of Knowledge!" she declared proudly. "Peel back all these layers of makeup and underneath you'll find a giant brain that's awesome at figuring out stuff."

"Wouldn't I have to peel back all the skin and muscles, too? And, like, pry your skull open?"

Pan laughed. "*Now* you're talking my kinda language."

"I'm learning," Javi said with a smile.

The van plunged into the jungle on the far side of the clearing, bound for the temple—and whatever dangers might lie ahead.

Much to her surprise, Pan found she was okay with that.

17

Annie, on the other hand, was not okay *at all* with the treatment she'd been receiving from her captors.

Her ribs still ached from the beating Lady Sasaki's minions had given her a half hour ago, and would continue to ache for some time, but she had managed to realign her dislocated left shoulder by slamming it a few times against the stone wall behind her. The cuts and bruises that speckled her face and body, however, were going to hurt for quite some time. The bottom line, though, was that at least she was still alive . . . for now.

Thank heaven for small favors, Annie thought sarcastically, and shifted her position on the rough wooden planks that served as a makeshift bunk. *Now if only I could get a decent mattress . . .*

She halfheartedly rattled her chains for what was probably the hundredth time, to check their strength. They were still as solidly bolted to the wall, still as unbreakable, as they had been five minutes ago. Annie sighed. On a normal day she would have shape-shifted into any number of forms to slip out of her bonds, but her supernatural gifts had been shut down by Frau Trude, a centuries-old German witch with a passion for turning children into firewood on cold winter days, and an obsession with candy-scented perfumes. The air in the cell was still heavy with the odor of peppermint, from the last time Trude had checked on her charge.

Still, Annie might be powerless but she wasn't helpless; her body might be battered, but her spirit hadn't been broken. And as for her captivity . . . well, this wasn't the first time she'd been locked away in a musty dungeon—she'd lost count of the jails and prisons she'd been a "guest" of during the past four centuries—so being chained to a wall in an abandoned temple (the etchings around her had clued her in to that) didn't concern her. Not as much as she was concerned by the location of her current predicament.

Halja's Island: discovered in 1616 by Dutch explorer Willem Schouten during his voyage across the South Pacific in search of new trade routes, but named by a German crewman in dubious honor of the mythological goddess of hell. The moment Annie had recovered from the catatonic spell one of Zaqiel's other magick wielders had cast in Japan to keep her quiet, she'd known exactly where she was: the last place on Earth she wanted to be. The last place on Earth she wanted *Zaqiel* to be.

But honestly, where else would he have gone after his resurrection? This was not only the site of his greatest defeat—at her hands, no less—it was also the source of his greatest pain. For it was here that the Almighty had banished His rebellious creations, His fallen angels, for their crimes against man and God. Only Lucifer— whose insane jealousy of humanity and mad desire to become a god in his own right had inspired the acts later committed by Zaqiel and his brothers—had been fortunate enough to escape similar punishment, and that was only because hell needed a building manager and Lucifer had ably demonstrated to his celestial employer that he was the perfect candidate. Lucifer's followers, however, were quickly forgotten as the lord of the underworld settled in to his new job—and continued his own dreams of destroying humanity, though in far subtler ways.

But God didn't forget. And He didn't forgive. Deep beneath this island, sealed up in a chamber, were His traitorous children—sentenced to experience unrelenting torment until the last days of the universe.

Until one of them had managed to escape, that is.

Two centuries ago, Zaqiel broke free and endeavored to right what he considered a great wrong. He traveled the globe, raising an army of monsters, and returned to the island with the intention of freeing his brothers, with the added bonus of unleashing a veritable hell on earth. And if it hadn't been for Annie and her own forces he might well have succeeded . . .

But that's all in the past, she reminded herself, *so there's no point in dwelling on it. Not when I can dwell on even* bigger *problems, like what I'm going to do to stop my crazy ex this time. Not disposing of Zaqiel's body after I'd killed him probably ranks as the dumbest thing I've ever done . . . well,* one *of the dumbest things I've ever done. In the top three, at the very least. If I hadn't been so softhearted—not to mention soft*headed*—as to still feel pity for him after all that chaos, the legend of a supernatural superweapon would never have started, I wouldn't have had to constantly move his remains from place to place so no one could find them, the vampire clans wouldn't have spent the better part of two centuries searching for them . . . and David Zwieback wouldn't have ended up buying them for his museum. And then Zaqiel wouldn't have been revived . . . or Karen turned . . . or Pandora killed . . .*

Annie sighed. *Isadora's right: I* do *need some time off. I've been so completely off my game recently it's a miracle I haven't been killed—permanently.* She smiled wistfully. *"Go find yourself a man," Izzy said. Well, I did think about asking David out for a drink, considering he and Karen are divorced, but after seeing how emotional David became when I brought Karen into the hospital, you'd have to be thickheaded not to realize he's still deeply in love with her . . . and I'm happy for them. Maybe there's a chance they can reconcile, if only for Pandora's sake. And a chance to help her come to terms with what she might become . . .*

The blasting concerned Annie, too. Every so often the walls had trembled from the vibrations of underground detonations; it had been going on for hours. A tunnel being cleared, she guessed. She had a strong belief as to where it might lead, and that worried her far more than being chained up in a dungeon.

The scrape of a key in the cell door lock interrupted her thoughts, and House Orlock's representatives entered. Elden, his sharply tailored Hugo Boss suit thoroughly out of place with the island's jungle setting, was the first in, as befitted his station as leader. His sidekicks, the African Noureddine and the Russian Alexi, weren't far behind.

Annie slowly swung her legs off the bunk, gritting her teeth against the pain that flared in her lower back, and sat up. "Oh, I see. Kiyoshi's thugs wore out their arms knocking me around, so now you three get a turn." She leaned to one side in an effort to see past the trio. "Is there some queue out in the hall I should be aware of?"

"Sorry, just us three." A trace of a smile curled the edges of Elden's lips. "Of course, that isn't to say there wouldn't be one forming up if Zaqiel offered everyone the chance to dole out some payback for all the troubles you've caused over the centuries. You're not very popular with . . . well, with pretty much every living creature in monsterdom, you know."

Annie rattled her chains. "I've heard rumors . . . ," she replied with a knowing smile. "So, why are you here, then? I would have thought you three had better things to do with your time. I mean, being the clotheshorse he is, I'm sure by now Zaqiel has a closetful of boots in need of a good licking. Don't let me keep you from your duties."

Perhaps mouthing off to her captors wasn't the smartest approach, given her current nonpowered status, but Annie had never been one to show fear to any monster. In fact, she firmly believed *they* should be fearing *her* . . . even when, as in this case, they had the advantage—for now.

Alexi snarled, clearly annoyed by her remark; Noureddine, though, seemed amused by his friend's reaction. Elden grinned and looked over his shoulder at the Russian, then held out his left hand. Alexi grunted, dug into his left trouser pocket, and extracted a handful of crumpled euro banknotes. He thrust a pair of hundreds into Elden's hand.

"What was the bet?" Annie asked.

Elden slid the bills into his jacket's breast pocket. "Alexi was certain that House Otoyo's brutes would have broken your spirit by now; I thought otherwise."

"And now I've made you two hundred euros richer." Annie held out a hand. "So where's my cut?"

Noureddine's eyebrows rose in surprise and he leaned toward his boss. "She's rather brash for someone in her position, isn't she?" he asked quietly.

"I've noticed," Elden muttered. "I'm beginning to think those beatings from House Otoyo made her even stronger-willed."

Annie cleared her throat with a loud *a-hem*. "You *do* know I can hear you."

"Bah! House Otoyo interrogators are crap," Alexi said. "*I* could break her spirit."

"Really." Annie flashed a wicked smile. "Care to bet on that?"

"Another time, perhaps," Elden interjected. "To answer your earlier question, the reason we're here is because His Majesty, the great, wise, and wonderful First Reborn Zaqiel, demands your presence."

Annie's eyebrows rose a touch. Elden's tone in reference to his master had an unmistakable ring of disrespect to it. *So then I wasn't wrong about Zaqiel's poor status among monsterkind, back at his coming out party in Yokohama. It's not just Dracula who's unhappy about his return, apparently it's the other houses as well. I wonder if Zaqiel is aware of this . . .* Mentally, she rolled her eyes. *No, of course he's aware of it, he just doesn't give a damn. That ego of his is so large he won't even consider the possibility that his "children" might turn against him if his plans fall apart again. Idiot.*

"Now just stay where you are and don't move," Elden ordered. "We're going to remove those shackles. If you try to escape . . ."

"You'll bore me with another clichéd threat?" she asked archly.

Elden frowned. Clearly her resistance to playing the frightened victim, compounded by her insistence on needling her enemies, was wearing extremely thin with him. *Probably has a lot to do with Zaqiel using him as an errand boy, too,* she thought. *Still, after helping him win that bet you'd think he'd ease off the death stare he's giving me. Some people just don't know the meaning of gratitude . . .*

Annie sighed melodramatically and held out her hands. Noureddine walked over with a small key ring in one hand—one key had no doubt been used to open the cell door, the other now came into play to unlock her manacles. The blocky iron bracelets fell away—to be replaced, vampire-fast in a flash of bright-new metal, by a pair of heavy-duty handcuffs that clicked around her wrists.

Annie sniffed disdainfully. "Well, at least they go with my earrings." Then she stood and purposefully strode toward the door, taking charge of the situation before Elden could order her around. The vampire and his burly Russian companion appeared to be surprised by her dominant attitude, and automatically stepped aside to let her pass before it dawned on them that she was supposed to be their prisoner. Normally Annie would have taken pleasure in her enemies' discomfiture, but at the moment she was biting down lightly on the inside of her lower lip as a way to distract her mind from focusing on the sore ribs she'd acquired from her sessions with Kiyoshi's minions. As she'd learned from all those previous dungeon experiences, showing weakness in front of one's guards was the equivalent of spilling blood into the ocean: the scent always drew the hungriest—and deadliest—predators.

Still, she hadn't the slightest idea where she was going. She'd been unconscious when she'd been transported to the island, and when she'd last been here almost two hundred years ago the temple—if it was the *same* temple—had been a mild curiosity spotted along the way to preventing Zaqiel's rescue attempt; with the world at stake there'd been no time for sightseeing. And after the battle, her only thoughts had been about getting off the island.

"Do you even know where you're going?" Elden asked from close behind her.

Busted. Annie came to a halt at an intersection of corridors. The ache in her ribs was flaring sharply and she was grateful for the respite. She twisted the pained expression on her face into a fierce snarl and turned to face her captors. "I'd imagine we're going wherever Zaqiel is. Knowing him, there's probably a throne room or a high priest's quarters on one of the upper floors that he's claimed as his."

"Right you are," Elden replied. He smiled condescendingly. "And that would be . . . where, exactly?"

Annie closed her eyes and concentrated. She might not be able to shape-shift or heal her injuries, but she could still sense Zaqiel's presence. *The echoes of love gone wrong?* she wondered. *Or is it just that there's so much anger radiating from his soul I can separate him from the darkness of an island full of monsters? Probably somewhere between the two.*

She opened her eyes and nodded toward a stone staircase at the end of one hall. "This way," she replied, and set off with her entourage in tow.

Yet despite the brave face she was putting on, Annie wasn't looking forward to her reunion with Zaqiel. Her lack of powers not only made her boringly normal, they made her extremely vulnerable. Zaqiel, on the other hand, was at the height of his angelic strength, and would take the greatest pleasure in loosening some of her teeth for old times' sake. But if he was expecting her to just stand there and take it while he tried to impress his sycophants . . . well, she wasn't the only one who'd come out of the encounter bruised and bleeding.

If she survived that long . . .

"What do you mean 'he's in a meeting'?" Elden asked testily as he waved a hand toward the set of golden doors at the far end of the makeshift reception area that House Otoyo had erected on the temple's top floor. "He's the one who ordered us to go fetch his girlfriend in the first place!"

"*Ex*-girlfriend," Annie stressed.

Head still tilted down toward the laptop computer that rested on a glass tabletop, fingers paused above the keyboard, the House Otoyo receptionist looked up at the vampire from the tops of her black eyes. "So I understand. Be that as it may, Lord Zaqiel is in the middle of a discussion with Lady Sasaki and her advisers and does not wish to be disturbed." She gestured toward a carpeted area on which a sofa, a coffee table topped with a selection of magazines, and a pair of comfy guest chairs had been set up. "Just take a seat. I will let you know when he is available."

"Who the hell puts a bloody waiting room in a jungle temple?" Elden asked.

"Just. take. a seat," the receptionist slowly repeated.

"Unbelievable," Elden said in exasperation. He turned to Annie and his sidekicks. "I guess we're taking a seat."

The quartet ambled over to the waiting area. Annie flopped down on the couch, with Alexi and Noureddine crowding her in on both sides; the latter grabbed a dog-eared *GQ* magazine and slowly flipped through it. Elden genteelly sat in one of the guest chairs, crossed his legs, and brushed dirt off one pant leg. Then he leaned back, closed his eyes, sighed, and muttered, "Ridiculous."

Annie looked around the room. The architecture reminded her of temples she'd seen in Southeast Asia; not quite Angkor Wat in Cambodia or My Son in Vietnam, but similar—right down to the birds nesting on the ceiling columns and the vines and trees growing in abundance inside the structure. Nature reasserting its dominance, *Life After People*-style. Untold centuries ago this top floor had been the entrance to the throne room of some now-forgotten island leader. It must have looked magnificent in its day, but as with the rest of the temple, time and weather had worn down its stone walls and soaring columns along with the ornate sculptures that loomed everywhere: representations of nightmarish creatures whose names were all too familiar to her but would never be spoken aloud—let sleeping elder gods lie, and all that.

House Otoyo, though, seemed less interested in admiring the artistry of ancient stonemasons and metalsmiths and more with bringing the remote location into the twenty-first century. It wasn't just office furniture they'd moved in, there were laptops and tablets and lamps in abundance, and industrial-level power cords that stretched across the leaf-strewn floor and out one of the windows; from somewhere down below the jungle echoed with the roar of generators.

All the conveniences of home, Annie thought. *Either Kiyoshi has had this setup in the works for some time, or she's more of a taskmaster than I realized. To have all this done in just a few days' time would be remarkable . . . loathe as I am to give her credit for being anything other than a monster worth destroying.*

Beside her, Alexi grunted in surprise. Annie looked over to find him staring at his cell phone; displayed on its screen was a Twitter page.

"They have Wi-Fi here?" Annie asked in surprise.

"*Da.* Lady Sasaki had them put cell phone towers on the roof." The Russian began typing on the keypad—not an easy task, given the thickness of his thumbs.

Annie's eyebrows rose. "Since when do vampires Tweet?"

Alexi ignored her, his concentration solely focused on updating his Twitter feed.

Annie frowned. "You know, it's rude to do that when someone's speaking to you."

"I could always shut you up, then," he rumbled softly—while still typing away.

"You could try," she replied evenly, "but then your followers would get to see what your death-cry looks like in a hundred and forty characters."

On her other side, Noureddine snorted a laugh as Alexi gave the huntress a mean side-eye.

"You're one tough bird, aren't you?" Noureddine asked Annie.

"Ask House Karnstein how tough I am," she replied. "They got to experience it firsthand a few nights ago."

He nodded. "Yeah, I heard about that attack on your home. Took out an entire squad of elites in under ten minutes, from what I understand."

"Under five." She turned back to Alexi and stage-whispered, "They didn't even have time to scream."

That got Alexi to stop Tweeting.

Annie smiled wolfishly at her captors. What she'd said hadn't been entirely true—it had definitely taken longer than five minutes for the battle that had torn apart her town house, and she'd taken a few rounds in the chest from a submachine gun before she could finish off the team leader—but it sounded good. And it *had* gotten the Russian's attention.

"Well . . . ," Elden said slowly, "that's certainly a conversation killer."

The Gothic Lolita receptionist stepped out from behind her desk to address the group. "The First Reborn will see you now."

"How big of him," Annie grumbled as she rose to her feet.

The receptionist escorted them to the golden doors, knocked softly, then pushed open both to usher the quartet inside.

Lady Sasaki's twenty-first-century decorative touches, Annie noted as she stepped past the threshold, had spread into the throne room as well, punctuated by a mission control setup complete with computers, plasma screens, and three-dimensional projected maps of the temple and its belowground levels. A power company's worth of cables snaked across this floor as well, all leading out another window and, presumably, down to more generators. And standing in the center of it all, looking like the epitome of a man overwhelmed by the technological complexities of the modern age, was Zaqiel. His gaze traveled across the images on three of the screens—a mountainous creature lumbering through the jungle some miles away, a crew of hard-hat-wearing workers assembled around an immense boring machine that was used to drill tunnels, a gigantic red spider closing in on a troll that had been stupid enough to get caught in its web—and Zaqiel shook his head, obviously impressed by two centuries' worth of advances made by the very humans he desired to exterminate. Not that such marvels would prevent him from unleashing hell on earth, of course.

His right-hand women, on the other hand, were thoroughly at home with their electronic accessories. Miyuki Sasaki reclined on a black chaise longue, attention riveted on a cell phone in her hands, thumbs skipping lightly across the keypad. She paused to giggle at something that appeared on her screen, then resumed tapping away. Miyuki's sister, Kiyoshi, was far more focused on running the ship. The clan leader barked orders into the Bluetooth headset clipped to her left ear as she fiddled with the screen of her tablet, calling up some graphic Annie couldn't see. Whatever it indicated, it appeared to please Kiyoshi, who turned to Zaqiel.

"The foreman at the main site reports success, my lord. The doors have been reached, and the workers are in the process of clearing the area. It seems the last round of executions you ordered . . . inspired the Mole People to double their efforts."

Annie frowned. Tunnel blasting that led to a set of doors meant only one thing: Zaqiel finally had access to God's subterranean prison for misbehaving celestials. But now came the million-dollar question: Find a way to stop him from opening those doors—unlikely, given the odds against her and the fact his people had already made it to the chamber—or allow Zaqiel to get inside and seal him up with his brothers? That might be doable. Either way, she'd have to wait for an opportunity to present itself.

She still preferred killing him, though. But that, too, required an opening to come along. For now, all she could do was stare daggers at his back.

Zaqiel must have felt them poking his spine because he turned to face her, a sly smile curling the edges of his lips. Kiyoshi's lips also curled, but in the form of an unpleasant frown.

"Sebastienne," he purred. "You're looking well."

"Despite the best efforts of your hangers-on," Annie replied, with a rancid smile directed at Lady Sasaki. "So why am I here, Zaqiel? Did you want to show me something, or did you just need a sounding board? If that's the case, if you're looking for someone to stroke your ego"—she nodded toward Kiyoshi—"go talk to your new girlfriend. I'm certain she'll be happy to do it." *Probably right before she drives a stake through your heart so she can rule alone,* she added to herself.

"Becoming jealous in your old age, my love?" Zaqiel asked.

"What, of you? Oh, please." Annie glanced around the room. "I'm not the one who's related to just about everyone in here, Mr. First Reborn. The thought that I'd be jealous of your being desired by your 'children' is actually a bit stomach-turning." She paused. "No, it's a *lot* stomach-turning."

Zaqiel bared his teeth. The rest of the monsters looked discomfited by the mental image Annie had provided—with the exception of Kiyoshi. It was apparent to anyone who observed her even for the briefest time that Zaqiel held no sexual attraction for her. The power over monsterdom that he possessed, on the other hand . . .

"Getting back to my question," Annie continued, "I imagine you had me brought here so I could witness your latest triumph."

"Something like that," the angel muttered.

"So a sounding board, then."

Zaqiel smiled coldly. "Of course. When this world falls and humanity is being wiped from existence, who better to listen to their death screams than you, my love?"

Jesus wept . . . , Annie thought. She hid a nervous chill by gesturing at the plasma screen that displayed the giant borer. "But why dig a tunnel? Why not just use the entrance on the volcano, like you tried on your last attempt?" She'd considered saying *your last* failed *attempt*, but decided it would be best to not push him too far. Not until she regained her powers.

"The volcano has been active in recent years," Kiyoshi explained. "That 'entrance' was an old lava tube that has since come into use. The Mole People's archivists, however, located records of a passageway three miles from this temple that had collapsed centuries ago. A passageway that leads right to the doors of the angels' prison."

"My lady," said a male tech seated near Kiyoshi. "I apologize for the interruption, but the perimeter alarm in sector five has been triggered."

Zaqiel grunted. "Another of the beasts roaming this island?"

"I do not think so, my lord," the tech slowly replied as he checked the information now appearing on his screen. "It's something smaller than those, and metallic. Some kind of transport, maybe?"

"Stop speculating, imbecile, and activate the camera in that sector!" Kiysohi barked.

The frightened tech jumped in his seat. "Immediately, my lady! I apologize for my . . ." His voice trailed off as he realized he should just shut up and concentrate on his task. His fingers fumbled their way across the laptop's keyboard as he accessed the video feed from whichever camera was located near the security breach and transferred it to one of the oversized plasma screens.

The image of the troll who was about to become a snack for the mammoth spider broke apart into static, to be replaced by a picture of a scratched and dented van as it entered the clearing around the temple.

"Who is this, now?" Zaqiel asked. Annie wondered the same thing. And if Zaqiel had no idea who the newcomers were, then there was hope—however slim—that it could be someone looking for her. Someone who could provide a distraction while she scrounged up a weapon that she could use to put the angel down for good . . .

She glanced around, but all she saw were electronic devices, useful only if she planned to beat Zaqiel to death with a laptop—and that would take too long. *Some temple this is. You'd think* someone *would have left behind a sacrificial blade or a rusted sword, but apparently the temple priests were too tidy for that.*

On the screen, the van slowed to a halt just inside the edge of the clearing. Who could it be? Her son Alexander was a smart kid; he would have known that Zaqiel's next move after rallying the troops in Japan would be traveling to Halja's Island to free his brothers. The only complication would be in getting the Vatican's approval to launch a mission. Not that Alexander would take no for an answer, even from the pope; not when family was involved.

Annie smiled wistfully. Thinking of her eldest child as a kid continually struck her as being absurdly funny, yet it was the undeniable truth. He might be in his sixties, now, but he'd always be her baby. *Then again, when you're as old as I am, almost* everyone *is a child . . .*

Her smile quickly faded, though, as the van's driver and passenger doors opened and out stepped . . . Pandora and Javier.

"Oh, my God . . . ," Annie whispered.

18

"Wow. Now *that's* what I call a temple," Javi said. "Hey, didn't they use this place for the first *Mortal Kombat* movie?"

"Never saw it." Pan gazed at the ancient stone towers as she adjusted the shoulder strap of her messenger bag. There might be no need for it, but she wanted the spear handy, just in case any trouble popped up. The mace that had been jangling alongside it in the bag was now in Javi's possession. Together, they were ready for anything. Maybe.

"You think anybody's home?" she asked.

"I think the better question is, do we *want* anybody to be home? I mean, since those vampire commandos we swiped the van from were coming to this island in the first place, you gotta figure they've got other vampire buddies waiting for them. Or maybe something even *worse* than vampires."

"Like . . . Zaqiel's already here?"

"Uh-huh. Him and the rest of Monster Nation. And what's the best place for them to hang out in? That temple over there. You see those things?" He pointed at a trio of large metal boxes that rested on towable bases. Thick black cables snaked out from the boxes, up the walls of the temple, and into a few windows on each floor. "Those are heavy-duty generators, like the ones my dad sometimes rents for his construction jobs. That means somebody's already set up in there—a lot of somebody's, if they need that much power. Maybe a whole vampire army, y'think?"

Pan sighed. "Y'know, before all this angels-and-demons crap started complicating my life, the thought of a vampire army taking over the world would've had me squeeing like a total fangirl. But now that I know it's all real . . . well, it's just another pain in my ass I have to deal with. Kinda takes some of the fun outta the whole love-of-horror thing, y'know?"

Javi nodded. "Yeah, I can see that."

"I'll get over it, though," she replied. "I *did* say 'some of the fun,' after all. No stupid angel's gonna ruin an entire genre for me." Not when she had so many good memories of experiencing monster fandom with her parents and her friends. "So how come you didn't think of what we might run into the whole time I was driving us here?" she added with a playful smile. Of course, she wasn't about to tell him that *she* should have thought of something like that herself.

Javi coyly looked away. "I don't know," he mumbled. "I guess I was kinda distracted."

Did he just blush? He totally did! It made sense, though. She'd caught him stealing glances at her when he thought she didn't notice, so that was probably what had been "distracting" him. Given how often he looked her way she must have made for a pleasant distraction. Obviously.

Obviously? thought Pan, surprised at the notion. *Wow. This new positive attitude thing is really taking hold, isn't it? And . . . I'm really kinda liking it . . .*

"So what do you wanna do?" Javi asked. "Get back in the van and look somewhere else?"

Pan shrugged. "I don't really know where else we *could* go, but hanging around here is definitely a bad idea. Eventually somebody's gonna notice us." She pulled her cell phone from her jeans pocket and held it up. "But it's not like we could call anybody for . . . help . . ." Her voice trailed away as she stared at the phone's lit screen. "That's weird. I've got a signal," she said in disbelief.

"What?" Javi dug out his own to check. "Huh. Me, too."

Pan's first instinct was to call Dr. Carlyle to find out the conditions of her parents, and let Dad know she was all right, but then she reconsidered. Even if Dad were just nursing a bump on his head, informing him that his little girl was on the run from vampires on the other side of the planet would only make things worse, because then he'd get all stressed out with worry. So, maybe it was best to hold off on that call.

"This is crazy," Javi said. "How can there be cell phone service on an island in the middle of nowhere?"

Pan made a quick inspection of the temple, her gaze sweeping over it from bottom to top. She located what she half-expected to find on the roof. "Those look like cell towers," she said, pointing at a row of metal cylinders. "You think we could call somebody for help?"

"Couldn't hurt to try. Maybe they've got cops here, or something."

Pan shook her head. "Doubt it. And even if there were island cops, they'd probably be working for the vampires. How about Alexander—you've got his number, right?"

Javi grimaced. "Yeah, but my dad would probably rip my head off when he got the long-distance bill."

"Better your dad rips it off than some monster, right?" As he nodded in agreement, she continued. "And besides, I think stopping a worldwide monster takeover kinda ranks as more important than blowing up your family's cell plan." She smiled. "Hey, maybe your dad can convince the phone company to give him a world-saver discount when the bill comes in. But, y'know, only . . ."

"Only if there's still a world left to save? Yeah, I see where you're going with that." Javi sighed. "I'm gonna be paying my dad off for this bill the rest of my life, I just know it . . ." Nevertheless, he accessed his phone's contact list and pressed Alexander's number. "Okay, it's ringing . . ." He grunted. "Crap. It went to voice mail."

"Well, leave him a message," Pan said hurriedly.

"I know, I know." He paused to listen to Alexander's greeting, then: "Alex! Hey, it's Javi. Listen, me and Pan—"

"Pan and I," she interjected, then mouthed *Sorry* for interrupting him. Correcting her friends' grammatical errors was something she'd picked up from her father, the former English teacher—not that Pan was the queen of proper diction or anything. She made just as many mistakes.

Javi waved a hand to signal it was okay. "Pan and *I* got kidnapped by those vampire commandos from the church and taken to this place called Halja's Island—"

"It's at the Pole of Inaccessibility!" Pan blurted out as she leaned in close to the phone. Just trying to be helpful. Javi winked at her. "Yeah, what Pan said. You probably heard about this place from Annie—it's where she mixed it up with Zaqiel last time."

The Pole of Inaccessibility. There was something about that name that kept nagging at her. Had she come across it in a short story, or a novel? A comic book, maybe? It was definitely in something she'd read. Pan knew it would come to her eventually, but the waiting around for her memory to kick in was *so* annoying.

All thoughts of mysterious global positions were cast aside, however, as she suddenly realized just how close she was standing next to Javi—like, right on top of him. With her hands resting on his chest.

Pan grinned, ignoring the blush she felt warming her cheeks. To hell with embarrassment, she thought. This felt . . . really nice.

Javi smiled and wrapped his free arm around her shoulders. "Look, Alex, you think you could get Natsumi to come pick us up? We got away from the vampires, but it looks like they were coming to a meeting, so that must mean— Hello? Hello?" He lowered the phone to glance at the screen. "I think the voice mail cut me off." He shrugged and put the phone away. "But at least we got to tell him where we are, so that's good. Now all we gotta do is wait for him to call back."

"Just not right here," Pan added.

Javi nodded. "Definitely."

As it turned out, there was someone else who also thought waiting in front of the temple for a callback wasn't such a good idea.

"KIDS! KIDS—GET OUT OF HERE!"

It took her a couple of seconds to recognize the speaker, but then Pan looked to Javi. "That sounds like—"

"Annie!" And once he'd said it aloud, Javi did exactly the same thing Pan knew she would have done in his position: he moved toward the temple.

But knowing it and doing it were two completely different actions, and given the potential danger they were facing, Pan latched onto his arm before he could get five steps away from the van. "Javi, wait!"

"That was Annie! We gotta go help her!"

He tried to pull away and she tightened her grip. "I know that, but what're you gonna do—run through a gauntlet of who-knows-what's creeping around in there to get to her? What good's it gonna do Annie if some monster's gnawing on your skull?"

"But I can see her! She's right there!" He pointed to a window at the top floor of the temple. Although she couldn't make out faces from this distance—maybe Javi had better eyesight—Pan could still see three people struggling. It looked as though two men were trying to pull her back inside, but Annie was putting up one hell of a fight to keep her position.

"GO, DAMN IT!" she yelled at the teens.

Javi tried to bolt for the temple steps, but Pan hung on and dug in her heels.

"Javi, listen. Us getting killed by just charging in isn't gonna do anything to help Annie. Remember what you told me back at the museum, when I wanted to go rescue Mom? About how being smart is knowing when's a good time to fight?"

"I remember you ignoring all of that and going anyway," he said, his gaze focused on that upper window.

Pan rolled her eyes. "Okay, so I was wrong and you were totally right. You're still right. I don't wanna leave Annie here, but you and me and a van and the spear—it's not enough. We need help."

Javi had no comeback for that—how could he? Pan knew she was making sense, and so did he. He stopped resisting . . . but then started to slowly retreat. "Uh. . . remember what you said about monsters chewing on our skulls?" He nodded toward the base of the temple.

Pan looked past him and gasped.

A quintet of the most feral dogs Pan had ever seen had gathered on the top steps outside the main entrance. The pack was held back by leather leashes gripped by two whatevers wearing dark blue robes. The deep shadows of their drawn-up hoods made it impossible to tell if there were humans or monsters in there, but considering both handlers stood perhaps seven or eight feet tall, Pan was leaning more toward the latter. The dogs were just as sizable, much taller than the average canine and bulkier, like mutant Irish wolfhounds, with coarse, rust-colored fur that stood out in tufts like porcupine quills. The low-decibel growls they directed at the teens made it evident they weren't here for belly rubs and playing fetch.

"Those are some really big dogs," Javi muttered.

"I don't think they're regular dogs," Pan said. "I think they're probably . . . I don't know, hellhounds, maybe? I mean, who'd be better at guarding the tomb of the fallen angels than devil dogs?"

"Okay," Javi replied. "They got a thing for eating people?"

"Kinda. They eat people's *souls*." Pan watched the hounds licking their chops, anticipating their next meal, and tried not to wonder if her soul tasted like chicken.

And then the handlers dropped the leashes. The hounds charged.

"Get in the van!" Pan yelled, and scrambled for the driver's side door, as Javi did likewise on the passenger side. She opened the door, but then paused long enough to turn toward the temple and cup her hands around her mouth. "Annie, we'll come back for you! I promise!"

"Come on, Cookie!" Javi urged.

Pan tumbled inside and slammed the door, grateful for having the foresight to leave the key in the ignition. In one smooth motion, she started the van, threw it into reverse, and stomped down on the gas pedal, sending the vehicle rocketing backward. She slammed on the brake and twisted the steering wheel, fishtailing the van around so it now faced away from the temple. Then it was back to the gas pedal. The van shook as it peeled out.

"You did *not* learn that from driving school!" Javi said with a grin. Then he glanced at his side-view mirror and the grin faded. "Aw damn, they're getting closer!"

" 'Course they are," Pan muttered. "Stupid monster dogs . . ."

The van roared back the way it had come, with hellhounds on its trail.

Annie awoke with a screaming headache, to find herself facedown on the temple floor.

It took her a few seconds to ponder why she was in her current position—she'd been standing upright a minute ago—but then she recalled the struggle with her House Orlock guards by the window, the baying of monstrous hounds, her cries to Pandora and Javier to get away . . . and then something had smashed into her face.

She raised her head off the cold stone, listening intently and holding her breath, fearful that her young friends were being torn to pieces. But instead of screams she heard the distant roar of an engine and the fading echoes of canine howls. The children had escaped; now she could only pray that they would somehow elude the pack.

The scuff of a shoe across the stones brought Annie's attention back to her predicament. Zaqiel stood close by, arms folded across his broad chest as he stared down at her.

"I'm curious," the angel said. "What exactly did you hope to accomplish with that display of idiocy?"

Annie struggled to a sitting position. "I was helping my friends." She raised her bound hands so she could rub the sore right side of her jaw. From the corner of her eye she spotted Alexi grinning at her—it had been his ham-sized fist that had smashed her into brief unconsciousness. She bared her teeth at him, and he cringed in mock fear before chuckling.

"Helping your friends." Zaqiel snorted. "You were merely delaying the inevitable, Sebastienne. I don't know how your friends arrived on this island—"

"Or how many others came with them, and are out there waiting to strike," she interjected. Probably none at all, she thought. There was no way Alexander would ever have allowed a pair of teen civilians to act as advance scouts for an attack. But Zaqiel wouldn't know that; neither would his sycophants, who didn't look quite as smug as they had just two seconds before. Annie could see the uncertainty in their eyes as they glanced out the windows, the trace of nervousness in their body language.

Zaqiel, not surprisingly, wasn't so easily swayed. "Your friends in the Church, if they were really out there, would have attacked already. But even if they are, they will be the first of the human filth to be wiped away once my brothers are free and our armies sweep across the planet."

Annie snorted just as derisively. "You said almost the exact same thing two hundred years ago, Zaqiel, and it was just as much a delusion then as it is now. Throwing a genocidal hissy fit just to get back at God? Do you really think that if you posed that great a threat to the Almighty, He wouldn't come down here and put a stop to you?"

That little jab got an unexpected response from the angel's followers, who slowly turned from the windows to stare at their leader. Nervousness was replaced with expressions of confusion . . . and suspicion. Apparently today's generation of monsters wasn't as easily gulled by the hyperbolic promises of an angel—especially one who'd had his ass handed to him by the very woman he was verbally sparring with.

The leader of House Otoyo, though, wasn't about to let Annie turn the troops against their esteemed ancestor.

"Isn't that your job, huntress?" Kiyoshi replied. Clomping across the stone floor in those ridiculously thick-soled Mary Janes she tended to favor, the vampiress inserted herself into the conversation by stepping between the former lovers. "Why should"—she glanced upward out of habit; Annie had yet to meet a monster who didn't when discussing God—"*he* intervene when he has his obedient watchdog to safeguard his most precious creations?"

Annie smiled sweetly, as though dealing with an imbecile. "God didn't give me the job, Kiyoshi, but I was happy to take it when the opportunity arose. I mean, you travel the world, make your own hours, get a good salary plus full health and dental benefits, *and* you get to kill all the weirdling vermin you want—who wouldn't want a job like that?" The smile twisted, became a sneer. "But if you'd like to ask God about His hiring practices, I'd be happy to send you to Him."

The blow that sent her reeling this time came from Kiyoshi. The clan leader had never seemed the type for physical assaults—at least according to her file in the Knights of the Apocalypse database, and Annie's own observations—so getting punched in the face by that very leader was doubly surprising. Somebody needed to update that file. And Annie needed to reassess Kiyoshi's threat potential.

Still, it wasn't that powerful an attack; certainly nowhere close to Alexi's. Annie remained on her feet and used her bound hands to wipe away the blood that trickled from the left corner of her mouth. She smiled. "You punch like a girl, Kiyoshi. A *human* girl."

Lady Sasaki snarled and drew back her fist—which was seized by the angel.

"Enough," Zaqiel growled, and looked to Annie. "You ask why God should pay me any mind when I pose no credible threat. The answer is, I wouldn't expect Him to; He paid little enough attention while my brothers and I had our run of this world. He was too busy playing with His own toys." He flashed a smile as he released Kiyoshi's hand. "I imagine the situation is much the same as it was then."

"What is that supposed to mean?" Annie asked.

"That at first my brothers and I were His favorites; then, when mankind climbed down from the trees, He forgot all about us"—Zaqiel snarled—"until it was time to punish us for our harmless deeds. Then He couldn't pay us enough attention."

Annie was stunned, at first, by his comments; then she became angry. "You consider raping human women to create races of monsters a harmless deed? You consider trying to overthrow heaven a harmless deed?"

"And when something new in the multiverse no doubt caught His eye," Zaqiel continued, ignoring her questions, "He tossed aside the monkey-children like discarded toys and never looked back."

"That's a lie," Annie said.

"Is it? You've been wandering this planet for four centuries, Sebastienne; you've seen the evils committed by His so-called favorites—the wars and genocides, the sadistic cruelties man has enacted upon his fellow man, with no end in sight. Where was God to put an end to that aberrant behavior? Hasn't He heard the sick and the dying cry out for mercy, for justice, every day, every hour, for millennia? Has He ever responded while I was away, even once?"

Annie faltered, lost for words. Zaqiel could still find ways to wound her—physically, mentally, and now spiritually. She looked around at her captors, and knew that any advantage she'd gained in creating uncertainty among his followers was lost. By causing doubt in their greatest enemy, Zaqiel had regained control of the situation.

"You ask me why God should pay any heed to my actions?" Zaqiel continued. "The better question is, why should He care what I do—why should He care about any of us?" The angel stepped close to Annie. "Admit it, my love: God abandoned you a long time ago."

She snapped his head back with a double-fisted uppercut to the jaw. He responded with an equally savage punch that caught her in the left eye and sent her crashing to the floor. Annie used the impact as momentum to roll to her feet, ready to launch another attack despite the odds against her and a severe lack of supernatural powers. But before she could move forward, a heavy foot slammed down between her shoulder blades and pinned her to the cold stone.

Annie looked back to find Alexi pressing down on her. The burly Russian smiled over his little victory and stepped down a tiny bit harder.

"You're just . . . begging me to . . . kill you, aren't you?" Annie growled through clenched teeth as the pressure on her back increased.

"Is it me, my love, or have you grown rather pious in your old age?" Zaqiel asked as he rubbed his jaw. He crouched down beside her. "I don't remember you being this devoted to any religion when we were together." He smiled. "Must be the company you keep these days."

"The sort of company that will put an end to you, Zaqiel," Annie replied. "If I don't do it first."

That got a chuckle from him. "You said almost the exact same thing two hundred years ago, Sebastienne—"

"Except I was true to my word," she countered. "Unlike a certain megalomaniac I could name."

Zaqiel sighed wearily. "And so we come full circle in our discussion." He stood up and addressed the room. "All of you get back to your posts. Soon the real work can begin: freeing my brothers from bondage . . . and tearing this world apart." He gazed down at Annie. "Perhaps you'd care to spend the remaining time in prayer? You never know, my love—maybe *this* time God will finally respond to your pleas."

The angel walked away, his laughter filling the stone chamber.

19

"Oh my God, they're eating the van!" Javi cried, although Pan almost missed hearing him above the ear-splitting shriek of metal being torn apart.

She glanced in the rearview mirror, and sure enough two large chunks were missing from the rear door on her side. And through the hole she could see one of the hellhounds preparing to take another bite. Then it chomped down and pulled back. The bottom half of the back door panel was ripped away with a metallic scream that made the teens wince.

"I . . . think they just made a doggie door," Javi said. He looked as worried as she felt. "Can you lose them?"

Pan's eyebrows shot up in disbelief. *Is he serious?!*

"You see how fast I'm driving?" she replied curtly, with a nod to the speedometer on the dashboard. They were doing better than fifty miles per hour, on unpaved jungle roads that hadn't seemed quite so hazardous at a slower speed on the way to the temple. It was a wonder she hadn't flipped the van over already, or broken an axle in the potholes that covered the dirt paths like moon craters. "What do you think I've been trying to do?"

It was a lost cause, though, and they both knew it. Not only had the hellhounds never broken stride in this miles-long chase, they'd actually gained ground with every step. And now they were turning the van into a chew toy.

"Okay," Javi said. "But can you *lose* them?"

She gave him a flash of withering side-eye, then couldn't help but laugh when she saw him grinning. "Jerk."

"Hey, just, y'know, trying to lighten the mood."

Pan smiled. "Okay. I'll let it slide this time." She took another peek in the mirror.

"If there is a next time . . ." With the back door torn open, and the hellhounds just beyond its ragged edges, it almost looked as though the four-legged beasties were already inside the van. *Monsters in mirror are closer than they appear,* she thought with a nervous flutter of her stomach.

Wait.

That's when the idea hit her. Maybe a crazy-stupid one, but an idea nevertheless. But if it didn't work perfectly, then the devil dogs really would be inside the van. Chomping on flesh and bone. Swallowing blood and souls.

She chewed on her bottom lip for a few seconds, checked the mirror again to see if the hounds were still right on top of them, and said, "Javi?"

"Yeah?"

"Hold on!" she yelled—and slammed on the brakes.

Javi's seat belt prevented him from rocketing through the windshield, but the strap dug into his chest pretty hard; Pan experienced the same. But in her opinion the momentary pain they felt was more than balanced out by the sweet, sweet sound of five hellhound skulls colliding against the rear of the van—just as she'd intended. Low whimpers filtered through the "doggie door" from the area below the rear bumper.

Javi rubbed his sore chest, glanced out the back, and turned to Pan. "Damn, Cookie, that was pretty hard core."

Pan smiled wickedly. "Yeah, well, I'm a cat person."

"Daaammmn," he said with a slow grin. "Okay. So . . . can you lose them *now*?"

"You are *really* trying to get on my bad side, aren't you?" she replied playfully. "Yeah, I think I can lose them now." She stepped on the accelerator—and the engine sputtered and died.

"Oh, crap," Javi muttered.

"No," Pan said forcefully. She turned off the ignition, then turned it on again as she pumped the gas pedal. It was something she'd seen Dad do a number of times with his old Chevy Impala and it always worked . . . eventually. But for Pan, in this particular vehicle, nothing happened. "Nononononono," she said through gritted teeth as she repeated the process. "I am *not* getting caught in a clichéd scene from, like, every low-budget horror movie ever made, just so a bunch'a stupid devil dogs can feast on my soul. It's not gonna happen." It was more of that positive thinking she'd been having since they landed on the island—but all the good thoughts in the world weren't doing a damn thing to make the engine turn over. So she tried the ignition/gas pedal combination once more . . . and failed again.

"I think maybe you're flooding the engine," Javi offered.

Pan's head snapped toward him. "Huh? What's that?" During the lessons she gave before Pan went to driving school, Mom never mentioned anything about flooding engines. Neither had her driving instructor. "Isn't that the thing that happens when you try going through a really deep puddle in a heavy rainstorm, and get stuck?" She waved a hand out the driver's side window. "Do you see any puddles around here?"

"Just . . . relax," Javi said gently.

"Okay," Pan sighed wearily, and slumped in her seat. "See? This is me, relaxed. Like a boneless chicken, my grandma Ellie would say."

That didn't last long.

The van shook as a sudden tremor rippled the ground around it. The teens yelped, then grasped the dashboard until the rumbling subsided.

"Holy crap," Pan said breathlessly. "They have earthquakes here?"

Javi and Pan exchanged a look, then leaned over the dash to peer up through the windshield. A smoldering volcanic peak loomed high above the tree line perhaps a mile or so from where they were parked.

"Wasn't that volcano, like, not even close to the temple when we were driving over?" Javi asked.

"It wasn't," Pan said glumly. "I . . . think I might've taken a wrong turn—"

"Or five."

"Hellooo," Pan said with a nod toward the back door. "Little distracted?"

"Excuses, excuses," he said with a wink.

Pan rolled her eyes at the smart-ass. "Yeah, yeah . . ." She pointed to the steering wheel. "So, what do you think?"

Javi nodded. "Give it a shot."

Pan glanced at the rearview mirror. There was no sign of the dogs through the hole in the rear door, but she could hear them groaning and huffing softly. Soon enough they were going to wake up, and if Pan didn't get this stupid van started, matters were going to take a definite turn for the worse. "I really wish Alex would call you back . . ."

"He'll call," Javi said. "I mean, with Sheena breathing down his neck, there's no way he's gonna forget about us—right?"

Pan laughed softly and reached for the ignition.

That's when she noticed the monsters staring at her.

They appeared to be human . . . ish. Men and women, tall, broad shouldered and powerfully built, some dressed in filthy jeans, work boots, T-shirts, and ball caps; the one standing foremost, probably their leader, wore a faded red T printed with an elaborate design and the words Deros Miners Union Local 832 arcing above and below it. The majority, however, sported coveralls in various colors, nylon safety vests with reflective strips, hard hats, and metal miner's helmets. Their features, though, were just . . . off; a weird sort of hybrid between human and animal. Beady little eyes that sparkled in the sunlight. Snout-like noses. Wide mouths with large, jagged upper teeth that protruded outward. Thick, brown facial and body hair that resembled fur pelts. Oversized hands—more like paws, really—with six fingers and long, slightly curved nails. Every one of the workers was covered in dirt, as though they'd just crawled out of a pit—and maybe they had.

Pan blinked a few times to make certain she wasn't hallucinating. Of course she wasn't; considering everything she'd learned about herself since meeting Annie, considering what she'd been through up to this point, the possibility that her mind might be playing tricks on her was out of the question. Mostly. Still, after ten years of monstervision and psychotherapy, old habits died hard, which is why she felt the need to ask Javi, "Do you see the Mole People, too?"

"Gah!" Javi practically leaped out of his seat in surprise as he eyed the silent onlookers. "Where the hell'd *they* come from?"

"Let's not stay around to ask, okay?" Pan turned the ignition—and the lead miner-thing opened its mouth and *squealed*. Loudly.

A pair of clawlike hands shot through the open driver's side window to grab a double fistful of Pan's hair—there were more Mole People on her side of the van! She cried out as broken nails raked her skin with the sharpness of serrated knife blades. Then the hands pulled back, forcing her to rise from her seat or risk a torn scalp. She felt other hands grab her shoulders and begin dragging her through the window, only to encounter resistance as the strap of her messenger bag—which she'd forgotten to take off—snagged on the inner door latch. The creatures yanked harder, and Pan's cry of pain became a full-fledged wail of terror as her hair started ripping out. Blood trickled down the back of her neck.

Javi jumped forward, one hand slipping around her waist to keep her inside the van, while the other shot past her face to smash into something just over her left shoulder. There was a howl that threatened to rupture Pan's eardrum, and then one of the hands gripping her fell away. Javi kept throwing awkward punches as Pan tried to force open the fingers tangled in her hair, but it became apparent that her head would be ripped from her shoulders long before she could break free. Left with no other option, she fumbled for the latch to open her door as grimy fingers wrapped around her face and neck.

"Let her go!" Javi barked, his fist pistoning as he continued raining blows on Pan's attackers. It was a valiant effort, but for every claw he knocked aside another quickly took its place. She could see in his eyes, though, that he wasn't about to give up.

Until someone interfered, that is.

The passenger-side door was thrown open and the red-shirted group leader grabbed Javi by the legs, to pull him out. Javi responded by kicking the miner-thing in the face, but it was a weak, off-balance blow delivered with the rubber sole of a sneaker. It was enough, however, to anger the creature, which grabbed the offending limb, opened his jagged-tooth maw—and chomped down on the boy's calf.

Javi screamed.

Then he was yanked from the van.

Pan's latch finally popped open and she tumbled onto the dirt path, momentarily free of her attackers as the door swung out to clip two of them; the rest stepped out of the way, then swarmed over her. Claws raked her face and hands, drawing blood; teeth sunk into the sleeves of her jacket, then began gnawing through the leather.

Oh God, they're trying to eat me!

Panicked, hair fallen over her eyes, Pan swung her fists and threw elbows, all the while screaming, *"Get off me! Get the hell off me, you bastards!"* She took some small reward in hearing pained shrieks as the rings she wore on all her fingers acted like makeshift brass knuckles to deliver bone-crunching punches. But then one of the creatures grabbed her head and slammed it against the side of the van. Pan collapsed in a heap.

Dazed, she could feel the Mole People pressing in around her. One kicked her in the stomach to roll her onto her back; bile scorched Pan's throat as it gurgled past her lips. Hands gripped her arms and legs to hold her down while another pair grasped her head and turned it to expose her neck. Pan ground her teeth, refusing to cry and beg for mercy like a victim in a bad slasher movie, yet she couldn't stop from whimpering softly as something razor sharp was pressed against her carotid artery—

That's when the growling caught everyone's attention.

The implement withdrew; so did the restraining hands. Pan swept aside her hair to find the Mole People slowly backing away, their attention riveted on the rear of the van. Pan knew exactly what was lurking there even before she looked.

Three of the hellhounds were awake. And they were really pissed off.

Pan froze as the beasts focused on her before turning to regard the new arrivals. Cat person she might be, but she'd watched enough nature programs on the Natural Geographic Channel to realize that the hounds were sizing up the situation, distinguishing easy prey (her) from potential threat (the Mole People). If the miners were smart, or scared enough, they'd keep right on backing up and leave the dogs to their meal.

Please, please *be stupid,* Pan thought. *You jackasses owe me at* least *that much for trying to kill me.*

But where were the other hounds? Pan lowered her head to take a peek under the van; sure enough, there were two more sets of canine legs on the far side, along with a collection of Mole People feet that shuffled around a large object lying on the ground. It took her a moment to realize what it was.

Pan gasped. "Javi . . ." But why wasn't he moving? Her stomach did a nervous flip. *Oh God, no . . .*

A shadow fell across her. Pan turned back to discover that the hounds on her side of the van had padded over to stand at her feet. She yelped and started backpedaling, pushing with her boot heels and elbows to scoot away from the beasts, which kept pace with her. Stalking her.

Easy prey, she thought as they closed in.

And then, thankfully, somebody got stupid.

One of the male Mole People took a step forward and, flexing his claws, hissed at the devil dogs. It was an action that Pan could only assume was meant to indicate, *Back the hell off, Scooby-Doo, this is* our *food.* At first the hounds didn't react, but when other Moles joined in to form a hiss-y chorus that sounded like steam pipes about to burst, they moved from a potential threat to a definite one and the dogs had no choice but to address the situation—which they did by charging the boob who'd interrupted their lunch.

The Mole Man squealed in horror—apparently he'd been under the impression that he could shoo away Satan's Rottweilers simply by acting tough—and fell back into his fellow miners. Rather than follow his example, however, the other union members surged past him to meet the challenge. Claws flashed on both sides, and then the fight was on.

The clamor of growls and barks and squeals immediately drew the attention of the group clustered around Javi. Pan watched as they abandoned their captive and went to the aid of their comrades; the remaining pair of hellhounds did likewise, racing around the back of the van to join their pack brothers.

The oddest thought popped into Pan's head as she watched the two sides clash: it was like being present at a reenactment of a battle scene from that Leonardo DiCaprio movie, *Gangs of New York,* only performed by devil dogs and giant moles. Then she remembered that the combatants were fighting over who'd have the honor of chewing the flesh off her bones, and decided it was time to be anywhere but right here.

She rolled under the van and quickly crawled on her belly—still sore from the kicking it had received—to the other side, where Javi lay. She grabbed his closest foot and gave it a shake. "Javi?" she whispered. *"Javi!"*

There was a soft rattle of breath. "P-Pan?" he croaked weakly.

Pan mouthed a silent thanks to the Man Upstairs, smiled, and pulled herself out from cover. Javi was alive, she was alive, and the dogs and Mole People were too busy fighting each other to realize she'd slipped away. Alex was going to call soon, she was certain of that, and then he and the rest of the Knights of the Apocalypse could swoop in here and save the day. Everything was gonna be okay.

Then she saw all the blood.

Javi's T-shirt had been torn away and his chest, arms, and neck were covered in blood, his normally light brown skin reduced to a sickly tan and riddled with deep, ragged bite marks.

The Mole People had been feeding on him. And from the horrified look she saw in his eyes and the tears that ran down his cheeks, he'd been awake the entire time.

Her own eyes brimming with tears, Pan clamped both hands over her mouth to prevent the scream she felt building. She knelt beside him and forced the smile back on her lips. "C-come on, lazybones," she said in a shaky voice. "Time to get up."

Javi turned those terror-glazed eyes toward her; they widened as though he'd just now realized she was at his side. Then his chest rose rapidly but shallow as he tried to draw enough breath to speak.

"R . . . r . . . *ruuunnnn.*"

It suddenly felt as though her heart had stopped. She couldn't move, couldn't think, couldn't speak, couldn't focus on anything but the words *He's dying* echoing over and over in her mind. Then: *Because of me.*

The sounds of battle punctured through the fog that had settled over her mind, and though she couldn't see what was happening on the other side of the van she turned in its direction anyway. Pan sneered.

No. He's not dying because of me; it's because of the Mole People and those stupid hellhounds. Because of the vampires and the monsters and that friggin' Zaqiel who's done nothing but make my life even more of a living hell than it used to be, when I just used to think I was crazy. They hurt my mom and dad and they took Annie prisoner, but I'll be damned *if any of those bastards are taking Javi away from me.*

She wiped her eyes with the heels of her palms, took a breath to steady herself, and moved to stand at Javi's shoulder. "Come on, we're going."

His mouth trembled slightly. "W-whaaa . . . ?" was the best that he could get out.

She bent over, hooked her hands under his armpits to lift him, and proceeded to drag the boy toward the tree line a few yards away. Using the van was out of the question. For one thing, she hadn't gotten the chance to see if the ignition worked, so there was no way to know if the engine would restart; for another, the hellhounds had already proven they could eat their way through the doors, so trapping herself and Javi inside a giant chew toy would be a really dumb idea. No, their best chance of losing their pursuers was to make a run for it—or as much of a run as one could achieve while yanking the other participant across the ground on his butt.

Keeping a grip on Javi was difficult; the blood from his wounds made him slippery, and Pan tripped a couple of times when her bag got tangled between her feet. Pulling him also took more effort than she'd expected—for such a skinny guy he was heavier than he looked.

"N . . . no," Javi whispered. "S . . . s . . . stop . . ." His voice faded as he drifted into unconsciousness.

"Shut up, Jeter," Pan muttered. "It doesn't always have to be boys rescuing girls, y'know . . ."

She struggled, she stumbled, she struggled some more, but eventually Pan succeeded in getting Javi off the dirt track, onto the grass, and out of sight among the trees. Then she kept going, wanting to put as much distance between them and the combatants as possible—odds were good that no matter who won the battle, the victors would come searching for their elusive meal. She thought about offering some encouragement to Javi, about how they were going out to get out of this predicament, about how he needed to hang on or risk pissing her off—or even worse, Sheena—but each time her fingers slipped in his blood, each time he took another labored breath, the words dissolved on her tongue.

Not that she was doing much better. Her head was still ringing from its impact against the van and from the Mole People's savage hair-pulling; her limbs quivered as the initial adrenaline rush that had been sparked by the attack began to wear off; and the combination of jet-black hair and an all-black ensemble in a hot, humid jungle was slowly cooking her in the afternoon sun. Her T-shirt and dyed locks were plastered to her skin, sweat kept pouring into her eyes, and she could feel the waves of heat rising from inside the leather jacket. And yet she kept moving—she had to, if they were to survive.

The withering sunlight had one positive effect, though: it dried up Javi's wounds. Maintaining a grip on him became slightly easier, if only because the blood covering him went from slick to tacky. Now it felt as though Pan had her fingers stuck to a glue trap for rodents.

If I can just find a place to hide out, I could try to heal him. But where the hell do you hide in a jungle? As she continued her back-treading progress, she gazed at her surroundings. Trees and more trees, bushes of various shapes and sizes, some really beautiful flowers, and a group of oversized plants that reminded her of Venus flytraps—big enough to fit a full-grown human inside them. Probably best to stay away from those.

Her boot heels slid off the grass and scuffed against dirt. Another path? Or had she somehow gotten turned around and brought them back to the same road? That would really, totally suck. Pan stopped to look over her shoulder.

It was neither. She'd stepped into a clearing that had been transformed into a construction site, which made it apparent just where the Mole People had come from. They'd probably been on break when they heard her attempts to restart the van's motor, and walked over to investigate. There were cement trucks and dump trucks and a pair of cranes, and at the center of the site was a ring of green nylon safety netting, set up around a concrete-lined hole in the ground that was perhaps fifty feet in diameter. An air vent, maybe? But the question was quickly forgotten as her gaze settled on the red-and-black metal platform with matching scaffolding that extended over the hole and ran straight down, and the cage-like box that sat atop it.

An elevator.

"Yes!" Pan said with a smile. They could hide out at the bottom of the shaft until the dogs gave up on eating them, or the Mole People went back to work, then return to the van and drive away. All she had to do was cross a couple hundred feet of open space, and pray that hellhounds didn't know how to operate elevators. Easy peasy.

That's when the howling started.

A chill ran down Pan's spine. She'd been so focused on getting Javi out of harm's way that she'd ignored the fight—and when it had ended. Now it was clear who had won . . . and what their next action would be.

Okay, don't panic. Panicking's only gonna make it worse. Just get to the elevator and you'll be fine.

The problem, however, was the *getting to* part. With devil dogs back on the hunt, speed was now essential, and dragging Javi the remaining distance would take much too long. That left only one option: carry him.

It took quite a bit of wrestling to get Javi into the right position, every moment spent dreading that the hellhounds would come bursting through the tree line, but eventually Pan managed to turn him around and drape him over her back. The toes of his sneakers were going to drag behind her, but there was nothing she could do about that. With his head hanging down over her right shoulder and her arms looped around his, she staggered around for a few steps until finding her balance. She wiped sweat from her eyes and took a deep breath to prepare herself for the next part.

"You are *so* gonna owe me when this is over," she muttered into Javi's ear. Then, hunched halfway over, messenger bag sweeping the ground by her feet, weary and scared and broiling in her dark clothes, Pan set off for the elevator.

Of course, that *had* to be the moment Javi's phone sounded. Pan didn't recognize the heavy-beat tune, but to her ears, in this dire circumstance, it was just about the loudest, most unwelcome noise she'd ever heard in her life. Because instead of tracking the teens, all the hounds needed to do now was follow the drumming and electronic screeching straight to their prey. After thirty seconds the music cut off— and then immediately started again.

I have never *hated freakin' dubstep more than right at this very moment,* Pan thought with a sneer. Still, she needed to answer that call; it could be Alex. She shifted Javi's weight so she could free her right hand, since the ring tone seemed to be coming from his right front pocket. Slightly off balance but still moving forward, she reached back, her fingers tracing a line along his thigh toward his pocket.

What're you doing? her inner voice chided. *Stop feeling him up and answer the damn phone!*

"I am ... *not* ... feeling him ... up," she wheezed.

Javi stirred. "Whaaa ... ?" he asked softly.

Pan blushed. "Nothing."

Okay, maybe she *had* been copping a feel, a little one, but it wasn't like it was intentional. Besides, how else was she supposed to reach his damn phone? Anyway, the end result was that she found the cell on the first try and pulled it out just as a third round of dubstepping began.

"Al ... Alex?" she gasped into the microphone.

There was a pause, then: "Hello, Mr. Maldonado. I'm calling to ask if you're satisfied with your provider's service. At—"

Pan ended the call and let loose a tiny scream of frustration between clenched teeth. A freakin' telemarketer? Seriously? For two seconds she considered smashing the phone in anger, but then her left foot struck metal and she forgot all about dubsteps and spam calls. Surprised, she looked up.

She'd reached the elevator platform.

Pan felt like howling with joy, only to freeze as a familiar growl reached her ears. She looked back and there at the edge of the clearing stood the five hellhounds.

Now it was time to panic.

Pan made a final dash for the elevator car, but as she hopped onto the platform Javi's feet caught on the edge, causing her to trip. As they went down in a tangle of limbs, Pan instinctively opened her hands to break their fall—and dropped Javi's cell phone. Which then bounced across the sun-heated metal ... and dropped over the edge into the shaft.

"No!" Pan cried.

A blur of motion in the corner of her eyes caught her attention. The hounds were racing across the construction site; they'd be at the platform in seconds.

Pan scrambled out from under Javi and frantically pulled him toward the elevator. They were *so close* to getting out of this; she couldn't fail now.

But just as she neared the door her foot caught in the messenger bag and suddenly she'd lost her grip on Javi and was flat on her back.

She sat up immediately, to find the hounds padding onto the platform. Back to stalking mode. Pan wondered if they were actually taking pleasure in this; if so, it was one more reason why she'd never cared for dogs. Then something lying beside her caught her eye; something she'd completely forgotten she was carrying around all this time; something that had fallen out of the messenger bag.

The Spear of Longinus.

Pan snatched it up and staggered to her feet, then positioned herself over Javi. It took all her remaining strength to keep her tired legs from collapsing, to hold the ancient weapon in trembling hands—the dogs could probably sense how weak she was—but she was determined to stand her ground. No stupid devil dog was taking her soul, or Javi's, without a fight. Not that she really wanted to stab them, just scare them off. As she'd told Javi once before, she wasn't a killer, even if somebody was trying to kill *her*.

. . .

Okay, so she was willing to make an exception for Zaqiel, but still . . .

The hounds edged closer.

"Go . . . home," Pan snarled. It was something Mom always yelled at the next door neighbor's dogs, back in Schriksdorp, whenever they got loose and started tearing up her front lawn. She swallowed nervously, then waved the spear at the demon canines as she repeated her command in a louder voice: *"Go. Home."*

The hounds stopped, then backed up a few steps. But it wasn't Pan that had made them cautious, it was the spear.

Its tip was glowing.

Pan once more felt the energy contained within the tarnished metal; the last time had been after the museum shoot-out, when she'd planned to use the spear on Zaqiel. As before, mystical power flowed into her, calming her frazzled nerves and clearing her head. Her body tingled with renewed strength, enough that she could stand fully erect and stare down her canine pursuers.

"Bad dogs!" Pan snapped. "Now get the hell back! Back!" She stomped her foot for added emphasis. Mom did that, too, with the neighbors' pets, although it never impressed them.

Surprisingly, this time it did, at least for Pan. All right, maybe it had a lot more to do with the spear than her "commanding" presence; that was fine. Whatever the reason, the hounds slowly retreated to the start of the platform—but that's as far as they were willing to go. They still had a soul-eating job to do, and clearly they wouldn't be sated until the teens' spirits were filling their bellies.

You'd think they had enough to eat already with all those Mole People, if that's what happened, Pan thought. *Probably happened. But there's always room for dessert, right?*

The hounds sat, eyeing her closely, no doubt waiting for the moment Pan dropped her guard. That, she thought with a grimace, might not be long in coming. Just like at the museum, the charge she'd gotten from the spear didn't last long; once it faded, given her injuries and level of exhaustion, she'd be too weak to stay on her feet. That's when the dogs would strike.

She glanced over her shoulder at the elevator, so tantalizingly close, then back to her canine enemies—still waiting, now licking their chops.

Never breaking eye contact with the beasts, she retreated until she was standing above Javi's head. "Javi? We gotta move."

No response. She looked down, saw he was still breathing, and took some comfort in that. Small comfort, though, because she'd have to move him again, and in her weakening condition she'd be lucky to make it to the door without passing out.

Pan sighed and wiped sweat from her brow with the sleeve of her jacket. "Well, it's not like he's gonna drag himself . . ."

She took a deep breath, exhaled sharply, and set about her task, looping her arms under his armpits and across his chest—taking care not to poke him with the spear—to begin the final leg of their journey. The going was much slower this time: her legs quivered with each backward step, her breathing—mixed with the occasional grunt—now sounded as labored as Javi's, and he seemed to have gained a ton of weight in the short time she'd taken to stop and defend him.

"You are . . . *so* . . . carrying me . . . next time," she groaned. And then her butt bumped against metal.

She'd made it.

Pan reached back and hit the call button for the elevator; with a soft grinding of gears the door slid open. She used the last of her remaining strength to scooch inside with Javi in tow, then stepped over to the controls. She glanced back at their pursuers—to find the hellhounds on the move, racing along the platform to catch up. They looked ready for their next meal.

Well, they weren't getting it here. Pan slapped the door-close button, then grinned and flipped the dogs The Bird. "Eat *this*, mother—"

The door's vertical, rubber safety bar made a *glonk* sound as it hit something; the door retracted.

Pan gasped and looked up and down for a cause.

Javi's feet were in the doorway.

"Damn it!" she cried in frustration, then threw herself down to grab his legs and yank him fully inside the car. With the beasts only steps away, she jumped back up and hit the button again. This time the door closed.

Followed by the sweet, sweet sound of five hellhound skulls colliding against it.

Pan breathed a sigh of relief, allowed herself a moment of Cheshire-cat-grinning giddiness to celebrate her success, and then gave the elevator's control panel a look-see. A red button for up, a blue one for down, a big red one for emergency stops, and two black—one marked for opening, the other for closing. Simple enough to operate.

"Down it is," she said and pressed the blue button. The elevator began its smooth descent.

A wave of dizziness washed over her, and she clutched the control panel for support. All her exertions, matched with the rising temperature of her overheated body, had caught up to her. She wanted to sit down and close her eyes, just for a minute—hell, what she really she wanted were a 7-11 Big Gulp of Cherry Coke and a long nap—but she had to take care of Javi. Somehow. As nice as it was to have healing powers, it'd be even better if she could use them when she needed to. Sure, they worked before—when she came back from purgatory or whatever, and when Natsumi needed her broken bones fixed—but so far they seemed pretty hit-or-miss. After all, if she had a superhuman healing factor like Wolverine in the X-Men, shouldn't it have cured her exhaustion, or at least made her head stop aching from all the scalp-pulling the Mole People did to her? So, no, she still didn't totally control her "gifts," as Annie called them, monstervision included. She had to try, though. She'd already made a promise that no one was taking Javi away from her; she was going to keep it.

She waited for the dizzy spell to pass, then turned around—to find Javi shivering from his injuries and blood loss. Pan's breath caught. He was going into shock.

"No," she snapped. She took off her jacket and covered his chest with it (*I think that's what you do when somebody's going into shock, right? Keep them warm?*), then knelt beside him and lifted his head onto her knees. "Javi?" she said softly. "Javi, c'mon, you have to stay with me, okay? What happened to all that talk about taking me out on a date? If you think getting chased and kidnapped and almost eaten by monster dogs is some kinda date, even for a Goth chick, then you totally suck at understanding women. I mean, not that it isn't cool doing it with you, it's just—"

The shivering became uncontrollable. His body seized with tremors and Pan wrapped her arms around his shoulders, unable to stop crying as she murmured encouraging words in his ears, telling him the shakes would pass, he'd be okay, she was right here for him . . .

Then he stopped breathing.

"*NO!*" Pan threw back the jacket and pressed her hands against his chest, willing the healing power to activate. "Pleaseplease*please* just work," she whispered as tears blurred her vision. "Come on . . . *COME ON!*" But other than a mild pins-and-needles sensation in her fingers . . . nothing.

CPR! she thought. That should work, right? She didn't really know what to do other than what she'd seen on TV or in the movies—something involving chest compressions and breathing into the person's mouth, she really should have taken that CPR class they offered at school—but a lack of proper understanding wasn't about to prevent her from attempting it. She crossed her hands atop his chest, over his heart, and started pumping. That was the easy part, but how long was she supposed to do it? Ten times? A hundred? Wasn't there a song you were supposed to sing while you did it to keep the beat—something really old that Dad used to sing in the shower? Was it Billy Joel? Or the Bee Gees?

Pan stopped at ten frantic compressions and bent over to breath into Javi's mouth. *I'm doing this all wrong!* she thought, wanting to scream in frustration, but she couldn't figure out an alternative. With her right hand she tilted his head back; with her left she pulled his jaw down to open his mouth. Then she took a deep breath, placed her lips over his—

And felt a familiar tingle in her chest—a low-level electrical charge that built in strength as it traveled along her spine. Her lips suddenly had the weirdest itch.

Pan didn't question the timing or cause of her power's activation, she simply lifted Javi's head into her arms, closed her eyes, and kissed him fully, allowing the energy to flow from her body into his to repair the damage. The transfer made her dizzy; she felt as though she were melting into him, and he into her. Becoming one.

Pain flared in her chest. Her heart pounded erratically; the scar burned hotly. She was pushing too hard, too fast, her body was warning her, giving too much of herself to heal him, as she had with Natsumi at the hospital; to continue was to risk her life. Pan knew that, but she wasn't about to stop. She'd told Javi that everything would work out fine, in the end. Now she had a promise to keep. Not even death was going to make a liar out of her.

A relaxing warmth suddenly spread through her body—a mild crackle of electricity that raised goose bumps on her arms and the back of her neck. It rejuvenated her, invigorated her. But how could that be happening?

Then the realization hit her: the warmth and returning strength were coming from Javi. He'd taken what his body needed and was giving the rest back to her. Helping her to recover as she had done for him. Easing her burden.

She felt the light touch of his hands on her face.

Felt him kissing her back.

Pan opened her eyes, saw the surprise in his own turn to gratitude. He smiled against her mouth. And though she wanted this intimacy, this *becoming oneness* to go on forever, she allowed him to gently break their connection.

"Th-thanks . . . Cookie," he murmured as he stroked her cheek. "But after we get outta here . . . maybe you could take a . . . a CPR course . . . so you don't go . . . busting up my ribs next time. Okay?"

Pan softly laughed, her pains forgotten, her fears dispelled. She lifted him so she could wrap her arms around him, and cried on his shoulder. Javi pulled her into a hug so tight it felt as though he never wanted to let her go.

They stayed that way, taking comfort from one another, as the elevator continued its descent.

20

Pan awoke—a little achy, a little stiff, but surprisingly well rested—to find herself alone, lying on a cot in a strange room with her head on a cushion, and without a clue as to how she got there. The last thing she remembered was holding on to Javi in the elevator, grateful to have him back, celebrating her triumphs over the hellhounds and the Grim Reaper. And then . . .

Had she . . . fallen asleep? While she was in the arms of a hot, *bare-chested* boy who was all toned and handsome and . . . and *bare-chested*? (Okay, his chest had been covered with dried blood—so . . . *ick*—but still.) A boy she'd rescued from death's embrace, just so . . . what? So she could take a nap on his shoulder? *Really?*

Her gaze slid down to a tiny pool of saliva on the cushion near her mouth. *Oh God, I probably drooled on him, too . . .*

Pan rolled her face into the cushion and groaned. *Curled up with the first good-looking guy I've met in I can't remember when, who's actually interested in me being me, and after saving his life I turn into a total drooling snoozefest. Gah. Some romantic I am.* Then a more important thought struck her: *Wait! Where is Javi?*

A feeling of dread chilled her skin and snapped her fully awake. Had more Mole People carried the teen off—to finish feeding on him? Or maybe the hellhounds figured out how to run an elevator, had made it to the bottom of the shaft, and Javi was now busy leading them away from her? She needed to find out. She tossed off the light blanket that covered her and jumped out of bed.

Too fast. The sudden elevation made her head swim and she had to sit down to avoid doing a face-plant on the floor. Head in her hands, elbows resting on her knees, Pan closed her eyes and massaged her temples, waiting for the dizzy spell to pass. A nervous flutter ran through her heart—not the onset of a panic attack, but a growing concern for what might be happening to Javi while she sat here feeling helpless. She took a breath, slowly released it.

It's just a bump in the road, it's not the end of the world . . . Seriously. Just calm down.

The light-headedness eased and Pan raised her head. "Better," she said with a nod, then rose to her feet at a more conservative speed. The room didn't start spinning this time, so that was a good sign, but her feet felt strangely chilly. She looked down to spy her pentagram-decorated socks. Her black leather calf boots, she now noticed with a slight turn of her head, stood neatly beside the far end of the cot, next to her messenger bag.

Pan smiled. Apparently before tucking her in, Javi had removed her boots and—she suddenly realized—washed off the grime and blood that had coated her hands. She touched her cheeks; her face felt cleaner, too.

He's either a natural gentleman, or his mom taught him real well, she thought with a grin. The grin wavered. *I hope he's okay . . .*

Pan sat back down and reached for the boots, eager to start her search. As she began jamming her right foot into the comfortably worn leather, she gazed at her surroundings.

It was an office of some kind, about ten feet wide and ten feet deep, with crappy "oak" paneling covering the walls and flooring made of dingy white-vinyl tiles. An air conditioner hummed softly on the wall behind the bed; after the sauna-like conditions of the jungle, the cool air was a blessed relief. A desk stood against the far wall, with a black ergonomic chair tucked into the leg well; the desk's surface was littered with papers, pens, and pencils, along with a scattering of empty candy wrappers and foam coffee cups. Seeing the wrappers brought an unexpected rumble from her stomach; when had she last eaten? Yesterday? Longer? Being on the run in a whole different part of the world had totally messed up her sense of time.

"Hey, you're up!" a familiar voice called.

Pan turned from the desk toward the lone doorway directly across from the bed—and there he was.

"Javi!" She jumped up, wobbling a bit in just the one boot, to greet him as he stepped into the room. Their embrace instantly erased her concerns and sent a pleasant chill up her spine.

When they finally pulled apart Pan took a few moments to examine him. Javi's jeans and sneakers were stained with dirt and dried blood, but he'd scrounged up an oversize, dark blue T-shirt from somewhere; emblazoned across the front was the symbol of the miners union the Mole People had belonged to. Baggy T aside, he looked much healthier—his skin tone was more like its normal color, the wounds on his arms and neck had all healed (presumably, so had the ones studding his chest), and his eyes shone a little brighter.

Am I good at this healing thing, or what? she thought proudly.

"What's with the staring?" Javi asked, with a lopsided smile.

"Just making sure you look okay."

"And do I?"

"*I'll* say," she replied with a grin, unable to avoid thinking of what he looked like *without* the shirt. "At least that makes one of us . . ." Pan glanced at the sweat-tangled mess of her hair, twisted strands floating inches in front of her face like Medusa's snakes, and used her hands to try and smoosh it into something less rat-nesty.

"Aw, c'mon, you look fine." With his thumb and forefinger, Javi gently tilted her head back, so he could do some examining of his own. "But how do you feel? You get enough rest? I know you used your healing power on me—by the way, did I thank you for doing that?"

"You being up and around is all the thanks I need," she replied.

"Well, I'll say it anyway: *Thank you.* If it wasn't for you, Cookie, I would've been in a really bad way."

If it wasn't for me you wouldn't have been in a bad way at all, she thought, but then quickly pushed it aside. *I thought you were done blaming yourself for stuff, "Cookie." Weren't you the one who said the monsters were responsible for what happened to Mom and Dad and Javi and Annie, not you? So just get over yourself.*

Old habits died hard, though.

So learn some new, *less blame-y ones,* her inner voice snapped. *Jeeeez.*

"—I'll find some way to pay you back," she heard Javi finish.

Pan shook her head. "You don't have to do that."

"Maybe, but I wanna. I know that doing what you did for me couldn't have been easy. I mean, I saw what happened when you fixed Natsumi's broken arm and ribs—you looked like you were ready to pass out after running one'a those Iron Man competitions. And I was . . . a lot worse than Natsumi."

She reached up to place her hand on his, gave it a squeeze, and tried to give her best comforting smile. "I'm fine." He didn't appear convinced, however, and guided her back to the bed. A good move, Pan thought, because she was getting tired of trying to maintain her balance in one boot.

"Let me get you something to drink," Javi said. While Pan struggled into her other boot, he walked over to the desk. Her eyebrows rose when she noticed the hitch in his step.

"You're limping."

He acted surprised. "Huh? Oh, yeah." For a moment, a hint of fear dulled the shine of his eyes—a remembrance of the attack he'd clearly rather forget—but then Javi shrugged. "That mole guy . . . when he was pulling me outta the van he bit my leg. There must've been venom or something in his teeth, 'cause I couldn't move after that. And then . . ." His voice trailed off and he looked away. "Y'know."

"Let me fix it."

He looked back up. "No, I'll be okay."

She frowned. "Javi, you're the shortstop on your school's baseball team; you're their fastest base stealer. If your legs aren't a hundred percent and you can't play your position, they'll kick you out."

He smiled, trying to play Mr. Cool. "I could always be the designated hitter. In high school baseball, they use a pinch runner after the DH gets a hit."

Pan was having none of it. The frown deepened. "Javi, I'm serious."

His smile faltered; it was obvious he agreed with her assessment. He'd probably been having the same thoughts while she slept. "Yeah, okay . . . but later. After you've got your strength back. You already did too much for me."

"And I'd do it again," she said, then added firmly, "I *will* do it again. Don't worry about me, Javi, worry about your future baseball career. You're gonna be in the majors, someday."

He grinned. "You've never even seen me play. How do *you* know I'm good enough for the major leagues?"

"Because I just know."

Javi chuckled. "Well, as my Tia Monacella would say, 'From your mouth to God's ears.' " He rolled back the chair, and reached into the leg well to open a small door. "There's a mini-fridge under here," he explained as he rummaged around inside. When he turned back he had in hand a pair of sports drinks, their colorful liquid contents glowing with neon intensity beneath the room's fluorescent lights. "Grape or fruit punch?"

"Grape, please." Javi unscrewed the cap and handed her the bottle. Pan guzzled half of it, not realizing until now just how thirsty she was. When she finally stopped to take a breath, she sighed with relief—and then belched. She smiled sheepishly and put a hand over her mouth. "Oops. Made a piggy. Sorry."

" 'Sall right," Javi replied with a grin as he sat down beside her. He took a drink from his own bottle.

Pan took a more ladylike sip. "How long was I asleep?"

"About three hours."

Pan started. *"What?"*

"Yeah, when the elevator reached the bottom you were pretty much in dreamland, so I carried you out. You know what was the first thing you said to me when I picked you up?" He grinned. " 'It's about damn time.' "

Pan grimaced. "Eep. Sorry."

"Don't worry about it," Javi replied. "I owed you. Then I spotted this trailer and thought it'd be a good place to get outta the sun, and to lay low in case there were any monsters lurking around. After I put you to bed I scoped out the area, but since I didn't see anybody I guess the crew and their boss were those . . . things we ran into."

"The Mole People."

"Yeah." He fell silent.

Pan's heart went out to him. He'd suffered so much at the hands of those monsters; for all the physical injuries she could treat, she could do nothing to heal the psychological wounds undoubtedly left behind by the attack. Still, she silently promised she'd do whatever she could to help him get past the bad memories. "Javi, I'm really sorry about what happened. If I'd gotten to you sooner, maybe—"

"What're you talking about?" Javi asked. "You don't have anything to be sorry for. You had your own stuff to deal with. If anybody should be apologizing it oughtta be me for not protecting you."

Pan's eyebrows rose. He'd said *what,* now?

She frowned. "I don't need protecting, Javi. I can look after myself okay."

"You know what I mean. I'm the guy—that's supposed to be my job."

That earned him an eye roll and a groan. "*Really?* You really wanna get into a debate on gender roles when it comes to fighting monsters?"

He paused, clearly uncertain about whether he wanted to cross that line. "I . . . don't know. Do I?"

"No," she replied with a warning smile. "You *really* don't."

" 'Cause I'll lose?" he asked with a sly grin. Then he shrugged. "Okay. I concede."

Pan laughed. "I accept. And besides, I could say the same thing about you."

"What, that it's *your* job to protect *me*?"

"Well, who's the one who dragged your unconscious ass across the jungle, and then had to outrun a pack of monster dogs that wanted to swallow *both* our souls? I don't remember you doing a whole lot of protecting me then, right? No, 'cause *I* was the one playing bodyguard."

Javi considered that for a few seconds, then slowly smiled. "Okay, maybe you got a point."

"So glad you approve," Pan replied sarcastically.

Javi stuck out his hand. "How about we call it even and just promise to watch out for each other?"

Pan smiled and they shook on it. "I can live with that."

"Good. So what do you wanna do, now that you're up?"

As if in reply, Pan's stomach rumbled again. Loudly. Pan, embarrassed, placed a hand on her gut. "Sorry."

Javi's eyes widened in surprise. "Whoa! I was just gonna mention getting something to eat. It's like your stomach read my mind!" He studied her closely. "Is that another one of your superpowers?"

"Wiseass." Pan averted her gaze and added quietly, "Could use a bathroom, too . . ."

Javi pointed toward the door. "Make a left right outside. Your jacket's hanging on the door. I tried to clean the dirt and stuff off the back of it." By *stuff* they both knew he meant his blood. "Hope I didn't ruin the paint job. It's really nice."

"Thanks." It had taken Pan almost two weeks to create the image on the back panel: a giant Satan head devouring souls, based on a sixteenth-century woodcut she'd found in a book. The flames on the sleeves were her work as well. "And don't worry—there are so many layers of paint on there you'd need a box of steel-wool pads to even make a dent in it."

Javi looked relieved. "Great. I'd hate to mess it up."

Pan smiled. Protective (okay, maybe a bit *over*protective), smart, funny, understanding, self-confident, gentlemanly—why couldn't she have run into Javier Maldonado a couple of years back, when her life had spiraled into a nightmarish crapfest? He might have been able to talk her out of some of the unfortunate choices she'd made during her dark days . . .

"Hey, you okay?" Javi asked with concern. "You just got this look in your eyes, like you were thinking about something really painful."

He was perceptive, too.

Pan lowered her gaze and concentrated on polishing her left-hand rings on the leg of her jeans. "I was just thinking . . . I wish I'd met you sooner," she said with a tiny smile, then shook her head. "Forget it."

"Why would I wanna do that?" Javi reached out to take her chin in hand, tilted her face back up. "Look, Cookie, I know you've had all kinds of problems ever since you were little and your monstervision kicked in, but that's all behind you—okay?"

"Really." Pan raised an eyebrow. "You're not gonna tell me I should stop dwelling on the past and just move on, are you? 'Cause I could get that from my therapist, Dr. Farrar, in one of our sessions."

Javi shook his head. "No. But I don't think it'd be a bad thing to, y'know, maybe look to the future and figure out where you want your life to go. And who you wanna make a part of it."

He was talking about himself, obviously. And he meant it, too. She'd felt that sincerity toward her before, and she could plainly see it now in his eyes, and in the way he smiled warmly as he gently caressed her cheek.

Pan swallowed nervously. "Are you *sure* you really wanna be part of my crazy life? 'Cause even though it's been established that I'm not crazy . . . pretty much . . . I have this feeling my life from this point on is never gonna be . . . normal."

Javi grinned. "Is that a promise? 'Cause that sounds kinda awesome."

He couldn't possibly mean that. "But after what just happened to us—to you—"

"Pan. Stop."

She did, mostly because she was surprised that he hadn't called her Cookie. Apparently he wanted to be taken seriously.

"Stop trying to chase me away."

Pan started. "What? I'm not."

"You *are*, even if maybe you don't know you're doing it. Now look, I get that you've gotten used to people treating you like some kinda weirdo . . ." He paused. "No, that's not it. You're not 'used to' it; you *expect* it. Every time you meet somebody, you're afraid they're gonna find out about your background, and the monstervision, and the doctors you've been seeing all these years, and run away screaming. It's been going on so long for you it's become . . . what's that thing they call it when you do something outta habit?"

"Second nature?"

"That's it," he said with a nod. "Second nature. Assholes in the past treated you like dirt, so you go into everything expecting the same from everybody. And when somebody new comes along and *doesn't* act like that you go on the defensive, 'cause even if they're nice to you, you're expecting them to make you look like an idiot later on."

Pan shifted uncomfortably. Maybe Javi was a little *too* perceptive, because he was hitting the proverbial nail on the head with his analysis. Not that she hadn't heard similar words from her therapists, from her parents, even from Sheena—but from a boy she'd met only a few days ago? Un-freakin'-real.

He took both her hands in his. "But it's different this time," Javi continued. "Did I run away when Annie showed you how to use your monstervision, up on the High Line, so you could see what Gothopolis looks like?"

"No," she replied slowly. "Because you'd already seen what Gothopolis looked like." And gotten one hell of a headache for his efforts, as he'd explained. Regular people, like Javi or her parents, could see the city of monsters that overlapped Manhattan, but it required a lot of concentration to see beyond the centuries-old magic spell that disguised its inhabitants. The end result of concentrating that hard, even for a short time, was a major headache. Dad had undergone the same experience, up on the elevated park, but at least he'd seen through the mystical veil long enough to confirm that his daughter had never been the crazy girl others had said she was.

"And did I run away when your dad talked about the hell that he and you and your mom went through when you started seeing monsters?"

Pan shook her head. In fact, Javi had looked as though he wanted to sweep her into his arms and offer comfort. Not out of pity, but of understanding.

"And wasn't I the one chasing that orang pendak that caused me to run into you at Penn Station? So I knew all about monsters and ghosts and all that stuff. Like I told you before, Annie's my godmother and my grandma Izzy used to go monster hunting with her—I've been hearing their stories ever since I was little. And the reason I was chasing that monkey in the first place was because I always wanted to go on those kinds of adventures; I wanted to be a monster hunter like Annie."

Javi smiled. "Don't you see? Even though we didn't meet until a few days ago, I was already part of your 'crazy life,' Pan." He leaned closer and added softly, "The question is, do you wanna be part of *mine*?"

For a few moments, Pan couldn't think of anything to say. She sat there, tongue frozen, heart pounding loudly in her ears, brain on complete lockdown, just staring into those sparkling brown eyes full of warmth and kindness.

And then she kissed him.

She hadn't planned on doing it—it was totally spur of the moment—but it felt like absolutely the right thing to do. Maybe it was the new-me attitude she'd adopted since learning the truth about herself that spurred her on. Or a desire to regain that sense of oneness she'd experienced while healing Javi. Or maybe it was simpler than all that.

Maybe it was just that she was falling in love with him.

When she drew back and opened her eyes, she found Javi grinning like an idiot. "Whoa," he said, breathlessly. "I'll take that as a yes."

Pan smiled. "You really should."

He grinned. "Awesome. So does this make us, like, boyfriend and girlfriend, now? I mean, if you're cool with that."

"Yeah. I'd like that." She kissed him again—a light one, this time, to prove she was serious. And, okay, because she wanted to. He had a really kissable mouth.

"Yeah, I'd like that, too." Javi slid an arm around her shoulders and she snuggled up against him. They sat like that for a little while, and then he chuckled.

"What?" Pan asked.

"I was just thinking maybe we should buy that orang pendak a fruit basket or something, to thank him for bringing us together."

Pan sat up and gave the thigh of his bad leg an enthusiastic squeeze. She didn't bother mentioning the slight tingle she felt running through her fingers. "Yes! That is *such* a great idea! When we get back to New York, and Mom's okay, I am totally gonna buy the biggest fruit basket for him and his baby. You remember that little baby of his?"

"The one who picked through your hair, looking for bugs to eat."

"Yeah." Pan grinned. "So cute . . ."

"I just hope my folks are okay with me dating . . . y'know, a *Mets* fan. My dad might kill me."

"Yeah, well, my dad probably won't be thrilled either," Pan replied, "but he'll just have to live with it. Mom won't care; baseball's never been her thing. But Sheen's a whole 'nother story."

"Nah, you don't have to worry about her," Javi said. "Sheena and me, we worked things out back at the hospital. We're cool."

"You mean, you guys are best friends, now?" Because that would be incredibly hard to believe.

Javi grinned. "Well, she still ain't crazy about me calling you Cookie, and we're never gonna work out the Yankees-Mets rivalry thing, so maybe . . . what's that thing—frenemies? I can work with that." The grin widened. "But only for you."

She patted his leg. "Aww, that's so sweet. Just don't go talking about all those world championships around her, okay? She's already got a shovel with your name on it, and a shallow grave all picked out."

"Whatever. I'll deal with it." Javi took her hand and gave it a squeeze. "Hey, you wanna see something weird?"

Pan's eyebrows spiked. "You know you're saying this to the girl with the monstervision, right? The one who took a little trip to purgatory and came back? You're gonna have to go a ways to find something *I'm* gonna find weird."

"Yeah, I know who I'm dealing with." Still holding her hand, Javi stood and gave it a playful tug. "Even so, I guarantee it's gonna blow your mind."

"Really." Pan grinned and rose from the bed. "Okay. But *after* I use the bathroom."

"God, and here I thought the hellhounds were scary-looking . . . ," Pan muttered as she stared at her reflection in the bathroom mirror. Hair in disarray, puffy bags under her eyes, right eye bloodshot—which, combined with its green sclera, gave the orb an oddly yuletide coloration—lips dry and cracked . . . *This* was the face Javi had been willing to kiss? Pan stuck out her tongue in disgust. "Blergh."

The bathroom was pretty small, with just enough space for a sink and a toilet and a spot on the wall to hang a couple of threadbare hand towels. She tied back her unruly mane and washed up, making use of the small bottle of dishwashing liquid that the construction boss apparently preferred over antibacterial soaps; the thick, orange-colored concoction smelled like tangerines. The towels, however, stank of oil and grease, so she unspooled great lengths of toilet paper to pat herself dry. The healthy glow of clean skin and the pleasant scent of artificial fruit brought a smile to her lips.

"Okay," she said, canting her face to get the best angle in the mirror. "This I can work with." She reached for her makeup bag, which rested on the sink. "Let the reconstruction begin . . ."

About twenty minutes later, she had a face she could live with—not exactly glamorous, but not the Creature From the Black Lagoon, either. Javi would no doubt be impressed, but he wasn't a girl—or a Goth—with a far more discerning eye. Still, as Mom would say, you make do with what you have. Which was totally true, given the current circumstances . . . but maybe a touch of powder wouldn't hurt . . .

She took out the silver-bat-stickered black compact and popped it open. There was a flash of purple light that made her yelp.

"Are we there yet?" rumbled a deep, familiar voice from the bathroom mirror.

Pan slowly turned to find a sharp-featured jinn gazing at her from the silvered surface. He looked extremely bored.

"Oh my God, Jerome!" Pan said. "I totally forgot you were in there!"

"Obviously," he replied in a droll tone.

"I am so, so sorry about that. It's just . . . things have been so crazy since we left New York, you wouldn't believe it."

"Try me."

There was a knock at the door. "You okay in there, Cookie? I heard you yelling."

Pan chuckled. "It's okay, Javi, I'm fine. I just forgot I was carrying Jerome around in my makeup bag and I kinda freaked out when he popped up."

"Oh. Okay. Hey, Jerome."

"Hello, Javier. Pandora is just catching me up on events."

Javi laughed. "That could take a while. Look, while you guys are talking I'll take a look around and see if we're still alone down here. Be back in a few."

"Be careful, Javi!" Pan called.

"You know I will," he said confidently. They heard Javi walk away, then the trailer door open and close.

Pan smiled. "Yeah, I know you will," she said softly.

Jerome sniffed dismissively. "I'll bet *he* forgot about me as well."

Pan grimaced. The spirit was probably right. "Yeah, well, like I said, things have been crazy."

"So you two are an item, I take it?" Jerome asked.

Pan started. "What makes you say that?"

"Your aura—it turned a warmer shade while you were talking to him. Love has that effect on it."

Aw, jeez. Pan blushed and turned away from the mirror.

"No, not *that* color," Jerome said. "That's just the color of embarrassment."

"Cut it out." Pan turned back to face him. "I thought you wanted me to 'catch you up' on stuff."

"And there was that 'Cookie' nickname—a play on your surname, I take it. What do you call *him*?"

Pan waved a dismissive hand. "Stop. You're worse than my best friend Sheena. Is this the kinda grief you give Annie?"

Jerome flashed a wicked smile. "All the time." The smile faded. "Where is she, by the way?"

"Still with the vampires and Zaqiel."

"And you haven't launched a rescue mission because . . . ?"

"Because Javi and m— Javi and *I* are alone on the island—we got cut off from Alexander. Just listen . . ."

Pan filled him in on her adventures, from when her group of would-be rescuers had departed New York all the way up to the run-in with the Mole People and the hellhounds, and her success in saving Javi's life. She left out the part about probably drooling on his shoulder while she slept.

When she'd finished her story, Jerome frowned. "So what you're saying is that we're stuck here in a construction pit until someone comes to rescue *us*, and then we can see about Sebastienne."

"Pretty much," Pan agreed. "And I hate it. I had this whole big plan in my head for how we were gonna save the day, and none of it's working the way I wanted it to. I just want my mom back to normal, but that's not gonna happen until somebody takes out Zaqiel. Except *that* can't happen unless Annie gets free, or Alex shows up with the cavalry, and there's nothing I can do to help with *any* of it!" She slapped the edge of the sink. "I feel so freakin' useless."

"Try living in a mirror for a thousand years," Jerome replied, "and see how useful *I* feel."

Pan nodded. "Yeah, I guess that would totally suck."

" 'Suck' doesn't even begin to describe it."

An old saying of Mom's popped into Pan's head: *As bad as you think you have it, somebody always has it worse.* A parental way of teaching a child perspective, and yet it was so true. It was just that, to Pan, it had always felt like *she* was the queen of the worst-case scenarios. Maybe it was time to step aside and let Jerome take the crown.

Pan smiled. "So what can two miserable people like us do to make the situation any better?" she asked wryly.

Jerome's head bobbed as though he were shrugging. "I suppose the proper response would be to stop feeling sorry for ourselves and press on . . . except I haven't a clue what we would be pressing on *to*."

"Me, neither." She chewed lightly on her bottom lip, mulling over the situation for a few seconds. She still couldn't think of anything and concluded with a shrug, "I don't know. Maybe Javi's got an idea."

There was another flash of purple light as Jerome returned to the compact's small mirror.

"Then let's go ask your boyfriend," he said.

"Ugh," Pan said in exasperation as she rolled her eyes, and closed the compact. "I don't know *how* Annie puts up with your crap."

"I heard that," came the muffled response.

21

"What should we do next?" Javi asked, then shrugged. "Y'got *me*. I was expecting a call from the Knights of the Apocalypse so they could tell me when they're gonna pull our butts outta here"—he reached into his back pocket and came out with a tangled mess of twisted wires and shattered plastic—"but it looks like somebody smashed my phone." He smiled wryly as he raised a quizzical eyebrow. "You wouldn't know how that happened, would you?"

Pan put on her most innocent expression. "You should ask the dogs about that."

"Uh-huh," Javi said with a knowing grin. He tossed aside the wreckage. "Well, good thing we still have *yours*."

Pan groaned. "Crap! I totally forgot about that, too! First Jerome and now the phone . . . I think this damn island's screwing with my long-term memory."

"Or it could just be you've had a lot of things on your mind lately—like me, for instance." Javi wrapped an arm around her shoulders and gently pulled her into a light kiss. When he moved back Pan grinned broadly, but then she playfully rolled her eyes.

"Oh, great—now I can't remember *anything*! My whole mind's gone totally blank!" She stared hard at him. "Who are you, again?"

Javi laughed. "Nice. Go call your girlfriend and tell her to get us the hell outta this hole."

Pan dug into her messenger bag and pulled out the cell. "Yeah, and maybe bring some sandwiches. I'm starving." Her stomach burbled in agreement.

"I can do something about that." Pan stared at him like he had three heads, and Javi laughed. "What? You think I'm making that up?"

"I think you're standing here wasting time when I could be eating. Go bring me food while I call Sheen." When he didn't move she waved a dismissive hand. "Go! Shoo! I've had enough of a trying day already; I don't need to add passing out from hunger to the list."

Javi chuckled. "Be back in a minute." He turned to go, then turned back around and pointed to his leg. "Hey, did you notice? I'm not limping anymore."

"I *did* notice," Pan said with a knowing smile. "Gee, I wonder how that happened . . . ?"

"I bet." Javi smiled slyly and then hurried off into the shadows.

"Run, Forrest!" she called softly.

Pleased with herself, Pan smiled broadly as she walked in the opposite direction, toward the airshaft. She stepped into the center of the mammoth opening and looked up. The first lavender brushstrokes of twilight painted the sky; she guessed that sundown wasn't too far off. And then who knew what horrors would come skulking out of the darkness, on an island filled with monsters?

"I'd rather not stick around to find out, thank you very much," Pan muttered as she pulled up Sheen's number and hit the auto-dial. The phone made buzzing sounds but the call never went through. Pan checked the screen, saw no bars lit up to indicate she had a signal, and grunted. "Crap. Too far underground, I guess." Which meant she'd have to go topside to access the vampires' Wi-Fi. Pan gazed up at the elevator landing so very high above. She thought she saw something move up there, but with the dwindling sunlight couldn't be certain. Were the hellhounds still lurking around, after all this time?

"Stupid dogs," Pan muttered with a sneer.

"Any luck?" Javi called.

"Nope. Can't get a signal." Pan turned to see him advancing—with a cafeteria tray loaded with food in his hands. Her eyebrows shot up. "Where'd you get all that?"

"I didn't know what you liked, so I just grabbed a bunch'a stuff." He set the tray down on a wooden crate. "Is that okay?""More than okay." Pan walked over, staring in disbelief at the selection of sandwiches and pastries, bottled iced coffees, vitamin waters, and sodas—all of them marked with a familiar demon-holding-a-coffee-cup logo. "Latte's Inferno?" she asked. It was her favorite coffeehouse franchise; the devil-girl T-shirt she was currently wearing—Javi's hospital gift to her—had come from one of their shops. "What, they started opening branches on Monster Island?"

"I'll show you later," Javi replied. "Eat first."

Pan used a metal drum next to the crate as a seat and hovered over the food. "Is that turkey cutlet and pepper jack on honey whole wheat? I'll take that. And one of the devil's food cupcakes for dessert."

"Whatever you want. I ate while you were sleeping . . . but I wouldn't mind one of these cream-puff things." He scooped one up.

Pan took a bite of her sandwich, was surprised to discover how fresh it was, and sighed contentedly as she chewed. "You wouldn't know how to make lattes, would you?"

"Sorry."

Pan shrugged. "That's okay. It's just that I could *so* use a mint mocha latte right about now. With extra whipped cream."

"I'll find you a barista on the *next* monster island we get stranded on," Javi said, and winked. "Promise."

Lattes aside, the food—washed down with ice coffee—was just what Pan needed to get back to feeling more like her old self. The restorative powers of a mild sugar-and-caffeine buzz helped.

"All good, now?" Javi asked with a smile from the other side of the table.

Pan smiled back and nodded. "All good."

"Great!" He held out his hand. "Then let me show you the surprise."

"This is the surprise?" Pan asked. She shook her head, still not quite believing what she was staring at. Before her stood a mammoth cargo container, similar to ones she'd seen in shipyards in movies, only this one sported the Latte's Inferno logo on the side, with a smaller logo above the lone door. Three large, extremely loud portable generators were connected to it, and the teens had to step well away to hear each other above the noise.

"It's *part* of the surprise," Javi replied. "This is where I got the food from."

"A coffee shop, on a jungle island ruled by monsters, in the middle of nowhere," Pan said. "That's just nuts."

"It's not a coffee shop, it's a refrigerator." Javi walked over to the door, opened it, and waved a hand toward the interior. "Take a look."

Pan did as he suggested. The container, front to back and side to side, was lined with rows of metal shelves, all stacked with countless boxes of prepared food and drink: sandwiches and full meals, desserts and snacks, water and sports drinks and sodas. The air, cold enough that Pan was grateful for the leather jacket she'd slipped back on, fairly vibrated with the muted roar of the generators outside. She stepped up to the first row of shelves to examine the boxes.

"Fruits and veggies not too popular with this crowd, huh?" she asked.

"This isn't exactly a salad kinda crew," Javi said. "Check out the stuff in the back."

Pan followed him to the rear of the container. Here there were no shelves, just loose, six-foot-high piles of cheap snack cakes from various countries and open boxes of moldy pastries and doughnuts.

"Everything's stale," Javi said. "I looked them over before. Some of the expiration dates go back a year or so." His lips curled in disgust. "I don't even wanna know how long the bakery stuff has been sitting around."

"But what's it doing here?" Pan asked. "They don't really expect somebody to eat this crap, do they?"

Javi shrugged. "Maybe they've got sugar zoms working the job. Those things would eat all of this without thinking twice about it." He paused. "I mean, if they could think at all."

Pan quirked an eyebrow. "What the hell's a sugar zom?"

"It's a zombie with a major sweet tooth," Javi replied.

"Oh, get out," Pan said in disbelief.

Javi raised his right hand as though he were swearing an oath. "It's the honest-to-God truth. I've seen them pawing through the Dumpsters and garbage bags in Annie's neighborhood. And let me tell you, a jittery zombie on a sugar high is nothing you wanna be around."

"And that's all they eat—junk food."

Javi shook his head. "I didn't say that. Sure, they eat other stuff—how do you think other sugar zoms get created? It's just that when they put the bite on you—"

"You get an incredible craving for chocolate-covered brains," Pan interjected.

"Pretty much."

Pan grinned. "Wow, you *do* have a crazy life, too."

Javi laughed and took her hand. "Let's get outta here."

A short time later, after packing her messenger bag with some water bottles and a selection of edible junk food, Javi slung the weighty satchel over his shoulder and led the way back to the construction site.

"So what's the rest of the surprise?" Pan asked as she closed the door behind them. "You said this was only part of it."

He pointed past the container, down a short row of others. "Over this way."

As they walked, Pan did a slow spin to examine their surroundings. "So where *is* everybody? With all this equipment and all that food, you'd figure there's gotta be a construction crew around here somewhere. Are they all on break?"

"There's nobody down here," Javi explained. "I checked. I think the things that attacked us were the work crew." He glanced over his shoulder toward the airshaft. "And I don't think they'll be coming back."

Pan took his hand and gave it a comforting squeeze. "That's fine with me. Whatever happened up there with the hellhounds, those jackasses got what they deserved."

"Yeah . . ." Javi squeezed back. "Thanks, Cookie. For everything."

Pan felt her cheeks redden just a touch. She'd always had trouble accepting compliments. "You'd have done the same for me."

"Well, sure, if I had superpowers like you."

Pan snorted. "If I had real superpowers I would've busted Annie out of that temple and kicked Zaqiel and all his monster thugs into the volcano or something."

"Maybe you can do that, too." When Pan gave him the side-eye, Javi added, "Well, it's not like you know everything about what you can do, right?"

"I'll stick to the monstervision and the healing stuff," Pan said. "That's plenty enough."

"And the sensing-the-spear thing."

"Yeah, that, too." She flashed a tiny smile. "But if I get any urges to leap tall buildings in a single bound you'll be the first person I tell."

"A Superman joke, huh? Nice."

"Well, I told you I read comics. Just not, y'know, the X-Men ones you're into." She gave him a playful nudge with her elbow. "But maybe there's some stuff you could recommend, right? 'Cause all I know about the X-Men is that Hugh Jackman should go shirtless in every movie."

Javi put some serious consideration into her suggestion; Pan could tell from the intense expression on his face. "Well, they did fight Dracula a couple times; I think I've got the trade paperback collection of those stories. And then there's the whole Brood storyline—they're giant space bugs that lay eggs in people, kinda like the Aliens from those movies."

"That definitely sounds like my kinda reading material."

Javi nodded. "Okay, when we get back home I'll lend you those." He glanced hesitantly at her. "Ummm . . ."

Pan knew that look; she'd given identical ones to her friends when they borrowed her things. She held up her hand, as he had done in the container, to swear an oath. "I promise you'll get them back in exactly the same condition you gave them to me."

Javi visibly relaxed. "Sweet."

Reaching the last of the containers, Javi came to a halt. "So here's the big surprise," he said, and gestured around the corner. Pan leaned forward to take a peek.

It was a tunnel. A semicircular, white-tile-lined tube as wide and well-lit—and probably just as long—as the Queens–Midtown Tunnel that connected Long Island City to Manhattan; it even sported a painted double-line down the center to divide lanes of traffic. To the left side of the tunnel were parked massive dump trucks, some loaded with mounds of dirt and rocks; to the right were a half dozen four-wheeled all-terrain vehicles, a couple of tricked-out Humvees, and a golf cart with the Mole People's union logo stamped on it. And arched above the entrance, someone had spray-painted in Day-Glo orange the haunting inscription that marked the gateway to hell in Dante's *Inferno*: ABANDON HOPE, ALL YE WHO ENTER HERE.

Javi pointed to the tunnel with a grin. "So?"

Pan knew what he was waiting for, so she placed curled-up fingers against the sides of her head, then flexed her hands away as she made an exploding sound with her mouth. Mind. Blown.

Javi laughed. "Told ya."

"It . . . doesn't really go to hell, does it?" Pan asked hesitantly. The one glimpse of it she'd had while visiting purgatory was enough to last her a lifetime—or in her case, a second lifetime. She wasn't eager to sign up for a full-blown tour.

"Don't know," Javi said. "I thought we could find out together, so I waited for you to wake up." Which, Pan thought, was really sweet of him to be so considerate. That way they could spend eternity roasting in the pits, together.

Pass, she thought.

"I figure it's gotta lead to the volcano," he continued. "They must've built this so they could transport all the dirt and rocks and stuff out of the work site at the other end. It's a pretty fancy tunnel for an excavation site, though." He barked a laugh. "Maybe Zaqiel's gonna start charging tolls."

Pan gasped. "I bet I know what this is for. They're trying to dig their way into the chamber Zaqiel came from—the one where all the other fallen angels are!"

Javi groaned. "Oh man, just dealing with one of them's a major pain in the ass— how bad's it gonna get if *all* of them get free?"

"It's bad already," Pan said quietly, thinking of her mother. "If they get loose . . . I think that'll be the end of the world."

"Jesus," Javi croaked in a shaky voice. "What do we do?"

Pan looked toward the airshaft; in the gloom of twilight, the elevator was barely visible. "We've gotta go back up. Alex has to know about what they're doing here, and I can't get a cell-phone signal this far down."

"Okay, but what if the dogs are still up there, waiting?"

Pan unconsciously raised her left hand and began gnawing on the cuticle of her thumb, using her teeth to scrape off the black nail polish—a nervous habit she'd inherited from Mom. After a few moments of contemplation and paint stripping she dropped her hand and shrugged. "I don't know. We'll just have to deal with it, I guess. They were afraid of the spear before, so maybe . . ."

"Umm . . . Okay," Javi replied with a nod. "So, let's go."

Pan could tell he was trying to act strong for both their benefits—such a totally guy-impressing-a-girl thing to do, in the face of danger—but the hint of worry in his eyes made it clear that he was as nervous as she felt. They'd barely escaped with their lives from the hellhounds. If the damn dogs were still up there, still hungering for souls . . .

No, it had to be done, Pan told herself. She and Javi had to go topside and place that call. The situation had gone way beyond a rescue mission, even beyond a battle to stop Zaqiel's plans. If the legions of monsters were already on the verge of freeing the other angels—although she had no idea just how they'd managed to get this far, when Zaqiel had been resurrected only a few days ago—then Alexander had to be informed immediately. He needed to spread the word. This was going to be an all-hands-on-deck emergency for the Knights of the Apocalypse . . . because the Apocalypse might really be on its way.

Pan exhaled sharply to steady her nerves, then took Javi's hand. "It'll be okay," she said with what she hoped was a confident smile, though she could feel it wavering along the corners of her mouth. Before it completely gave way, she stood on her tiptoes and drew him into a brief kiss.

"What was that for?" Javi asked with a confused smile. "Not that I'm complaining."

"You looked like you could use one." Pan grinned. "So could I."

"Works for me," Javi said with a laugh. "C'mon, let's go call in the troops."

Hand in hand, they began jogging toward the elevator—only to stop when they heard it activate. As they watched in a mixture of shock and horror, the car rose toward the ground-level platform.

"Oh crap," Pan muttered.

"You think the dogs figured out how to use the elevator?" Javi asked.

"That would reeeeally suck." Pan shook her head. "But no. I think somebody else is coming."

"Or some*thing*." Javi looked at her. "Wanna stick around to find out?"

"Not so much." Pan glanced around. "Is there someplace we can hide?"

"I wouldn't go back to the office trailer," Javi replied. "There's only the one door, and the windows are too small to crawl through to get out that way. We'd be trapped if they came in. Same thing for that refrigerated container. And all these other containers have locks on them."

The solution struck them both at the same time; in unison they glanced over their shoulders at the tunnel—which was the last place she wanted to go.

"You thinking what I'm thinking?" Javi asked.

"I'm thinking this sucks even more than the idea of devil dogs learning how to use elevators," Pan muttered. She sighed "Let's go" and joined Javi in running full-out for the entrance.

As they drew closer, however, Javi changed direction and headed for the ATVs. By the time Pan reached him, he'd already taken a seat on one and switched on its ignition. When he revved it up she'd expected it to roar like her mother's motorcycle; instead it sounded like the gas-powered lawn mower Mom had her trim the front lawn with.

"You know how to ride one of these things?"

"Sure. My folks have some property upstate, and Dad lets me use the quad he's got in the garage there. I think that's 'cause he's thinking of buying a new one for himself, but I don't really care. As long as it's running, I'm happy enough with the old, beat-up one." Javi nodded toward the back of the ATV. "Hop on."

Pan was happy to do so, lightly wrapping her arms around his waist as she settled against his back. It was a nice fit, she thought.

"Hang on," Javi warned. The ATV lurched toward the tunnel and Pan tightened her hold. And laughed.

Because in spite of the dangers that might await them at the end of that tunnel, in spite of the horrors that might be following them, she'd finally found someone to share this whole crazy, monster-filled life with.

22

She couldn't stop staring at the blood on the floor.

The construction site elevator was crowded and hot and its clanking gears and chains were loud enough to rattle her teeth, but Annie's attention was completely focused on the sticky pool of dried blood in which she stood. Blood that she feared belonged to either Pandora or Javier.

Zaqiel and his party—of which Annie continued to be an unwilling member—had discovered the teens' van parked amid the scattered remains of what Kiyoshi Sasaki had said was this site's work crew. During the time that the group lingered at the massacre, Annie spent it convincing herself that neither her young friend nor her godson could be among the victims, but with so many body parts scattered across such a wide area, doubt and dread gnawed away at her confidence. Her hopes had risen a tiny bit when Annie spotted a set of boot prints weaving through the jungle up to the elevator platform—a type of tread that didn't match any of the work boots she'd noticed among the carnage. Coupled with the drag marks that accompanied the footprints, which indicated to her tracking skills that someone had been pulling a body—presumably alive—from the attack and up to the elevator platform, Annie could only believe that the kids had survived long enough to elude the hellhounds that the party had found sitting at the edge of the airshaft. But then to find all this blood in the car . . .

"Impressed with our work?" Zaqiel asked, interrupting her thoughts.

Annie pushed aside her dark thoughts and gazed at the construction site below her. "You did *not* build all this in a few days' time. You couldn't have. Temporal magic?"

"Precisely," Zaqiel replied. "The Sisters of Time are mine to command, as well."

Annie doubted that was true. The Sisters were many things—witches whose lineage dated back to the seers of ancient Greece, manipulators of history, devourers of memories, destroyers of lives—but sycophantic followers of a fallen angel was not one of them. And since Zaqiel hadn't bothered to involve them in his last bid for worldwide domination, their participation this time would more than likely have been someone else's idea.

She gazed over her shoulder at Lady Kiyoshi Sasaki, who stared daggers back at the huntress. The leader of House Otoyo clearly didn't enjoy having to stand in the back of the elevator with the help, although her bubbly sister, Miyuki, seemed amused by the close quarters. Crammed into the car along with Annie, Zaqiel and the two sisters were a half dozen of the clan's gun-toting thugs, Kiyoshi's second-in-command, Hiromi Takami (also armed), and Frau Trude, the wizened old crone who made certain that the power-dampening spell on Annie remained active. Add in the five blood-crusted hellhounds and their trainers, and it made for one oppressively hot, smelly elevator.

"How much did it cost for the Sisters' services?" Annie asked Kiyoshi. "The souls of a school bus full of children? The still-beating hearts of a hundred holy men? I understand their prices have gone up in the last century."

"I promised them your corpse," the vampiress replied coolly. "They were particularly interested in your brain."

"For my memories, of course. How far back were they willing to go?"

"Three years."

"Three years?" Annie frowned. She didn't know if she should be grateful that the workers could travel back in time only so far, or insulted that four centuries of memories were worth so little.

"A sufficient amount of time," Kiyoshi said, and gestured at the site. "According to the Mole People's records, and verified by an ancient religious work one of my clansmen discovered, this area we're entering was part of the original construction: an antechamber connected by a tunnel to the doors of the prison"—there was that upward glance again—"*he* had the angels construct. The tunnel had been sealed once the work was done."

Annie raised a quizzical eyebrow. "And would the name of this 'ancient religious work' happen to be *The Book of Enoch*?"

Kiyoshi eyed her with great suspicion. "Yes," she said slowly.

"Was it the Diana Huntermeyer translation, from 1830? That's probably the most famous one."

Kiyoshi frowned. "Yes."

"I thought so," Annie said with a sagely nod. "That's *my* translation. Your clansman probably found it online, on one of those public-domain book sites." She paused. "I don't remember anything about a tunnel, though. Are you sure that's in there?"

"*Your* translation?"

"Well, it can't always be about staking vampires and beheading angels, now can it? I do have other interests; translating ancient texts just happens to be one. You see, about a year after my . . . breakup with Zaqiel, I started thinking about the stories he used to tell me. About his life before the fall, and the 'harmless' acts he committed, and the punishment God brought down on his head, and those of the other Fallen.

"And I wondered if there was some way to verify his tales. One day I mentioned this to a Knight of the Apocalypse and he recommended I read this tome called *The Book of Enoch*, to learn the truth about Zaqiel's stories. It was supposedly the firsthand account of Enoch, the great-grandfather of Noah, who was commanded by God to bear witness to His judgment on these hundred and ninety-nine fallen angels who'd attempted to overthrow Him with the aid of the children they'd fathered." Annie flashed a condescending smile. "Sorry. I said 'children.' I meant to say meant 'horrific, bastard offspring.' "

"Yes, we all know the story," Kiyoshi said.

"Anyway, I found a few copies of the book in the Vatican library, even though the Church doesn't treat it as scriptural canon. Most were Latin and Green translations, but there was also one in its original Ge'ez-language form. Well, I didn't speak Ethiopic, but I had a feeling that perhaps something might have been lost—you know how some translations are—so I taught myself, and then got to work. It took two years, but what Enoch described was certainly a revelation . . . no pun intended." She glared at Zaqiel. "Good thing for you I didn't know Enoch's book even existed, back when we were lovers. If I'd had any idea what sort of a monster you really are, I'd have cut off your head a lot sooner."

Zaqil snorted. "Before or after I'd have torn out your throat?"

A soft giggle from the back of the car interrupted Annie before she could respond to the angel. Together, she and Zaqiel turned around to find Miyuki smiling at them. "You sound like an old married couple."

The huntress looked uncomfortably at the angel, and he at her, then both turned back to stare at the work site.

The elevator came to rest at the bottom of the shaft and Zaqiel threw open the car's door. Annie stepped right beside him, taking a small amount of pleasure in blocking Kiyoshi on the way out.

"What I don't understand, Zaqiel," Annie said, "is, why not send your lackeys into the past to resurrect you? I'd tucked your coffin away in the darkest corner of a UK warehouse so long ago I'd forgotten it was there. If some time-traveling vampire had pulled the Spear of Longinus from your chest three years ago, there's a good chance I might never have been aware of your return until you'd already put your plans in motion." She flashed a knowing smile. "As hard as it is to believe, even *you're* capable of subtlety, Zaqiel. When you want to be."

"I've waited a century for my revenge, Sebastienne," Zaqiel replied. "What are a few days in comparison?"

Annie snorted lightly. She knew an evasive answer when she heard one. "You mean you'd already considered it and the witches refused to comply. You had to settle for sending back construction workers to dig out the tunnel and let the project catch up to the present day." Her eyebrows rose slightly. "The Sisters of Time, concerned about disrupting the timeline—*that's* a first."

Or perhaps it was an indication that Zaqiel was destined to fail, just like before. After all, the Sisters were descended from seers—they might not be able to travel into the future (as far as Annie knew), but they could certainly look into it. And having observed future events, they'd probably decided that no matter how much or how little the timeline might become screwed up by an early awakening for Zaqiel, the risks weren't worth the effort because the outcome was inevitable.

Or perhaps this was all just wishful thinking.

Kiyoshi shoved her way past just as two of her minions grabbed Annie by the shoulders; they sharply yanked the huntress into her proper place in line—behind the clan leader, of course. Annie didn't bother resisting, her attention given to the two sets of tracks she spied leading away from the center of the airshaft on a meandering course. One set of treads belonged to the same boot that had terminated at the elevator platform. The other was a running shoe of some sort, its stride pattern longer than the boot, which indicated its owner was taller than the boot wearer. In her heart, Annie knew the footwear belonged to Pandora and Javier, and she glanced skyward to offer a silent thanks to the Almighty and a request that He continue watching over the teens. She considered asking Him for a little assistance in quashing His fallen child's latest rebellious act, but then decided not to—God helps those who help themselves, and all that. Besides, she'd been able to stop Zaqiel once without calling on God to step in. Of course, she'd had an army at her back at the time . . .

Then her heart skipped a nervous beat when she realized that the kids' winding path led to what appeared to be a reconstruction of the Lincoln Tunnel on Manhattan's West Side—except that the destination at the far end of this particular passageway was a great deal more dangerous than anything found in New Jersey. Even worse, she spotted a fresh set of tire tracks—no doubt created by an all-terrain vehicle similar to the ones she saw parked nearby—heading down the tunnel's roadway.

Inwardly, Annie sighed. It was bad enough the kids had somehow arrived on the island, apparently without adult supervision; did they have to make matters even worse by actively seeking out trouble? "Out of the frying pan and into the fire" was a cautionary sixteenth-century idiom; it wasn't meant to be a lifestyle choice.

Says the woman who's made a career out of jumping from one bad situation to the next, Annie thought with a small, wry smile.

The smile faded, though, when she saw the hellhounds straining at their leashes, pulling their trainers in the direction of the ATVs. They'd caught the teens' scents and were eager to renew the hunt.

Zaqiel also noticed the dogs' behavior. He examined the vehicles, took note of the tire tracks, and turned to Annie. "Your latest protégés possess admirable survival skills, my love, to have escaped the carnage in the jungle . . . but not a great deal of intelligence." He gestured toward the tunnel. "They evade death by tooth and claw, only to venture into the very heart of suffering and despair? Ridiculous. But if it's any consolation, they will be the first humans to die when my brothers are released. I'll see to it personally."

"Normally at this point I'd say that if you harm those children I'll kill you," Annie replied with a sneer. "But since I plan on doing that anyway, why bother?"

"Enough," Kiyoshi snapped at her, then turned to Zaqiel. "My lord, why do you continue to tolerate this disrespect, from the very creature that betrayed you at your greatest hour? If you desire that she bear witness to the fall of humanity, then so be it, but at least permit one of my clansmen to cut out her tongue so that we no longer have to listen to her incessant chattering."

"I don't know why *you're* so upset with me, Kiyoshi," Annie said. "I might have failed to assassinate Zaqiel back in Yokohama, but I *did* eliminate a good number of your clan elders in the process. If anything, you should be thanking me for simplifying House Otoyo's bureaucracy."

Kiyoshi frowned but said nothing, because Annie had spoken the truth. Ever since the Sisters Sasaki had taken control of House Otoyo, rumors had quietly spread through the underworld of how Kiyoshi's plans to modernize the organization and greatly expand membership always met opposition from the elders, who had little use for change. Masters of the old world, they'd grown comfortable in their ways and, like so many other weirdlings of their generations who'd survived this long, saw no reason for their personal worlds to become infuriatingly complicated by their having to figure out things like smartphones and apps and tablets. Yesterday's monsters were a millennium's worth of seniors out of touch with modern times, with no desire to play catch-up with today's technology. And as for social media as a recruiting tool, why bother when vampires still added to their ranks the old-fashioned, neck-biting way? Fangs before Facebook, the argument basically went.

By gunning down a number of the old guard, Annie had eliminated some of Kiyoshi's most strident obstacles. Of course, now Lady Sasaki had the exalted Zaqiel to take orders from, but Annie had a firm suspicion that Kiyoshi had her own method in mind for handling that problem . . .

"I would be happy to remove her tongue, my lady," said a pleasant voice in Japanese. All eyes turned to Kiyoshi's male second-in-command, Hiromi Takami. Like the other, more youthful members of his clan, Takami wore the leather-and-lace of an Elegant & Gothic Lolita clotheshorse, only his tastes were distinctly feminine: a black cropped jacket with matching skirt, a black silk blouse, a small satin top hat rakishly perched on the left side of his curly auburn wig. He carried off the look magnificently, right down to the makeup, but the predator's smile that he directed at Annie, and the six-inch-long, double-edged dagger he slid from his jacket, ruined the ensemble.

"You stay out of this," Annie warned him. "Or you're not going to like where that knife ends up."

"A most generous offer, Hiromi," Kiyoshi said, ignoring Annie, and turned to Zaqiel. "My lord?"

For about ten seconds Annie could practically see the gears turning in Zaqiel's brain as he weighed his options. On the one hand, his enormous ego demanded that Annie be present when the world burned, so he wasn't about to have her killed. On the other, having her present without the ability to deliver a running commentary, should any complications arise, undoubtedly had a certain appeal. Decisions, decisions . . .

"Later," he replied. "I want the pleasure of hearing her cries of anguish as she watches her young friends die, then her moans of hopelessness as she witnesses the subjugation of the human race." He glanced at Takami. "Then you may cut out her tongue."

"You've really thought this out, haven't you?" Annie asked.

Zaqiel stepped over and halted inches from her face, then grabbed her lower jaw between thumb and forefinger and squeezed until Annie snarled in pain. "My sweet, beautiful murderer," he growled softly, "I have had two hundred years in hell to plan your demise. It will be slow and agonizing, and each time you die I will wait for you to revive . . . and then I will start the process all over again. The Sisters of Time may have laid claim to your mind, but I will rip apart your soul. And it. will. take. *centuries* before I am done with you."

Every word of it was true; she could see it in his eyes.

The urge to make a snide comeback was strong. Annie had heard similar threats more times than she could remember, and none of her enemies had ever lived long enough to make good on their promises—but there was something different about Zaqiel's. It was more . . . heartfelt. Of course, it had all the earmarks of a standard villain speech—promises of unending torture, the mention of a timetable to explain just how long he'd been plotting his revenge—but there was a passion in the way he said them that always eluded the madmen she'd faced in the past.

Except Zaqiel wasn't a madman. A celestial being fallen from grace, certainly; an angry lover determined to punish the woman who'd betrayed him, definitely; a child destructively lashing out at his father for favoring other children over him, without a doubt. But not a madman. And though his words might not be as powerful as he imagined—at least from Annie's perspective—metaphorically kicking him in the shins just to score ego-boosting points might not be the right course of action to take. Perhaps a lighter touch was needed to defuse the tension.

Annie slid her aching jaw out from between his fingers and smiled pleasantly. "You always *did* know how to sweet-talk a girl, Zaqiel."

His eyes narrowed. "You think I'm *joking*?"

Inwardly, she groaned. Damn the man's severe lack of a sense of—

Her thoughts scattered as he punched her hard enough to knock her off her feet.

Annie crashed onto the hard-packed dirt, but used her momentum to roll to a crouching position. If she weren't handcuffed, she would have already been leaping for his throat, gun-toting vampires be damned.

"Did that *feel* like a joke to you?" Zaqiel demanded.

Annie snapped her head back to sweep aside the hair that had fallen over her eyes, then spat out a phlegmy wad of blood. *So much for the lighter touch,* she thought as she fixed the angel with a steely glare. "It *felt* like the last hand you'll ever lay on me before I send you back to hell."

The angel snorted derisively, then turned to Kiyoshi's followers.

"Pick her up. There is still work to be done."

Kiyoshi gestured to a pair of clan members, who yanked Annie to her feet. Frau Trude took a few moments to examine the cuffs to make certain they hadn't broken.

"I'm fine, thanks," Annie told the old woman, voice dripping with sarcasm. Trude glared at her with bloodshot eyes, then hawked up a thick spitball that she deposited at Annie's feet. "Aren't you adorable," the huntress said with a sneer.

Kiyoshi turned to her second in command. "Get the vehicles."

Another pair of guards hurried over to the Humvees parked by the tunnel entrance and drove them back to the group. Zaqiel, the Sisters Sasaki, Takami, and three guards joined the driver of the first vehicle, while Annie was shoved into the backseat of the second transport, between a guard and the crone. The hellhounds and their trainers piled in as well, and the Hummer quickly filled with the combined stench of sweaty fur, drying blood, fetid dog breath, the strong cologne of vampiric male fashionistas, and the even stronger, too-sweet scent of a wizened hag's perfume.

Annie grimaced at the tight quarters. "Cozy," she muttered sarcastically, then turned to Frau Trude. "What perfume is that, exactly? You smell like a candy factory threw up all over you." The crone cleared her throat, preparing to loose another phlegm discharge, but Annie leaned over to place an index finger firmly against her lips. "I might not have my powers, you sack of dust, but spit on me again and I'll rip out your tongue and feed it to these dogs."

Trude, wide eyed, stared at Annie for a couple of seconds, then at the hellhounds that seemed to understand what the huntress had said, then back to Annie—and swallowed the loogie with an audible gulp.

"Good girl," Annie said in a condescending tone, and sat back. She would have crossed her arms for an additional show of superiority, but the handcuffs made that impossible.

The Hummer lurched forward and followed Zaqiel's vehicle into the tunnel, and Annie's thoughts immediately turned to Pandora and Javier. Somewhere up ahead they were about to encounter nightmares out of legend; creatures of the purest evil; horrors that no human had beheld since biblical times. Annie didn't just fear for their lives, she feared for their souls . . . and their sanity.

"Oh my God, this is totally insane," Pan said in awe. "And I oughtta know, being an authority on the subject and all."

Javi turned to look over his shoulder at her. "Really?" The tone of his voice made it clear he was actually saying, *I thought we were done with all the crazy-girl talk.*

Pan grinned and gave him a nudge in the back. "It's a joke."

"Oh, okay," he said with a nod. "Just checking." He slowly looked around. "But you're right, it is kinda nutty. But . . . it's also kinda amazing. Y'know?"

Pan smiled and rested her chin on his shoulder. "Yeah."

Still seated on the ATV behind Javi, she gazed around the enormous chamber they'd arrived at. This end of the tunnel was unfinished for the last two hundred or so feet—no smooth pavement, white tiles, or fluorescent lights here, just hard-packed dirt inside a concrete tube, with two rows of lightbulbs hanging from the roof—and the road continued for another quarter mile before curving into a twisty downward slope that ended roughly fifty feet below at an extremely busy work site. Perhaps as many as a hundred figures—at this distance it was difficult to discern features or genders (or even species)—in hard hats and miner's helmets labored under high-powered lights mounted on mobile aerial platforms; the LED lamps illuminated the bottom of the cave with the brilliance of a midday sun. The focus of their work was a pair of bronze doors that stood thirty or forty feet high and were decorated with ornate symbols. The doors looked thick and heavy, and at some point in its history the left-side panel had slipped off its hinges and come to rest against its partner; the task of the crew seemed to be getting the door back on track so both could be opened. A chill ran up her spine as Pan wondered what might be lurking behind them . . . and if Javi would be interested in sticking around to find out.

It wasn't just the doors that were captivating, however. The ceiling of the cavern rose high above the teens, supported all around by the uplifted arms and tentacles of fifty-foot-high statues of bizarre and disturbing creatures whose identities Pan couldn't even begin to guess at. She'd never really seen mythological monsters before, not outside illustrated collections of folklore and legends, but had a firm suspicion that these statues were accurate representations of living terrors that had once walked the earth—and hoped they didn't have modern-day descendants. Because as much of a horror fangirl as she prided herself on being, the last thing she'd ever want would be to run into these kind of gargantuan beasts in real life.

Still, the statues *were* pretty amazing works of art . . .

Pan hopped off the ATV, pulled out her cell phone, and started taking pictures.

"Seriously?" Javi dismounted and looked back the way they'd come, no doubt expecting someone, or some *thing*, to come charging out of the tunnel.

Pan spared him a glance, then went back to shutter-bugging. "What, you think I'm gonna stand here, in some giant cave that no human being has seen in, like, forever, with incredible statues that look like this and *not* take pictures? Now *that* would be crazy." She frowned. "It's just so dark in here I hope these shots come out. The lights down there help . . . a little, but it'd be so much better if this cell came with a flash."

"Well, not having a flash isn't such a bad thing," Javi replied, and jerked a thumb in the direction of the work crew. "I mean, do we really need to get everybody's attention down there by you playing Jimmy Olsen and lighting up the place?"

"I guess not . . . ," Pan said noncommittally. He had a point, but she'd still rather have a cell with a flash. "Hey, you think they have Wi-Fi here, like they do up top? 'Cause if we don't find a way to call Sheen and let her know where we are, between the ghoulies down there and whatever's probably coming up the tunnel behind us, we are gonna be royally screwed." She tried to sound lighthearted about their predicament, but inside her stomach was nervously roiling. Seeing no bars displayed on her cell didn't make her feel any better.

"I don't think we're gonna find a hotspot around this place," Javi said, looking around.

"No, just some really big doors and a lot of awesome statues . . ."

Javi grunted softly in response, his thoughts clearly elsewhere. He put his hands on his hips and stared at the ground in silence; from the way his eyes narrowed, Pan could tell he was trying to formulate a solution. She snuck a picture of him standing there, looking all serious and thoughtful and handsome. After a minute or so of gazing into space, then staring down the tunnel, his jaw set firmly and he nodded, apparently in agreement with himself. "Okay."

"So what's the plan?"

He pointed to a pair of boulders that stood to the left of the tunnel entrance. "First, we stash the ATV behind those rocks. Then we go up to that ledge up there"—he indicated a platform about twenty feet up, accessed by a rough footpath that started just beyond the proposed hiding spot—"and wait until whoever's coming goes by. Then we get back on the ATV and tear outta here for the elevator."

"And hope the hellhounds gave up waiting for us."

Javi grimaced. "Oh, yeah . . . Forgot about them. Damn."

Pan waved off the problem. "One thing at a time. It's a good plan; let's go with it."

With Pan using the handlebars to steer and Javi pushing from behind, they maneuvered the ATV into its hidey-hole facing forward (for an easier getaway), and then began cautiously picking their way up the path. Javi took the lead, occasionally stopping to offer a hand up when Pan wasn't yanking on one of his pant legs for support. Soon enough, they reached the platform and took a seat. From up here they could see everything without being seen, the shadows deep enough that the teens were safely out of the glow of the work lights.

Javi slipped off Pan's messenger bag and scooted up to the edge of the platform to watch the activity below. When he spoke, he did so quietly to avoid having his voice echo in the chamber. "Y'know, this high up, it kinda reminds me of sitting in the upper deck at Yankee Stadium. You should come to a game and see what it's like."

Behind him, Pan stuck out her tongue in distaste. Yankees. Blergh.

"Y'know, we could've waited *on* the ATV behind the boulders, and not bothered coming up here—but you'd already thought of that, didn't you?" Pan scooched up beside him and pointed to the work crew. "You just wanted a better spot to check out what they're doing, without them noticing."

"I'm sure I have no idea what you're talking about."

Pan grinned. *Liar.* "Well, to be completely honest, I would've suggested doing the same thing if you hadn't."

Javi turned to face her. "Really?"

"Are you kidding? Those doors are—what, like a bazillion years old? That means whatever's behind them must be just as old—or even older."

"Older than a *bazillion* years?" Javi asked playfully.

Pan gave him a tiny nudge in the ribs. "You know what I mean. This is the island Zaqiel escaped from, and yet he comes back, not once but twice, to rescue his 'brothers.' Which means they must still be here, maybe even right behind those doors. Don't you want a peek of what's on the other side before we have to leave?"

"Well, when you put it that way, sure," Javi replied. "But opening something that God's involved with? That kinda stuff never works out. You ever see *Raiders of the Lost Ark*?"

"Only a bazillion times," she replied with a sarcastic edge.

Javi chuckled. "Okay, you made your point. I'm sorry."

"Apology accepted," she said lightly. Javi nodded, then went back to observing.

Pan did likewise, got bored after a while, and began rummaging through her bag, pushing aside the Spear of Longinus to reach the junk food that she'd taken from the refrigerated shipping container. "You hungry? I could go for something."

"Nah. I'm good."

Her fingers brushed against cellophane wrapped around a pair of familiar round shapes. With a smile she pulled out a package of chocolate-frosted devil's food cakes. Her favorite brand, too. She slid the food under her jacket to muffle the sound of the cellophane snapping open, pulled out the first cake, and took a whiff of the frosting. Pure heaven.

Javi glanced at the snack, so she held it out. "Want a bite?"

He smiled. "Nah. You enjoy it."

"Oh, I will," she replied.

Javi chuckled and turned back to observe the excavation—then started. "What the hell . . . ?"

Pan leaned forward to see what had caught his attention. "What's going on?"

The crew had stopped working. As one, they tilted back their heads and sniffed the air. The wheezing noise generated by a hundred people snuffling sounded like an inflating bellows with a leaky bladder.

Their supervisors noticed the halt in production. One of them bellowed an order in what Pan assumed was Mole People-ese, high-pitched and screechy-sounding like a bat using echolocation; probably telling them to get back on the job. The workers ignored him and continued sniffing. They were definitely locked on some kind of scent.

"Oh crap," Javi whispered. "The Mole People *are* using sugar zoms, like I thought." His shocked gaze moved from the corpses to the snack cake in Pan's hand. *"And they can smell that."*

Pan's breath hitched in surprise—and then she shoved the entire cake into her mouth, in what she knew was a lame attempt to hide it from the walking dead. She didn't know what else to do with it. "Forrryyy," she mumbled, shards of frosting tumbling from between her lips.

"It's okay," Javi replied. "It's not like they can see us up here in the shadows." He glanced down to confirm that belief . . . only to find every sugar zom staring at them. Well, in their direction, anyway.

"Don't move," he whispered.

Pan swallowed her mouthful of food. "You mean they can't see us if we stay still? What are they—zombies, or T. rexes from *Jurassic Park*?"

"Their eyesight's not so good, so they have to rely on their sense of smell mostly," Javi replied. "Least that's how Annie explained it to me. But if they see us running, they'll swarm up these rocks like crazy. You and me and a bag full of junk food—for sugar zoms, that'll be like one of those feeding frenzies you see on Shark Week."

"Yeah, but would we be the main course, or the dessert?" she asked with a smile. Sure, it was a lame joke, but she was trying to keep the mood light—and not think about zombies turning them into an all-you-can-eat buffet. Except now she couldn't think of anything *but* that. Stupid zombies.

"I don't think it matters to them . . . ," Javi replied. The tone of his voice made it apparent that, although he'd heard her question, he hadn't realized it was a joke—he was too occupied looking away from her. At what, though?

Pan glanced downward. The sugar zoms were starting to mill around, their noses still locked on something they couldn't possibly still be smelling. *I ate the damn cake already! What's their problem?*

She minutely shifted her position—her butt was starting to fall asleep—and heard a tiny crinkle of cellophane in her lap. Pan looked down and grimaced. She'd forgotten there were *two* snack cakes in the package.

"Hey, does that look like a doorway to you?"

Pan started. "What?"

"Over there," Javi said. He was holding his left hand against his chest, so as not to move around too much, with his index finger pointing past him in the direction of even deeper shadows that filled the space between the legs of a squid-headed statue about twenty or twenty-five feet away.

"What am I supposed to be looking at?"

"There's, like, a hole in the rocks over there. I think. It kinda looks like a doorway."

"What—like a caretaker's entrance, or something?"

Javi turned to face her. "Or where the pizza delivery guy delivers his pizzas?" he asked with a smile. "I don't know. But do you see it?"

Pan craned her neck out a tiny bit. She could see something, maybe a hollowed out part of the wall. "Yeah . . . Could be a doorway. But wait—a doorway everybody missed?"

"Like I said, the sugar zoms have bad eyesight. And they're not too bright, y'know what I mean? They're *zombies*. And those"—he sneered—"Mole People've probably been too busy trying to keep them under control to scope out the area. Anyway, their job is to clear the big doors, so you gotta figure that's what they've all been focusing on."

The sound of shouting drew Pan's attention to the gathering below. She swallowed nervously. "Not any more they're not."

Ignoring the commands of their Mole People crew bosses, the zombies were clambering up the rock face in search of chocolaty goodness. And making pretty good headway—the way some of them hopped from place to place as they ascended reminded Pan of mountain goat footage she'd seen on some nature show.

"Holy crap, I didn't know those suckers could *climb*!" Javi said as he jumped to his feet.

"I thought you knew everything about sugar zoms," Pan said as she joined him.

"Well, I didn't know *that!*"

The scrape of rubberized soles against dirt made Pan turn to her left. A few yards away stood a trio of zoms that had already reached the pathway, cutting off the teens from the ATV and escape. They stumbled forward, the stumps of their withered noses twitching as they homed in on the nearby food. Their features were beyond gaunt, the skin so tight it appeared the skulls had been shrink-wrapped in discolored flesh, the eyes so recessed into their sockets they gave the impression of fireflies flitting around the depths of animal burrows. Water-thin lips drew back to expose rotted teeth and swollen, black tongues.

Real zombies, I'm actually seeing real-life zombies, she thought in wonderment. The horror fangirl in her squeed a bit at the notion, despite the danger bearing down.

A hand dropped onto Pan's right shoulder and she loosed a tiny yelp, but it was just Javi. "We gotta go," he said.

"No kidding," Pan replied. She grabbed her bag and she and Javi bolted for the hole in the wall. Pan hoped with all her might that it really was a doorway and not some tiny alcove created by the volcano.

Without breaking stride she threw the remaining snack cake at the approaching zoms. It distracted one corpse, who stopped to shove it into his mouth, but his two companions kept right on shuffling. They smelled bigger game.

Then they started running.

Pan sucked air through clenched teeth. "Running zombies? Oh man, those are the worst . . ."

More zombies swarmed onto the path to join the chase, and all of them were quick on their feet. It didn't take long to shorten the distance between the horde and its intended meal.

"Damn, those things are fast!" Javi yelled. "I don't think we're gonna make it!"

He was right. These zombies were hungry and nothing was going to stop them from gorging on flesh and blood and entrails and brains.

Nothing, Pan suddenly realized, except maybe a messenger bag full of junk food.

She fumbled to open the clasp.

Javi reached the doorway—and, thankfully, it *was* a doorway—first, scrambling up a pile of rocks and small stones to reach a platform at the feet of the statue. He held out his hand. "Come on!"

Pan took it and leaped up to join him, but then she turned around and reached into her bag. She heard Javi, who'd stepped toward the hole, come to a halt. *"What're you doing?"*

"Creating a diversion," she said as the bag's clasp came free. "Hoping to create one, anyway . . ."

As the zombies closed in, Pan began hurling snack cakes and pastries as far as she could throw them; a few she hard-balled into the faces of the ghoulies that got within grabbing distance of her legs. The tactic worked: within seconds she'd transformed a surging crowd of flesh-eaters into brawling sugar addicts competing for a bagful of sweets.

"Choke on it!" Pan crowed. *"Choke on it!"*

Grinning, she turned to find Javi staring at her in shock. "What the hell?" he asked.

She gave him a tiny shove. "Just go. *Go!*"

Beyond the doorway was a tunnel just wide enough to accommodate their walking side by side. They quickstepped along the dusty corridor until the glow of the construction lights faded from view; then Pan halted.

"Hang on a second." She dug into her bag and pulled out a six-inch-long, paper-wrapped tube that she tore open. Into her hands dropped a plastic cylinder that she snapped in the middle and then vigorously shook. A bright blue light filled the tunnel.

Javi raised a quizzical eyebrow. "A glow stick? Gonna use it to do some magic, like Natsumi?"

Pan laughed. "No. I got stuck on a crowded N train once, in the tunnel going to Manhattan, and the power went out . . . and then I had one of my monstervision episodes. It got kinda . . . freaky for me for a while. And when the power came back on, I made a promise to myself to never get caught in a situation like that again."

"So you're afraid of the dark?"

Pan shook her head. "Not afraid, I just got . . . cautious about it. Remember who you're talking to: the girl who sees monsters everywhere. Being trapped in the dark, with the air getting all hot and stale, feeling all those bodies pressing against me and thinking way too much about what their owners might look like . . ." Pan drew a breath, then exhaled sharply, pushing back the memory. "Let's just say that every time somebody used their cell phone or tablet to light up the car, my imagination got really creative." She shook the miniature light. "So, I always carry a couple of glow sticks . . . just in case."

Javi appeared to be at a loss for words, uncertain whether to offer sympathy or make a joke. After a few seconds he said, "Sure come in handy."

"That they do," Pan said with a smile.

They trudged ahead, not having a clue where the tunnel might lead, but Pan figured that anywhere that led away from a ravenous horde of corpses was better than standing around, waiting to be eaten.

"So you wanna tell me what that was about, back there?" Javi asked. "With the sugar zoms."

"Oh, what, the 'choke on it' thing? It's my favorite line from *Day of the Dead*," she explained. "Y'know the George Romero movie? A bunch of zombies are chewing on this guy, and that's what he yells at them while they're gnawing on his intestines." He gave her the side-eye. "What? It just seemed appropriate."

Javi shook his head. "Man, you are one weird chick."

Pan laughed. "You just figure that out now? I'm like an iceberg of weirdness, Javi—ninety percent of the *really* strange stuff is below the surface."

" 'An iceberg of weirdness.' Is that anything like an artichoke of knowledge?" he asked with a sly grin.

She grinned back. "Could be."

"And if I put them together, would I get an artichoke iceberg of weird knowledge?"

Pan chuckled. "Yeah, that's me, all right."

The smile they shared, however, quickly faded when the sounds of boot heels echoed from the darkness behind them.

Something was coming—and moving toward them fast.

23

"Well, look at that," Dalibor said as he pointed at the rental van. "You see, Jenna? And here you were so certain I'd forgotten where we parked."

Leaning heavily on his commanding officer as he hobbled along on a wounded right leg, Dalibor flashed a weak smile. He was obviously trying to sound lighthearted for her benefit, but Jenessa wasn't in the mood for levity. She was looking for revenge. And blood. And those two damnable children who'd stolen the van would supply her with an opportunity to obtain both, once she got her hands on them.

Jenna looked around the clearing. There were enough signs to suggest a battle had been fought here—the corpses, the torn-up ground, the damage to the van—but apparently only one side had suffered casualties, since all she saw were the chewed up body parts of Mole People. So either the other combatants had taken their dead or wounded with them . . . or the island's scavengers had carried off the bodies to feast upon, and would be back for seconds. If that were the case, Jenna needed to get her people out of the area immediately, because they had already experienced the dangers that stalked Halja's Island . . .

Jenna looked over her shoulder at the remains of House Karnstein's new strike team. Along with Dalibor, only Casper Andritsch and Florian Herzog had survived the jungle predators; the others—Michelina Tagwerker, Keenan Phibbs, and Anastasya Stogryn—hadn't lasted long once the team had started their pursuit of the teenagers. Anastasya, the witch, could have brought the team's dilemma to a quick end by teleporting them to the van, but she couldn't concentrate on spells, her brains a little too scrambled by some Taser-like device the boy had used on her. She never got the chance to clear her head . . .

Jenna pushed aside the unpleasant memory. "Casper, check out the van. See if it's still operational."

Andritsch nodded once, then jogged over to the vehicle. He made a quick sweep around it, peering through the windshield and checking underneath to make certain there were no deadly surprises waiting.

"It's probably only suitable for the junk heap, now." Dalibor *tsk*ed. "We're never getting our deposit back."

Jenna sighed. "Not now, Dalek."

Andritsch plopped down in the driver's seat. "They left the key in the ignition." He twisted it once and the engine roared to life. "Looks like we still have about a third of a tank."

"Best news I've heard all day," Jenna grumbled. Still supporting Dalibor, she guided him toward the van while Florian provided cover. With the luck they'd been having since launching this mission, Jenna wouldn't have been surprised if the Mole People scattered at their feet suddenly rose up in zombie fashion, hungry for undead flesh.

"I don't see the children," Dalibor said as his gaze swept the killing field. His eyebrows arched a touch as he turned to Jenna. "They couldn't be responsible for this . . . could they?"

Jenna snorted. "Dalek, the girl has some low-level preternatural abilities—anyone can see that, if they look close enough—and she's certainly clever, but to do all this? Never. And the boy is just . . . human. Worthless."

"Not as a meal," Florian remarked. "And I'm starving."

Dalibor's softly rumbling stomach agreed.

"You can have whatever's left over," Jenna replied, "after I'm done with him. Although I can't promise there'll be much blood to drink once I've torn him apart."

"And the girl?"

Jenna paused, thinking of the terror in Anastasya's eyes as her throat was ripped out by a monstrous trapdoor spider that had leaped from an underground lair. That had been the start of the siege; after Anastasya went down it became a blur of teeth and claws, made worse by the realization that with the young witch's death the team had lost their means of escape.

And as she ran with her "children," laying down a barrage of fire but unable to save Michelina and Keenan from the beasts that were drawn to the gunshots and the screaming and the blood, one image remained foremost in Jenna's thoughts: the leering grin of a teenaged punk-rock reject as she abandoned her captors to their fates. To their deaths. Oh, for the chance to obliterate that infuriating grin . . .

"The girl has a lot of suffering ahead of her before she dies. First she'll watch her boyfriend get his due, and then . . ." Jenna flashed a malicious smile. "She'll be a long time dying."

"Unless the two of them have already been wolfed down by whatever these Mole People fought," Dalek said.

"Possible, but something tells me that anyone who's this much of a pain in the ass has some talent for survival—"

"Like some people I know who shall remain nameless," Dalibor mumbled playfully.

Jenna nudged him to shut up. "—and isn't going to die so easily." She pointed to two sets of deep grooves carved into the blood-soaked ground that curved around the van and into the tree line. "So let's follow these tire tracks and see where they take us. Perhaps they hitched a ride with the victors of this skirmish."

"You think one of the other houses came to their rescue?" Dalibor frowned. "That would mean the Spear of Longinus is in their hands. That won't go over well with Lady Karnstein."

"What the lady doesn't know won't hurt us, Dalek," Jenna replied quietly with a sly smile. "So let's make certain that once we've regained the spear there's no one left to tell the tale."

Whether the list of potential targets included Lord Bohumil Schovajsa's handpicked team members, Casper and Florian, was a question Dalibor knew better than to ask, and Jenna wasn't willing to answer. For now.

The charge in the air became apparent soon after the Humvees entered the tunnel—it prickled Annie's scalp, raised gooseflesh on her arms, and made her teeth itch. Powerful, ancient energies had been released by the excavation and that worried her. In fact, though she'd be loath to admit it out loud, it terrified her. Because what she sensed was just the slightest hint of the darkness that would be unleashed if Zaqiel freed his brother angels. At first, it would sweep across the globe, weakening every mystical barrier, every "perception filter" that separated the worlds of men and weirdlings; at full strength, it would shatter the spells that protected both realms from the great beasts that had stalked the lands in ages past. Madness and chaos and death would erupt, followed by decades of war as humanity fought to survive. But in the end, the monsters would win . . . just before they turned on one another.

The soft squeal of brakes pulled Annie from her depressing reverie.

"What the hell is this?" said the driver.

Annie leaned forward to get a look though the windshield, only to have a rather smelly dog butt rise inches from her face. The hellhounds wanted to see, too.

Annie grunted in disgust and turned to the right-side rear passenger window. Beyond the guard crowded in beside her she could see hordes of people running around, as though in a panic. A riot, perhaps, or were they fleeing from something they'd freed along with that dark energy?

The guard raised a hand to his right ear and nodded, apparently listening to an instruction through an earpiece Annie hadn't noticed earlier. He threw open his door and the howls of the damned filled the Humvee, quickly matched in volume by the hellhounds' defensive barking. The guard jumped out with Annie a step behind him. He turned to glare at her.

"Being your prisoner doesn't mean I have to go deaf sitting in there," she said with a nod toward the dogs. The guard grunted but said nothing.

Now that she had an unobstructed view, Annie could see that the Humvees had stopped just outside the tunnel, in a vast chamber whose ceiling was supported by statues of the same great beasts she feared would return.

"Not good," she whispered, and turned to focus her attention on the melee occurring on the cliff face below the roadway—men and women pushing, shoving, biting one another as they fought over small objects that occasionally glittered under the work lights. It was only when one of them bounced high enough to see clearly that Annie realized they were fighting over cellophane-packaged junk food.

The workers were sugar zoms—at least that was Javier's name for sugar-addicted corpses. It made sense: sugar zoms were mindless, unfeeling lumps of flesh who would never stop working, so long as they were supplied with ample amounts of sweets. Presumably they were being kept well fed to have reached Zaqiel's objective, but what could have whipped them into such a frenzy?

She looked to the other Humvee. Zaqiel and his entourage had also stepped out, and all appeared as confused as she felt. For someone who'd expected to be celebrating a moment of triumph in his ex's presence, the angel seemed ready to tear off someone's—anyone's—head for this embarrassment. Rather than give him reason to focus that anger on her, Annie turned her head so he wouldn't see her smug grin.

And then a powerful shout echoed off the cavern walls:

"Choke on it! Choke on it!"

Annie gasped—she recognized that voice. She scanned the darkness for its source, and found it beneath one of the statues on the far side of the cave. A girl stood on a platform above the chaos, and though her black clothes were difficult to see, the blond streak in her hair and the red-faced devil-girl face printed on her T-shirt stood out like beacons.

"Pandora," she whispered. And if Pandora was alive and well, then Javier should be close by her—at least that was Annie's hope. Pandora cackled at the mayhem and then dashed into a hollow space between the statue's feet.

Annie snarled. She needed to get up there, to help the kids—who knew what new danger they might be running toward? But in order to help them, she needed a distraction to provide her with a means of escape so she *could* get up there.

Something heavy slammed into her hip and shoved her aside: the hellhounds, no longer willing to sit in the Humvee. And with them came their handlers, along with a disheveled, dog-slobber-covered Frau Trude, who staggered a few steps to get her bearings and then went about straightening out her rumpled clothes. The *thunk* of a door on the other side of the Humvee signaled that the driver was coming around to join the group.

Moving cautiously so as to not draw the attention of her keepers, Annie eased behind Trude, then leaned forward to murmur in her ear. "Chaotic scene, wouldn't you say?"

The hag nodded. "That's putting it mildly. Are those things zombies?" She *tsk*ed. "Disgusting creatures."

"Yes. And did you know this particular kind of zombie is addicted to sweets?" Annie asked. "Can't get enough of them. They'd tear a person apart just to get their hands on a week-old Danish." She slowly unfurled a predator's smile. "Can you imagine what might happen if they ever encountered someone who smells like a candy factory?"

It took a few moments for the words to sink in, but soon enough the realization dawned on Trude; Annie could see it in her startled expression when she turned to face the huntress.

Then she shoved the old biddy toward the horde.

Annie's guard spun to subdue his charge but she was already in motion, kicking high to break his nose with a boot heel. The small silver cross embedded in the rubber—overlooked by Zaqiel's minions, who'd expected to find more conventional weapons on her person when they initially searched her—branded him across the lips and down his chin. The stench of burned meat mingled with Frau Trude's confectionery vapor trail.

Moaning as he clutched his face, the clansman stumbled into the witch and both went down in a heap—right on the edge of the riot.

As expected, once the sugar zoms caught a whiff of Candy Crone and Barbecue Face it was as though a dinner bell had rung in their heads. They howled loud enough to make both the living and the undead wince in pain, then swarmed across the rocks, desirous of this latest treat.

The driver, momentarily distracted by the sight of his compatriot being smacked down by an allegedly helpless prisoner, discovered Annie wasn't quite so helpless as she grabbed him by the lapels of his morning coat and dove into the surge, followed closely by the hellhounds with their surprised handlers in tow. Perhaps realizing that Annie was one of the few living beings in this cave that still possessed a soul, the dogs weren't about to allow a tasty meal to get away. The handlers, unable to control their hellish pets, were just along for the ride.

Jumping into the middle of a zombie mosh pit to escape her captors might not have been the wisest course of action, but Annie was a firm believer in seizing an opportunity when it presented itself. Like starting a feeding frenzy by offering a candy-perfumed witch as an appetizer. Or grabbing the driver before making her break: without her powers she wouldn't be able to kill him, but he'd certainly make an effective battering ram to clear her a path. And he did, especially with all the panicked arm flapping he was doing to beat back his attackers. The hellhounds and handlers, though, had no barriers between them and the horde—they shrieked and yelped and whined as the sugar zoms tore into them, and then fell silent.

"Return to your work!" Kiyoshi ordered the ravenous horde bearing down on her.

Good luck with that, Annie thought. Sugar zoms were rather hive-minded when it came to filling their bellies: when one zombie felt like eating, *all* of them felt like eating, and nothing was going to distract them from chowing down . . . unless it was an offer of more food, as Pandora had demonstrated. Kiyoshi might as well have barked commands at the Humvee she and Miyuki were backed against—the result would have been the same.

Takami stepped in front of his clan leaders, an Israeli-made Bul Cherokee 9mm pistol in hand, and began snapping off head shots with precision. He was quickly joined by the Sasakis' bodyguards with their Austrian-manufactured Steyr AUG A1 Para 9mm submachine guns, and the cave reverberated with the rattling echoes of high-caliber gunfire.

The bullets had little effect on the tsunami of corpses that swept over the top of the ridge. Frau Trude's and the branded guard's screams were cut short, replaced by the sounds of teeth rending flesh and scraping bone. Anything that was edible was fair game for the zombie workers—including their angelic leader. Zaqiel was shocked to find a trio of sugar zoms attempting to take bites out of him. He spread his ebon wings wide and took to the air, only to be knocked down by a dozen enemies that used the Humvees as springboards to reach him.

Annie, meanwhile, had made some headway in her escape, but she was quickly running out of vampiric shield—the zombies had already chewed off the driver's legs and forearms. A few more bites and Annie would find herself holding a headless torso, until that was ripped from her grasp—and then what would she use for protection?

But then a familiar tingle coursed through her body—a pins-and-needles sensation like sleeping limbs beginning to wake up.

Or supernatural powers returning.

Annie batted aside a pair of burly zombies, then stole a glance over her shoulder. Somewhere in the bloody melee behind her, Frau Trude was now less a witch and more a snack tray, and with her passing went her magical influence over Annie. The spell that had shut down the huntress's abilities was broken.

She was free.

Annie didn't bother wasting energy cheering or gloating. She was free of the spell, but not of the frenzy she'd helped create. And though she'd put distance between herself and Zaqiel's entourage, the opening that Pandora had slipped through was still too far away to simply run for it.

Unless, of course, it wasn't Sebastienne Mazarin making a break . . .

As the remains of the driver were snatched from her hands, the huntress's form blurred. Skin and muscle and bone and hair shifted, rearranged, and settled into a new configuration, all in a matter of seconds; the handcuffs slipped off wrists that were momentarily as thin as twigs. And when the change was complete, where the fearsome La Bella Tenebrosa had stood there was now a slack-jawed wreck of a work-crew corpse. At first the dead stared at her in confusion, then she was immediately forgotten as they pushed past her to join their compatriots at the buffet.

She moved against the tide until she reached a spot on the small cliff that she could climb, and soon reached a rough footpath below the opening.

"Sebastienne!"

The roar echoed through the cave, louder than the zombie hordes, louder even than the gunfire. In spite of knowing better than to reveal herself, Annie looked back. Bloody and bare-chested, Zaqiel hovered high above the war zone on tattered wings that weakly flapped to keep him airborne. Even from where she was standing Annie could see the fire in his eyes as he pointed right at her zombie form. Their old psychic love connection had given her away.

She abandoned her disguise and ran, lunging through the doorway and haring down the tunnel beyond. She had no idea where she was going, but anywhere away from Zaqiel and a ravenous mob was good enough for now.

She slowed, however, when she noticed a bright blue light up ahead. "Pandora?" she called out cautiously. "Javier?"

The tunnel echoed with the sound of both teens yelling "Annie!" Then the blue light sped toward her and Annie was able to see the source of the illumination: a glow stick held by Pandora. The girl's smile was almost as brilliant.

The teens fell into her arms, and Annie hugged them as though they were her own children.

"What in God's name are you doing here?" she asked, then looked over her shoulder. Was that the scrape of a footstep she'd heard from the tunnel's entrance? It was probably her imagination, but better not to take chances. She gently urged the teens forward. "Tell me along the way. We need to move."

"But where are we going?" Javier asked as they walked. "Do you know where this thing leads?"

"I haven't a clue," Annie admitted. "The last time I was on the island, I wasn't thinking too clearly to go exploring after the battle."

"And why was that?"

"Because I'd just killed my evil boyfriend, my mother had lost a hand—thanks to Zaqiel—and I was a little distraught. As soon as the fighting ended and his forces ran for the hills, I got the hell off this island. Exploring his prison was the last thing I was interested in doing. I left the cleanup work to the Knights of the Apocalypse and never came back."

"I don't blame you," Pandora said in agreement. "Oh, and speaking of killing your evil boyfriend . . ." She handed Annie the glow stick and began rummaging through the bag slung over her shoulder.

"Ex-boyfriend, thank you," Annie said firmly. "What are you looking for?"

"This," Pandora replied as she held up the Spear of Longinus.

Annie's eyes widened in shock. "Where did you get that? More importantly, *how* did you get that?"

"Alex helped us," Javier replied.

"Alex," Annie said. "You mean *my* Alexander?"

"Yeah, *your* Alexander."

It was impossible to believe. "You're saying my son Alexander willingly put the two of you in harm's way in order to obtain the spear? That doesn't sound like him at all. What sort of half-assed plan did he have in mind . . . that involved risking the lives of *children*?" Annie snarled. "If he wasn't too old to ground, I'd lock him in his old bedroom and he'd never see the light of day again."

"For your information, it wasn't his plan," Pandora said. "It was mine. Javi and me and Sheena—you remember Sheena? You met her at my dad's museum. Anyway, Javi and me, and Sheena and her boyfriend Uwe, were coming to rescue you. With Natsumi's help."

"How did you meet Natsumi?" Annie waved off Pandora's answer before she could utter it. "Never mind. So you and your friends convinced a witch to teleport you here—"

"Well, not here," Javier interjected. "We thought you'd still be in Japan. We were gonna rescue you." He shrugged. "Didn't work out that way, though."

"So, stealing the Spear of Longinus and launching a rescue mission—that was your entire plan?"

"No," Pandora said. "There was . . . other stuff. I was still working on it."

"Nah, that was pretty much it," Javier replied. He smiled at the sour expression she directed at him. "C'mon, Cookie, you know there wasn't much more to it than that." He looked to Annie. "But hey, it's not like Alex's bosses were in any rush to save you. And with Pan's mom getting sicker, we got tired of waiting for somebody to do something. So we stopped at your place to pick up some weapons." When Annie glared at him, he quickly added, "But no guns. And when Alex showed up, he tried to talk us out of doing this."

"Not very successful, was he?"

"Again: not his fault," Pandora said. "And he's not the only one who offered to help. Your mirror-genie guy, Jerome, wanted to come. He's in my compact."

"He's *what*? Oh, for God's sake," Annie said in frustration. Bringing a soul-devouring mirror demon to possibly the greatest source of evil in the world, and expecting him to help in their foolish quest . . . Madness. Utter madness. It took all of Annie's willpower to not bellow at the teens. She settled for clenching tightly to the glow stick in a death grip. "And Alexander approved this insanity?"

"No," Pandora said. She returned the spear to her bag and took back the glow stick before Annie broke it in half. "Look, let me just start at the beginning, okay? It'll all make a lot more sense when you hear the whole story."

Annie came to an abrupt halt. "Tell me later . . . ," she said quietly. They'd arrived at the end of the passage, and though Annie couldn't see anything beyond the glow of Pandora's dance-club party favor, she could tell from the acoustics that they'd stepped into a much larger space.

The dark energy she'd felt on the drive over was stronger here, though that didn't surprise her—the closer to the source they moved, the more powerful the flow. The gooseflesh she'd experienced earlier had intensified to the sensation of ants crawling over her skin; the prickling of her scalp had become an itch that wouldn't let up. What did surprise her was that Pandora seemed unaffected by the power—with her preternatural gifts, the girl should be incredibly sensitive to the presence of such evil, and yet here she'd been chattering away as though the three of them were strolling through Central Park on a sunny day. Was that because she was a horror fan, and felt comfortable in such a bizarre and deadly setting? Was it because she was mentally blocking it out, as she had tried to do with her "monstervision" during all the years she thought she was mentally unbalanced? Or perhaps it was the perceived indestructibility that most youngsters possessed, only at a higher level; after all, Pandora had fought her way back from purgatory. Why fear dying when you have the power to turn away the Grim Reaper?

Or maybe you're just overthinking the situation, Annie thought. For all she knew, it could just be that Pandora was too excited about this grand adventure she'd found herself in to focus on the dangers that undoubtedly lay ahead. Annie had noticed that same look in Javier's eyes, when he'd assisted his godmother in tracking down the orang pendak under Pennsylvania Station. But that in itself was a worrisome trait, because as Annie knew from experience, it was always the most adventurous humans who threw caution to the wind . . . and who suffered the greatest . . .

"Hey, you hear that?" Javier asked. "I think they stopped shooting."

Now that he'd mentioned it, Annie realized it *had* become deathly quiet in the outer chamber. She looked over her shoulder and saw the glow of work lights about a quarter-mile back, outlining the off-kilter doors that the sugar-zom crew had been preparing to open.

"Sounds like Zaqiel settled his work-stoppage problem," Annie remarked.

"That means they'll be coming through those doors next," Pan said.

Annie nodded. "Which means we shouldn't be standing here when they do." She placed a hand on Pan's glow-stick-holding hand and gently pushed it down. "Put that away, just for a minute. I can see better in the dark."

"Oh, yeah? What're you, part owl?"

"When I need to be," Annie said with a knowing smile.

Pan gazed at her for a moment. "Oh, I get it. You're gonna do some shape-shifting stuff, right? Cool." She did as requested, sticking the plastic tube under her jacket, and the corridor was plunged into darkness. "Spoooky," she whispered.

Annie shushed her and concentrated on the transformation. In a split second her eyes changed to those of an owl and she began scanning their surroundings. It was a much larger corridor, as she'd suspected, but it wasn't made of volcanic rock—this was a man-made construct of marble, lined with unlit torches and the same types of grotesque statues that held up the ceiling of the outer chamber. From where Annie and her young companions were standing, it extended another quarter-mile or so and ended at what appeared to be a cavern as large as the one they'd left behind, its entrance framed by the legs of a four-legged sculpted beast. However, it wasn't the design of the hallway or its garish statuary that sent a chill through Annie's body, but the words that were carved into the vaulted ceiling. The twenty-foot-long letters were in a language she didn't recognize, possibly one lost to time, but as she watched the ancient script blurred, shifted, and reset in an English translation, apparently for her benefit:

THIS PLACE IS THE END
OF HEAVEN AND OF EARTH

I remember that phrase from when I was translating The Book of Enoch—*it's what one of the angels said to Enoch, when it was describing the prison that had been fashioned for the Fallen. Who knew it would turn out to be the basis for a warning sign?* Annie mentally shrugged. *Well, at least it's not as clichéd as "abandon all hope, ye who enter here"* . . .

"See anything?" Pan asked.

"Probably more than I care to . . . ," Annie replied.

"*That* doesn't sound too ominous," Pan muttered. "So is it okay for *us* to look, now?"

"Hmm? Oh, yes. Sorry." Annie stopped gazing at the ceiling and shifted back to her normal eyes. "Go ahead."

Pan removed the glow stick from her jacket. "So, what's the plan? Did you find a way outta here?"

"Not a clearly marked one, but there's another chamber at the end of this corridor," Annie said. "Hopefully there's an exit." She glanced back at the outer doors. "It's not as though we can leave the way we came in . . ."

They set off at a jog, Annie taking the lead with the glow stick. The thought that they were running into even greater danger was foremost in her mind; she was certain the teens shared that sense of dread. Or did they?

God, I really hope they're not enjoying this. She glanced over her shoulder just to be sure, and inwardly groaned. *Oh for pity's sake, could their smiles be any wider?*

The "fun," however, came to an abrupt end when the corridor shook from the force of an explosion that knocked all three off their feet.

Annie lost her grip on the glow stick as she fell, but quickly rolled to a crouching position. She shifted back to night vision to locate her young adventurers. "Are you kids okay?"

"I'm good," Javier replied.

"Me, too," Pandora said. "What the hell was that?"

Annie shifted back to normal sight and looked toward the main entrance. An immense cloud of dust rolled along the hallway, but through it she could see the blaze of work lights on the far side of the bronze doors, which now wobbled on broken hinges.

Isn't that just like Zaqiel? Annie thought. *Why wait to straighten the doors and walk in like a normal person, when you can simply blow them out of their frame? Then again, he and patience have* always *been worlds apart.*

"They're coming in," she said as the hinges groaned under the massive weight. "Stay down and cover your ears!"

The teens followed Annie's example just as the hinges snapped. The thick doors slammed down with an echoing boom that seemed to last forever. Dust and debris rushed down the corridor, enveloping the trio in a choking cloud of volcanic grit.

And that's when every dormant torch on both sides burst into flame.

Annie and her friends winced as their eyes adjusted to the lighting. Through the dark spots dancing in her vision, Annie watched as four figures in combat gear entered the hallway to make a sweep of the area. She wondered where the soldiers came from, but then pushed aside the question. Right now, the need to escape overrode the desire for answers. Annie ran over to the kids and helped them to their feet.

"I think somebody set off an alarm," Javier said as he gestured, squinty-eyed, at the torches.

A rumble of stone grinding against stone, soft at first, then growing in volume, interrupted Annie before she could respond. She looked upward. Was the ceiling about to come down? No, other than some little bits that the explosion and door collapse had knocked loose, it looked fairly stable. Then what was causing that noise?

"Behind you!" Pandora said, and pointed over Annie's shoulder.

The huntress turned to see the statue that framed the entrance to the next chamber breaking into chunks that slammed onto the floor. That didn't concern her as much as the fact that with each section that fell away, a piece of dark brown flesh was revealed. Then four sets of sharp toenails. Then a pair of tusks that jutted out from the sides of a mouth lined with jagged teeth. Then, finally, a pair of amber-hued eyes . . . that slowly opened.

There was a monster within the stone. And it was waking up.

The beast pulled away from the wall and the rest of its covering dropped off and shattered. It stood ten feet high on all fours, was thickly muscled, and possessed a wide, blunt head that was some hideous combination of canine and bovine features.

"That's a really big guard dog," Javier remarked as he and Pandora moved beside Annie.

"It's . . . Behemoth," Annie said hoarsely.

"A behemoth? That's one way of putting it," Pandora said.

"No, that's its name," Annie replied. "It's mentioned in the Bible—the Book of Job. 'His bones are as strong pieces of brass; his bones are like bars of iron. He is the chief of the ways of God: he that made him can make his sword to approach unto him.'" *Funny,* Annie thought, *the things that stick in the back of your mind when it comes to monsters.*

"And what does that Bible verse mean in today-speak?" Pandora asked.

"It's pretty much indestructible. And only God can kill it."

"Oh," Pandora said softly, then added in a stronger, sarcastic voice, "Well, sure. Why should *anything* be easy to deal with on this freakin' island?"

Behemoth shook off the remaining bits of stone, took a deep breath, and roared; in such a confined space, the sound felt like a physical assault—Annie and the teens staggered back, as though struck.

Then it focused on the three creatures at its feet.

"Don't move," Annie whispered to her charges. From the corner of her eye, she watched as Javier cautiously reached out to take Pandora's hand; the girl gave a reassuring squeeze. Apparently they'd done some serious bonding since she'd last seen them, so even though they'd ignored her command to remain still, Annie had to smile. They made such a cute couple, how could she be angry?

Behemoth lowered its head and sniffed them individually, with Pandora receiving an extra whiff . . . and a closer look. *It probably senses her gifts, or the Spear of Longinus,* Annie thought, *because there's no possible way it could consider her a threat. Not with a fallen angel and an island full of weirdlings right behind us.*

It seemed that Behemoth agreed with that belief, because after giving Pandora the once-over, it snorted dismissively and looked beyond the trio. And though Annie daren't turn her head to glance over her shoulder, she had a pretty good idea who it was that had caught its attention.

"Stand aside, beast!" the angel bellowed, his voice amplified by the hallway's acoustics. "Zaqiel of the First Reborn has come for his brothers!"

Behemoth bared its teeth—and then charged.

"Run!" Annie said to the teens, and all three raced for the next chamber. She looked over her shoulder to see what was developing. There was an army of monsters gathered behind Zaqiel; apparently Kiyoshi had called in the troops while she and Miyuki sat in the Humvee during the zombie uprising. And as Behemoth bore down on the legion, a multitude of gun-mounted laser sights shone brightly in the dusty corridor and focused on the Almighty's guard dog.

The shooting started immediately.

Pandora and Javier both yelped and hunched over to avoid being struck by the stray bullets that whizzed past them. Annie, however, was more focused on the entrance to the inner chamber—and the stone slab that was dropping down from the top of the doorframe. Apparently another security measure had been engaged.

With a final burst of speed, the trio dove under the ancient stone and slid to a halt on the other side. The "door" closed with a teeth-rattling impact, plunging them into darkness.

"*This* can't be good," Javier said.

"Y'know, I am *really* starting to hate this island," Pandora said sarcastically.

"Nobody move," Annie commanded. "And I mean it this time. Just stay where you are. I'll come get you."

In response, there was a rattling sound that Annie recognized as Pandora rummaging through her messenger bag, followed by a snap of plastic and the bright yellow flare of a glow stick that revealed Pandora sitting cross-legged on the floor, a wicked smile on her lips. She held the tube just below her chin so that the glow created strong, deep shadows on her face. Monster lighting, it was called in the movies, and undoubtedly a term with which the young horror fan was familiar.

"Anybody up for telling ghost stories?" she asked playfully.

"Maybe another time," Annie replied. "Right now I'd rather concentrate on the story of how we got out of here."

And that's when the wall-mounted torches in the chamber burst into light.

It took Annie a moment to realize that the yelp she'd heard hadn't come from one of the kids, but from her. That was a pleasant surprise. Four hundred years of adventuring and monster hunting, and apparently there were still some things that could startle her.

Still, she grinned sheepishly at her young friends. "Sorry about that."

Not that the teens heard her. Pandora had jumped to her feet and joined Javier in looking past Annie in astonishment.

Annie sighed wearily. "There's another giant guard dog behind me, isn't there?"

A smile slowly lit Pan's features. "No," she replied softly. "Much cooler."

Annie gazed at her in confusion for a couple of moments—what the hell was so cool about a beast that could swallow you whole in one bite, that had only ignored them because better prey was available?—and then turned to face whatever this new sight was.

It took her breath away.

24

Despite the seriousness of the situation, Pan couldn't help but grin as she heard Annie gasp in disbelief. Not that she could blame the huntress for reacting that way—the chamber was a pretty astonishing sight.

It was round and somewhat conical, the stone-block walls rising to a point in the center. The ceiling wasn't as high, the floor space not as wide as the one outside the main doors, but it was big enough to house the collection of marble angel statues that lined the circular wall on three levels. It looked as though there were a couple hundred of them, all tucked into alcoves with the exception of four that encircled a marble column placed right below the center-point of the ceiling. Heads tilted back, arms raised, hands clasped in prayer, it appeared as though the angels were pleading the heavens for forgiveness—but if the rest of the bunch were as evil as Zaqiel, those pleas were never going to be answered. Or it could be that they were begging the angel positioned at the top of the column to do something. He, too, had his hands raised, but his hands were open, and in his palms rested a large red jewel that glowed brightly with an inner light—a representation of an offering to God, maybe? That's what Pan would have given as an explanation, if she'd ever painted a scene like this, but she had a feeling the jewel's purpose had a deeper meaning.

"Huh," Annie said, disrupting Pan's thoughts. "This reminds me of tholos tombs I've visited on Mycenae, like the Treasury of Atreus." She pointed upward. "You see the way the ceiling curves to a point in the center, like a beehive? That's what 'tholos' means—beehive. I've just never seen one this old, before." She rolled her eyes. "Well, of course I haven't—after all, this tomb predates even the ancient Greeks."

"Guess they had to get it from somewhere, right?" Javi said.

"So, Annie, does this mean when you're not hunting monsters, you're some kinda tomb-raiding archaeologist?" Pan asked.

"I've dabbled," Annie said with a smile. "But long-lost tombs aside, right now I'd be happy to just discover an exit."

"I hear that," Javier agreed. "And speaking of hearing . . ." He paused, then cocked his head to one side. "I'm not hearing anything from outside."

Pan joined him and ran a hand over the stone, then knocked on it a couple of times with her knuckles. "This thing must be really thick," she remarked, and pressed an ear against it, " 'cause I'm not hearing a thing, either. Maybe Cujo took out Zaqiel and the rest?" *I hope.*

Annie pressed her own ear against it. "I can't tell, but as much as I'd like for that to happen, if only to make all our lives easier, I'd have to say no. Zaqiel's come too far this time, to let some ancient guard dog stop him now."

"But you told us only God could put down that Behemoth-thing," Javi said.

"That could have been biblical hyperbole. After all, bullets and bombs didn't exist in the days of the Old Testament, just swords and arrows."

"And spears," Pan added, with a tiny shake of her bag.

"Exactly. But we'll let the monster dog . . . thing worry about that while we find an exit. If Zaqiel and his followers make it past Behemoth, that door won't keep them out for long." Annie glanced around the chamber. "Let's look for an access tunnel, like the one we walked through to get here. There have to be others."

"How'd Zaqiel get out?" Pan asked.

"A lava tube on the east side of the volcano, but that's unusable. Apparently it's gone active again, which is why all this excavating and tunneling was going on."

Pan's gaze shot straight toward the ceiling, and the concave depression at its conical top. "Wait. We're under the volcano?" The thought of all that molten rock pouring down on the trio, through what appeared to be a ready-made inverted funnel, popped into her mind and she took a step back, bumping into the stone door. A solid reminder of there being no escape through the way they'd entered.

Annie placed a hand on her shoulder and gave it a comforting squeeze. "Relax. I don't think we're in danger of a cave-in anytime soon."

Pan raised a quizzical eyebrow. "What, are you a volcano expert, too?"

Annie grinned. "I'm multifaceted."

"So why're there access tunnels in the first place?" Javi asked. "And those giant doors out in the hall. I mean, what's the point in building a prison to keep angels in, if you're gonna give them a way to get outta it?"

"Maybe to let the prison guards in?" Pan asked. "If it's a prison, you've gotta have some guards, right? If only to make sure your prisoners haven't escaped."

Javi started to reply, then paused to consider the point. "Oh, yeah," he agreed with a nod. "Okay, that makes sense."

"Although, y'know, they'd have to be really *big* guards, if they needed doors like those."

Javi chuckled. "Yeah. But if there are guards, how come we haven't run into any of them?"

"I'd imagine it's been a *very* long time since anyone has set foot in here," Annie said. "This chamber predates Noah's flood, according to the material I've read, which probably means this 'prison' has been left unattended for millennia. And Zaqiel never mentioned anything about guards when he told me his story about escaping from here."

Then who's been setting the torches on fire? Pan wondered. But she kept that thought to herself, not certain she wanted to find out. It could just be that God invented motion sensors that activated the torches—yeah, okay, maybe that was a little far-fetched—but if whoever was working the lights was anything like the Mole People, she could do without meeting them.

"You sure your boyfriend just didn't kill them, and not bother to mention that part?" Javi asked.

Annie grunted softly. "That wouldn't surprise me at all. And he's my *ex*-boyfriend." She shook her head, as though to dispel a bad memory. "Let's find that exit."

They moved deeper into the chamber to begin the search, but Pan's focus was on the statues in the center.

"I've got a better question," Pan said. She gestured around the chamber. "We've got a ton of angel statues, and those giant monster ones of I don't even know what they are . . . but what I'm not seeing is anything like prison cells or whatever. So if this is the place where Zaqiel was locked up, where are the other angels?"

Annie paused and looked away for a moment, as though reluctant to answer. Then she nodded toward the statuary. "You're looking at them."

Pan started. "What?"

"Oh, get out," Javi said.

"I'm serious." Annie stopped and threw out her arms, then did a slow 180-degree turn to encompass everything in the chamber. " 'And the archangel Uriel said to me: 'Here shall stand the angels who have connected themselves with women . . . here shall they stand till the day of the great judgment in which they shall be judged till they are made an end of.' All one hundred ninety-nine Fallen . . . well, one ninety-eight, not counting Zaqiel." She pointed to the angel at the top of the column. "See that one? That's Jeqon, who started the whole mess. He put the bug in the others' ears about how God was casting aside His first-generation creations, the angels, to focus on His latest experiment: what eventually evolved into humanity. And when mankind flourished, and angels like Jeqon felt they'd been knocked off the pedestal as God's favorites, that's when Jeqon convinced Zaqiel and the others it was time to revolt."

"Wait," Javi said. "I thought Zaqiel was the leader."

Annie shook her head. "No, he was just a follower. One of the first vampires, true, but still nowhere close to holding a power position. Jeqon was the mastermind behind the uprising."

"And *I* thought it was Lucifer who led the revolt," Pan said.

"That was against heaven, and before Jeqon's uprising. Besides, their goals were worlds apart from one another: Lucifer wanted power and eventually got it—only not in the way he'd expected; Jeqon and his followers just . . . wanted to get laid." She flashed an awkward smile. "Sorry."

Pan grinned. "Hey, no problem. We're all adults here." *Do* not *give Javi the sly-eye*, she warned her inner femme fatale. *Go focus on the statues or something.*

"Get laid and wipe out all humans, you mean," Javi said.

"No, that became Zaqiel's goal after he escaped from—" Annie waved at the statues—"this." She smiled wryly. "He has a tendency to hold grudges a long time, if you hadn't realized that yet."

"I'll say," Pan agreed.

"Where'd you get all this info from?" Javi asked Annie. "I don't remember hearing about this stuff in church—ever."

"It's from a tome called *The Book of Enoch*. It's one of the Apocrypha—the books of the Bible that were cut out because they didn't mesh with the Catholic Church's teachings."

"And this Enoch thing is all about Zaqiel and the rest of the fallen angels?" Javi asked.

"Yes, plus some of what Zaqiel told me when we were . . . together matches up with it. But I'll tell you all the details later." She gestured toward the left side of the chamber. "Take a look over there and see if you can find a passageway. I'll look on this side."

While Javi and Annie split off to start their search, Pan walked toward the ground-level statues . . . or angels, if Annie was to be believed. But that couldn't be right, could it—angels turned into statues and imprisoned underneath a volcano until Judgment Day? Maybe it was more of that "biblical hyperbole" Annie had mentioned, from that "lost book," because the alternative sounded pretty cruel, even if that Jeqon guy and his angel bros had been a bunch of total scuzzballs, like Zaqiel. Or was it really all that surprising? Wasn't God more of an ass-kicker in, like, the Old Testament, zapping people into pillars of salt and smacking down Egypt with all those plagues and stuff? So maybe turning angels into statues wasn't outside the realm of possibilities. Well, whether it was God being mean or this *Book of Enoch* thing exaggerating, she had to find out.

"Pandora, what are you doing?" Annie asked. Apparently she'd taken notice of her young friend's action.

"Don't worry, I'm not gonna touch anything," Pan assured her. "I just wanna take a closer look."

"That's really not a good idea," Annie said. There was a note of worry in her voice that made Pan roll her eyes. What were a bunch of statues going to do—get up and start flying with their big marble wings? Seriously, Annie . . .

Pan came to a halt beside the group clustered around the base of the column. Up close, the statues were even more amazing, with a high level of detailing she'd never seen on gravesite memorials in her numerous rambles through cemeteries. If they really were angels, they must have gotten the full Medusa treatment, like in Greek mythology. *If* they really were angels. She leaned forward and stared hard into the eyes of the one next to her, but all she saw was lifeless stone.

"Nope. You're just a statue, aren't you?" she murmured, more to assure herself than to expect an answer. She wasn't sure how she would have reacted if it *had* answered. Still, the openmouthed expression of horror etched in its cold features—an expression she noticed was echoed by the others around her—sent a chill up her spine.

"Hey, ladies," Javi called out, "I think I found the way out."

Pan looked over to find him standing on the chamber's second level. Confused by how he'd managed to get there, she backtracked his position and spotted a ramp that curved up from the main floor. Handy. Then she watched him step into an opening hidden by shadow; he returned a few seconds later.

"There's a stone staircase over here that goes up," he said, "so it's gotta lead topside, don't you think?"

Annie stared at the opening for a few moments. "How the hell did Zaqiel ever miss that?"

"Maybe 'cause you gotta be looking for it?" Javi offered.

"He lied to you, about how he got out," Pan said to Annie, and rolled her eyes. "Big surprise, there."

"No, not about this," Annie replied with certainty. "Otherwise why go to all the trouble of digging that tunnel out in the main chamber?"

"Maybe he avoided the easy way out 'cause that old lava tube was cooler," Javi said, and jerked a thumb toward the exit. "There's a *helluva* hot breeze running down the steps that's making me think the volcano's right outside." He shrugged. "But, y'know, if this is the only way we're gonna get outta here . . ."

Annie exhaled sharply—not a sigh, but definitely a sign of exasperation. "Then I guess we don't have a choice."

Great, Pan thought dourly, and glanced at the conical point of the chamber roof. Now that she was under the centerpiece, it sure did look a whole lot like a spout you could pour lava through, flooding the chamber with molten rock and burning alive anyone trapped in here . . .

"Pandora? You coming, or staying?" Annie asked playfully.

Pan snapped out of her depressing thoughts and spun around to see Annie starting to cross the chamber, headed for the ramp that led to the second level. The huntress waved her over. Pan smiled sheepishly. "Sorry. I got a little distrac—"

"*Nnnnnnn . . .*" It was less than a moan, more than a whisper, a soft whimper that choked off her breath and raised the hairs on the back of her neck. And it came from right beside her.

Slowly, she glanced down toward the angel she'd examined . . . and found bright blue eyes looking back. And despite her love of all things horror, despite the real-life terrors she'd been facing since the Spear of Longinus entered her life, terrors she'd confronted head-on with little hesitation . . . she screamed.

Boot heels pounded on the floor, and then Annie was standing next to her. She grabbed Pan by the shoulders and moved her aside, placing herself between the girl and the statue. "Come away, Pandora."

"But . . . but he's alive in there!" Pan tried to pull out of Annie's grip, to touch the angel, but the huntress's fingers dug in hard. Then she began pushing the girl. "What're you doing? We have to get him out!"

"We're doing no such thing," Annie said sharply. "Now come on."

"Hey! You guys okay?" Javi called down.

"We're fine, Javier," Annie replied. "Stay there. We'll be up in a minute."

Pan tried to plant her feet, but Annie was a hell of a lot stronger than Pan had imagined. With what appeared to be little effort, she forced her young friend toward the ramp. "Annie, no!"

"He's a fallen angel, Pandora, just like Zaqiel," Annie snapped. "Just like the rest." She spun Pan around to face her, then swept her hand toward the statues. "Look at them! Spiteful, hateful creatures who turned their backs on God out of nothing more than petty jealousy, and then took out their aggressions on every woman they could find. Do you know where most of the monsters in the world come from? They're the offspring of the Fallen and the women they violated. Vampires, werewolves—practically all supernatural creatures of great evil can be traced back to the Fallen. Why do you think he's called Zaqiel of the First Reborn? He and some of the others in here were the first vampires! *Think* of what they're responsible for! Why in God's name would you ever want to unleash that evil on the world again?"

The anger that raged in Annie was so vividly displayed on her face that Pan found it difficult to respond with her typical sarcasm, or even to look the huntress in the eye. "I . . . I didn't know," she muttered. "I'm sorry."

For a moment, Annie said nothing. Then she gave Pan's shoulders a comforting squeeze. "So am I." Pan looked up, to be greeted by a warm smile. "You have to understand, Pandora: being sealed—alive—in stone for all eternity is the least these bastards could suffer for all the misery they brought into the world. I wish the punishment had been a lot more severe, but apparently the Almighty couldn't bring Himself to just erase the whole lot from existence. He loved them too much to destroy them." She laughed—a sharp, brief note of disbelief. "Can you believe that? He wanted to give them time to contemplate their actions and atone for their sins. And if it took until Judgment Day for that to sink into their thick skulls, well . . ."

"So this is God's idea of . . . tough love?"

"No, this is God's idea of punishing a roomful of deserving assholes." Annie winked. "Now are we done debating? I'd like to leave before—"

With a deafening boom that sounded as though the volcano had erupted, the main door exploded inward, and before either Pan or Annie could duck for cover, the concussive force of the blast threw them across the chamber.

Then everything went black.

25

Where's all this blood coming from? Pan thought dimly. She'd been staring down at the small pool of it for what felt like hours, and as she continued watching more blood dripped in front of her eyes, adding to it. She also couldn't make sense of why she was lying on the ground, propped up by her forearms, or why her head ached so much.

Her eyes itched like crazy, but then the air was filled with dust, swirling like fog in the light breeze running through . . . wherever here was. The dust coated her hands, the arms of her leather jacket, and probably her hair, and she could feel it sticking to her face—her tongue, too. It tasted really nasty. Blergh.

A flash of light caught her eye, and Pan turned her head to see what looked like soldiers standing around, sweeping the area around them with laser thingies. The red-haired female soldier who seemed to be in charge looked kinda familiar, but Pan couldn't place her. It'd come to her, though, eventually; that's how it usually worked—when she wasn't thinking about it, the woman's identity would pop into her thoughts. Then the wind shifted and the soldiers were lost in the dust. It was funny, though: she couldn't remember hearing the soldiers come in, and she couldn't hear them now; there was just this annoying ringing in her ears. Or was her whole head ringing? That'd be weird. Maybe she should get up and ask the soldiers; if nothing else, they could perhaps tell her where all the blood was coming from . . .

A hand gripped her shoulder. Pan rolled onto her right arm and looked back to find Javi crouched beside her. He, too, was covered in dust, and his jeans and T-shirt were peppered with tiny rips that shone with the blood of fresh cuts. His arms and face bore similar traces, as though a lot of somethings small and sharp had sliced across him. Was that the source of the blood she'd been staring at?

No, the cuts weren't deep enough.

She saw his lips moving, but all that came out was a muffled *wah-wah-wah* trombone-ish sound, like the voices of all the adults in the Charlie Brown holiday specials she used to watch on TV when she was little. Pan smiled. She'd always loved *It's the Great Pumpkin, Charlie Brown*, with its connection to Halloween. Still, it was so weird that Javi would try communicating with her in such a funny way.

But then her ears popped, and suddenly she could hear *everything*: the dust-hidden soldiers talking, someone barking orders in the distance, the thunder of feet stomping across broken ground, and Javi hoarsely whispering "Are you okay?"

"Why are you whispering?" Pan asked—maybe too loudly, considering the panicked look that lit up Javi's eyes. He placed an index finger to his lips in a shushing gesture and gazed past her, no doubt to see if anyone had heard her. "Sorry," she said—again, a bit too booming for Javi's comfort. Well, once her ears— or her head—stopped ringing, everything should be back to normal.

Javi helped Pan stand up—she felt a little too weak-kneed to do it herself—and guided her around a mound of debris and into a shadowed alcove beneath the ramp. Seeing it, and a glimpse of an angel statue on the next level up, dispelled some of Pan's murky thinking and reminded her of where they were, the explosion they'd been caught in . . . and the danger they now faced from a horde of armed monsters. Once the teens were concealed by darkness, Javi sat Pan down and started rummaging through her messenger bag. He pulled out a bottle of water and a packet of tissues.

"Let's take care of that cut on your head, before we do anything else." He opened the bottle, poured some water on a fistful of tissues, and gently pressed them against her head in certain spots, from her forehead to just above the hairline.

"Am I . . . bleeding?" Pan asked. That *was* a whisper, wasn't it? She was still having some trouble figuring out proper volume levels. But at least now she knew the source of the blood from before.

Javi lifted up the tissues just enough to take a peek. "Yeah, but it already stopped; I think it's starting to heal. I was just cleaning up the dried blood." He smiled weakly, no doubt trying to allay her fears. "Good thing you're, like, Wolverine's sister, with that super-first-aid power, huh?"

Pan grunted noncommittally. "So what's going on?"

"Zaqiel's people blew a big hole in the door, and a part of the ceiling fell in; that's why there's so much dust. You and Annie got caught in the blast; me, not as much."

Pan gasped. "Where's Annie?"

"Right behind you," replied a gravelly whisper that made both teens jump.

They shifted around to find Annie sitting a few feet away. She looked as bad as Pan felt, which was considerable: hair disheveled and coated with so much dust it looked white, clothes torn, face bloodied, and cradling her right arm in her left. Was it broken? Dislocated? Pan couldn't tell. She was just relieved to see her alive.

Despite her aches and throbbing head, Pan crawled over to give the huntress a light hug. She felt Annie stiffen and heard her inhale sharply through clenched teeth. With a start Pan realized she'd brushed against Annie's injured arm.

"Oh God, sorry, sorry," she said as she moved to back off.

Annie, however, slid her good arm around Pan's shoulders and leaned forward to lightly kiss her on the forehead. "It's all right, Pandora," she murmured gently. "I'm just glad to see you." She reached out to squeeze Javi's arm. "Both of you."

"How did you get back here?" Javi asked. "I tried looking for you, but with all the monsters coming in . . ."

"I'm a shape-shifter, remember? I turned into a scarab beetle and scuttled my way over." She grimaced. "The effort took a lot out of me, though. It's hard to concentrate on maintaining a form when you have a broken arm."

Pan groaned inwardly—now she felt twice as bad for leaning on Annie when she hugged her. She reached out. "Here. Let me fix it."

Annie shook her head. "This is just a minor annoyance, and it's not the first time it's happened. Give it a few more minutes and I'll be good as new. You're not the only one with recuperative powers."

"Seriously?" That was certainly news to Pan, but apparently none at all to Javi, judging from his knowing smile.

Annie nodded. "So concentrate on healing yourself first. That's a nasty cut you have."

"I'll be fine." *Once my skull gets done ringing, that is.* "Anyway, Javi said it was almost healed."

"I said it was *starting* to heal," he replied, and leaned forward for another examination. "Okay, it looks a little better. At least it stopped bleeding. Just take it easy, okay?"

"I'll do my best," Pan replied with a wink.

Annie stared past the teens and cocked her head to one side, as though she was listening to something. "Did you happen to see what was going on before you came in here?" she asked them. "The chamber's gotten too quiet."

Pan looked over her shoulder. With the dust still swirling around, she couldn't see much beyond shadowy figures moving about, but Annie was right: it *had* gotten really quiet.

"Can't really see much out there until the dust settles," Javi replied. "Want me to take a peek, anyway?"

Annie paused a moment, then nodded. "If you wouldn't mind. But be careful."

"You got it." He gazed at Pan and smiled gently as he gave her hand a squeeze. "Back in a minute." Moving in a crouch, he returned to the artificial barrier created by the partial ceiling collapse.

Concerned for his safety, Pan watched him as her stomach fluttered nervously, and she unconsciously began scraping her bottom teeth against her right thumbnail, stripping off the polish.

"So . . . you two are an item, I take it?" Annie asked.

Pan stiffened. "Uh . . ."

"I think that's wonderful."

Pan did a slow turn to find Annie smiling at her. "Really?" she asked haltingly.

Annie laughed softly. "Did you know your aura turns bright red when you're embarrassed? It's adorable."

"So I've heard," Pan muttered, certain that her aura must now look positively nuclear in these shadows.

Annie's smile broadened in response. "And to answer your question, yes, I do think it's wonderful. You're an amazing girl, Pandora, and Javier is lucky to have found you."

"And I'm lucky to have found him." Pan smiled awkwardly as she looked away. That new, more positive attitude she'd been developing didn't seem to mind blurting out the truth when the opportunity arose. "I mean, that's kinda how I feel about it," she added quickly. "It's just . . . I haven't had a lot of luck with, y'know, guys and stuff."

"Because of your gift?"

Pan shrugged. "Yeah, I guess. Among . . . other things." Gift—Annie's word for the monstervision that had plagued Pan for the last decade. Seeing monsters everywhere you looked had never felt like a gift; more like a curse. And as for the "other things" . . . well, they didn't need to get into any of that right now.

Annie smiled warmly and gave her arm a tiny squeeze. "Then take it slow and follow your heart. I *promise* you, Javier will *never* give you a reason to regret it."

Pan squirmed a little. The last time she'd followed her heart the path had led to Ammi, and that, to put it mildly, hadn't turned out so well. And sure, Annie could just be giving Pan the hard sell because Javi was her godson and she wanted to fix him up with the strange girl with the dye job and the neon aura who was *of her kind* (sorta), and because she thought they made a cute couple. But Annie's opinions and promises meant little to Pan. What mattered was that Pan *wanted* to be with Javi. And he wanted to be with Pan.

Things were different, with Javi. He wasn't another Ammi—he was so much better. And at this point in her life, especially with all the crap she'd recently been going through, didn't she *deserve* better? Abso-damn-lutely. *This* relationship was gonna work out, Pan told herself firmly. If they survived long enough to get off this freaking island, that is . . .

She smiled. "Thanks, Annie."

Annie reached out to lightly stroke the girl's cheek. "I want nothing but happiness for the two of you."

"You and me, both," Pan said with a grin.

The soft patter of footsteps heralded Javi's return. "Looks like they sent in an advance team to see if we're around, but now they're just standing around by the statues in the middle. I think with all the dust and debris they didn't notice the gap down here."

Annie frowned. "That won't last long."

Then Javi looked to Pan with a hint of fear in his eyes. "I couldn't make out faces, but I saw one of them had red hair."

Pan swallowed nervously. *That's* where she knew the redhead from! The vampire squad they'd stolen the van from and ditched in the jungle had finally caught up with them. She sighed wearily. Could this day *ever* stop sucking?

"And Zaqiel?" Annie asked.

"Didn't see him."

"That's odd. He's never been the type to hang back." She took a couple of moments to mull that over. "Kiyoshi probably didn't want him charging in until they had secured the chamber, just in case I was lying in wait." She flashed a wicked little smile. "It must *kill* him to be taking orders from a woman."

"I just wish it'd kill him for real," Pan remarked.

"You and me, both," Annie replied with a wink.

"So what's our next move?" Javi asked. "Like you said, it probably won't take them long to spot this little cubbyhole and decide to check it out."

Annie slowly raised her injured arm and stretched it out, then flexed her fingers a few times and rotated her shoulder. "Good as new," she said with a smile. "All right, here's what we'll do: While I create a diversion, you kids run for Zaqiel's escape route."

That sounded like a terrible idea. "Annie—," Pan began.

"Once you make it to the surface," the huntress continued, before Pan could voice her objection, "contact Alexander and tell him to rally the troops—and to hurry. Then go find a hiding place in the jungle and *stay there*." She glanced from one teen to the other. "You do have a phone, don't you? Otherwise this will turn out to be a terrible plan."

Javi smiled slyly at Pan. "Well, I *used* to have one . . ."

Pan dug into her pocket and pulled out her cell. "It's already a terrible plan . . . ," she muttered.

"I'm open to suggestions," Annie replied in a pleasant tone. That caught Pan off-guard, because it sounded as though the huntress with all the monster-fighting experience actually *wanted* alternatives offered from the newbies. That was . . . unexpected, but Pan appreciated the invitation.

Unfortunately, "Uhh . . ." was all she could come up with. "Sorry."

Annie patted her on the knee. "Don't worry. It's only your first adventure. Next time the ideas will come faster."

"Umm . . . okay." *Next time?* Pan thought. *We'll be lucky if we make it out of* this *time alive!* But if Annie was so certain of it, then . . . okay. Maybe being on the island had boosted Annie's positive attitude, as well.

The huntress started clambering toward the wreckage barricade. "Come on. We'll have to wait for the right opportunity, and we won't spot it sitting back here."

"Not to mention you wanna see what's going on," Javi said.

Annie paused to look back and flash him a smile. "Not to mention I want to see what's going on."

Pan tucked the phone back in her pocket and joined the hunchback procession. The trio crouched behind the debris to find that the dust had mostly settled, making visibility better. But without that cover to hide their movements, Pan realized Annie's plan was going to be more difficult to carry out. And yes, the vampire hit squad—or at least some of its members—that she and Javi had escaped from had shown up. They looked really pissed.

Pan sighed. Apparently the day wasn't done sucking just yet.

"And here comes the bastard now . . . ," Annie murmured.

Zaqiel strode into the chamber. His Goth Loli entourage followed, all of them gazing silently at their surroundings—except for one girl in pink who was taking numerous cell-phone photos while she excitedly chattered away in Japanese. Pan glared at the vampire as she paused to take a selfie with the angel-surrounded center column in the background. Was that the same Loli she and Javi and Sheen had encountered in the museum's basement—the one who'd tried to put the bite on her dad? It totally was; Pan was certain of it. And if that was the case, then the other girl in black had to be her sister—the monster who'd set everything in motion by reviving Zaqiel. Okay, Pan thought, so now there were two *more* somebodies she'd like to introduce to the Jesus spear in her bag.

That would be extremely difficult to pull off, though, because the Goth Lolis and the vampire soldiers weren't the only monsters to contend with. Grotesqueries of all shapes and sizes lumbered and stomped and slithered into the chamber: a real-life-horror convention whose attendees had walked straight out of myths, legends, and folklore—and nightmare. And to make matters even worse, two of the largest creatures—who looked like gray-skinned, horned cousins of the Incredible Hulk— sauntered in, oversized battle-axes gripped in one hand while with the other they dragged the bloody head of Behemoth between them.

Pan gasped. "Oh, no."

Annie grunted. "Terrific. So much for the Almighty's unkillable watchdog . . ."

As she watched the angel strut around, Pan scraped her teeth against the nail of her right middle finger, ignoring the flakes of black polish that accumulated on her tongue. On the one hand, she had to admit to herself that, as much as this mad monster party appealed to her inner horror fangirl, she was kind of terrified by the notion of being trapped in a room full of bloodthirsty cratures that included the very one who had killed her not so long ago. On the other, though, she wanted so badly to rush out there, Spear of Longinus clutched in both hands, and impale him with it so she could get some much-needed revenge for what he'd done to her, and to free her mother from his vampire spell.

You tried that before, her little inner voice chimed in. *Out in front of the museum, when you wanted to rescue Mom? Remember how that worked out for you? It's how you wound up dead.*

Pan closed her eyes. She hadn't forgotten; she'd never forget. Her body involuntarily stiffened as she recalled the pain of the spear slicing through her chest; the crunch of bones as it shattered her rib cage; the unbelievable agony as her heart was cleaved in two—

A hand touched her shoulder. "Pan? You okay?" Javi asked gently. "You're crying."

"What?" Pan blinked and felt a pair of big tears roll down her cheeks. She swiped at them with the heels of her hands and flashed an awkward smile. "Just thinking about stuff, is all. I'm okay."

Javi squeezed her hand. "It's all gonna be fine, Cookie. I'm not gonna let anybody hurt you."

Pan smiled wryly at her protector. "I thought we agreed we were gonna look out for each other. Equally."

"We did," Javi replied with a nod. "And if something comes up, I'm holding you to your end of the deal. But it's not a bad thing to, y'know, reassure the other person when they might need to hear it—is it?"

"... No." Pan clasped his hand with both of hers and smiled good-naturedly. "No, it isn't. Thanks." She glanced past Javi to find Annie beaming at them. "What're *you* grinning about?"

Annie's smile widened. "I was just thinking what an absolutely adorable couple the two of you make."

Both teens blushed.

"Annie ... ," Javi groaned in exasperation.

"So what's going on?" Pan asked. Anything to change the subject ...

Annie did the finger-to-her-lips shushing gesture, then pointed toward their enemies.

Zaqiel walked toward the center of the chamber, occasionally looking up and around to gaze at his stone-encased brethren. From this distance it was impossible to see his expression, but to Pan his light tread seemed to indicate he was pleased with what he saw.

The angel threw his arms out wide. "My brothers!" he bellowed. "I have returned, just as I had promised long ago. Returned to set you free!"

"Returned to pat himself on the back, is more like it," Annie murmured in disgust. She saw Pan return the shushing-finger gesture and shrugged. "Sorry."

"These are the other Fallen, my lord?" asked the Loli in black (Kiyoshi, wasn't it?). Pan couldn't be certain, but there was something about the way Kiyoshi said "my lord" that made it sound as though she found it really distasteful to utter the words. No doubt she was used to being in charge, and didn't enjoy having to bow and scrape for her new master.

Good, Pan thought with a haughty sniff. *Serves her right.*

"Indeed, they are," Zaqiel replied, and did a slow turn as he pointed to certain figures. "Azazyel. Kokabe. Danjal. Samjaza. Hananel. Simapsiel. And all the rest." He gestured toward the quartet of angels grouped around the marble column. "And here: Asbeel. Gadreel. Penemue. Kasdeja. Our mighty generals in the war against the Almighty's pets."

He pointed to the figure atop the column. "And high above them all: Jeqon—our hallowed leader, who inspired us to undertake our ill-fated quest for righteousness, for respect."

"For chaos, you mean," Annie growled softly.

"Hey," Pan said quietly to get her attention. "So if Jeqon's the fearless leader, and Zaqiel was just one of his soldiers but likes to *act* like he's the big boss, would I be in wrong in thinking that the *last* thing Zaqiel wants to do is free him so he can go back to taking orders?"

"No, you wouldn't," Annie replied. She frowned as she turned back to observe her ex. "I wonder what he has in mind . . ."

She wasn't the only one with questions.

"How will you free them, my lord?" Kiyoshi asked.

"You see the jewel that Jeqon holds?" Zaqiel replied as he pointed to his former commander. "That is both the lock that imprisons my brothers, and the key to their release."

"And . . ." Kiyoshi looked toward the ceiling for a moment. ". . . He just left it out in the open like that, for anyone to find." Her voice was tinged with disbelief.

"A cruel trick of the archangel Michael. The means of our escape, simply for the taking, in a chamber populated by immobilized prisoners. And to place it in the hands of Jeqon, so that he could stare at it for all eternity yet be denied the mobility to use it . . . A good jest, wouldn't you say?"

More like a sick joke, Pan thought.

"So, wait a minute," Javi murmured to Annie. "If he knew all along how to free the other angels, why didn't he just do it once he got out?"

"Because he's a total d-bag?" Pan replied.

"Not to mention completely self-centered," Annie added. "When he became comfortable with the new life he'd fashioned for himself, he forgot all about his 'brothers' until he got bored and started dreaming of building an empire. Then he rediscovered his concern for their well-being, because without their assistance he can't become the king he imagines he should be."

"He got bored with *you*?" Pan snorted. "He *is* a d-bag."

Annie chuckled. "Thank you—" She started. "What in God's name is he doing now?"

Zaqiel had walked over to one of the Hulk's cousins and extended his hand. The ogre or whatever it was nodded and handed over his ax. Considering the thickness of the handle and the enormous, two-headed blade, Zaqiel shouldn't have been able to lift it, let alone hold it, but that's exactly what he did, and apparently without any great effort. Then the angel spread his wings and took to the air.

"No!" Annie gasped, and moved to stop him.

Pan and Javi were instantly on her, dragging her back into hiding as the huntress struggled to shake them off.

"Quit it, Annie," Pan snapped. "There's a whole army out there. You'd never get to him."

"Yeah, what're you, nuts?" Javi whispered hoarsely. "You trying to get yourself killed?"

Annie sat back with a weary sigh. "It's too late, anyway."

Together, the three watched as Zaqiel flew one full circuit of the chamber, building up speed. Then he swooped down, raising the ax as he dove straight at Jeqon—and shattered the immobilized angel with one mighty strike.

The monster congregation gasped in shock as the stone pieces that rained down changed back to flesh and bone and blood. Then they began cheering.

Javi, wide-eyed with shock, whispered hoarsely, "That's . . . that's messed up."

Pan put both hands over her mouth as she felt her stomach turn over. Closing her eyes she fought the urge to throw up, succeeded, and then looked to Annie. "I . . . I guess that's how he solves the boss problem," she croaked. The huntress nodded grimly. Pan swallowed the last of the bile burning her throat and asked, "So what happens now?"

The answer came in the form of shattering crystal, as the jewel that Jeqon had held struck the floor.

"Close your eyes!" Annie barked, and threw herself on top of the teens.

Whatever was inside the crystal exploded in a supernova-like burst of light that, even with her back turned to it, Pan could still see through her eyelids—and which brought cries of terror from the children of the night.

"Come on!" Annie grabbed Pan by the hand and yanked her out from the hidey-hole.

When Pan opened her eyes, the first thing she saw was one of the Hulk's cousins on fire, flailing his arms around as he screamed in pain. He wasn't the only monster suffering: at least a dozen more burned while others writhed in anguish from unseen injuries. For a couple of seconds Pan actually felt sympathetic toward them, before she remembered what they were and pushed those feelings aside. But then her gaze drifted to the charred spots on the floor that she knew had been living creatures just moments before, and it felt as though a weight had settled in her stomach.

Guilty conscience? she wondered.

"Why didn't that happen to us?" Javi asked, motioning to the carnage. "How come we're not burning up?"

"Keep moving," Annie said, and pulled them along.

Pan did as she was told, but couldn't turn away from the gruesome spectacle in front of her. She knew she should find some measure of satisfaction in the deaths of Zaqiel's followers, but was surprised to discover she couldn't. Despite the hell her life had been plunged into, despite the suffering her own parents were undergoing, she couldn't help but think how sad it was to see such fantastic beings—monsters she'd read about and fantasized about and, in some cases, even admired most of her young life—reduced to this state.

But I thought you wanted every one of them dead, her inner voice said. *Isn't that what you wished for, back at the museum when you thought Mom had died?*

That was true, and she had to admit that she still wouldn't mind seeing Zaqiel get his comeuppance in some nasty, fatal way.

Pan stumbled up the ramp and realized that Annie was leading her and Javi to the escape route. She gave her head a little shake to clear her thoughts and focused on escape. She noticed Javi observing her and offered what she hoped looked like a confident smile. "I'm good," she said. "It's all good."

That's when the entire chamber began quaking.

Javi groaned. "This day just keeps getting better and better, doesn't it?" he said, voice dripping with sarcasm.

Annie released the teens so they could all have a better chance of staying on their feet, but that became increasingly difficult as the vibrations grew in strength. Pan tripped over her own feet and sprawled at the base of an angel statue . . . to stare mutely at the normal-looking toes that wiggled to life as their stone casing flaked off.

Down on the main floor, the monster party broke up as the survivors ran for the tunnel. Even the Goth Lolis wasted no time hanging around to see what would happen next. Whatever death trap Zaqiel had led them into, they wanted no further part of it. It was a smart move, because chunks of the ceiling began crashing down.

"I think the whole place is coming apart!" Javi said as he helped Pan up.

"That's not the only thing!" Pan pointed to the angel's exposed foot; with each vibration, more of the celestial being was being revealed—as were the faces and limbs of the angels on both sides of him.

The eyes of the angel directly in front of Pan snapped open, then narrowed as he regarded her. The stone encasing his jaw fell away, and he uttered his first word in untold millennia in a raspy, hate-tinged voice:

"Huuuumaaannnn."

Pan immediately took a step back and bumped into Javi, who muttered, "Aw, crap . . ."

Pan thought he was commenting on the angel, but when she turned to face him she discovered he was gazing at Annie—who was facing down Zaqiel.

"Where the hell did *he* come from?" Pan asked.

"I guess that explosion knocked him for a loop, but it didn't kill him, and then he saw us leaving, so . . . ," said Mr. Obvious, but Pan thought a sarcastic remark was the last thing Javi wanted to hear right now.

Annie's back was to the teens, so Pan couldn't see her facial expression, but her body language told Pan everything she needed to know. Knees slightly bent, weight resting on the balls of her toes, arms away from her sides with fists clenched . . . she was preparing to attack her ex.

An ex who was still in possession of a rather lethal, double-bladed weapon.

"Annie, are you crazy?" Pan cried. "He's got an ax! You don't have anything!"

The huntress looked over her shoulder and flashed a predator's smile. "I know. Puts him at a disadvantage, don't you think?" She pointed at the exit. "Now get up those stairs while I keep him busy!"

Pan saw the angel's brow furrow in confusion as he glanced at the stone steps. "Where the hell did *those* come from?"

"Missed those the last time you were here, did you?" Annie said. "Too bad you won't get to find out where they lead."

And with that she rushed Zaqiel. He grinned evilly and tightened his grip on the ax handle as he stepped forward to meet her charge.

Javi gave Pan a gentle but firm push toward the exit. "Come on! Annie can look out for herself."

Pan considered staying to watch what happened in the monster-hunter-versus-monster battle—because if Zaqiel was going to meet his end here and now she wanted the satisfaction of seeing it firsthand—but then she realized that the revived angels near her and Javi were shaking off their initial lethargy and taking notice of the two representatives of the much-hated human race who were standing in their midst. And from the rage-contorted expressions on their faces, it appeared that a few thousand years of enforced contemplation for their prior bad acts hadn't done a thing to change their attitude about who needed killing once they were free.

This time, Javi's shove was none too gentle. "Go!" he barked. And this time, Pan didn't hesitate. She pelted up the steps with Javi close behind, both teens occasionally bouncing off the rough stone walls as the chamber continued quaking.

"Annie isn't gonna try and take *all* of them on, is she?" Pan asked. Because in all honesty, with a ton of ancient bad guys coming out of the walls and the place falling down around their ears, that would be colossally stupid.

"Nah, she'll be happy just putting Zaqiel in his place," Javi replied. "Besides," he added with a nervous laugh, "it's not like *all* the angels are going after her."

There was something about that laugh that troubled Pan. As she continued climbing—and where the hell was the end of these stairs, already, all this panicky vertical running was really wearing her out—she took a glance over her shoulder and almost tripped over the next step.

Back at the entrance, the teens had picked up an entourage of a half dozen or so fallen angels. They were a little wobbly after their long sleep, clearly trying to get their limbs to work properly, and occasionally a wing or two from the angels in front would pop open and block the Fallen behind them, but as they worked their way up it was apparent from the determined looks on their faces that they were either planning to tear apart the humans trying to escape, or just making a clumsy dash for the fire exit—which still probably involved tearing apart the humans trying to escape, if only so Zaqiel's minions could reach the door first.

Could it be tomorrow, already? Please? Pan thought as she forced her tired body to keep moving. *'Cause, like, I am so done with this whole sucky day.*

She lurched forward, running on all fours now, with her hands pushing off the steps in front of her to keep her moving, certain she'd never reach the top before the angels caught up to her and Javi . . . and then suddenly she was stumbling into the open, to land stomach-first on a warm, flat stone. She inhaled deeply to catch her breath, only to fill her lungs with hot, sulfur-tinged air that sent her into a major eye-watering coughing fit.

Hands grasped her shoulders and she instinctively spun onto her back, throwing punches as she came around. They missed, but that turned out to be a good thing.

"Whoa, Cookie! It's me!" Javi said.

Pan sat up and wiped her eyes. "Sorry! Sorry!" she croaked.

Javi grinned and helped her to her feet. "Don't worry about it. Anyway, we've got bigger things to worry about—like, how do we get down from here?"

Pan studied their surroundings. They were on a cliff a hundred or so feet below the peak of the volcano, which loomed right beside them—hence the sulfury air—with a moonlit view of the night-shrouded jungle. But for all that she could see, the one thing that didn't present itself to her slightly bleary vision was a staircase or a Stone Age elevator or even a natural waterslide that would lead to ground level. As far as she could tell, the only way off this cliff was to go back to the chamber—and that path was currently blocked by ascending bad guys.

"You sure those superpowers of yours don't include flying?" Javi asked.

"Don't I wish," Pan replied as she took another glance down the cliff face. It sure looked like a long way down from here . . .

"Those angels are gonna be here any second," Javi said. He glanced at the entrance to the staircase, then held out his hand. "Gimme the spear."

Pan raised an inquisitive eyebrow. "The spear? What're you gonna do with it?"

"Use it to fight," he said simply.

Pan nervously bit down on her lower lip. "Javi . . ."

"Hey, who's the one with the three twenty-two batting average, huh?"

Pan couldn't help but smile, remembering how she'd asked him for his baseball stats back at the museum, when he had a lead pipe in his hand and they, along with Sheena, were preparing to rescue Mom and Dad. "Okay, so you can hit better than me, but the spear isn't a bat, y'know. It's not even as big as a bat."

"If I can swing it, I can hit with it," Javi said confidently.

". . . Okay." Pan opened her messenger bag. "But what am I supposed to fight with while you're belting homers, A-Rod?"

"You seemed pretty good at swinging those fists around a minute ago," Javi replied with a smile. "I think you'll do okay. Besides, some of those rings you're wearing look pretty lethal."

Pan nodded in agreement—and then froze. When she'd reached for the spear, her fingers brushed against a familiar piece of hard plastic. *Wait a minute. Isn't that . . . ?* She peeked inside the bag to confirm her suspicions.

It was her compact. The same bat-stickered compact that the mirror demon Jerome was hanging out in. A sly grin slowly lit Pan's features. "Hey, Javi, I think I know how—"

"Look out!" he cried, and pushed her down, using his body to protect her from whatever threat had just popped up.

A heavy weight crashed onto the ledge about twenty feet away, the stone cracking under the impact. Based on the silhouette of the object against the moon, it seemed to be a man dressed in armor, hunched over.

Then he stood up and spread his ivory wings, and Pan realized he was an angel—but not one of Zaqiel's. This one was too limber, his wings too spotlessly clean. Her eyebrows rose in surprise. An angel who'd made a dramatic three-point landing like

Iron Man in the movies? Did they do that kind of stuff in heaven? Apparently so . . . unless this one was just showing off for the mortals lying at his feet. Probably the latter, she decided. Based on her experiences with Zaqiel, modesty didn't seem to be one of the angels' greatest attributes.

The more important question, though, was whether this particular angel had arrived to help, or make things worse.

Moving with deliberate slowness to avoid giving the impression they might be a threat, Pan and Javi untangled themselves and stood up. The celestial being, though, paid them no mind—his attention was focused on the chamber's stairwell.

"So at last the day has come, when the Fallen regain their freedom. And of course it had to happen on *my* watch." He sounded really bitter.

Pan softly cleared her throat. "Umm . . ."

The angel slightly turned his head in her direction.

"Hi," Pan said sheepishly, then pointed to the entrance. "There's a whole bunch of, uh, bad angels coming up those steps. They oughtta be here any second."

"And you're the one who set them free." His left hand settled on the pommel of the sheathed sword that was hanging from his belt.

"Oh, crap . . . ," Javi muttered.

Pan started. "What? No! It wasn't us, it was Zaqiel! You know Zaqiel—used to be one of you guys?"

The angel grunted. "I know Zaqiel."

"Okay, well, he's the one who's trying to take over the world with his monster armies. And to do that he just set all his Fallen buddies free to help him out. We didn't have anything to do with that!"

"Yeah," Javi agreed. "We just, y'know, got dragged into all his craziness."

"And I'm supposed to believe you're a complete innocent in all this?"

"What, us?" Javi asked. "Well, of c—"

"No. Not you. *The girl.*"

Pan opened her mouth to respond, then paused, caught off-guard by his attitude. She exchanged glances with Javi, who appeared equally confused.

"Well . . . yeah," she said haltingly. "Why wouldn't you believe that?"

"Because I remember you, sinner," the angel growled. "I remember the painted harlot."

"W-what?" There was something blood-chillingly familiar about those words, but she couldn't put her finger on what it might be. She knew, however, that she'd definitely heard them before, in that same anger-tinged voice. And that made her take a step back.

Javi moved in front of her, to act as a protective barrier. Pan decided that at least this one time, she wasn't going to argue about it.

The angel faced the teens, but his gaze was fixed solely on Pan. "You escaped your punishment when last we met, but there will be no escape for you this time—of that you can be certain."

"Pan, what the hell is he talking about?" Javi asked. Like Annie before him, he was subtly moving into a combat-ready position—weight resting on the balls of his toes, fists low but at the ready.

"I-I don't know," she stammered.

Then the angel turned his head so that his face was bathed in moonlight, and Pan instantly recognized him.

Six foot six or seven. Built like a steroid-pumped body builder. Chiseled features and full lips like those of a top-level male model. And a particularly foul mood caused either by hating vampires so much, or by hating to work a late-night security detail.

It was the angel she'd encountered in purgatory. The one who'd called her a painted harlot because of her gothy appearance. The one who'd tried to cut off her head and send her to hell before she'd managed to dislodge the Spear of Longinus from her chest. And he remembered exactly who she was: the one that got away.

A situation he was clearly determined to correct.

"Yes—hell! That is the place where you belong, demoness." The angel grasped the hilt of his sword and drew it; the blade instantly burst into flame. *"And hell is precisely where you're going!"*

The blade swept down, and Pan screamed.

THE VAMPIRE WAR REACHES
ITS DRAMATIC CONCLUSION!

THE SAGA OF PANDORA ZWIEBACK · BOOK 3

BLOOD&IRON

STEVEN A. ROMAN
BESTSELLING AUTHOR OF THE CHAOS ENGINE TRILOGY

ABOUT THE AUTHOR

STEVEN A. ROMAN is the bestselling author of the novels *Blood Feud: The Saga of Pandora Zwieback, Book 1, X-Men: The Chaos Engine Trilogy*, and *Final Destination: Dead Man's Hand*.

His short fiction has appeared in the anthologies *Best New Zombie Tales 2, The Dead Walk Again!, Doctor Who: Short Trips: Farewells, Untold Tales of Spider-Man, The Ultimate Hulk, If I Were an Evil Overlord, Lorelei Presents: House Macabre, The Almanac of Vampires*, and *Tales of the Shadowmen 4: Lords of Terror*. He also wrote the comic books *The Saga of Pandora Zwieback Annual* #1 and *Stan Lee's Alexa*; the graphic novels *Lorelei: Sects and the City, Lorelei: Building the Perfect Beast*, and *Sunn*; and co-wrote the Marvel Comics animated short film X-Men: *Darktide*.

Steve's current projects include the novels *Blood & Iron: The Saga of Pandora Zwieback, Book 3*.